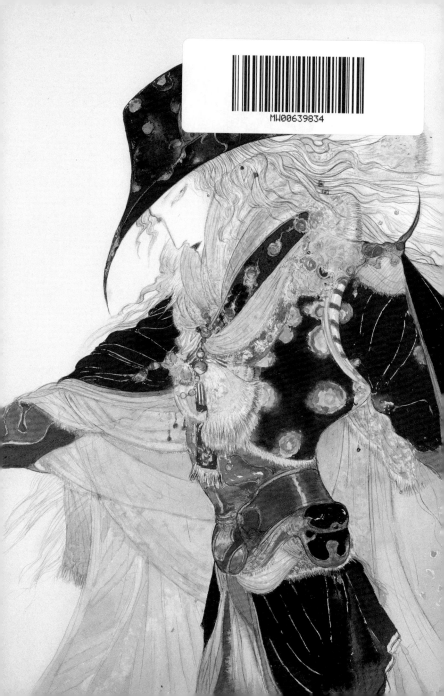

VAMPIRE HUNTER D

Other Vampire Hunter D books published by
Dark Horse Books and Digital Manga Publishing

VAMPIRE HUNTER D

VOLUME 12

PALE FALLEN ANGEL

PARTS THREE AND FOUR

Written by

HIDEYUKI KIKUCHI

Illustrations by

YOSHITAKA AMANO

English translation by

KEVIN LEAHY

Dark Horse Books®   Digital Manga Publishing

Milwaukie   Los Angeles

VAMPIRE HUNTER D 12: PALE FALLEN ANGEL PARTS THREE AND FOUR

© Hideyuki Kikuchi 1995, 1996. Originally published in Japan in 1995 and 1996 by ASAHI SONORAMA Co. English translation copyright © 2009 by Dark Horse Books and Digital Manga Publishing.

Cover art by Yoshitaka Amano

English translation by Kevin Leahy

Book design by Heidi Whitcomb

Published by
Dark Horse Books
A division of Dark Horse Comics
10956 SE Main Street
Milwaukie OR 97222
darkhorse.com

Digital Manga Publishing
1487 West 178th Street, Suite 300
Gardena CA 90248
dmpbooks.com

Library of Congress Cataloging-in-Publication Data

Kikuchi, Hideyuki, 1949-
  [Kyuketsuki hanta "D." English]
  Vampire hunter D / Hideyuki Kikuchi ; illustrated by Yoshitaka Amano ;
  translation by Kevin Leahy.
      v. cm.
  Translated from Japanese.
  ISBN 1-59582-012-4 (v.1)
  I. Amano, Yoshitaka. II. Leahy, Kevin. III. Title.
  PL832.I37K9813 2005
  895.6'36--dc22
                                          2005004035

ISBN 978-1-59582-131-7

First Dark Horse Books Edition: March 2009

10 9 8 7 6 5 4 3 2 1

Printed in the United States of America

VAMPIRE HUNTER D

Pale Fallen Angel

PART THREE

A Foggy Road Through the Rocks

CHAPTER 1

I

The fog rolled in just after noon. With the sinuous moves of an alluring dancer the milky white water particles clung to the driverless carriages and D, who rode beside them.

Hemmed in on either side by great craggy chunks of rock, the road ran on like a slender ribbon. You couldn't really call it a path through the bottom of a valley—it was quite literally a road weaving between the rocks. And as it was usually easier and easier to stray from the road the thicker the fog grew, it was obvious the stone bulwarks would come in handy.

It was nearly noon. Once they traversed this pass and spent another half day crossing the plains, their destination of Krauhausen would be waiting for them at twilight.

They were finally there. But how many people harbored this relief in their heart? Naturally, there were no voices from the coffins sealed away in the carriages, and D sat astride his mount with a cold, clear expression from which no hint of emotion could be gleaned.

It was about thirty minutes after they started down the foggy road that the Hunter's eyes took on a faint gleam. Stopping his horse and doubling back, he then rapped lightly on the carriage door.

What is it? the baron asked in a voice no one save D could hear.

"Don't you know?" asked D. His voice could likewise be heard by the baron's ears alone.

No. What's happened?

"This isn't the right road. We seem to have lost our way."

The road had vanished at some point without their even realizing it.

That's not like you. Although I must add that I didn't sense anything, either. Is it due to the fog?

The Nobleman was apparently mindful of that, at least.

"Probably," D replied.

Even with his ultra-keen senses, the fog seemed like nothing more than ordinary water particles.

"What do you make of it?" the Hunter inquired, but not of Balazs.

"It's just plain old fog. Even I don't have a clue why we've lost our way."

At that response from his left hand, D ran his gaze over the rocky mounds to either side of them.

"Those rocks are real enough," the hoarse voice continued. "You fixing to wait here until the fog lifts?"

"No."

"I get you," D's left hand said as he raised it up high.

In the palm of it, human eyes and a nose swiftly took shape. Its mouth opened.

The *whooosh* that resounded wasn't the sound of it drawing breath, but rather the groan of the wind. The fog eddied as it coursed into the palm of the hand.

Ten seconds passed. Twenty seconds.

And then, when the trailing edge of the milky whiteness had been swallowed, someone exclaimed in astonishment, "Well, I'll be damned!"

The voice came from the very same mouth that had devoured the fog.

But even before it had said a word, D had noticed the same thing.

They were on the very same road as before. With great chunks of stone lining either side, the path ran straight for another hundred and fifty feet before breaking to the right.

Something strange is going on, the baron's voice was heard to say.

"We're back in the same spot again," D replied before turning around. "While we were lost, the amount of ground we covered was roughly a hundred feet. I have to assume that something was done to us during that time."

A mere hundred feet. Though that didn't seem like much, getting both D and the baron to advance down that otherworldly road for such a distance before noticing anything was miraculous.

"Know anything about this?"

The Hunter's query pertained to who might've set them up.

Dr. de Carriole could manage it.

"Do you know what moves he's likely to make?"

A number of them. He was my tutor in my infancy.

"Then I'll need you to keep your eyes peeled."

And with these words, D flicked the reins of the horses drawing the carriage. Accompanied by the creak of wooden wheels, the horses stepped forward. They approached the turn in the rocks.

D took the turn first.

Thirty feet up ahead, there lay a dark figure. Lying face down, the person was dressed in black garments, and wore a coat in the same hue.

Like D.

It certainly looked as if the attack had already started.

D dismounted.

Stop, the baron ordered him. *It's obviously a trap. Don't go near him.*

However, they couldn't very well leave someone lying there across the whole road.

White clouds floated in the blue sky. To either side of the path, flowers swayed in ivory beauty. And on the road lay a corpse.

Perhaps D intended to accept this invitation. Going over to the remains, the Hunter bent down.

It was just then that the corpse turned over.

A pale face looked up at D . . . with the face of D himself.

For just a second the two exchanged looks, but then D swiftly stood back up and drew his sword. There was a flash of stark light from his blade, and the head of the figure on the ground was removed from its body.

"It's a doll," said D.

At that point, he felt like something was softly pulling away from his own face.

Sure enough, wood was visible where the head had been severed from the figure at his feet.

What a strange thing to do, the baron said, his voice wavering with perplexity. *If that was the work of Dr. de Carriole, I don't recall him having any such ability. D, do you sense anything out of the ordinary?*

"Not a thing," D replied succinctly as he tossed the wooden remains to one side of the road and got back on his horse. But one thing gnawed at the heart beneath those black garments.

The two carriages passed by in silence, and the only one out in the white sunlight to hear the dwindling creak of the wheels was the severed head of the doll. But as it lay exposed to the sun, the smooth, polished wood of its face was now flat and utterly featureless. The countenance of the gorgeous Vampire Hunter had vanished without a trace.

Though it was daytime, the room was hemmed in by a thick darkness. The darkness jelled even further, forming two figures that were darker still—a stooped old man, and a young man who stood bolt upright and completely motionless behind him. The old man was draped in gold brocade, and he wore a long robe. The unusually lengthy garment fell across the floor behind him like a shadow.

Suddenly putting his right hand to his ear, the old man said, "It's finished!"

"And you think that'll take care of the Hunter?" the young man asked.

Apparently the old man had succeeded in something, and while the other man might have been his apprentice or at least his subordinate, the young man didn't seem at all delighted by this. To the contrary, he sounded quite skeptical.

"The spell has been cast. There can be no doubt of that. However—"

"However what?"

"There is one thing that troubles me," the old man said, his expression horribly intense as he slowly turned toward the young man.

While there were other reasons why the darkness of the chamber was fraught with tension, if one were to claim it all sprang from the old man's look, no one would ever doubt it. Hidden beneath age spots and wrinkles and a hoary goatee, his face was like that of an ancient mummy, his thread-thin eyes brimming with a yellow light, while tremendous intellect, evil, and willpower all spilled from his green irises.

"The mask you made of him, Zanus—is it perfect?"

"Do you doubt me?" the young man—Zanus—asked in a hard tone.

"Not at all. I recognize your skill. After all, your 'transference' hex proved effective," the old man said with a nod before turning back the way he'd faced originally.

"Then I shall proceed according to schedule," the young man told him, bowing as he prepared to take his leave.

"Our foe is the same man who slew the water warriors. You mustn't let your guard down. Be on your toes," the old man said, his voice trailing after the young man.

Once Zanus had left, the old man didn't move for a while, but eventually he took a seat on a nearby settee and mumbled introspectively, "Baron Byron Balazs . . . I wonder if you remember me? Do you still recall the name of the hopeful tutor who saw in you the salvation of your race?"

"Dr. de Carriole," a voice called out from somewhere in the darkness.

As the old man spun around reflexively, his expression was awash with a respect and fear that made it clear he'd guessed who it was that addressed him.

"Oh, my—when did you get here?" the old man—Dr. de Carriole—said with head hung low, while in his heart he chided himself. His laboratory was equipped with warning systems that should've been able to detect even the slightest difference in the makeup of the air.

"I am always around you. It wouldn't do to have you using the fruits of your strange research against me, now would it?"

"Surely you jest," de Carriole replied, but to himself he thought, *That was a century and a half ago.*

That one time alone the old man had tried to put up some resistance. To this day, even he himself didn't know what had come of it, for although he'd tried, nothing had changed at all. The assassins he'd sent had vanished without a trace, and the source of the voice had appeared before the doctor, just as always. And from that day to this, de Carriole had gone without a single soul ever censuring him or accusing him of any wrongdoing. Because after that, he'd sworn allegiance to the source of the voice in the darkness.

"Is my son coming?"

From this question, the voice could belong to none other than Vlad Balazs.

"Indeed he is. He'll be here in half a day," de Carriole replied.

"So, even with all your power, you still didn't manage to slay him? That comes as little surprise, given that he has that Hunter for a bodyguard."

De Carriole turned with a start toward the depths of the darkness. He could see through the gloom as clear as day. They both could. Yet his eyes found nothing save inky blackness.

"Are you familiar with 'D,' then, sire?" he asked.

"No."

The doctor was at a loss for words.

"I don't know D," the voice continued. "Or, at least, any manhunter by that name. However, he does bear a distinct resemblance to another great personage whose name I do know. Or so it would appear."

"A great personage . . ." de Carriole began before breaking off.

It must've been centuries since he'd been surprised twice in a single day. His skin, which had died ages ago and had only been reinvigorated by reanimating drugs, now rose in goose bumps.

The voice mentioned "a great personage." To the best of the doctor's knowledge, there was only one person on earth he would refer to as such. However, from the way he spoke, it seemed it had to be someone else. In which case—

Memories swirled and flowed. One by one, his brain cells were lanced by the point of a needle, active cells and slumbering cells alike. Cells that had long ago fallen into disuse and ancient brain cells that his brain had even forgotten existed. And in one of them—he found it! However, it gave off only a momentary flash before fading into eternal darkness. Freezing the flash would be impossible. But he tried to comprehend it. Forgetting all about his surroundings, de Carriole focused his entire consciousness on that one point. The actual memory of the concrete information took shape for only an instant—and then it quickly slipped away. De Carriole's concentration pursued it, and a split second before it was swallowed by the nothingness, he brushed the tail end of it.

"Now I remember . . ." he mumbled, not because the information he'd wrested from his brain needed to be spoken, but because it threatened to leave him again. "That great personage . . . did indeed have . . . just one . . . But . . . it couldn't be . . . It's simply not possible . . . that a filthy ghoul . . . a Hunter of the Nobility . . . could be *his* . . ."

"Perhaps that is the case. But then, perhaps it is not," the voice said gravely. It was as much a confession that he himself couldn't judge or comprehend the situation. "If the latter is true, then to us, he is merely Byron's cohort, and we shall have no choice but to eradicate him. But if the opposite is the case, there's much to be feared."

And saying this, the voice gave a low laugh.

Is he prepared to bare his teeth even against the great one's very own—de Carriole thought, terrified by the concept. In a manner of speaking, he would be making a foe of the great one himself. And the Nobility as a whole were bound by that great personage's regard for his family like no other rule.

"Make ready, doctor! Make ready!" he was told by a voice that echoed both high and low from the darkness. "Before they enter my lands or after makes no difference. Use every means at your disposal if you must, but slay them."

"Kindly leave it to me. You can rest easy while de Carriole handles everything."

It was just then that a sound like a long, long sob was heard from nowhere in particular.

II

It was a woman, and no doubt she was incredibly distraught. Her grief was so great it'd driven her mad, yet still she couldn't help but lament—that was the impression anyone would've gotten.

"Aside from yourself, there is one other who understands that my son is approaching. But I have to wonder, why is it that what should be a song of triumph is instead a wail such as would greet the dead?"

The voice was tinged with laughter.

"Dr. de Carriole!" it added.

"Milord!" the robed figure exclaimed, visibly shaken.

"You had best go. Not surprisingly, that's enough to rend even my heart. I would not have anyone else hear that voice."

"I understand," the old man said as he bowed his head, and at that point he realized that the source of the voice was no longer with him.

"I understand," he repeated to himself. "But who are *you* to speak of how it rends your heart?"

And once he'd spoken, a chill surely ran down the old man's spine. But no bolt of lightning fell from the heavens to strike him down.

A few minutes later, de Carriole descended a lengthy spiral staircase to a depth even he was unsure of toward a certain chamber. In scattered places on the stone walls atomic flames burned with a blue light, casting flickering shadows on the steps and walls.

His descent ended abruptly, as always. As he stood in a vast hall paved in stone, guards sheathed in armor closed on him from either side. All of them were synthetic humans. They weighed over a ton each thanks to the heavy alloys, but their footfalls didn't even make a sound. Their long spears came to bear on the doctor, the tips glowing red.

"Out of my way!"

Before the doctor had finished speaking, red glows extended from the ends of the spears to his chest and exited through his back. The rock wall behind him turned red hot, and in no time at all, holes two inches in diameter were bored into it.

When these guards were imbued with life, the first thing they'd been set to do was to slaughter absolutely anyone who happened to come here.

"Idiots! You know nothing of the world. Out of my way!"

As the doctor took a step forward, a blinding band of light shot from the sleeve of his robe and mowed through the guards. And when the light returned to his sleeve once more, the old man walked over to the door that lay before him.

The remaining guards couldn't move a muscle, their spears at the ready but otherwise frozen in place. Though the volume of light was sufficient, there was something frosty about this subterranean illumination that gave all beneath it the doleful aspect of lifeless sculptures.

Halting before a door, the old man put his right index finger to his mouth and bit the tip of it slightly. The drop of blood that quickly welled up fell into a hole that opened in front of the lock, and less than a second later, the sound of the lock being undone rang out.

Taking the golden doorknob in hand, de Carriole trembled. He had just reflected on the person he was about to see and what would transpire. While heaving a deep sigh, he pushed open the door. It took just as long for the door to open as it did for his sigh to end.

And then the voice that sounded like some despondent lost soul once again reached the ancient sorcerer's ears. Who was this woman who wept in the untold depths of the earth, surrounded by guards who would slay any who drew near?

In scattered places along the lengthy corridor were set doors that seemed to be of bronze. On either side of the doors atomic fires burned.

Casting vague shadows on the floor as he advanced, the old mummy of a man looked as if he were guided by the woman's plaintive cries.

In no time, a door appeared ahead of him, as enormous as a castle gate. The voice was spilling from behind it. However, it seemed utterly impossible that those echoes—thread-thin, low, and full of grief—could make it through the great door that towered before him.

When he reached the foot of the door, de Carriole put his blood into this lock as he had done with the last. Extracting his DNA, memory circuits within the lock then matched it against the list of people who were authorized for access before giving the OK for the door to unlock. It took but a millisecond.

Splitting down the middle, the door opened to either side. It was fifteen feet thick, and once de Carriole had gone through it, he looked up at the ceiling. It must've been over thirty feet high. He was greeted by light that was like that of the evening.

There was water as far as the eye could see. As proof that there wasn't even a ripple from the wind, the dead-calm surface of the water displayed no tendency to cling to the light as it spread in a placid expanse. There was no end to it. No matter how hard you looked, you simply couldn't see beyond it.

The floor at de Carriole's feet formed a stone staircase with about ten steps, and the lowest one was underwater. At the bottom of the staircase there floated a boat made of bronze. The reason it wasn't moored was because there was no movement of the water.

The woman's voice continued to wail, rustling across the water.

Like some investigator who'd sought that voice for a century, de Carriole climbed into the boat, took the oars that were stored in it, and began to paddle through the water. The ripples spread. It had been a long time since this expanse of water had known any kind of wave.

After rowing for about ten minutes, de Carriole then ceased and listened intently. His eardrums confirmed that the woman's voice was coming from right below the starboard bulwark. Leaning out, he peered through the surface of the water.

Just below the boat, a woman drifted with threads of blood flowing from her body. No, that wasn't entirely correct. The woman was trapped in a single spot for all eternity. Her long black tresses didn't drift, or sink, or float at all, but rather stayed twined around her body and the white dress that she wore, while eyes the same hue as her hair peered up with a quiet emptiness. The smooth line of her nose left an impression that carried over to the rest of her body, right down to the tips of her fingers, causing the old man to wonder for the first time in years if perhaps the water hadn't washed all possible hardness out of her. And the woman's lips. Bloodless and paler than even her skin, he had to wonder why they alone seemed to stand out. It was because they were moving. And through their sensuous and heartbreaking trembling, the voice was produced.

"Milady," he called out to her after a short time had passed. "Milady, it is I—de Carriole. I've come because there's something I must tell you."

It took time for the words to penetrate the water that separated the speaker and listener.

"Thank you for coming, de Carriole," she said, her heartbroken tone becoming emotionless as she greeted him.

The old man prostrated himself.

"Have you responded to my voice? To my cries of deepest woe?"

"Indeed I have. Milady has been privy to things even I myself do not know."

"Being underwater, I can hear the sound of the stars moving and the world turning. The sound of coffins opening, the baying of wolves, the wailing of the sun as it sinks beyond the horizon, and the jubilant cries of the darkness."

"Incredible."

"My child has returned, hasn't he?" the woman's voice inquired.

"Indeed he has. He is now but a half day from the castle."

"And what of *him?*"

"He seems rather agitated."

"I should think so."

"Although this is merely my own interpretation, I would say that Lord Byron has returned after acquiring power surpassing his father's."

"And *he* knows it, too. How splendid," she said with a laugh, her voice buoyant even underwater. "Then I take it you are in charge of the efforts to hinder him, are you not?"

"Yes, milady," he replied without any hesitation.

"And I'm sure my child will make it through."

"No," de Carriole responded flatly. "I won't allow that. Lord Byron's life will surely be taken before he enters this land."

"You mean to suggest that a member of the Nobility would fall to humans?" the woman said, chuckling once again.

"Zanus has already gone out to meet him."

The woman's laughter ceased.

"Zanus has?"

"Indeed."

"So, that's who's gone, is it? I see . . . Perhaps Byron *will* be slain."

"It is as you say, milady. And the Hunter acting as his bodyguard is already under our control."

"This is merely the prelude, de Carriole. Merely the prelude."

"Yes, milady. The next person you lay eyes on shall be Lord Byron or myself—and the other one shall never look upon you again."

"It was so good of you to inform me of this, de Carriole. You have my thanks."

"Think nothing of it."

And then, without any further words of parting, de Carriole began to row the boat away again. But his vessel came to a dead stop just as the stone staircase and the doorway began to take shape.

"Milady," he muttered.

He was working the oars. He could even feel them digging into the water. And yet the boat didn't move an inch. He then saw something calmly reach up for the gunwale from the surface of the water. It didn't take him any time at all to realize he was sinking.

"Am I to take it that you don't wish me to lay a hand on Lord Byron? Very well, then."

Rising, he held his right hand out parallel to the water's surface. Water had already begun to creep into the boat over the gunwales. From the sleeve of his robe something like a silver thread shot out with a trail behind it, but it mixed with the water and quickly diffused.

As the water rose to his ankles, de Carriole set one foot out of the boat and onto the water's surface. He didn't sink. The other leg followed—but even after he'd put his entire weight onto the water, its surface supported him as if the soles of his shoes were resting on a stone floor.

He watched coolly as the bronze boat sank like a petal off a flower. The shore was still quite some distance away. Letting out a single sigh, the aged scientist slowly began to walk back on the path he'd created across the surface of the water.

III

While they still had about an hour to go before leaving the rocks, one of the cyborg horses twisted an ankle. Inspecting it, D discovered that an artificial ligament in its heel had snapped. He decided to take a rest so that he could repair it. The condition of the other horses would also need to be checked.

VAMPIRE HUNTER D · PALE FALLEN ANGEL PART THREE | 17

"Once we're through here, we'll head for the plains," D said as if addressing someone. "For your foes, that'll be the last redoubt. They'll be coming at us full force."

Not necessarily, Baron Balazs countered. *No, they may come at us, but they won't play their trumps until after we're in the village. I'm sure that's how Dr. de Carriole would do it.*

"Do you know the names of the most powerful opposition in Krauhausen?" D inquired.

First of all, there's Zanus, the voice replied. *Though he's Dr. de Carriole's star pupil, I don't know all that much about him, only that while the doctor continues to grow older and older, Zanus seems to stay just around twenty. If he's not a Noble, he'd have to be a synthetic human. Ordinarily he serves as the doctor's assistant, but it's said that he can act autonomously when the need arises. As for his ability—I really don't know. From all that I've heard, he's a fearsome opponent— that's all they say.*

"Who's next?"

Chlomo the Makeup Lover, the baron replied, a ring of distaste to his voice. *He's the captain of my father's personal guards, and from morning till night the man plays with cosmetics. And he applies them not only to himself, but to others as well. Although I don't know exactly what that accomplishes, one theory has it that the person he applies them to takes on a personality befitting that makeup.*

"And the third?"

Sai Fung of the Thousand Limbs. He's a martial-arts genius. They say that using only his bare hands he can beat opponents armed with ranged weapons. It seems that the brutalized remains of his enemies look as if they've been pummeled by a thousand people. And those are our three greatest foes. In addition, there are their underlings. They are also formidable. Each is probably worth about ten ordinary soldiers.

"Yet they haven't come out to meet us."

Once he finished inspecting his cyborg horse, D settled into a hollow in a nearby rock. No matter how exceptional a Vampire Hunter he might be, so long as he had Noble blood in him, he would find it far more exhausting than a human being to labor out in the sun. By nature dhampirs sought darkness in the daylight, yet at the same time, their recuperative powers transcended those of ordinary people.

With the carriages parked out in the sun and D melded with the darkness formed by the rock, the road through the boulders was visited by an ancient stillness that early afternoon.

It was perhaps a few seconds later that the horses whinnied.

D came out of the hollow.

Cut free of the carriages with a flash of his sword, the cyborg horses galloped forward. They and D alone had noticed the flapping of wings closing on them from beyond the rocks. It wasn't a sound that human hearing could easily detect—it was a hum even fainter than the buzz of a mosquito.

Perhaps whatever was approaching sensed something out of the ordinary, but as a noisy trio came around one of the rocks to close swiftly on D, a stark flash of light blazed from behind the Hunter. All but one of the sounds were lost, but as the streak of light was drawn back into the carriage, strange ripples passed across the black surface of the last noisy invader. Most likely it was some kind of vibration.

The flapping of its wings was replaced by a groan as the object collided with a rock on the opposite side of the road—and exploded. More than the explosion itself, it was the sight of the fireball that devastated the rock wall that made it clear it'd been some kind of incendiary bomb.

The fireball swiftly spread, assailing D and the carriages as the Hunter rolled over. A shock wave accompanied the hundred-thousand-degree flames. The pair of carriages were easily knocked on their sides and slammed against the rock face. Even now, blistering winds beat against the vehicles.

A few seconds passed—after the flames had raced away down the rocky road, only the tempestuous wind was left in their wake.

Are you okay, D? the baron's voice inquired.

The road belched white smoke like some burnt and twisted caldera, while out in the middle of it sat a black shape that hadn't been there before. Flames swayed here and there and black smoke poured from the shape as it rose gracefully. It had taken on human form. That of the most gorgeous young man in black.

"Are you okay?" the Hunter replied, the baron's question apparently having served to prove that the Nobleman still lived.

D said nothing more as he struck the shoulders and chest of his coat to extinguish the flames. No one there noticed the crude belch of satisfaction that escaped from his left hand. With a coat made of special fibers—heat resistant, cold resistant, and impact resistant—and a left hand that could gobble up flames, D had safely emerged from the fiery inferno.

In the far reaches of the plains, a steam-powered coach was parked. The steam engine at its rear looked like a cylinder crowned with a bell, and on top of it a man sat cross-legged.

"Look, a fire's broken out," he muttered, adding, "but—"

With one hand he held a pair of binoculars to his eyes. As for the other hand, it had been engaged for quite some time now in scratching roughly at his back through a fishnet garment. He was reaching over one shoulder to get at his back—but astonishingly enough, his hand hung all the way down to his waist.

"—I don't think that's all it'll take to finish off Lord Byron. Especially not with the man called D as his bodyguard."

His tone was that of a casual conversation.

A reply came from inside the coach.

"I realize that. The firebombs were simply a test. I checked into something I wanted to know."

"That's good. So, what exactly did you cook up?"

"A face transference."

"You can't be serious!" he exclaimed as the hand stopped scratching away at his waist. "You went and—If you screw this up, Zanus, you'll be—"

"I'm ninety-nine percent confident."

"You could be ninety-nine point nine nine nine percent sure and it'd still be a far cry from perfect. Who were you gunning for, anyway?"

"D."

"Holy shit!" the man cried, reeling backward.

His momentum had him just about to fall off the engine, or rather, he actually dropped about three feet, and then stopped there. His long right leg was braced against the bell-shaped head.

"What complete madness! That pretty boy's not of this world, you know. I don't care how damn good you're supposed to be at making masks, that's just plain suicide!"

"No, it's not," Zanus countered in a voice brimming with self-confidence. "As I believe I just told you, the results have been verified. As a success, I might add."

"Is that a fact? I find that hard to swallow . . . even for that son of a bitch Chlomo."

Like a water strider skipping across the surface of a pond, the man lithely hopped back to the very end of the engine, where he let out a great laugh.

"Don't let me hear any more of your idiotic guffawing, Sai Fung!" Zanus said, his voice charged with wrath.

"Okay, dammit, okay! But that son of a bitch Chlomo—"

But once he'd spoken, his mouth hung open in apparent surprise as he cautiously peered around in all directions with a look of fear that was not an act. What's more, he sensed a chilling air from inside the coach that was normally unthinkable.

"Don't talk about him," Zanus ordered.

"I read you."

Standing up gracefully on top of the engine, the man—Sai Fung of the Thousand Limbs—brought the binoculars up to his eyes once again.

"Hot damn! Now this is something! Let's hurry up and get the hell out of here. The whole damn neighborhood's waking up!" he exclaimed.

Presently, there was a sound from inside the cylinder like a robot or a set of gears going into action, and with a keen whistle white smoke shot out in all directions from exhaust vents around the joint of the bell-shaped head. This unconventional vehicle that didn't rely on horses turned around at a good clip and began speeding back to the village of Krauhausen, which lay a quarter of a day's trip away.

But what did Zanus mean by a success? And who was this third man named by the baron as one of the three greatest warriors in Krauhausen and so feared by the other two—Chlomo the Makeup Lover?

Before they had come out of the rocks, D noticed the wall of smoke rising high into the heavens.

"Looks like a brush fire," said his left hand. "Those flames earlier probably started it. The wind's blowing toward the village. Our best bet is to just wait here."

From where D sat, that seemed like the wisest plan, too.

Flames shot up from the grass, and the gusting wind only served to fan the fire. Everything in their field of view was tinged with voracious hues of orange and black.

Just then, the earth shook terribly. The rocks to either side of the group creaked, and sparks flew where they banged together. The instant a diagonal crack opened across a massive boulder that looked to weigh a hundred tons, D had already doubled back and whipped the hindquarters of the horses hitched to the lead carriage. After sending the second carriage—Miska's—on its way as well, the Hunter was about to take off when the ground sprang up as if something incredibly huge was wriggling below.

The rock went flying. Both D and his horse flew into the air, too—almost straight up. After rising nearly thirty feet they halted, and as the mount and rider dropped straight back to earth, that hundred-ton boulder came right down on top of them.

Literally escaping by a hair's breadth, the figure in black leapt from the back of the horse as it was quickly crushed into an unrecognizable pile of meat, electronic parts, and steel framework, and he then flew like an arrow toward the exit from the rock-lined road. The way he curled into a ball and shot from the exit, it seemed as if he was riding the shock waves of the massive boulder that'd fallen behind him.

Out in the middle of the flames a good sixty feet from the rocks, D tried to see where the carriages had gone, but even with eyes that could see through the black smoke as if it weren't there, he could find no trace of the two vehicles anywhere.

"Oh, that baron should do just fine, I'm sure. Even if he can't get out of his carriage by day."

Flames blew into the left hand as it spoke.

"The village is on the other side of this," the left hand continued. "If we don't hurry up and go, the fire will spread here, too. There's no telling when the wind might change."

A mass of flame shot up by D's side.

"Oh, looks like there's a nest of firebugs or something down there. One false step onto that baby and that'll be the end of the story."

The voice was moving forward. Stepping right through the flames, D broke into a run. The ground was spitting up fire, and the air shimmered in places from the heat. A mass of flames went up. The hem of the Hunter's coat flashed out, and the flames dispersed feebly in all directions.

"Wow! I thought without a horse you'd be in a bad way, but it doesn't look like it makes any difference at all on flat ground. You're something else!" the hoarse voice remarked.

As D ran, he turned and looked back. There were footsteps following him. And more than just one set—the quaking of the earth testified to that.

A terrific force struck the ground, echoing like a tremor.

D's eyes caught a shadowy group rolling forward like a fog beyond the flames. It was spearheaded by a massive swarm of giant black caterpillars covered by needlelike bristles. Behind them was a pack of ten-foot-long plains rats, followed in turn by three-headed boars and burrowing pythons—and this mob of plains-dwelling creatures stretched as far as the horizon in a wild stampede. Fearing fire, they raced off in search of someplace safe, and if caught in their path, even a fire dragon would be crushed by the hoard. One giant black caterpillar already engulfed by the flames couldn't help but slow down, but in a heartbeat it was caught up in the stampede and crushed underfoot before it even had time to let out a scream.

It was only another three hundred feet to D. Even he didn't possess the speed necessary to outrun them. There was only one thing to do.

"You've got no choice but to get up on their backs," said his left hand.

Two hundred feet.

A hundred fifty.

However, when they had closed to within a hundred feet, the strangest thing occurred. Perhaps it was something they saw, perhaps something they sensed, but the caterpillars in the foremost rank tried to halt en masse. Sparks flew madly, but of course they couldn't stop the stampede. The force of those behind them surging forward promptly crushed those in the vanguard, and those responsible then suddenly tumbled forward.

D leapt backward. From midair he saw it.

Between himself and the rampaging beasts, the earth had split open in a straight line. The sight of the creatures falling one after another into that black abyss resembled nothing so much as the dead being swallowed by hell. The chasm continued to grow. It even stretched to where D would land.

"This is incredible!" the left hand exclaimed with misplaced admiration as D drifted, right toward the black and bottomless abyss.

The Destroyer and the Princess Fair

CHAPTER 2

I

I t was just then that a black streak of whip came seemingly out of nowhere. Winding tightly around D's waist with a crisp snap, the whip carried him from the edge of the abyss out onto the burning land. As he came back to earth, D didn't stand, but rather rolled with a shower of sparks. The earth was still breaking open.

And from the abyss there loomed a vivid wall of pink. Looking wet as a heat shimmer in this world of flames, it rose up to a height of over thirty feet, then fell to the ground, crushing grass and fire beneath it. D was already sixty feet ahead of it. And while it was a flat, thick slab of meaty tongue, it nevertheless began to pursue D in inchworm fashion, only at a daunting speed. In no time it closed the distance to thirty feet.

Just as the great wave of flesh was about to come crashing down, there was a flash of white light. Bright blood billowed out like a snowstorm.

Without a backward glance at the crazed spasms of the ten feet of tongue he'd carved open, D dashed on. Behind him, another wave was closing. Another beefy tongue had lolled from the pit.

The tongues seemed to be those of the earth itself. Now there were three of them after D—seizing some sort of small animal, one of them swiftly dragged it back into the abyss.

One above him and the other below, the pair of undulating waves of flesh were once again ready to consume D when a band of light mowed through them. The fleshy tongues that even D's blade hadn't been able to sever were easily sliced into four pieces, and ignoring the death throes of the tips flopping around on the ground, the main portions were drawn back into the abyss.

The shadowy form of a carriage appeared in front of D. Beside it stood the baron, but once he'd seen D, the Nobleman quickly opened the door and climbed into the vehicle.

"Looks like he was waiting for you. So, was that flash of light just now his too? For a full-blooded Noble, he sure holds up well in the sunlight," a hoarse voice remarked.

Without replying, D raced over to the carriage and swiftly climbed into the driver's seat. The second he took up the reins, the whole world tilted violently. Fifteen feet to the right of them, another maw had opened in the earth. The vehicle's wheels tore into the ground and the carriage raced forward. The crevice was right behind it, instantly swallowing the same ground the vehicle had just covered.

"Wha—what the hell is all this?!" the Hunter's left hand bellowed.

"An earthwyrm," D replied. Apparently his interest had been piqued as well.

The left hand muttered pensively, "An earthwyrm? Then there's nothing we can do."

Inhabiting regions more than fifteen hundred feet below the planet's surface and reaching lengths of up to thirty miles, these enormous creatures had been considered mere legend until a scant four thousand years earlier. When certain circumstances forced the Nobility to construct a subterranean city, a team of their scientists came into contact with an earthwyrm in a spot ten thousand feet under the northern Frontier, and as soon as they struck part of its enormous body, they were simultaneously writing new pages in the histories of both biology and biological warfare.

The titanic earthwormlike creatures dubbed "earthwyrms" were endowed with what was an ideal system for an organism to remain alive—they drew the very soil into their bodies and converted it to energy. In a manner of speaking, they were like holy men who were said to live off the dew.

Already ageless and undying and hindered only by their inability to operate by daylight, the Nobility harnessed the creatures' energy, creating soldiers that were not only as immortal as their creators, but that could also continue to fight outside any time restrictions. The Greater Nobility who controlled the Frontier and the polar regions worked on making their own personal armies of the creatures without notifying the central division, while others among them were more overt about raising the flag of rebellion. After three centuries of fighting, the central executives who'd somehow managed to kill or contain the Greater Nobility prohibited for all time the production of immortal soldiers and sealed all information about their life-sustaining processes in the core of a superdense star far out in the Milky Way. In order to keep their secrets completely safe, the rest of these earthwyrms would need to be exterminated, but where that was physically impossible, a special concrete material they couldn't penetrate was poured from the surface of the earth almost all the way down to the magma in regions where they were suspected of dwelling. The one that'd been prodded into activity by the waves of heat now scorching the surface world had either broken out of whatever had sealed it away, or else it had managed to remain free from the very beginning.

This was just *one?* The body of each individual earthwyrm had innumerable energy intakes—in other words, mouths and tongues. If they moved their body, they could destroy everything on the surface and send it all falling into the depths of the earth. They were like a kind of living Armageddon.

"We're not gonna make it. We'll be swallowed!"

As if in response to the cry from his left hand, D reached out with his right and grabbed the wooden lever next to the brake—something that hadn't been there until two days earlier. From a compartment on the underside of the carriage a pair of black globes were released, disappearing into the crevice that pursued the vehicle.

How far underground was his foe? A thousand feet, by D's estimation.

It was three seconds later that a new rumble traveled up through the spinning carriage wheels. A dull explosion could be heard off in the distance.

"It's stopped! Looks like that did the trick."

As he listened to the voice from his left hand, the Hunter's ultrakeen senses did indeed tell him the crevasse was no longer pursuing them, but his exquisite face was emotionless as he stared straight ahead, as if everything had gone according to plan.

Two days earlier, the group had encountered a traveling blacksmith in the middle of a forest. A traveler could ask for no stauncher ally. The last remnants of a band of craftsmen trained in secret techniques passed down from antiquity, they could use the very latest electronics technology that puzzled even the Nobility. Serving travelers and villages on the Frontier, they could upgrade their customers' tools and weapons, doing conversions to the hardware or even crafting new items on the spot when necessary.

D had requested that the blacksmith augment the carriage's armaments within half a day's time. But there was more to the vehicles of the Nobility than mere elegance. Their sleek bodies were layered with panels that could disrupt three-dimensional radar and ultrasound systems, and many of the intricate carvings concealed equipment that would unleash laser beams or ultracompact missiles, spearheads or iron arrows. Once the doors were closed, the entire carriage was transformed into a fortress sealed tight. And that was merely the standard equipment. The higher a Noble's rank, the more enemies they had, and their vehicles would be adorned with the staggering array of armaments and defensive equipment dreamt up by their personal teams of scientists.

In the entire human world, the only ones with the technical skill to match the Nobility and even scorn those accomplishments were the tribe of traveling smiths. The vibrating body that had deflected the enemy's insectoid incendiary missiles and the weapons compartment on the underside of the carriage were both the traveling smith's handiwork. The work had been done by a man who seemed to barely be in his twenties.

After taking his payment, he'd rapped on the body of the vehicle, saying, "Now she's a match for your average Noble's tank or even a pillbox. Part of that's my skill, but of course, she was pretty solid to start. Well, the folks riding inside will be able to tell when they see it, I wager."

Traveling blacksmiths didn't discriminate in their trade. Humans and Nobility were treated equally, and because of that, they were distrusted and despised by a portion of mankind—a situation not unlike that of someone else there.

Finally, he gave D a clap on the shoulder and said, "Looks like someone worked on it once before I did. That's okay—I kicked the offensive and defensive capabilities of that up a notch, too. My treat. Godspeed to you."

"You have our thanks."

The young man's eyes went wide, and he said, "That's not what I'd expect to hear from you, but don't mention it."

D had watched in silence as the steam-driven truck raced off into the distance.

It was about twenty minutes later that the wildfire reached its denouement. An automated plane dispatched from parts unknown had scattered vast amounts of firefighting chemicals.

"That'd be the Nobility's fire-prevention systems, I guess," the Hunter's left hand muttered.

Even with all the Nobility's scientific skill, it was impossible to anticipate every disaster or fluctuation of nature. Due to this, in regions where an area of a certain size was recognized as having artistic or scientific merit, a fully automated firefighting system was sure to be installed, and this was perhaps the most positive factor in the Nobility's legacy. The people needn't ever be deprived of the beauty of lakes that reflected the setting sun, windswept prairies, and life-giving forests that rang with endless birdsong. But those who'd managed to create that system were fading with the setting sun, while those who appreciated that accomplishment the most were the same ones who'd destroyed its creators. The firefighting plane just now must've been driven by some remnant of the software for such a system.

"We seem to have made it through," the baron's voice remarked.

"Where's Miska's carriage?" D asked.

"There's a little river and a linden tree about a dozen miles from here. That's where she is."

However, when they arrived less than ten minutes later, the linden tree cast a supple reflection on the glittering water of the river, but Miska's carriage was nowhere to be seen.

"Do you think someone spirited her away?" the baron inquired as D stared off at the far edge of the plain, as if to suggest that was the source of those responsible for the abductions.

"Your father?" the Hunter inquired.

"Probably," the Nobleman replied, and by that he included those working for Lord Vlad.

"If they headed straight into Krauhausen—" D muttered before falling silent.

"—Miska is in danger," the baron continued. "All will be well so long as they don't wake the Destroyer that slumbers within her. But if she were to be subjected to some cruel torture, the Destroyer might awaken to protect its host."

"What do you think they'll do with the girls?" the Hunter asked in a voice like ice.

And for the first time, the baron may have noticed the fundamental difference between D and himself.

"They won't kill them right away," he replied after a short pause. "I know how he is. He's certain to use them to try to destroy us. But even I'm not sure exactly what form that will take."

With gravity to his tone, he called out, "D, I don't suppose I could get you to extend our arrangement until the three of them have been rescued?"

"No," he replied frostily. For the gorgeous Vampire Hunter, they were no more than an unnecessary factor that had come up while he was performing his duty. As was Hugh, who was still among the missing.

"I thought you'd say that."

Unable to think of anything else to add, the baron let his voice peter out.

A short while later, he remarked, "Come to think of it, the two girls would've been better off riding in my carriage. Why did you have them in with Miska?"

II

It was Zanus and Sai Fung that had made off with Miska's carriage. While fleeing the danger zone and heading back toward Krauhausen, their curiosity ultimately got the better of them, and they were watching the wildfire when Miska's carriage came along. Needless to say, the traveling blacksmith had also worked his magic on the lady's vehicle. Had the men tried to test just how firm its defenses were, they wouldn't have come away unscathed. But they were able to easily make off with it after hearing a voice from within the stationary carriage say, "You there—well, if it isn't Sai Fung!"

Sitting cross-legged on the end of the steam engine, the man almost fell off from sheer surprise.

"That voice—Lady Miska?"

"Indeed, it is I, Miska. How have you been?"

"Er, as you can see, I'm fit as a fiddle," he replied with a hasty thump to his chest.

Exiting the vehicle, Zanus looked up at him suspiciously and asked, "An acquaintance of yours?"

"Yeah. As you know, I used to be a mercenary, and before that I was actually a bodyguard in this place called Winslow. This is the granddaughter of the lord of that region, who took care of me back then. Imagine meeting out here like this!"

"I was aware that you'd relocated to this area. So, are you now a retainer to the lord of Krauhausen?"

"No, nothing of the sort," Sai Fung replied, because he had an inkling of how Miska's journey here had gone.

"Splendid. And just what are you doing out here?"

"Well, at present, my job is keeping an eye on the plains. Oh, this is my partner Zanus."

"And do you swear you have no allegiance to the local lord?"

"On my oath."

"Very well. Then, could you kindly tell me how to get to Fisher Lagoon's establishment?"

"What?!" Sai Fung exclaimed, his eyes going wide.

Zanus followed suit.

"Lady Miska, that place is actually—well, are you certain you're not somehow mistaken?"

"No, that's the place. Grandfather left word that something of great importance to me had been entrusted to the owner of said establishment."

"Your grandfather—excuse me, I mean the good duke—is he well?"

"He died. Betrayed by the villagers. And that's what brings me to this region."

"I see. But if you're headed to Fisher Lagoon's, Lady Miska, have you nowhere else to go?"

"No," she replied flatly, her tone colored by an anxiety that was like a draft under the door.

"In that case, why don't you come and visit the home of one of my acquaintances? Needless to say, he's not a Noble, but someone extremely close in position to the Nobility."

"And who is this person?"

"Er, a scientist by the name of Dr. Brosmen. He lives in a splendid mansion. Of course, it's still the home of a lowly human, but if you can stomach that, it should prove rather pleasant."

Miska's voice fell silent. Her agitation was made manifest.

After a bit, she said, "Alas, my business is at Fisher Lagoon's. That is where I must first go."

Clucking disappointment on the inside, Sai Fung suggested, "Then I shall show you the way."

"That won't be necessary. I must wait here for my traveling companion."

"Pardon my asking, but who might that be?"

"I'm not at liberty to say."

That made Miska's connection to the baron crystal clear. While they were aware that a second carriage accompanied Byron Balazs's, they hadn't known the identity of its occupant.

"But look at the flames. Are you sure they'll make it through?"

"Without fail."

Silent up until now, Zanus interrupted at this point, saying, "And you then intend to enter Krauhausen with him?"

Miska fell silent. Although she had no direct connection to the matter, Byron and his escort definitely had hostile intentions toward Vlad Balazs, and entering the latter's domain in their company would be too risky.

As if he could see into her troubled psyche, Zanus said, "As I recall, the proprietor of Fisher Lagoon's is one 'Taboo' Horton. He and I go way back."

Used by confidence men in the Capital who preyed on girls fresh off the Frontier, the trick was as old as time, and Zanus himself seemed somewhat doubtful of whether or not it would work.

"Ah, that's a different matter, then," Miska said with delight.

In every society there were innocent hothouse flowers that would wilt with the first cold wind—and apparently even the Nobility were no exception.

"Arrange a meeting with him for me right away. Can you do that?"

"As you wish. However, at the moment he's off in the eastern part of the Frontier on business, though he's scheduled to be back within a day or two. Until then, perhaps it would be wisest to stay with Dr. Brosmen."

"Indeed. Let's do that, then," Miska said, assenting with the greatest of ease.

No sooner had she entered the village of Krauhausen than all the strain of the battle up until now began to work against her. Though she was somewhat forlorn, the real reason she was taken in so quickly by the pair's honeyed words was because she'd led the life of a princess. Normally having nothing but scorn for humanity, the Nobility didn't believe they could be deceived by their inferiors, and thus were prone to being caught off guard. This was the fundamental reason why the humans had been able to rise en masse against them. And that was how Miska came to be separated from the baron. But there may have also been another reason, known only to her.

It was dusk when the white carriage arrived at Dr. Brosmen's mansion—or just a little before. Claiming that the plains were dangerous, the pair urged her to make the trip at top speed. But in their hearts, they were motivated by the thought that the baron and D might make it through the flames. When the white carriage halted and its door opened, it wasn't surprising that the two men gasped in astonishment. The pale beauty who stepped down was followed by a timid yet unmistakably human pair, and girls at that. They finally realized the other reason Miska had agreed to accompany them.

"Do what you will with those two. It's been a long journey."

And saying this, Miska entrusted the pair to Zanus before she began to leave with Sai Fung.

"As soon as I have any word on Taboo, I'll get in touch with you, perhaps even as early as tonight," Zanus called out to her.

After going through a number of gates, they were passing through the garden when Sai Fung asked, "What's on your mind?"

"Nothing," Miska replied in a slightly irritated fashion.

"Then forget I asked. I just thought that perhaps you might still be concerned about those two girls."

"Don't be absurd. Why would I care?"

"First of all, it's rather unexpected to have a human come out of a Noble's carriage. Even more so when it's members of the fair sex coming from a Noblewoman's vehicle. Lady Miska, I can't help wondering if perhaps you've grown fond of those girls."

"Sai Fung, spewing any more of that nonsense will be—unpardonable!"

"Yes, milady. Begging your forgiveness," the man known as "Sai Fung of the Thousand Limbs" said, tensing as if from a jolt of electricity. That was the effect the Nobility had.

"I was thinking that you might be a liar. Look. This garden is positively a shambles. And that tower up ahead of us is even worse. It's like the lair where some sorcerer leers down at the world below. You're not trying to mislead me, are you?"

"No—not on your life!" Sai Fung said, swinging a long hand in front of himself dismissively.

Actually, the garden of this mansion he'd said even a Noble would find passable was truly desolate. Long ago, it must've been impressive in scale and elegance, but the shrubbery had died off, and the marble paths and fountains were so sadly blanketed in dead and rotting leaves you could make out the layer of humus. What's more, there was an unpleasant miasma flowing from God-only-knew-where and the smell of chemicals, both of which assailed Miska's far superior olfactory sense and repeatedly left her on the brink of gagging. This was clearly a place of egregious death and decay. And the symbol of that was the tower that menaced the heavens—the same structure that'd just stopped Miska in her tracks. No, having seen the gigantic tree that the Dark Water Forces had used as their base, the scale of it wasn't amazing, but the general lack of glass windows and the antennae jutting out in all directions like countless horns—along with fragments dangling from them that could've been either cords or netting—all oozed a ghastly aura that was not to be rivaled. There was something here beyond imagining.

But seeing that even Miska, a Noble with that species' typical paucity of fear, was ready to freeze in her tracks, Sai Fung grinned in his heart of hearts. Both he and Zanus were de Carriole's personal soldiers. The only reason they'd become known as servants of Vlad Balazs was because de Carriole had loaned them to Vlad. And they had led Miska not to Vlad's castle but here because their first duty was to their true master. Using this woman, perhaps he might be able to do something about Byron Balazs. Lord Vlad would then come to hold de Carriole in even greater esteem, and as his servitors, the two of them would also rise in stature.

"Although this may be an overwhelming place, I assure you the master knows how to treat Nobility. Please, step this way."

Sai Fung put his hand to the massive front doors. True to form, the squeal of the hinges rang out like an agonized shriek, and once the doors were open, the pair was blasted by air that carried an eerie tinge. Though it was heavy with the smell of chemicals, the atmosphere wasn't completely intolerable.

As they stood there swathed in a murky light, an old man in a gown appeared from nowhere in particular with a candlestick in hand. His upper body was so hunched over it hung parallel to the floor. The eyes set in his mummylike face were shut so tight it seemed like he didn't need the candlestick at all, but once he'd stopped a few steps shy of Miska, those same eyes snapped open and emitted a weird light.

"This is our master—"

"De Carriole is the name."

His voice, like a snarling cold wind blowing out of the netherworld, made Miska forget that his name wasn't the same one Sai Fung had told her, so it wasn't until a few seconds later that anger suffused her countenance.

"That's not the name I was given. You've tricked me!"

"Don't be ridiculous. That was merely a bit of forethought to relieve your tension, madam," Dr. de Carriole said in a vapid, murky tone.

Though Miska wasn't familiar with the name de Carriole, Sai Fung and Zanus thought that since she'd been with Byron awhile, she might know about him. Anyone who knew his father Vlad knew that de Carriole was the feudal lord's confidant—an extension of him, so to speak. The mere mention of his name would've undoubtedly kept Miska from accompanying them. However, from Miska's reaction as she stood before that freakish old scientist, Sai Fung realized that his deception ultimately proved unnecessary.

"What are you?" Miska inquired.

"One who serves Vlad Balazs."

"What?!" she exclaimed, turning to Sai Fung and glaring at him with a red gleam in her eyes. Her eyebrows and lips rose instantly. The pair of fangs that poked from her mouth left the woman's Noble and vampiric nature on display.

"Cease this," the old man said in a low voice.

Turning back to him, Miska peered into his eyes. The Noble red glow in her eyes swiftly faded. Holding her gaze as she swayed unsteadily, Miska then bent her knees a bit and prepared to pounce on the old man. But something delivered a short, firm tap to her shoulder. The old man's cane. That alone left Miska immobilized, as if she'd been turned to stone.

Swiftly pulling his cane back, de Carriole then jabbed it into the woman a little to the right and above the ample swell of her left breast.

Sai Fung gasped aloud. The cane had gone right through the pale beauty's chest and poked out through her back without the slightest resistance.

Miska didn't move at all. All emotion and vitality were gone from her face.

"Which of the two has become insubstantial, the young lady or my cane?" de Carriole muttered in a disturbing tone. "So nice of you to sell out the granddaughter of someone to whom you were once so indebted."

His words of praise could've also been taken as a dire condemnation. It was unclear what the old man made of Sai Fung worrying his lip as he looked down at the floor. But employer or not, it was strange that the fighting man didn't show the slightest hint of anger at that remark.

"As for the young lady—since she was traveling with Lord Byron, she should certainly be brought to Lord Vlad. However, before we do that," the old man said, peering into the paralyzed beauty of her face, "there's something that intrigues me. This face also holds the face of something else that lurks within her. However, exactly what that is—"

And then, the old man turned to Sai Fung and said in a tone that made the man swallow hard, "I thought that to find out what that other thing is, we might pit it against you—how about it?"

"Fisher Lagoon's" was a towering mansion at the western extreme of the village of Krauhausen. In terms of scale, it was a far cry from the castle Vlad Balazs kept in the center of town, but on the other hand, it was every bit as opulent. Every night, richly colored lamps lit more than a hundred windows, while everything from the strains of classic instruments like the violin, harp, cello, and oboe to electronic music patterned after that of the Nobility flowed serenely from the structure. No expense had been spared in procuring the finest furnishing, food, and drink from the Capital—to say nothing of the supple women. The village of Krauhausen maintained the greatest stock of "resources" in the region, and it was for this reason that it had a constant stream of visitors, not only from neighboring villages, but from far across the Frontier as well. Actually, the entire mansion was a huge entertainment center—an enormous pleasure palace.

In one room of the building filled with coquettish female tones and reeling with the aromas of alcohol, perfume, and expensive cigars, Taki and May sat across a great black table from a giant of a man with only one eye. This was the man who'd lent his name to the establishment—one Fisher Lagoon.

Behind the two girls, Zanus leaned back against a section of wall by the door and kept a frosty gaze trained on all three. Before they'd been seated here, he'd told the two girls, "The owner of this place is quite prominent. And he has a deep sense of morality on top of that. If you explain your circumstances to him, I'm certain he'll sympathize and agree to help you."

And now, as the giant scrutinized them thoroughly, his good right eye gleamed with apparent lechery as he declared, "Good enough. Fifty thousand for the older one, and thirty for the other."

It was "the other"—May—that suddenly stood up. Whipping around to face Zanus by the door, she jabbed a finger in the giant's direction and said, "You tricked us! He's nothing but a slave trader!"

Shrugging, Zanus replied, "Well, there's not much we can do about that. Just tell yourself it's better than winding up with that Noblewoman."

The second Zanus smirked, May's face flipped right in front of his eyes, both of her feet slamming right into the bridge of his nose before she used that as a springboard to fly at Lagoon's face.

At the same time the girl was being plucked out of midair, Zanus gave a shake to his head, a stream of blood trailing from his nose.

"What are you doing?! Let go of me!" May shouted.

"Are you trying to get yourself killed? Stop it!" Taki exclaimed as she fought to restrain the girl's wildly thrashing hands and feet.

What was it she feared?

On the far side of the big desk sat Fisher Lagoon's massive form, the giant looking on with clear amusement but not moving a muscle. It was only when Zanus took both girls by the scruff of the neck and dragged them back to their chairs that any emotion stirred in the giant's face, which had the same dark sheen as worn leather.

"Knock it off," he said in a voice that somehow called to mind the growl of a carnivore.

"These little bitches are out of line," Zanus said, putting his hands on the shoulders of both. His fingers didn't exactly sink into them, but neither May nor Taki could move in the least. "Mister Lagoon, let's forget the whole deal. The only thing that's gonna satisfy me now is to hang the two of them from Madison Bridge."

"Sorry, but since we've already set the price, they're my property now. Get your hands off them. Now, take this and go, will you?"

A thin gold bar was placed on the table.

"No, save it. I wanna make these bitches listen to their own necks snapping."

"Zanus," the giant said, his eye vested with a terrible gleam.

But Zanus didn't respond at all. "You ready to see your whole place wrecked on account of these two?" he asked in a soft tone.

Smiling thinly, the giant remarked, "Vlad would be heartbroken, I'm sure. Over the loss of such a good subordinate, that is."

"Fine," Zanus replied, letting his white teeth show. "Show me a little more sincerity, then."

The giant's hand slid across the tabletop, and three more bars of gold appeared.

"Thank you. That's what I'd expect from the owner of a place like this. You really know your way around. Well, they're all yours, then."

Taking his hands off the girls' shoulders and collecting his bars of gold, Zanus then departed in high spirits.

Now left alone with the giant—Fisher Lagoon—Taki and May remained frozen in their seats. Ordinarily, the act of taking the two of them from Zanus should have lent him some humanity or perhaps earned him some gratitude, but as he sat there before them, the intensity that radiated from him in some ways surpassed that of Zanus.

"We were tricked, you know. Let us go," Taki said.

Without changing his expression in the least, he declared gravely, "I paid more for you two than I intended. And you'll have to work it off. We get all kinds of folks here. Out of them all, we'll give you the kind of clients new girls have the hardest time with to get you used to the work."

Running his eyes over the list of names on a screen set in his desk, he said, "Tonight, it'll be—oh, is that Mister 'Porky' I see? And then there's—"

Here his breath escaped him. On their first day, the two "new girls" got to see something rarely witnessed by anyone: a look of fear on Fisher Lagoon.

III

When D and the baron arrived, the village was dissolving into the twilight. However, it was bright. Blindingly so. Along the streets, torches and atomic lamps glowed warmly, while tables and chairs were set out haphazardly where the people could while away their time with steins of beer and monster chess and pleasant conversation. Though the yard of each and every house had its gate closed, light still spilled from the windows, while at bars, restaurants, and even the general store—anyplace one might get a drink—every door remained open, ready to welcome all guests. The sad strains of a gypsy violin rang in the baron's ears as he sat in the driver's seat, while fireworks tossed by children exploded in a rainbow of colors around the feet of the mounted D. When the baron and D were spotted, it came as little surprise that folks' expressions changed and the street musicians halted their performance, but once they'd passed, they left no wake at all as the same jovial atmosphere returned.

"Strange place, isn't it?" the baron said to the Hunter. "On all the vast Frontier, this is the only place where villagers enjoy such a vibrant nightlife while their feudal lord remains in power. It's been this way ever since I left."

"When was that?" asked D.

"There is no sense in our kind speaking of time," the baron replied, but after saying this, he smiled wryly. "Pardon me. I can't help but keep thinking of you as a Noble."

"That's a laugh!"

Narrowing his gaze, the baron asked, "Did you say something?"

D tightened his grip on the reins with his left hand and replied, "No."

Getting the feeling he'd heard a tiny cry of pain, the baron strained his ears, but he heard nothing further.

"Should you happen to be concerned about the two girls, there's a hotel called the Rivers Inn if you turn right at the fourth intersection. Take a room there. I'll give you more information as it becomes available."

This meant that their journey would end at that point.

In less than two minutes they arrived. It was just an ordinary intersection.

"I'm in your debt," the baron said, handing D a heavy sack. "There's what we agreed upon. See you."

D said nothing, but halted his horse, as if watching his employer's back to the very end. The dark carriage passed by without a sound. After watching it melt into the darkness at the end of the road, D turned right at the street corner.

The Rivers Inn was about ten minutes away. Many inns in Frontier villages were humble affairs, but as the communities grew larger, they were often divided into separate lodgings for merchants and general travelers. But the Rivers Inn was neither. To put it bluntly, it was for millionaires. The first floor boasted a restaurant, bar, and casino, while the parking lot was filled with the very latest gasoline-powered cars and steam-driven vehicles, all polished and gleaming in the moonlight. The standard carriages were all drawn by at least a half-dozen horses and were lavish, adorned with gold and other precious metals.

Winding the reins of his horse around a hitching post that seemed to have seen no use at all, D then stepped into the foyer. The singing voices that soared to the accompaniment of the piano and violin dropped like dominoes as D moved toward the front desk. Even the bodyguards who kept a razor-sharp eye on the patrons in the hall and lounge couldn't move in the least, as if they'd been struck dead. A grim reaper in black had intruded on this world of multicolored splendor—but what a gorgeous reaper he was. Although the people had been turned to statues in part by the ghastly aura that surrounded D, they were also lost in his handsome features.

Tell anyone without the finest carriage and clothing that we're full—those were the orders the man at the front desk had been given, but the second he saw D step through the door, he forgot all about the fearsome manager's mandate.

"Do you have a room?"

"Indeed we do. The very best suite. However, I hardly think it would be up to your standards, sir."

"A single will be fine. Kindly give my horse some synthesized protein later."

"Yes, sir. And the payment for your stay will be—unnecessary."

As D stared at him, the clerk at the front desk returned to his senses and told the Hunter the correct charge. Paying for three days for the time being, D took the key and was headed over to the stairs when a coquettish voice and porcine laughter spilled from the bar off to the left.

"Mr. Balcon, you can't be so cruel to a girl who just got here today," said one of the women in a tickle of a voice as she writhed in a virulent tangle of bodies.

"Do I look like that sort of reprobate?" replied a corpulent man who looked to easily weigh four hundred fifty pounds.

While the arms of the women were wrapped around his neck and torso, their eyes feverishly embraced the tall figure behind him—a young man dressed in a black suit. Neither his face nor his build resembled that of Balcon. From the way he carried himself and the look in his eyes, he had to be a bodyguard.

"I'm only going to engage in some gentle conversation. Unlike those other dirty old men, I'm not out to take a 'peek and a poke' at the private areas of some young virgin. You see? My interest, in fact, is purely in staying up all night talking," he bellowed, an explosion of vulgar laughter filling the hall before flowing out toward the entrance.

When he arrived at Fisher Lagoon's in a carriage drawn by six galloping horses, Balcon was promptly surrounded in the front hall by the women who accompanied the madam. Though he had the poorest imaginable excuse for a chest, a chin that disappeared into five or six rolls of fat, and a belly that sagged like a sow's ass, the hands that reached for the bulge in his pants were prompted in part by a professional approach to customer satisfaction, but the proof that the act was mostly motivated out of very real interest was the way every last woman had her eyes rolled back in her head and drool spilling from the corner of her mouth as she moaned incessantly.

This was the result of the sexual stimulants mixed into their daily meals and aphrodisiacs in the incense that even now filled the air. The longer they stayed, the worse it became, and in fact, spending a mere week in this house would make these women slaves to the endless swell of carnal cravings that came from within, smothering the will to escape and leaving them animalistic bitches in heat who did as their master and his clients commanded and pleasured them in any way they desired. And although there were naturally many clients who sought that sort of woman, the calls were even louder for virgins pure as the driven snow. As a result, "scouts" of sorts set off for neighboring towns and villages and even went all the way to the Capital to find fresh girls to meet Fisher Lagoon's endless demand.

"You have the girl from the earlier communiqué, I take it?" Balcon asked the foxlike madam.

"But of course, Mr. Balcon. Have we ever said we had a girl and not delivered? She's up in the penthouse suite, sure enough, just awaiting your arrival, Mr. Balcon. Although the girl did arrive just today, so she may be somewhat impertinent. Please try to keep that in mind. And another thing—" the madam said, lowering her voice to add, "though we don't mind a few broken arms and legs, you mustn't kill her."

"I know, I know. That last one—Giselle was it?—I was drunk then. But as you can see, I'm practically sober today," he said as he coughed a cloud of seemingly inflammable breath on the madam.

Stopping and looking all around, Balcon said, "By the by, is that old dog Lagoon not going to come out to greet me today either? Five years I've been coming here, and in all that time, I can't remember the owner showing his face even once. Don't you think that's a bit rude of him?"

"Begging your pardon. You see, the boss's motto is that no matter how pretty our girls are, folks would lose their taste for taking their pleasure if they were to see his face. But that's fine, isn't it? After all, a greeting from the boss wouldn't change the thrill from the girls in the least."

As the crafty old woman stated her case plainly and stared at Balcon in an unpleasant manner, something seemed to suddenly occur to the rotund man.

"Well, there are places like this in even the smallest villages, but it really seems strange that you could build a bawdy house this big and showy right in plain sight of a Noble's castle and make so much hoopla without ever bringing down their wrath. Though they fulfill their own desires by drinking blood, the Nobility have a thing about stamping out the human pursuit of pleasure. Why, there have even been establishments that drew just a little attention to themselves, and as a result not only the patrons and staff, but also the proprietor and his family were all slaughtered. Most peculiar. I can't get over this. What's more—" Now it was his turn to lower his voice as he said, "I've heard rumors. They say the owner of Fisher Lagoon's is actually the bastard son of a Noble. And an unbelievably high-ranking one at that—"

No sooner had he said that than the madam's expression paled.

"What are you trying to say? The boss is a genuine, full-fledged human, mister. A Noble's child would be Nobility. And didn't you yourself just state one of them would have nothing to do with running a house like this? And a Noble's child that wasn't Nobility would be a dhampir. Even that would be half Noble. They'd be bowled over by spending too long out in the sun long before you or I would, but they could lose an arm without it being any major concern. I swear to you, the boss is human. I've seen him out in the sun buck naked, and when he got stabbed in an argument with a testy customer, he needed major surgery. Although I'm the only one he shows it to, from time to time he lets me see that he's still got the scar from it on his belly. And knowing all that, Mr. Balcon, do you still insist on seeing smoke where there's no fire?"

"Don't be absurd," Balcon said as he turned away in a snit, his fears allayed by the madam's harangue.

And yet, the madam grinned from ear to ear. That was part of her job consciousness, and she realized they couldn't afford to allow such a valued patron to grow any more sullen. She was a true professional. A young man in black stepped smoothly to the fore and said, "That will do."

His voice was sweet, but had a great power to it. The girls around Balcon writhed at the sound of it, with one of them even kneading her ample breasts.

"I'm heading up to the penthouse. You come with me," Balcon said to his dashing bodyguard as he swung his great belly around, adding for good measure, "The other guy can watch the carriage. You think he'll be okay?"

"He'll keep a good eye on it. That's about all he can do in the shape he's in."

"Come to mention it, he sure is a confident, creepy customer. Maybe we'd have been better off not bothering with him."

The nondescript elevator arrived then, and only the madam and the two men got into it.

Just as it went into motion, the madam recalled what they'd been discussing.

"Who is this creepy character you're talking about?"

"This guy we picked up in Shabara Canyon on the way here. He's missing one arm and so covered with bruises we thought he was a goner, but somehow he's still alive. What's more, he asked us to take him to the village of Krauhausen, and said that in return he'd act as a bodyguard. There's folks out there that really take the cake. Well, he was so dead set on this, I figured we'd take him along and score some positive karma. But to tell the truth, I have to wonder if he'll live to see tomorrow."

"Have you taken him to see a doctor?"

"Rubbish! What sense would there be in taking someone who can't be saved to the doctor? Now that would be a true waste of good money."

While Balcon was speaking, the elevator halted and the group stepped out onto a roof where the moonlight danced with the night breeze. Some sixty feet away, the shape of a building could be discerned, with windows lit by lascivious red lamps. The rooftop was bordered on either side by the darkened forms of enormous trees. Yet each of them was more than three hundred feet away, so there was no fear of penniless perverts trying to use them to get a free peek at the action.

"Here's the key, sir. I'll be going now."

Both the madam's words and the sound of the descending elevator faded, and as Balcon started down the torch-lit pathway, his eyes were already shamefully bloodshot and his breathing ragged while his tongue hung out. As a matter of fact, he'd even forgotten all about the bodyguard following along behind him. However, and perhaps this was to be expected for someone of his sort, there was one tiny point of risk management of which he remained aware: the sound of his bodyguard's footsteps. As long as they continued to trail after him, he would be safe.

At first glance, the man simply looked like a tall lady-killer, but in the "Capital of the West" he was counted among the five best warriors. His specialty was the throwing knives that he had concealed within his suit coat. Balcon himself had seen the man drop five flame beasts charging at a hundred twenty miles per hour in a second.

In the time it took him to reach the door and use the key to open it, there was no change at all to the sound of his bodyguard's steps.

The room he entered was a small but lavish living room, and next to it was the bedroom. As Balcon surveyed the bizarre implements of torture laid out in the living room, his face seemed to melt in rapture. For what he excelled at was tormenting tender young girls with the cruelest of devices. Seeing the girl tied spread-eagled on the bed in a bedroom without curtains or screens, he was positive that tonight would indeed be pleasurable. With her limbs lashed to the four bedposts by cords, the girl apparently hadn't been drugged at all, and as she noticed Balcon approaching, she struggled madly. It went without saying that nothing could excite a man like him more than that. A black whip in one hand and an electric cattle prod in the other, he stood at the foot of the bed and focused a gaze that could no longer even be described as human on the crotch protected only by the girl's thin pair of panties.

"There's a good girl, missy. Uncle Balcon's going to have fun with you all night long."

And saying this, he held the cattle prod up so the gagged girl could see him switch it on. Blue lightning danced across the tip of it, making the girl's eyes go wide in terror. And that was everything he desired in a woman.

"We'll start out with the light stuff. This prod. Come now, there's nothing to be afraid of. All I'm going to do is singe your privates a little, okay?"

But even as he started to bring the cattle prod down between her thighs, the girl didn't move a muscle. Her eyes were staring right at Balcon—no, over his shoulder, and on realizing this, he also noticed that the young girl's gaze didn't contain the merest hint of fear.

As he was about to turn, the man felt an icy steel grip close on the scruff of his neck and the wrist of the hand that held the cattle prod, freezing the portly Mr. Balcon solid. Slowly craning his neck around, he looked over his shoulder and managed to see a dark figure—a handsome young man in black. However, this beauty was neither that of Balcon's familiar bodyguard, nor that of anything of this world.

Beneath her gag, the girl shouted something. Although the cloth stuffed in her mouth prevented any words from escaping, she'd exclaimed, "D!"

Hunting the Hunter

I

Indeed, it was D that stood there.

But how had he found this place? Or reached the rooftop? And how had he managed to sneak into the penthouse, of all places? Even with his senses blurred by the pink glow of lust, hadn't Balcon still focused on the sound of the footsteps behind him that reached the penthouse without him ever detecting anything out of the ordinary?

"Who—who the hell are you?!"

Although there was no way Balcon's windpipe could be crushed by a hand gripping the scruff of his neck, his face already looked purple. It was due to an incredible strength, and to the ghastly aura billowing at him from the face of unearthly beauty right before his eyes. One of D's hands released Balcon, and then there was a *swoosh* through the air as freedom was restored to all four of May's limbs.

Intense, ungodly—there was just no way to describe his skill with a sword.

Balcon wasn't even watching. Though agonized and on the verge of asphyxiation, he could only gaze at the gorgeous visage in adoration. It was at that point that he finally remembered the name of the young man.

"Such a . . . looker . . . It couldn't be—you couldn't be . . . D?"

"Besides her, there was supposed to be another 'new girl,'" the young man in black said in a low voice.

To Balcon, the voice seemed that of a demon of darkness, immeasurably heavy as it echoed from the depths of the earth.

"Where is she?"

Did that mean that D had come for Taki and May?

Having been splayed out so indecently, May was still ashamed even now that she was free, and something hot spilled from her eyes.

"I—I don't know. There were some good girls . . . that's all I heard. A young one and one not so young . . . and when they asked which I wanted, I asked the ages . . . and chose the young one . . ."

"I know!" May shouted as she wiped away her tears. "They've taken Ms. Taki to 'the castle.'"

A gasp squeaked from "Porky's" throat.

Putting more strength into the fingers around the base of the man's neck, D asked, "You know anything about that?"

"Well . . . uh . . . if you're talking about castles around here . . . Lord Vlad's is the only one. Come to mention it . . . he also has a real taste for . . . young girls' blood."

And having said this much, Balcon gave a squeal and lost consciousness. D had finally pressed all the way down to his windpipe.

Making a light swing of one arm with the clumsily collapsing blob of flesh, the Hunter sent the man flying all the way to the far wall of the bedroom, which he crashed against before moving no more.

"Thank you," May said as she stood up, already dressed in the clothes that'd been discarded by her pillow.

"Any injuries?"

Though D's question was clinically cold, his voice seemed to come from heaven above.

"Er, no."

"Let's go," D said, turning his back to her and walking toward the door.

Following after him, May stepped outside, where the strong nocturnal winds tossed her hair. The rustling from the trees to either side of the building rolled over them in waves. As the torch flames grew thread-thin, their flickering light revealed a figure in black lying on the ground halfway between D and the elevator. Balcon's bodyguard.

Aside from the fact that D had overheard talk of "new girls they just got in today" back at the Rivers Inn and had followed Balcon's carriage out here, the manner in which he'd managed to get up to the penthouse without drawing anyone's attention now became clear. To wit, there was a special wire thin as a spider's web stretching from a branch of one of those trees three hundred feet away and wound around the roof's railing, and the Hunter had come across it. It went without saying there was a grappling hook at the end of the wire. Throwing it three hundred feet through wild night winds was no great challenge for D.

The house was surrounded by a pair of moats and three sets of walls, with electronic eyes and human guards maintaining a strict level of security round the clock, and even for D it must've proved moderately difficult to sneak in, but there was no time to waste in taking care of the dirty old man.

However, he hadn't known Balcon would be going to the penthouse, and when he got over onto the roof, it was purely good fortune that he ran into the pig of a man coming out of the elevator. After the madam left, the Hunter had knocked out the bodyguard and followed the fat man into the penthouse. Only someone with D's ungodly skill could've kept Balcon from hearing any change in the sound of the footsteps to his rear.

But D's feet came to a sudden halt then.

Shocked, May leapt off to one side and hid behind the iron pillar of what seemed to be a laser antenna. Though she looked as hard as she could, she couldn't make out anything aside from the prone figure.

But then that shadowy figure got right up. The motion was so fluid, it almost seemed he must've laid down on purpose from the very start. Without a second to lose, there was a flash from his right hand. Although the knives flew with the speed of a swallow, it was perfectly natural coming from the bodyguard in whom Balcon had had such complete trust. But D batted one after another aside with his bare hands, catching the very last in his left hand and using it to split the bodyguard's head like a piece of bamboo before hurling it off into the darkness to one side.

Just before a cry of pain rang out, a cloudlike mass blowing into D's face was painted red by the torchlight. In a heartbeat D made a massive leap back, but it was too late to avoid the trails of the red cloud that streamed off his chest and other parts of his torso.

"How do you like them apples? I did it, D!" a voice called out from somewhere in the distance as a man in a cape stepped unsteadily from behind a row of gas cylinders.

It was easy to see in that haggard face so near to death the features of the man he'd once referred to as Crimson Stitchwort.

"Got you with my mist, didn't I? It can get through any kind of clothing . . . work its way into your body . . . And in no time . . . it'll take root, D . . ."

And then the man who'd been run through the heart finally gave up the ghost, tumbling forward to fall on his face.

No doubt he was the one who'd breathed new life into the unconscious bodyguard. Having escaped the *coup de grace* from D back in the Shabara Canyon, Crimson Stitchwort was caught in the massive collapse and injured almost to the point of death, yet to have his revenge on D and the baron, he'd latched onto Balcon and come all this way. But D had no way of knowing all of this. And since Crimson Stitchwort had surely never dreamed he'd run into D here of all places, it was yet another strange coincidence.

"D—are you okay?" May asked as she raced toward him.

"Stay back," D commanded her sharply just as the elevator doors opened to spill light and human shapes out onto the rooftop.

The three men who swiftly fanned out in a semicircle around D and May were guards at the establishment. And behind them was

an even larger figure that seemed to oppress the very darkness with his towering form.

"You've got real nerve and skill sneaking into Fisher Lagoon's. I don't suppose I could trouble you for your name before we tear into you?"

Having said this much, a certain astonishment suddenly seemed to fill the giant. And not just him, but the three guards as well.

Just then, a shift in the wind's direction sent the torch flames illuminating D's face off in another direction, allowing his handsome features to sink back into darkness. However, that had more than sufficed.

"My oh my, what a pretty boy we've got here," the giant said, and then he suddenly realized something. "Oh, so you'd be—D? Ah, just goes to show you can't believe everything you hear, I suppose. You're about ten thousand times better looking than they make out."

His words trailed off there.

As Lagoon stared intently at D, faint ripples seemed to travel through the giant's expression. Not even D could tell whether they were of surprise or puzzlement.

D quickly went into action. Although it invited a rapid loss of strength that caused him to stumble, all the guards' eyes reflected was an attack by this person of inhuman beauty. They were all paralyzed by the unearthly aura D gave off.

Their weapons groaned. A trio of arrows loosed by steel bowstrings that could bear five tons were absorbed by the gorgeous figure in black, two of them being deflected by one of his hands while the third and final one sank deep into the right side of his chest.

"Ah!" exclaimed May—and Lagoon.

D backed away unsteadily, grabbing hold of May with his right hand and pulling the arrow from his chest with his left before hurling it like a missile. It penetrated the forehead of the guard who'd shot D, killing him instantly.

While the heart was a different matter, the right side of a dhampir's chest wasn't a vital spot thanks to their Noble blood.

Especially not after the arrow had been extracted—the wound would close almost immediately. But the unsteadiness in D's steps was troubling, as if that one arrow had unleashed all the sickness in his body.

Racing over to the railing with May tucked under his arm, he grabbed hold of something in the air with his right hand.

"Hey!"

"He's got something strung up there!"

Instead of firing a second volley of arrows, the guards saw D's unsteady steps and decided to take matters into their own hands, discarding their bows and drawing the bastard swords from their hips as they rushed him.

"Stop!" Lagoon bellowed, his gigantic form trembling with the cry, but it was unclear for whom it was intended.

Up on the railing with the hem of his coat spreading like the wings of some supernatural bird, D slid off toward the depths of the forest along with May. His right hand held May now, while his left had a tight grip on the steel line strung through the air.

Until he saw the naked blade D held in his teeth, Lagoon didn't know why the two men who'd charged him had toppled backward in a bloody mist. And by the time he got to the railing, the shapes had dissolved into the darkness. There was only the cry of the wind.

The gigantic bordello owner turned what could be called a strange-looking face toward the rustling forest, and his words sounded almost like an incantation as he muttered, "That face . . . It can't be, it just can't. We'll meet again, man called D!"

Around the same time D was arriving on the bordello's roof, the baron reached the gates of the opulent castle in the center of the village. On the way there, no hidden defenses had been unleashed on him, and precisely because of this, his heart truly burned with fretfulness at his inability to guess what the enemy—his father—might be planning. There was no chance the lord was unaware of his arrival. Despite the fact that the monitor eyes of the automated surveillance system had been trained on him ever since he'd crossed the double moat, the drawbridge had lowered into place, and when the baron reached the main gate, the sentries opened it without saying a word.

At some point he'd gotten out of his carriage, and now he stood alone in a vast hall within the castle. He no longer seemed fretful. Even if he actually were, he wasn't the sort of young man who would let it show on his face or in his bearing. He was gazing silently at the throne before him. Glittering with gold and jewels, it was the seat of the man he'd left behind some twenty years earlier. There was no sentimentality in this. He'd come here to do a job he never should've had to do.

"How good of you to come!" a voice called down to him.

This was the shape the father and son's reunion took.

"Or perhaps I should say, 'How good of you to come back'? What's become of the Hunter guarding you?"

"Good question."

That was the first thing he said to the lord of the land.

"I don't know," he continued. "We parted company on the way here. After he performed his part splendidly."

"What a pity. At present, I'm more interested in him than I am in you."

There was no sign of his father. The dreary hall was devoid of so much as a single insect. And yet, the baron was gravely aware of the presence of the lord of the castle.

"State your business—though I know what it is without asking."

"As I promised twenty years ago, I've come to take your life," the baron said, a smile and murderous intent spreading across his beautiful countenance for the first time. The smile grew because he'd finally been able to say what he'd been thinking for so long.

"You still remember that? Oh, by the look on your face, it would appear you've gone through quite intensive preparation. I'm sure Yona and Frazetta would be overjoyed to see you."

Those were the names of two loyal subjects who'd wept as they watched the baron's departure two decades earlier.

"Lord Vlad," he called out to his father, "you made a promise to me not to lay a hand on them when I left the castle. Don't tell me you weren't true to your word."

"Of course I was. Oh, don't look at me that way. That look in your eye is the very reason I would have you killed!"

"That's right—and you, my own father, at that. Father, now it's my turn."

"I know. No need to get excited. Don't hate me just yet. I shall show you I'm a man who keeps his word. Come out, Yona! Frazetta!"

His cry ushered in a pair of presences. The figures who appeared in the baron's field of view seemed to suddenly materialize in midair. They were indeed the same old vassals whom he'd trusted more than anyone in the past, and who had loved him in return. However, as the baron gazed at the approaching pair, it was a tinge of grief that spread through his eyes.

When the pair stopped about six feet in front of him, the baron said nothing, but extended one hand. The pair reached out as well. And then, the instant their fingertips were about to touch, their heads fell off in a bloody mist, and in the span of mere seconds they were reduced to ashes in the pile of clothing they left behind.

As the baron quietly shut his eyes and bowed his head, mocking laughter exploded above him.

"I'll have you know I haven't breached our agreement. Those loyal to you were to remain safe until the day you returned to this castle with your head filled with nasty notions about killing me. Or was I a day early? Ha, ha, you'll have to restrain yourself and pardon such a tiny error."

"Very well. I shall do just as you say. I will restrain myself," said the baron. "But only until Lord Vlad shows himself before me. And let that be soon."

Before the baron had even finished speaking, a flash of white light shot from the interior of his cape.

The streak of light that D's left hand had judged as faster than even the Hunter mowed around the perimeter of the hall, slashing through each and every one of the marble pillars and splitting all the intricate sculptures on the walls in half before they dropped to the floor. The rumblings and great crashes that followed were further adorned by shattering fragments of carved arms and legs.

Amidst the fray, the baron alone stood bathed in a blue light. Solitary and sad as a god of destruction.

When the rumbling in the heavens and earth quickly subsided, the baron then inquired, "Still won't show yourself?"

His blue eyes were crystal clear, and a smile even graced his manly and intrepid visage. Such a gorgeous god of destruction he made.

"Here I come now," Vlad responded in a way that seemed to suggest he had little other choice. "However, before I do that, there's one other person I'd like you to meet. Come out."

Perhaps the self-confidence in that voice allowed the baron to predict what would happen next. From behind a toppled statue, a pale figure appeared like a goddess of devastation, and her name spilled from his lips.

"Lady Miska—what are you doing in this accursed castle?"

II

"What did you do to her?" the baron demanded as he faced the heavens. "What have you done to this woman, Lord Vlad?"

"Not a thing—at least, I didn't do anything," the voice replied. "What was done to her was the work of your old physician friend, Jean de Carriole."

"Indeed, it was," another voice remarked. It came from behind the baron.

This alone must've been enough for the baron to tell who it was, because he didn't turn to look at the strangely hunched mummy of an old man as he said to him, "So, you still live?" There wasn't a mote of emotion or concern in his tone.

"Milord, it is an incredible honor to see you once more," the old man said with a deep bow as he expressed his sincerest excitement.

"What have you done to the lady?"

"Well, she has an extremely dangerous being dwelling within her flesh. No, not really in her flesh, but in her psyche."

It was the same entity known to the baron as the Destroyer.

"And so?"

"After some discussion with the princess, she expressed her wish to have the Destroyer removed. And I have agreed to fulfill that desire."

"You of all people should be up to the task. I've said as much myself. However, what worries me is what comes after that. Exactly what do you intend to do with the extracted Destroyer, Jean de Carriole? I don't want to hear that you removed it merely to have it return because it 'has nowhere else to go.' And I don't think you're the kind to do such a thing anyway. So, what are you plotting?"

"This is most unusual," de Carriole said as he circled around the baron, finally walking over to stand by Miska's side. "I have no intentions save offering the princess my assistance. The reason for her present listless condition is that I've anesthetized her so that I might safely perform the operation."

"Then take her and go. But know that I absolutely will not tolerate a failure on your part."

"Understood. Never fear," the old man told him as he took Miska by the arm and left.

Though the baron may have seemed cold, there was a certain logic to his actions. First, any connection between Miska and himself normally would've ended completely with their arrival in the village of Krauhausen. Next, the baron had to acknowledge the painful fact that de Carriole alone could banish the Destroyer within Miska. And no matter what the human de Carriole might think of Miska, he wouldn't be able to do anything that might put the Noblewoman at a disadvantage—that was a rule that bound all who served the Nobility. All de Carriole could do was separate Miska and the Destroyer, and release her safe and sound.

"Lord Vlad, this has proved an interesting diversion, but that's more than enough for the first act. It's long past time we returned to the business at hand. Show yourself!"

"Before I do, I have one more bit of entertainment I'd like you to see."

With a different ring to it now, the voice drew the baron's attention to the top of a heap of rubble. There, a figure in a bluish purple cape suddenly stood. At more than six feet eight, he stood a full head taller than the baron, but his figure looked perfectly square due to the unusual broadness of his shoulders. His lengthy face was black—not like that of a Negroid, but rather with a metallic luster to his skin that made the outline of his eyes, nose, and mouth all imperceptible. His naked chest was also pitch black, and against it swayed a medallion of jewel-encrusted gold. But even more conspicuous was the dazzling scepter clenched in the blackness of his right hand. The crimson stones set in its head glittered mysteriously.

"Lord!" the baron called out to him.

As if in response, one half of the cape Vlad had closed over his chest opened like a wing. The sight of the young lady it exposed, or perhaps even the suspicion that she would be found there, was enough to make a low rasp of breath escape the baron.

"I'm told Taki is her name. She was sold to a brothel, and thereby came into my possession. I hear she's a virgin. She certainly has an exquisite throat."

"Don't touch her, Vlad!" the baron shouted as he stepped forward.

Smiling but not saying a word, Vlad pulled Taki close.

Perhaps under some spell, Taki remained just as she was with a vacant look in her eyes.

"What a fool you are to be Nobility, yet fear the taste of human blood. I procured this girl so that I might show you a true banquet of blood."

A band of light split the speaker in two, lengthwise. The blinding streak that traveled from the crown of his head down his forehead and out again through the crotch was slowly working to push the two halves of Vlad apart. The thick band then became a thin thread. And it took less than a second for that thread to dwindle down to nothing and disappear.

The baron didn't unleash a second attack.

Black hands had wrapped around Taki's waist and pulled her right up against the Nobleman.

Seeing the black lips part, the baron caught sight of the deep red maw and white fangs, but there was nothing he could do. The lips obscured the nape of Taki's neck. A disgusting overlay of black and white continued for about two seconds, and then the lord took his lips away. They were damp and red.

The baron watched this outrage without comment not because it was simply the Nobility's everyday manner of "feeding," but because the display had a traumatic effect on him due to his genetic makeup and personality. But the instant Taki's head jerked back and he saw the pair of raw and swollen wounds at the base of her neck and the vermilion stream that spilled from them, he ran toward the pair like a wild horse.

It was a split second later that the ground beneath his feet, or rather, the floor of the entire hall, suddenly sank. Unable to do a thing, the baron fell dozens of yards. What awaited him was cold water. Gurgling loudly, it sucked him under and shoved him away.

The legends spoke of this. How vampires weren't able to cross running water.

As the baron desperately worked his arms and legs, his ears caught a haughty laugh, and voice bellowed down to him, "If you are in fact any part Nobility, you can drown down there. But if you should happen to be spared, you shall be cursed for all eternity!"

†

D and May were out on the edge of town in an abandoned shed that housed a water wheel. But though the enclosure might be described as a shed, it was hardly on the scale for merely using the water wheel to mill flour. The wheel itself was easily three hundred feet in diameter. It literally stretched up into the heavens like God's very own lathe. Beside the shed, the river that even now kept that great fifteen-feet-thick disk in perpetual motion flowed by at an appreciable pace. It would've been more correct to call the shed where D and May were a power station. Although the village had switched over to more efficient solar power two decades earlier, the vast interior of the building still contained everything from enormous energy transformers to countless machines, tools, and even living quarters.

It was on one of the beds in the aforementioned accommodations that D lay. After rescuing May, he'd raced out to the edge of the village and entered this place when they happened upon it. May had gone into the kitchen to look for some tea, and putting the kettle on an electric heater there was fortunately still enough power to run, she'd returned for a moment to find D lying down. Since he was hardly the sort of young man who'd take it easy and let a little girl do all the work, May decided to peek in on him and see what he was up to, and she was shocked by what she saw. From the chest of D's black raiment, three plants with crimson blossoms had sprouted. This Frontier maiden immediately realized they were the color of blood. The flowers drained D's blood so they might gain that mysterious luster.

The girl was frozen in astonishment when D ordered her, "Go someplace else."

Seeing the slim scalpel he held in his hand, May raced over despite herself, shouting, "No, we've got to get you a doctor!"

"A doctor can't cure this," D said. "Besides, if we take too long, our pursuers will catch up with us. And Vlad has probably heard about us by now."

The Hunter explained the situation to the eleven-year-old girl. That in itself was proof that he viewed her not as a child, but as a woman who dwelt out on the Frontier.

"And you plan on taking care of that—alone?"

"Go," D told her.

"No, I wanna help!"

"There's nothing you can do."

"Even if there were, would you tell me?" she shot back, not even sure why she had spoken. Perhaps it was some feminine instinct that compelled her to rise to the challenge and not let this gorgeous young man get the better of her. "You just hold on a minute. I'll go fetch some hot water."

Hastily returning to the kitchen, she transferred the steaming fluid in the kettle to a larger pot, added water from the tap, then wrapped both arms around it and staggered back to where a truly ghastly scene was unfolding.

D had already carved one of the stalks out of his own flesh with the bloody scalpel and was about to start in on the second. The roots of the flower he'd thrown down on the floor looked to be nearly three feet in length, and when she thought about them burrowing through his body, May nearly dropped the pot. What's more, the blood that leaked from the roots had collected in a small puddle on the floor.

Saying nothing, D moved the scalpel through the flesh around the second stalk as if he were merely sketching a circle. May's eyes were riveted. As if fearing what would come next, the red blossom's petals trembled. Grabbing hold of its roots, D yanked it right out.

An indescribable cry assailed the girl's ears. A scream unleashed by the flower.

"Wait," she called out to D as he was about to set to work on the third stalk, and once she'd set the pot down on a simple table, May fainted dead away.

The next thing she knew, she was lying in bed. Though the lights had been extinguished, a watery light filled the room, and there were birds singing outside. It was dawn.

Realizing that she must've been unconscious all night, May got out of bed. Although the bed on which D had lain and the floor were both soaked with blood, the pot was gone. The girl thought he must've carried it off again so that she wouldn't see anything more unpleasant than necessary when she returned to her senses.

"D?!"

Exiting the living quarters, she found the door to the shed open. May scurried out into the still-feeble light. Wooden steps ran from the main entrance down to the riverbank, and the girl was surprised to find a figure in black standing by the side of the loudly gurgling flow. The wind fluttered the hem of his coat.

"D!" she called out to him, but on finally noticing the massive shape above her, May looked up and froze in her tracks.

She'd ridden the great Ferris wheel at the sprawling amusement park in the western Frontier—but this was five times its size. A cold, wet mist struck her face—spray sent out by the water wheel. Once the sun rose high enough, she wondered if the shadow of the water wheel would cut across the whole village of Krauhausen, or even cover it completely.

It was soon thereafter that her attention shifted from that imposing sight to the young man by the water's edge. Though the Hunter didn't even turn to look at the girl as she ran toward him, May neither thought that he disliked her nor that he was cold. No matter how he might comport himself from day to day, hadn't he raced to her aid like a genie when her life was in danger? Having been there right by his side, she knew better than anyone how he'd risked his life in doing so, for the pain he'd suffered from the bloody blossoms the night before was something he'd been subjected to in the process of saving her. And although she wanted to thank him at the very least, she couldn't find the words. The young man in black had a sternness about him that blocked any attempt to approach him. May wasn't exactly sure why that was the case.

D suddenly turned in her direction. His chest was covered by his black raiment, as if nothing had ever happened.

"D . . ."

That was the only word she could form. There were a million things she wanted to say. However, the gorgeous young man was there, as powerful as any mountain. And the rescue, the monstrous flowers, the blood that had been sucked from him, the intense operation he'd performed—none of that mattered.

"Something flowed past here last night," D said.

"Huh?"

"By the time I got out here, it'd already gone by, though—"

Eyeing the glittering water, D then started back toward the shed.

May didn't follow him. She wanted to let the morning breeze blow over her.

As he was disappearing into the shed, the sunlight shone onto his beautiful form. On the opposite side of the river—from the far depths of the forest—the morning sun was beginning to rise. For a second, it occurred to the girl that perhaps D had been out there waiting for the dawn. And although she had no particular reason for feeling as much, May found that notion profoundly sad.

III

The village of Krauhausen was bisected by two rivers, one running from east to west and the other from north to south. Flowing, oddly enough, in almost straight lines, the two rivers intersected at Vlad's ancient castle. The crystal-clear waters were drawn underground beneath the heavy ramparts, the river from the east exiting to the west and that from the north coming out again in the south. As might be imagined from the proportions of the water wheel, the current was quite strong, and not a year went by without a number of people drowning not only out between the mountains but also in the village itself. The villagers had dubbed the river running north to south the Pierce, and the one from east to west the Spear.

Downstream along the Pierce, a bizarre little booth had been set up since early in the morning. A pair of chairs sat on opposite sides of a folding table. Although this was a common arrangement for fortunetellers, there wasn't the customary crystal ball or astrological charts. The only thing that sat on the table was a small mirror.

There were quite a few travelers either hastening into Krauhausen or merely passing through in the wee hours of the morning, and they couldn't help but notice the booth. At first, most would get a look in their eyes that said, *What's the story with this?* but on noticing the person who stood beside the booth, they'd be taken aback, staring rather intently at the proprietor's face until their eyes met. At that point, their expression would once more be one of shock, and the travelers then wasted little time in leaving.

In the hour or so since dawn, ten travelers and three wagons had passed the booth, and all of them had displayed the same reaction. And then the eleventh and twelfth came along—a father accompanied by his daughter, by the look of them. Though the father was about to keep right on going, his daughter stopped in her tracks and pointed at the man who stood beside the booth.

"Look, Papa. That man—he's really pretty!"

Having business that night in another village, the father was clearly in ill humor as he turned to look from further down the road, but as he did so, his eyes went wide. Was he dreaming? The man who stood there was wearing a coat that borrowed all the colors of the rainbow. Since the father knew that Krauhausen was a bustling village, the sight of a man wearing such an insane riot of hues didn't make much of an impression on him, but the face was another matter. Quite long—to the point where some might describe it as a horse face—it was still graced by round eyes, a nice high nose, lips as long and thin as blades of grass, and nigh-translucent skin. No matter how you looked at it, it was a face that was the very embodiment of youthful beauty. Knowing all the while that it wasn't the kindest thing to do, he began to compare him to the daughter by his side. However, his daughter didn't mind in the least, as she was completely absorbed by the man's performance.

His performance?

In one hand the man had a three-tiered cosmetic case, while he gripped a brush between the fingers of the other and was in the process of making up his own face.

"Voilà! Finished!" he said as he took the brush away from his eyelashes.

The father and daughter gasped.

On closer inspection, his eyes were too narrow and their lids were weirdly broad. Although his nose ran in a nice sharp line, his nostrils were permanently flared out to either side, making his nose seem like a naked figure sitting cross-legged in the middle of his face. And his lips looked like plump sausages that'd been glued onto him. Yet he appeared to be the most dashing lad in the land.

That was the power of makeup. Eye shadow that looked positively moist cast shadows, and foundation that duplicated subtle skin tones had been spread to make the three-dimensional lines of his nostrils lie flat in two dimensions. Needless to say, those faint wisps of lip came from the way his lipstick had been applied.

"What do you say, miss?" he said, gesturing to a seat, which the girl then headed for with unsure steps.

"Hey! Joanna!" her father shouted in an effort to stop her.

"Never fear. I'm Chlomo, a makeup artist who works exclusively with travelers heading into town. My whole purpose is to make your lovely daughter even more beautiful. As far as payment goes—I don't want any money."

"No charge?" the father said, a penurious grin flitting across his lips, but he quickly wiped it away, adding, "I don't know . . ."

"I wanna do it," his daughter pleaded, staring at the tough-looking man wearing makeup.

Under greater scrutiny the true face of the man—Chlomo—became apparent. And it was for this very reason that the wondrousness of the makeup he'd applied put her feminine instincts into overdrive.

Up until now, every traveler who'd passed by had been male.

While there was some insistence along the lines that it would be fine and it was free, the father still found the guy vaguely unsettling, but on reconsideration he knew this couldn't be some kind of monster out first thing in the morning. Ultimately, he had no choice but to let the girl do as she wished.

Having the daughter take a seat, the artist settled into the chair across from her and set to work. Her makeup was complete in under a minute. In addition to being executed at an alarming speed, the job was also peerless in its precision. The eye brush flashed out; the powder puff sprinkled iridescent powder.

"How do you like it?" Chlomo said as he held a mirror out for her, having returned to his own unadorned horse face. No doubt he'd decided that as a dashing young man, he'd be hard pressed to impress the girl no matter how much he improved her appearance.

"It's incredible!" the girl exclaimed with delight. She had to wring the words from her throat. With eyes of peerless allure and cheeks as pink as cherry blossoms, the face reflected in the mirror could be none other than that of Venus newly born from the foam of the sea.

"What do you think, sir?" Chlomo said, but the girl's astounded father was unable to form a reply. He appeared dumbstruck by his daughter's transformation, or, worse yet, filled by an emotion of an entirely different sort.

"My . . . It certainly is something . . . That you could make her so . . . so sexy . . ."

Both his gaze and his voice were vacant.

"It's just wonderful, Papa. Look—I'm the most beautiful woman in the world!"

Grabbing the hem of her skirt, the girl twirled around.

Chlomo followed right behind her, and when they were a short distance from her father, he asked her in a hushed tone, "Do you like it, miss?"

"Of course I do. Thank you. You're the greatest makeup artist in the world!"

"No, I'm just someone with a love of cosmetics. But miss, your face is actually based on a beautiful model."

"A model? Well, that's okay. There shouldn't be any harm in there being two people this good looking."

"Of course there wouldn't. However, there's more to consider. Said model was actually an exceptionally wicked woman."

"A wicked woman?" the girl said, stopping in her tracks and gazing at Chlomo with uncertainty.

"Yes, indeed. So conceited with her own beauty that she made men support her, dumping them in a heartbeat when their money ran out, stealing her acquaintances' boyfriends, and eventually ordering men to rob banks, steal livestock, kidnap, and commit murder—she could make them do anything. But the worst thing of all was—"

From a short distance away, the father watched Chlomo whisper something to his daughter. Just as he was thinking, *Something ain't right about all this*, his daughter turned in his direction. For all her newfound beauty, her face was now far stiffer than it had been seconds earlier.

"What's gotten into you?" he asked in spite of himself, feeling rather unsettled.

"Oh, nothing," his daughter replied with a shake of her head, and then she drew the knife she wore on her hip for protection and drove it into her father's chest.

"Y—you . . ."

When the father fell without another word, Chlomo raced over to take his pulse, gave a nod, then felt around inside the father's shirt pockets until he pulled out a fat wallet. Admiring its weight once or twice, he then slipped it into his own coat pocket before turning to the girl standing there dazedly with a bloodstained knife in one hand.

"The worst characteristic of the model I chose was that she always killed the men she'd used. The father who'd raised her was in particular danger. Here endeth the lesson," he remarked with amusement.

Then circling around behind the girl, he rested one hand gently on her shoulder and whispered into her ear once more, saying, "If we were to let such an utterly wicked individual live, there'd be no room for law and order in this world. And we couldn't have that."

A second later, the girl bent backward. A steely tip poked out between her breasts.

Putting one foot against her back as she convulsed, he simultaneously pulled his bastard sword out and kicked the girl's body into the river that ran under the road.

"Well, that's the end of your makeup," the dashing young man said, grinning as the splash of the water reached his ears.

Once the spray she'd created had sent ripples great and small traveling out across the river, redness spread through the water a short distance away and the slight form bobbed to the surface, floating off with the water's mighty current. Her father's body was promptly sent after hers.

"I made more than I expected. I can close up shop for the day."

How did those words sound to the corpses as they flowed off into the distance with heads hanging low and blood trailing behind them like swaths of red fabric?

Raising his gorgeous face suddenly and furrowing his thin eyebrows, Chlomo looked upstream and muttered, "Oh, looks like someone else has been up to my tricks."

His eyes had gone right back to the surface of the river. In one area, the river grew much wider, and as it did, the flow became more sedate than in narrower parts. Thanks to this, all kinds of junk got hung up on wooden piles or trees that'd toppled at the water's edge. About fifteen or twenty feet upstream from where he'd disposed of the father and daughter, he'd spotted someone's arm snagged on a branch of a fallen tree, while the rest of the person was underwater. His remark about someone being up to his tricks was merely a joke in poor taste about there being another corpse in the water. Or it was only supposed to be a joke, but as Chlomo stared at the body, his eyes shone with amazement. In a cape so blue it called to mind the depths of the sea, and with a form that looked manly and strong even swaying beneath the water, there was no way this was a human. It was a Noble. And considering the matter that had the only Nobility in Krauhausen in an uproar of late—for he'd been working for de Carriole and Vlad—he knew it had to be *him*. The highborn scoundrel who'd come to assassinate their lord was none other than Baron Byron Balazs.

But what would he be doing out here?

The answer was simple: last night he'd paid a visit to the castle and met with an ambush. Chlomo didn't think that it served him right. Although he was one of Lord Vlad's mightiest three—along with Zanus and Sai Fung—the other two had originally been working under de Carriole, so their loyalty to their lord wasn't especially great. In particular, the reason Chlomo could leave it to Zanus and Sai Fung to stop Byron from attacking while he was out robbing and murdering first thing in the morning was because he planned on taking off anyway and leaving Lord Vlad to fend for himself if things started to go poorly—to put it plainly, he was a self-centered bastard or, worse yet, a psychopath.

What fun! Nothing like a little murder in the family, he chortled in his heart of hearts.

At that point, the only thing sticking out of the water—the baron's pale hand—twitched. Actually, the baron's hand hadn't been hit by direct sunlight, but rather it had lain in the shadow the leaves of this toppled tree cast on the water's surface. However, if the sun were to rise even a tad higher, the shadow would recede, leaving the back of his hand exposed to the rays of the sun. And it had just risen that little bit. Despite being covered by clothing and the armored back of his glove, the Nobleman's skin reacted quite sensitively to the sunlight. His immortal flesh had now begun to voice a protest against the force that kept him from shielding himself.

"Interesting," Chlomo muttered as the evilest look of amusement surfaced on his face.

Quickly walking over to where the toppled tree lay, he placed a hand on one branch and leaned out over the river. And just as he was about to grab hold of the baron's wrist, his own wrist was instead caught tight in the baron's fingers.

"Holy!"

Judging from the way the cosmetic-obsessed freak squealed, he was actually something of a coward. Nevertheless, once he'd seen that the fingers that'd caught hold of him would go no higher, he seemed to consider himself safe, and using all his might, he hauled the baron's body up onto the fallen tree. However, the log was already exposed to direct sunlight. The baron didn't say a word, but his body convulsed. Wisps of white smoke had begun to rise from the damp beauty of his countenance.

"This won't do one bit."

On seeing that the Nobleman had collapsed, Chlomo slung his body over one shoulder and dashed into the dense forest nearby as fast as his legs would carry him. In less than two minutes, he had set the baron down in the bushes in the deepest depths of the darkness, where not even a sliver of light made it through the branches. Panting to catch his breath, he once again looked at the face of Byron Balazs.

"What a good-looking man. Truly worthy of making up. Now, to get this done before he comes to."

And having said that, he took out his makeup supplies, the bizarre nature of which had been amply demonstrated in the horrible murders that had just taken place.

In this corner of the forest that was like the darkest depths of an urn, what sort of makeup job would he perform on the baron? And what were his intentions?

The Woman in the Water

CHAPTER 4

I

Although to May's eyes D appeared to have recovered completely, the truth of the matter was that even now, a heated battle was taking place within his flesh. The bloodsucking blooms Crimson Stitchwort had unleashed were far more virulent than the ones the Hunter had once removed from the baron's lungs. Toxins excreted from the tips of the hairlike roots were able to transform even the blood of a dhampir like D into something vile—the blood itself turned into poison, for these flowers loved polluted blood. Moreover, the instant they were about to be extracted, they released ten times the normal amount of toxins, as if they intended to drag their victim down to hell with them. Even now they contaminated D's blood and coursed through his body.

D possessed the ageless and immortal flesh of the Nobility, and his blood had the ability to cleanse itself of impurities. But would that take twelve hours, or a day, or three days more? Until just before noon, he remained motionless in the water wheel's shed—or rather, in the factory.

May was worried about Taki. The night before, that fat pig had said that Taki was in Lord Vlad's castle while D had him by the throat. He'd also stated that Lord Vlad was quite fond of the blood of virgins. It might be that it was already too late.

What's D doing? she thought, but when she looked, she found the gorgeous figure in black walking around the factory without making a sound. Not in contemplation, but more likely he was taking everything in. From time to time, he would run his hand over some machinery whose purpose was utterly foreign to May.

Hurry up and go save her!

Though she felt exasperated, as a woman of the Frontier, she recognized the hard facts when they reared their ugly head. He had neither a duty nor an obligation to save them. His job was to deal with the Nobility—to hunt down vampires. And while it was as strange a thing as could ever be imagined that he would play bodyguard to a pair of Nobles and wage a constant deadly battle all the way to their destination, given that the gorgeous young man had a strange personality far removed from that of both humanity and Nobility, it wasn't completely beyond comprehension. For that very reason, May found it utterly impossible to fathom why D had broken with his own creed and rescued her the previous night.

In that case, he should help Taki too, May thought, but she didn't say anything. The gruesome surgery he'd performed there in the hut had made it clear exactly how dearly he'd paid just to rescue her. Now he'd completely healed—or so it seemed. But she couldn't bring herself to say that now he had to go save Taki.

It was almost noontime.

In the vast building, a third voice—one that couldn't possibly be there—remarked in a hoarse tone, "Looks like rain, eh?"

Streaks like silken threads fell at an angle beyond the window.

"Doesn't look to be just a passing shower. That throws a wrench into things."

Making no reply, D gazed at the ever-growing torrents of rain.

An hour after high noon—that was the time the Nobility were at their weakest, their "hour of doom," as it were. The biorhythms of those slumbering in coffins would reach their nadir, and the Nobles would be practically unable to move a muscle. Even Baron

Balazs hadn't been able to speak to D during that period. And his father, Lord Vlad, would be no exception, either.

The rain fell with a dull thrum.

What happened at such times?

Based on readings taken by a number of the Nobility's scientists, the drop in their biorhythms would be less than usual for high noon. Although rain was indeed one of the forms of running water that constituted a weakness for vampires, by blocking out the sun at noon, it actually served as a kind of antidote—like using a snake's venom to make antivenin. However, for a dhampir like D, it was nothing short of a major ordeal. The rain only aided the Nobility because they were shielded by their coffins. On the other hand, D would be forced to expose his skin to running water. His muscles would lose both strength and speed, his form would grow heavy, and horrid chills and fever would assail his body by turns. Most Vampire Hunters avoided doing battle on rainy days, as Nobles in their coffins would be ready then for hired assassins.

Picking up his saddle, D walked over to May. As the girl stood bolt upright in shock, he said to her, "I'm leaving town."

The girl's eyes were tinged with understanding—and with despair.

"Or would you like to hire me instead?"

It was a few seconds later that there was a booming toll in May's head, like that of a great bell.

"Me—hire you?"

"I'm a Hunter. I make no distinctions between employers."

"But . . ." May realized that something warm was rising in her chest. Raw emotion. "But, I don't have any money."

"You can pay later," D said in a cold tone.

"In that case—in that case, you're on. D—you're hired. Save Taki!" "Understood," said D.

They now had a contract.

"I'm going to the castle. You should—"

Stay here, D was about to say, but then he turned and faced the windows again. The rain already blanketed the world like smoke, making the entire scene one of blurred shadowgraphs. And he had heard the sound of hoofbeats in the distance.

"They're coming," remarked a hoarse voice that May couldn't hear.

"The enemy's here. There's a boat tied up outside at the dock. Get in it and wait."

Although the Hunter spoke softly, there was a resolute steeliness to his tone, and May dashed for the back door with a face void of emotion.

Seeing that she'd gone, D then advanced to the center of the shed, where he stood silently. Five seconds passed. Then ten.

The sound of the iron-shod hooves came to a halt right in front of the shed.

"Ten of them," his left hand said.

"Come on out, Hunter!" a voice was heard to call through the door via a microphone. "We know what you are. Come on out into the rain. Or if you've got a problem with that, we'll give you five seconds before we blow this shack sky high. Five . . . four . . ."

When the voice reached "one," D stepped through the door.

Through the world-shrouding rain, the figures that had already dismounted and the pair who still remained in the saddle came into focus.

"Allow us to introduce ourselves," a young man on horseback said, his lips twisting into a grin. "As you may already know, I'm Zanus. A servant of Lord Vlad. And this is Sai Fung of the Thousand Limbs."

"You sure went and made a fine mess of things," Sai Fung said with clear disbelief. "Forcing your way into Fisher Lagoon's, making a fool out of one of his clients, and cutting down guards to boot. That's no ordinary whorehouse, you know. In a manner of speaking, it's the other sanctum here in the village."

"That's more than enough out of you," Zanus said, glaring at Sai Fung.

"What's the problem? We're gonna kill him here and now anyway. If we send a Vampire Hunter into the hereafter without him even knowing why, there's no guarantee he won't come back as some kind of ghost," the other man replied, but it seemed that he really just liked to talk too much.

"You know why it is that his house can go about its business so flamboyantly? Well, this is just between you and me, but the place has the Sacred Ancestor's—Oof!" he groaned, the wind knocked out of him by the leg Zanus had driven into his side.

Though Sai Fung's face contorted with pain, his normal expression quickly returned as he continued impassively, "At any rate, no one's allowed to spill blood there. You're the first one to ever break that rule. Matters of right or wrong aside, I'm impressed with you, and it's on account of that we wasted no time in hunting you down. When the lord caught wind of it, he was royally pissed, which is why he had folks spread out all night searching the whole village. This place was spotted thanks to a mountain dove with a TV eye mounted in it. Of course, it would've been better if it'd been in the morning. Due to the downpour we've got now, it had to get pretty close before we could tell."

And having brought that to a close, Sai Fung caught his breath.

"Do you recall the name Galil?" Zanus inquired coldly. "He led the Dark Water Forces—who you probably slew—but those you see here were modified after that into the most elite corps of the entire army. Try not to let yourself get butchered before it's our turn, D!"

And saying that, Zanus gave a toss of his chin, and the shadowy figures who up until that point had been standing there in the driving rain croaked in reply and began to advance on D without another sound. Some splashed through puddles as they advanced. Some had their torsos still half-melded with the ground. But the strangest of all did some of both—slipping in and out of the water.

Standing there impassively, ready to meet them, D said, "Last night, a young lady and a man paid a call on your master. What happened to them?"

"Oh, wow!" Sai Fung exclaimed, raising one hand and drawing a glare from Zanus once again. "I heard about that from Dr. de Carriole.

By 'a man,' you must mean Master Byron. Sad to say, the young lady in question had her blood sucked before his very eyes, and then he was dumped into the running water. I wonder what's become of him now. Probably still down there, a bloated meal for the fish. The whole story just brings a tear to my eye."

"Once we knew you'd arrived, security around the castle was increased tenfold. Nothing can get in, be it god or demon. Not that it's anything you'll need to concern yourself with anyway. Get him!"

At the command Zanus barked, two of the water warriors leapt at D. Rain spattered off the bastard sword each held in his right hand. Although D didn't appear to move at all, the two attackers seemed to take it upon themselves to slip right past him on either side, crashing into the door behind the Hunter. With a sound like a slap in the mud, they were promptly smashed flat. All that remained were viscous black stains.

While it was unclear when D had drawn the weapon, the sight of the dully gleaming blade in his right hand made the two men on horseback look at each other.

"Hell, they'll just be throwing their lives away," Sai Fung said as he gazed with pity at the half-dozen water warriors still surrounding D. "Stand back. I'm coming through."

"No," Zanus countered. "I let you deliver that Noblewoman to Dr. de Carriole. Now it's my turn to have some fun."

Digging his heels into the belly of his cyborg horse, he advanced on his mount through the rain.

"You look weary; you know that, D?" Zanus called down to him from horseback. Astonishingly enough, he'd been able to ascertain D's physical condition from the last bit of swordsmanship. From a stroke of such ungodly speed no one should've detected anything out of the ordinary.

"Let me share something else with you. You're already under my spell."

Surprise was shown not by D, but rather by Sai Fung.

"Go!" Zanus bellowed, and this time a trio of figures rushed D at his command.

After each and every one of those around him had been reduced to something that was neither muck nor clay, fresh blood erupted from both of D's shoulders.

"Your arms didn't seem to move very well. That would be thanks to the doll you found out on the road through the rocks. It had the same face as you, didn't it? Well, that's because it's you. And through that doll, you yourself are now a puppet under my control."

II

"How do you like this, Hunter? I made another one!" Zanus said, reaching around to his back with his right hand, and holding a fresh and lovely visage glowing in that same hand when it returned. It was D's face—or rather, a mask of it.

In antiquity, it was believed that photographs or masks that reproduced someone's face had the magical ability to draw the soul out of their subject, and the masks crafted by this Zanus character seemed to exhibit the very power mentioned in those old tales. For the briefest instant, D's soul would be transferred to the two masks that were identical to him and he would fall under the control of their creator, Zanus. Just enough time for him to fire a stake through the Hunter's heart.

The remaining water warriors crushed in around D, and a second later, a flash of white light sliced off their heads, melting them away.

But look. Bright blood was gushing from D's right side.

"All while under my spell—you're good," Zanus remarked with unexaggerated admiration as he pulled tight on the reins. Whinnying, his cyborg horse poised to advance. "At long last, it's me you'll face. Keep your gloves on, because you'll be needing them to knock on heaven's gates."

The grayish horse and rider raced through the driving rain. Zanus's right hand already gripped a longsword.

Even covered in fresh blood as he was, D stood like a solitary piece of black ironwork. His face looked at the other. It was at just that instant that a crack ran down the length of the beautiful mask the man held up so high.

"Ah!" Zanus cried out in desperation on noticing the crack, but only after he'd bounded for D.

The black-garbed figure of unearthly beauty who'd leapt up over his head brought his blade down with a might and speed that showed no sign in the least of being spellbound, splitting the mask maker from the tip of his head to the middle of his chest with one stroke.

A vermilion hue swirled through the ash-gray world.

As D came back to earth, the wall of rain slapped against his face, seemingly whipped by the wind. Yet his eyes didn't so much as blink as he watched a shadowy form dwindle in the distance with a thunder of hoofbeats, the man already so far away that it would be impossible to give chase.

Whatever kind of swordplay he'd used, not a drop of gore remained on D's sword as he returned it to his back, turning then to face the shed.

From behind him, a voice that didn't seem like it could've come from anything living rolled across the ground.

"Could it be . . . that I . . . underestimated you? You . . . the man they call . . . D?"

It was Zanus's voice. While he had indeed been slashed from the crown of his head to the breastbone, he still sat on his horse gripping the reins. His entire body—and the back of his horse—were soaked with blood. And blood continued to spill from the wound, but perhaps he was running dry, because the gore was washed away by the torrential downpour to reveal a terrible gash and skin as pale as paraffin.

Ordinarily, D would've been merciless in delivering the *coup de grace* at this point. What stopped him? Was he strangely moved by the willpower of his foe?

"Just tell me . . . one thing . . . How come . . . my mask . . . didn't . . ."

Though the words came from a dead man, D didn't reply.

At that point, the rain that hung like a screen between them was blown off in another direction by the wind. Zanus's face was already a rictus, and when his eyes lit up with amazement, it then swiftly took on a look of comprehension and even tranquillity.

"So, that's it? The real thing . . . was just that handsome . . . was he? In that case, I guess I wasn't up to capturing it . . . with my own hands . . . My mask . . . must've been an embarrassment . . . You pretty boys are a whole different ball of wax," Zanus muttered in the end, the words of admiration slipping from him as his body fell out of the saddle and hit the ground.

Not even bothering to check the corpse, D walked back to the water wheel and its shed in the driving rain.

May raced over to him. Disregarding his instructions to stay in the boat at the dock, she couldn't help but stay and watch the deadly battle out in the rain. The fresh blood dripping from one side of his black raiment tinged the girl's retinas with crimson. Stopping cold for just a heartbeat, May then quickly tore one of the sleeves off her blouse and attempted to press it against D's wound.

"Don't," D said tersely as he walked deeper into the building.

"Why not? I've got to patch you up. Dhampir or not, you're hurt real bad!"

"It'll heal soon enough."

Though soft, his refusal came in a tone infused with a force and a weight that paralyzed May, but she swiftly mustered her courage again.

"No way. There's gotta be germs everywhere around here, after all. Now, let me have a look at it."

Surprisingly enough, D halted, saying nothing as he showed her his side and the black clothing that covered it.

Pushing the fabric aside a bit, May let a cry of "What in the world?" slip out.

The flow of blood had stopped as if there'd never been any bleeding in the first place, and the blood that clung to him had dried into complete blackness. Utterly at odds with everything she knew, the healing that'd taken place was almost miraculous.

But even for a dhampir?

Yes. No one had ever mentioned anything about an ordinary dhampir displaying such fierce recuperative abilities.

In any case, May hadn't been able to help at all.

As the girl stood there frozen in a daze, D took two or three steps before halting and turning to her with one hand extended.

"I'll take that," he said.

May's face was beaming.

The young man, beautiful and cold as a crystal-clear winter night, hadn't forgotten how to take the feelings of others into consideration.

Holding the cloth to his wound, D said, "We're leaving right away—get your stuff together."

Their hideout had been discovered.

"Okay."

As the girl gave a vigorous nod, her eyes reflected the figure of D slowly sinking to the ground.

"D?!"

Dashing over, May turned her eyes to D's wound. He was down on one knee.

The cloth was deep red and soaked.

"How?" she exclaimed despite herself.

Just then, from between the cloth and the wound, something resembling a bloody root suddenly wriggled out. No, it most definitely *was* a thin root. The seeds Crimson Stitchwort had sown in D's body had drunk his blood and grown to the point where they were now breaking out. Although D's taking that blade in his side had been due to the falling rain and to Zanus's spell, the effect of the menace within him had also been great.

As the root tried to wriggle free, D grasped it firmly and jerked it right out. With the sound of ripping flesh, a bloodied mass appeared. Seeing that it had the form of a disturbing flower, May had to fight desperately to keep her consciousness from slipping away.

"What is that thing?" she asked.

D stood up again, throwing the fearsome vampire bloom on the ground and crushing it beneath his foot. A copious amount of blood surged out around it, like ripples on a pond.

Before May could do anything, he told her, "Wait a second," then entered the staff quarters in the back.

Closing the door, he took a seat on the edge of the bed and pulled out a knife with his right hand.

What was he going to do? Perform an operation. He was going to carve his own chest open in order to root out the bloody blossoms that riddled his body and even now continued to strengthen their hold.

Though his gorgeous face had lost what little color it normally had, not a hint of pain lingered on it as D cut open the left side of his chest. Fresh blood gushed out. Merely furrowing his brow a bit, D coolly held the knife, slicing a cross into his chest and then sticking his right hand in through the opening.

Each flower left a bloody trail behind as it was pulled out, and ten minutes later, they numbered a half-dozen.

Covered with a thin sweat, D gave the knife a small flick to clean off the beads of blood before ordering in a low voice, "Show yourself."

The door opened slowly.

"So, you noticed me after all, as I might've expected," a strapping man in a black mask muttered with delight from the doorway.

His mask had openings for neither his eyes nor his mouth. He was, quite literally, entirely featureless. From the way he wore the combat belt around his waist and the artless angle of his longsword, one got the feeling this was no run-of-the-mill fighting man, but a daunting professional. The reason D hadn't taken any action earlier despite noticing the man's arrival was because he hadn't sensed any murderous intent.

With a light shake of his black-mask-shrouded head, the man said, "Well, that's not good. Just looking at you makes my head swim. I didn't think there was any man in the world as good looking as all that."

Having said that with a sigh, he continued, "At the request of a certain person, we're to guard you. Kindly get your gear together."

"And who is this certain person?" asked D. There wasn't anything at all in his voice to hint at the fact that he'd just opened his own chest and performed an operation.

"Even we don't know that," the man replied. "All I can tell you is that we got the request in the middle of the night last night, and we were told where you could be found. Now, if you'd kindly come with us."

"Not yet," D replied, opening a compartment on his belt and taking a small leather bag from it.

Once he'd sprinkled a brownish powder on his wound, the man in the black mask shouted to him with some agitation, "Hey!"

Sparks went up. A mass of black smoke drifted into the air. As it spread, it carried the pungent odor of cooked flesh. It was gunpowder that D had sprinkled on the wound. Though this was a common method of sterilization out on the Frontier, it did seem a little rough when someone did it right before your eyes.

"There's more to you than we ever heard," the man in the black mask said, not so much because of the actual treatment, but more likely because not a single trace of pain had shown in D's expression. His surprise was all the greater when he saw the Hunter stand again at the edge of the bed without any real effort.

Exiting that room, D found five more people in black masks standing in the center of the hut, protecting May. It was clear from the way they carried themselves that they were all highly competent. To hire a half-dozen pros of this caliber—or perhaps even more—their employer must've been extremely well to do. Apparently May understood that the men were on their side, for while she looked somewhat uncomfortable, there was no sign of fear in her.

The group went outside, all of them dissolving into the rain like black smoke.

Avoiding the main road, they took a byway that came to a fork. If they were to keep going straight, it would bring them right into town, while branching to the right would lead to forbidden territory—the home of Vlad.

Halting his horse, D asked, "Where is this hideout you mentioned?"

The first of the black masks replied, "In a certain warehouse on Thornton Street in town. You'll see soon enough."

"Just take the girl and go," the Hunter told them.

May turned and looked at D in amazement.

"Where are you going?"

"I have an employer of my own, you know," D said, raising one hand to May.

By the time he'd raised it, he'd been reduced to a black silhouette the rain bounced off.

"Wounded like that? He's a hell of a man," a black mask said in a rusty tone. "So, he's headed off to Vlad's manor, is he?"

D had already melted into the rain.

"Well, not even the man known as D is a match for Lord Vlad," he continued in a tone that made it seem a truth not even May could deny.

III

D halted at a spot where the mightily flowing river made a broad turn to the right. Once that turn had been made, the manor would be visible. A blue pendant glowed mysteriously against D's chest. The sensors searching for him and all other electronic devices were rendered ineffective. Or rather, they'd be completely unable to catch D's form. His foes would have no choice but to rely on spyglasses with old-fashioned lenses, or the naked eye.

Tethering his horse to a nearby tree, D went down to the riverside. For some time now the cawing of crows could be heard. D had recalled the weird birds that sailed through the sky above Lord Vlad's manor. Making a detour around the manor, he'd gone around to its rear. During their journey, he'd heard all about the manor and area surrounding it from the baron. And the Nobleman had never said anything about the flow of the river being gentle. As it struck the rocks along the riverbank, the water bared white fangs.

D entered the river quietly. It wasn't very shallow. The first step found him waist deep, and the next made his shoulders vanish. His traveler's hat alone floated like a piece of black jetsam, and then that, too, quickly disappeared from view.

Needless to say, D was moving underwater. And the river's flow was sucked under the manor about five hundred yards ahead.

Ordinarily, water would be necessary for drinking and other uses. However, the Nobility's castles had no need of water. Although they had a use for the river, they wouldn't really consider the water itself important, and the castle contained machinery that could make it rain. D didn't know why Lord Vlad's manor had this most exceptional need for water. But taking the long view of the structure of the castle and the river, he'd deduced where the water would enter.

In no time, he came to an enormous black intake that was like a cavern. Thick iron bars ran the full height of its opening. It came as no surprise that measures had been taken to guard against underwater intruders. D grabbed hold of two of the bars, one with either hand.

Did he intend to bend them? Even with the blood of the Nobility within him, it would be impossible for a dhampir to bend those inch-thick rods of a special metal alloy. Especially not underwater, where the Nobility were at their worst.

Air bubbles rose from D's lips. And at the same time, an inky streak spilled from the corner of his mouth to spread like a net. Blood. He'd bitten his own lip.

His right arm made a rough jerk, and the iron bar bent like rubber. The one in his left hand followed suit. Twisting his body to slip through the bars, D had a bewitching blood light in his eyes as he was swallowed by the blackness of the hole. Having drunk his own blood to unleash the Noble power within him, D had transformed his handsome features into those of a vampire so cold and cruel the devil himself would've gone to great lengths to avoid him.

Once the flow had grown gentler and a blue light shone down from above, D started back toward the surface. There were no signs of life. When he surfaced, it was by an inspection catwalk that ran alongside the waterway. There were doors at either end of it. Making a quick check of his surroundings, D then headed toward the entry before him. It was a computer-operated door. There was a gleam of blue light from his chest. The door opened without a sound.

An incredible sight greeted D. Black pistons of ridiculous proportions ran the length and breadth of the room, and all were in motion. For every turn of the arm that drove them, white steam sprayed out from nowhere in particular to obscure D's form like some mist-shrouded beauty. The arm had to be easily one hundred and fifty feet long, and the base to which it was attached was unbelievably high and wide, probably tipping the scales in the area of a thousand tons. The sound of each and every rotation was fierce, ringing out like dreadnought-class thunder, and had this not been D, he would've gone mad, or perhaps he would've ruptured his own eardrums first. No doubt this equipment met the horrendous energy needs of the castle. The black machine that flickered through the white wall of steam was like a giant from some other world slaving away for all eternity, raw and breathtaking.

"That's a hell of a setup, ain't it?" a voice said from the vicinity of D's left hand.

"What do we have here?" it added a second later, letting its own suspicions slip out as D's eyes also left the titanic machinery and turned to the walkway ahead.

Twenty-five or thirty feet ahead of him stood a woman in a white dress. Her whole form was wrapped in pale white light that could almost be described as phosphorescent. So lovely and graceful was her figure, the Hunter's left hand let slip a cry of "Oh, my!"

However, it quickly added, "She's a dead woman, right?"

And as if that remark had reached her, the woman collapsed into nothing.

Hastening over, D found that nothing was left of the woman; not even her clothes remained. There was only one thing there: the stone walkway, which was utterly soaked.

When the palm of his left hand was placed against it, it told him, "This ain't true water. The river water's been one hundred percent filtered out of it. I guess you could say the woman was made out of water. No, I'm just joking. Bwa ha ha!"

Before the laughter had ended, D made a great leap to the right and threw himself into the waterway.

From between the machines, a form like a gigantic stag beetle appeared and closed on a puddle on the walkway made from water that'd dripped from D on his way over there. The front half of the beetle's body turned to face the waterway. While it was unclear what it intended to do, D had long since been swept away to the watery depths. In a manner of speaking, the beetle was a kind of patrol car making its rounds in the manor. D was right to suspect that his intrusion had been discovered.

Less than a minute after he'd entrusted himself to the flow of the waterway, D suddenly found himself surrounded by a vast, open space. Water stretched endlessly on all four sides. The flow that'd carried D here no longer had even a trifling effect on the world, while the blue light was the only saving grace of the motionless void. Making for the light, D started to rise toward the surface.

"This is one weird place," his left hand said. Its voice was muffled. They were still underwater, after all.

Sticking just his head out, D looked all around. The ceiling was curved in a great vault and had lost the coarseness of natural stone. This was most likely a natural cavern that had been modified.

"Water flows here from the river. But for what? There ain't so much as a minnow down here!"

At that point, D turned his gaze down into the water and said in a low voice, "No, there *is* something."

A pale woman's face was gazing up at D from below. Her gaze, which could be described as earnest, carried all the solitude of her watery existence, while her white dress seemed to speak of long years that it hadn't been allowed to flutter despite being underwater. It was definitely the same woman as earlier.

"When did she . . . ?" D's left hand muttered, and that was probably the very same thing the Hunter was wondering. For not even D's ultra-keen senses had detected the woman's approach.

D sank into the water once more. Perhaps he thought the woman really wasn't suited to being out of the depths.

"Welcome, O mighty one," the woman said, her voice ringing in his head. It wasn't telepathy—the woman's lips were actually moving. And her voice did indeed echo in D's head.

"Are you the baron's mother?" D asked in his usual voice. It was quite strange how it sounded normal even underwater.

"Oh! Is my child well?"

"Didn't you see him?" said D.

"You mean—he has come here?"

"Indeed."

"In that case—in that case, my husband . . ."

"Your son was out to get his father. Would his father have any compunction about doing the same to his son?"

"No, he would not."

"If he were slain," D said coolly, "what would be done with his remains?"

"They would go into the subterranean incinerator or the river."

"Someone else—a young woman—should've been brought here as well."

"I know nothing of that."

"Where is Lord Vlad's bedroom?"

"In the north end of the basement. Or at least it was. Long ago."

The last phrase seemed tied to boundless thoughts. There wasn't resentment or anger or even grief. The only emotion in this woman was a calm as still and clear as the waters that surrounded her.

Just as D was about to kick away through the depths, the woman called out to him, "Could I not trouble you to hear a certain tale? You, who have the blood of the Nobility in you but are no Noble, who have the mind of a human but are not human—I should like one such as yourself to hear this. To hear our tale."

The woman's voice held emotion for the first time. And that meant chaos and destruction for this placid world.

"Wow!" the Hunter's left hand remarked.

A fierce turbulence that would've left any ordinary person unable to keep their eyes open speared through the crushing depths of the water, tossing D like a toy.

The woman could do more than merely drift peacefully.

Just then, the waves that traveled through the water carried a different sound.

"An intruder has been detected," said a voice that reached them underwater—the voice of a machine. "No one's come this way, have they?"

"Leave me!" the woman said, her lips moving.

"Pardon the intrusion."

"Oh, now there's something you don't find much. Fear in a machine's voice. It seems the lady ain't just a sunken stiff."

While it was unclear just where the left hand had learned such colorful terminology, it fell silent after that.

"I'll hear you out," said D.

The woman's violent emotion had already been lost.

"You see, a month before my child—Byron—was born, a certain august personage came to our manor," the woman began, speaking through the water. "Ah, yes—he has an air about him that is so very much like yours, the great one does."

All she could remember was a giant figure in black standing there in the center of the great hall—this is what the woman told him. Her husband and their retainers had prostrated themselves, and when she followed their example, that great personage declared, "Your child shall be born in a month's time—but I want to perform a certain procedure on him immediately, and I shall take custody of him for three months once he is born."

"Forgive my impertinence, but what are you trying to say?" Lord Vlad had asked.

"I shall make a new Nobility!" he answered instantly.

That reply caused the woman to tremble. Persistent rumors circulated about the great one abducting large numbers of human girls and also performing bizarrely inhuman experiments on Nobility. She thought her husband would object. However, with the great one before him, her husband consented readily, saying, "This is a great honor. Kindly do as you see fit, and allow us to serve in any way that we may." And as he expressed his approval, he smiled so broadly his cheeks seemed fit to burst.

For the following month, the woman was troubled. The mixing of human and Noble blood—that was the sort of thing the rumors described. For a woman of purebred Noble upbringing, that was every bit as cruel as plummeting straight to hell. Especially when that fate might be her child's. She worried, contemplating everything from running away to killing both her baby and herself, but she was unable to pursue either course of action. Knowing well what weighed on his wife's mind, the lord had her under strict surveillance.

Presently, the day of the delivery came and the great one called upon them once more, taking the infant away just as promised. After her husband returned from seeing off their guest in the most obsequious fashion, the woman rebuked him violently.

"Why didn't you try to stop him? How could you let him take our treasure? I despise you. And I shall never forgive you, for so long as I live," she said, spitting the words out like a gout of blood.

In reply, her husband merely said, "Wait three months."

For the woman, those three months were like flesh being shaved from her bones. And then her baby returned. The shadowy figure that towered once again in their hall set the peacefully slumbering babe on the floor and turned to leave without speaking a single word.

Her husband called out to his back, "Were you successful, or was it—a failure?"

There was no answer.

"Byron grew up without incident. He was showered with blessings by my husband, myself, and everyone else. And as my child grew, my hatred waned."

Watching her child grow into a fine young man, the woman swore to herself that she would protect him no matter what happened.

The change, rather, came in her husband. It was when Byron was five or six that she noticed a disapproving gleam drifting through her husband's eyes whenever he looked at the boy. With each passing day it only grew in intensity, until it took the form of cruel violence unleashed on Byron's person. One day, his coffin was taken from its place in the basement and left out in the sunlight unbeknownst to anyone. A timer had been set on the lid so that it would open at a certain hour. Byron's entire body was burnt, engulfed in flames.

"I'm not sure whether or not you know this, but when a Noble's flesh is charred by the rays of the sun, it never again returns to its original pallor," the woman said sadly. "Perhaps that would've been for the best. Ever since that incident, my husband's feelings toward our child could only be described as murderous . . . ever since our child's skin returned to normal *that very same day*."

Destruction and Rebirth

CHAPTER 5

I

Miska was with de Carriole in a certain location. Naturally, she wasn't there of her own free will—all freedom of mind had been taken from her when she first met him. Her eyes were still vacant even now, and she made no attempt to flee despite the danger, but lay on a table like a lovely doll.

She was in a laboratory.

Surrounded by countless drugs and pieces of glassware, an atomic generator, a forge, and the like, de Carriole was seated in a chair beside her. And sitting there, he looked like some evil old jailer ready to torture the captive beauty with his vile "experiments." However, the deep wrinkles of the old man's face drew closer together, and a shadowy suffering seemed to cling to his features like the wings of a bat. In fact, he'd been deliberating this way for nearly a full day. Going through the pile of parchment scrolls he had close at hand, he quickly ran his eyes over them, as he'd done more than a hundred times before, yet still he did it once more. He then banged a scroll against his knees with both hands. For this great sorcerer who was said to be able to call forth the devil himself, such displays of pique were rare.

"This will never do. There seems to be no way at all to remove the Destroyer from this girl. It's impossible to separate the two of them safely."

Rising to his feet, he glared down at Miska as she lay on the table. Ordinarily, it wouldn't have been strange for his eyes to have held despair, but they were ablaze with malevolence. It was because of this disposition that de Carriole had become a sorcerer feared by even the deadliest serpents, but it did not help him overcome his current obstacle.

"If they are separated, the girl will die. That is unpardonable. What's more—?"

Just as he was speaking, an odd-timbred voice announced from a circular window up by the ceiling, "Sai Fung is here."

The black figure was that of a large raven. Its gaze gleamed with purple. Crystals had been set in place of its eyes.

Shooting a glance of displeasure not at the raven but at the distant door, de Carriole commanded, "Send him in."

Without the slightest delay the door opened and the man in question stepped in. He then informed the old man that Zanus had been slain.

"Zanus?! When was this?" the ancient sorcerer asked, his eyes glowing with a spark far too base to be termed hope, but after Sai Fung replied, the light swiftly faded and the old man returned to the seat he'd been about to vacate.

"No, it's too late now. At least, to use a dead body. Even for him, it would be too great a load to bear."

The ring of what some might term obsession in his voice finally prompted Sai Fung to ask with some discomfort, "What are you talking about?"

Although he made no reply, the great sorcerer seemed to suddenly think of something, and he turned an incredibly intense gaze on his subordinate.

"Wh—what is it?"

"What if I were to use you?"

The look in his eye and his tone of voice both defied description. Sai Fung's hand reflexively reached for the bastard sword on his hip.

Subordinate or not, the deadly determination in the man's eyes made de Carriole shake his head in futility.

"It's no use. You wouldn't last a minute."

"What in the world have you been going on about all this time? Have you no words to ease the passage of Zanus's soul?"

"I'll give you his pay."

"Well, that's another matter, then," the man chortled. "Go ahead and take all the time you need for contemplation. You've heard my report. I'm heading back to the manor."

"Wait," the old man called out to stop him, and then he rose from his chair, walked over to a large desk that was close by, and grabbed the flask that was warmed by the flames of an atomic lamp. About half an inch of pale purple liquid had accumulated at the bottom of it—the result of his completely focused efforts since learning about the connection between Miska and the Destroyer.

As his master approached with the flask in hand, Sai Fung raised one hand to stop him, saying, "Kindly wait just a second."

For an instant, the strangest phenomenon occurred. While it was clear he'd only raised his right arm, it seemed to blur into an overlap of countless limbs. However, as de Carriole stopped right in front of him, the old sorcerer's eyes saw just one image of Sai Fung's right arm.

"What in blazes do you wanna do with me? Don't tell me you want me to drink that funny-colored concoction."

"Correct."

"Just stop it."

The baron had counted this man among the three greatest warriors, but Sai Fung grew pale as he backed away. It seemed he'd had more than enough of his master's potions.

Grinning at the naked fear of his subordinate, de Carriole told him, "Relax. I'm not going to turn you into a purple phantom again. This is a fortifying elixir."

"What's that supposed to mean?" Sai Fung asked, his eyes narrowing even further.

"It's a drug that will turn flesh into steel. Drinking just a drop of it would transform you into a superman capable of smashing through the walls of the manor's reactor with a single blow."

"By all means, let me drink it."

"But in return, your whole body will be reduced to dust in an hour."

"I retract my previous remark. And why would you concoct something so useless in the first place?"

"In order to make a vessel."

"A vessel?"

Fluttering his white beard, de Carriole turned to the table where Miska lay and said, "There's something horrible within that young lady. It slumbers at present, but once awakened, it would destroy everything on the face of the earth."

"You can't be serious," Sai Fung said, as people so often do, but he knew that where supernatural phenomena were concerned, this great sorcerer neither lied nor even joked, so he said nothing more to question his master.

"I sorely desire to have it under my control. But in order to do so, I must separate this entity—which we can refer to as the Destroyer—from the girl by whatever means necessary. However, as things stand now, I wouldn't be able to control it. Until I can, I need another body—one under my command—in which I might let it sleep."

A hand dotted with age spots gripped the flask tightly.

"In that case, you have plenty of servants and homunculi in your mansion."

"Balderdash!" de Carriole bellowed at Sai Fung, crying the word like a man unhinged. "You think any old body, filthy and frail, would serve to confine something that could destroy the world? The Nobility! A Noble's body would do the trick. The girl is proof of that. However, being pledged to Lord Vlad's service, I am unable to use Nobles in my experiments. That is why I prepared the fortifying elixir, but, as expected, it simply won't do. The initial form can't withstand the energy the elixir produces."

"Is this Destroyer character really all that strong?" Sai Fung inquired with trepidation. Although his head knew what his master said was the truth, his heart couldn't accept it yet.

He immediately regretted posing such a rash question.

De Carriole's lips warped into a smile.

"Want to see?" he asked, his voice practically a whisper.

Based on past experiences, nothing good could come of this. It would be bad, and on an incredible scale.

"Do you want to see?" the great sorcerer asked again. His eyes glowed maniacally.

"Uh . . . sure," the man replied, unable to refuse.

De Carriole's highly disturbing smile grew ever more daunting.

"Excellent. Then I shall show you just a little."

And saying that, the old man tottered back toward Miska, hunched over all the while. As if pulled along on invisible strings, Sai Fung followed behind him.

Before reaching Miska, de Carriole took a summoning bell that sat on the desk and gave it a shake. The crystal-clear peal was swallowed by the air. Setting it back down while its signal remained a mystery, the old man stood by Miska's side and raised her pale right arm.

"As a result of my examinations, I've determined that this is the easiest spot to get the Destroyer to come out."

Though Sai Fung stared intently, he couldn't find anyplace odd on the bone-china skin that was unique to the Nobility.

"I can't see it either. So of course you wouldn't be able to," de Carriole said boastfully.

While one hand held Miska's arm, a silver needle gleamed in the other. The needle was a good twenty inches long.

"However, a machine I constructed indicated that this pressure point served as an entrance and exit for the Destroyer. Allow me to demonstrate a small fraction of the Destroyer's power!"

Right here and now? Sai Fung thought as a shudder raced through his body, but de Carriole's needle remained motionless, and the sorcerer turned around.

The same door by which Sai Fung had entered opened again, allowing a colossal figure to enter.

"A golem . . ." Sai Fung muttered.

Awkwardly planting one foot after another on the stone floor, the imposing figure walking toward them was most definitely a humanoid shape sculpted from clay.

Sorcerers often had odd jobs that were impossible for humans, and although there were various means of dealing with this issue, the most widely accepted was the "animated doll." Formed from bronze or earth, or even from flowers or air, these dolls were given life by the miraculous concoction that made them. Of them all, those shaped from clay were said to be the toughest and most obedient, and sorcerers, necromancers, and Nobles pitted them against each other to test their abilities.

"This is bad news. That's a combat model!" Sai Fung squeaked in a pathetic tone. "Breathe life into one of these guys when there's no fighting to be done, and there'll be hell to pay before you get it back to sleep again. This one in particular is always nasty when it gets up, isn't it?"

"Exactly," de Carriole said as he raised the needle in his right hand and gradually brought it closer and closer to Miska's pale arm.

A *clang!* resounded from the floor.

The golem had clapped its hobnail-studded iron boots together and taken a position there, arrow straight and utterly motionless. Standing eight feet tall, it weighed in excess of twelve hundred pounds. With those proportions, it wasn't exactly cut out for housework. Battle—it was for that purpose alone the humanoid weapon had been given life.

"I'm so glad you're here." Staring intently at Sai Fung, de Carriole said, "Kill him."

"Wha—?!"

Before Sai Fung could even begin to voice an objection, the golem turned noisily and robbed him of any breathing room.

"Hey! Knock it off, boss!"

As the man backed away, his hip slammed into another table, rattling it badly. Even after Sai Fung had stepped away from it, the table still didn't stop shaking.

Creaking across the floor, the golem rushed at him. It was like a massive steam locomotive barreling forward. Knocking desks and tables aside that must've weighed several hundred pounds each, it extended both arms as it closed on Sai Fung. The sounds of bottles and other equipment shattering seemed to go on forever.

The monstrosity closed with a speed and a force that were both inescapable. As its two arms came together in an iron ring, a lithe form leapt out from between them on a course that angled off to the right. It was Sai Fung. But how in the world had he managed that? His bound was made at an angle and with a speed which were both impossible for a mere mortal. What's more, both his arms were straight out in a rather natural pose, and he stopped as if stuck to the ceiling. Incredibly enough, he was still at an angle.

"The thought of not being able to do anything but run pisses me off, you know. Is it okay if I reciprocate, boss?"

At his question, de Carriole—who'd been watching the whole incident from start to finish from down on the floor—smiled with a strange affability and replied, "Very well, then."

"I've got permission now," Sai Fung said, his expression filled with a dauntlessness that made his fear up until now seem like a sham. "Have at you, mud pie!"

A black shadow suddenly covered the man's face. The giant was right in front of him. The tremendous twelve-hundred-pound form had kicked off the floor and sailed up to him, up more than thirty feet. And now it didn't seem the least bit interested in merely grabbing him.

It was a gargantuan clay fist that ripped through the air on its way to Sai Fung's face. But the term "clay" was misleading, because de Carriole had kneaded it and mixed in various materials to give it the strength of steel.

However, Sai Fung's form suddenly disappeared from right under the giant's nose. He was right behind the golem, hanging from the ceiling, his pose not changed in the least. But how had he done that? He still had both hands resting at his sides.

Without breaking its pose from the hook it'd thrown, the golem began its descent.

Sai Fung made a leap that brought him skimming along the giant's back. A bastard sword glittered in his right hand.

The golem's left arm quickly twisted around behind its back. It slammed into Sai Fung's shoulder—or so it appeared for a heartbeat, and then the man made a vertical descent to the floor. There was no conceivable way he could zip around like that. It was almost as if countless unseen arms and legs propelled his body in any possible direction. As Sai Fung made a light landing, the massive form came crashing down right in front of him. Its own weight plus the acceleration meant a force of over five tons on impact—but the clay colossus took it with just a slight bend of both knees. It whirled around with unbelievable speed.

Humbled perhaps by the sheer power of the giant, Sai Fung stood stock still.

The giant's right arm was already raised as high as it could go. It came down with an explosive *whooosh!* Right at Sai Fung's head.

A strange sound rang out. And an odd scene played out.

The grinning Sai Fung stood there with both arms extended, while above his head—and not more than a quarter of an inch from him at that—the golem's fist had stopped dead.

"Too bad," Sai Fung said as he drove the bastard sword in his right hand deep into the giant's heart.

II

"That will do."

Halted by de Carriole, Sai Fung pursed his lips as he stepped back. His bastard sword had already been pulled out of the golem's chest and returned to the scabbard on his hip.

The giant took a booming step forward. It hadn't lost its will to fight.

A white flash skimmed through its waist. The light had shot from the hem of de Carriole's robe. It was almost laughable to see how the giant came to a stop without a second to spare. Noticing how it had halted with one foot extended but still a fraction of an inch from touching the floor, Sai Fung groaned.

Approaching the giant, de Carriole struck its waist. Though it touched the end of its foot to the floor, the giant stopped at that.

"Drink this."

Taking the proffered flask from the old man's hand, it raised it to its mouth.

As the clay sculpture downed the mysterious elixir, Sai Fung could only stare in amazement.

"Make good your exit. Even I can't stop it any longer," de Carriole said as he dashed over to Miska's side.

While it wasn't exactly in character for Sai Fung to remain there, as a warrior he was anxious to see with his own eyes the strength of the giant now that it had quaffed the fortifying elixir.

The golem bounded almost immediately. Its speed was considerably greater than Sai Fung remembered.

"Oh, shit!" Sai Fung exclaimed as the massive form dropped from above, leaving him no time to escape. The sole of a shoe twice as large as his face was about to smash him—and then the giant rolled. It actually looked as if it had been flipped away. But neither of Sai Fung's arms was in a position to do that.

Leaving a shattered table on the floor, the giant was in the process of getting back to its feet when a voice called out from behind it, "Over here!"

Perhaps it realized that was the voice of its master, but the hatred blazing in its eyes was that of a warrior who'd just confirmed the presence of a new foe. As it got up, the giant twisted its body. Glittering shards of glass and ceramic fell from its back, scattering across the floor.

What the golem saw was a woman with a long needle being driven into her pale arm, and the old man who held said needle. A blue point of light clung to the woman's wrist where the needle went into her. As it was drawn out again, the room was simultaneously filled with an air of terror.

Was this fear from the golem, de Carriole, Sai Fung—or was it perhaps the very air in the room that was terrified?

The skylight was blown out, glass and all. The wind that came rushing in performed a crazed dance.

"B-boss?!" Sai Fung exclaimed. For some reason, his whole body had been enveloped by a red fog.

In front of the giant—beside de Carriole, to be exact—a pale, mistlike mass had formed. Issuing from Miska's wrist, it had only stopped growing when de Carriole once again covered the place where the needle had pierced the Noblewoman.

So, that was the Destroyer?

For a few seconds the madness vanished from the crazed golem's eyes, but they soon blazed with a new and fervent emotion— murderous intent against his foe. And then, with booming thuds, it barreled at the pale mist.

When the woman's story had ended, D looked up at the surface and said, "Time to go."

Whether that remark was addressed to his left hand or the woman was unclear.

"Kindly wait a moment," the woman said, stopping him.

Glowing like something out of a dream, her pale hands undid the bosom of her dress. Her breasts were large and beautifully formed. A finger touched the right breast and red blood streamed out like a thread, forming a small vermilion ball about eight inches from her.

"Drink," the woman said. "In order to safely escape this underground lake, you shall need my permission. That's what this is. Although as a Hunter, I'm sure you may find it disturbing to drink the blood of a Noble, kindly accept my offer. If not, you have no prospect of defeating my husband, no matter how powerful you may be."

This avowal was most surely what she truly felt, without any shadow of mistruth.

D said, "I've come here to destroy the one who would drink that."

And then he raced toward the surface. Indications of the form swimming away traveled through the water.

For the first time ever in this underwater world the woman muttered to herself, saying, "So beauteous a man—and so strong. But against my husband . . ."

It was thirty minutes later that D arrived at Vlad's bedroom. The woman had said it'd been located at the north end of the manor's basement once, and so it remained even now.

Although the woman in the water had informed him that escape from the underground lake would be impossible, D was now at the large and magnificently carved door, dripping wet from head to toe but otherwise completely unharmed. The ranks of fiendishly powerful foes that had once pierced de Carriole's body stood in D's path, as did barred doors, but when his pendant glowed, the former fell silent and the latter opened without a sound, permitting the young man in black to pass. Along the way, D had encountered a few of the stag beetles—guards—but his sword had pierced the thick armor of each and every one, allowing him to make his way to the master's private quarters without falling victim to any of the numerous labyrinths or traps. Never stopping for a second, D pressed forward.

Though the great door looked as if it were opened and closed by an old-fashioned key, it was, in fact, under computer control. A series of three doors opened, each of its own accord, when the gorgeous young man came to them. And when the last of them opened without a sound, D saw a bronze coffin lying on the floor in a vast chamber, covered by a canopy and defended by five canals, one nested within the next. This was the basement, of course, but the windows were still covered by heavy curtains.

In darkness devoid of a single ray of light, D's eyes glittered with a quiet intensity. His feet were already on the walkway that bridged the canal. Since leaving the underground lake, he hadn't stopped even once. But he halted when he heard a sound spill from the coffin.

A sound? No, a cry of pain. A curse. Denunciations from the dead on one who would defile his sacred resting place.

"Oh, this guy's pretty pissed. Looks like he really doesn't want you opening his coffin. It's still daylight outside."

As his left hand had indicated, the cries from the coffin grew louder and more violent as D stepped forward.

Crossing the last canal, D stood before the coffin and reached for the lid. He tore it off with one pull. The locks shattered.

After taking a look inside, it was naturally his left hand that remarked, "Oh, my!"

D's dark eyes reflected the bloodshot eyes and waxy face of the girl staring up at him quietly. Pale arms stretched out toward the Hunter's face.

"D . . ." said Taki.

D had made silent note of the abhorrent teeth marks that marred the nape of her neck. As Taki tried to rise, his left hand delivered a blow to her solar plexus, and the girl slumped forward.

A small recording device had been placed in the head portion of the coffin. The masculine cries of pain had issued from that.

A presence formed behind the Hunter. Whoever it was might've been hidden quite well, and all five of D's senses had certainly been focused on the coffin. However, this was still D. Who could've deceived his ultrakeen senses and kept their presence a secret?

D didn't move. He'd sensed that the second he took a step or even so much as lifted a finger, his foe would strike with lightning speed.

"So glad you could come, man known as D," said the voice from behind him. "I wish we could sit down and have a drink in recognition of your long and wearying trip, but I'm afraid neither

of us is in a position to do so. The least I can do is make your death an easy one. Or should I say your *destruction?*"

A low laugh made the speaker grow tense.

"Death or destruction—that's a distinction a human would make. Either one is fine, but do you think you can do either to us?"

"A-ha!" the voice behind him said, sounding quite impressed. "So, you're not alone? How interesting. I don't know where it is in D that you hide, but I shall send you both to the hereafter. Turn around."

The second D complied, he would probably be hit with some unknown attack.

D didn't move.

As the Hunter stood stock still without any apparent tension or fear, the source of the voice seemed to sense something.

"Why do you not face me?" the voice from the darkness asked in a tone far darker and crisper.

"Is that what you really want?" the Hunter asked.

Did he really want D to turn around?

The voice fell silent.

As the young man in black stood there, motionless and defenseless, an aura like nothing on earth swirled from every inch of his body—and any who felt it would never see another peaceful awakening.

"Why, this is . . . You're just so . . . ."

The content of the words that finally spilled from him aside, there was a weight to them equal to the cries of pain that had issued from the coffin a short while earlier. However, the voice quickly regained its ring of confidence and maliciousness.

"So, it is true. You actually are the great one's—"

The air grew taut, freezing the next word.

A flash of white light streaked toward D's back, but was deflected. Shifting his back ever so slightly, D had parried the attack with his sheath.

At the same time, the man in black became a bird in flight, sailing backward. What D saw was a gigantic hazy figure shrouded in darkness. No matter what it was, it didn't seem like it could possibly have a means of protecting itself from the blade of D's sword.

Putting the speed of his descent and his own weight behind the sword, he brought the blade down. The instant he felt it slice only air, white-hot pain seared through his right shoulder.

III

D's body limned an arc with all the speed of a striking bolt of lightning. Leaving a trail of black blood behind him, he touched back to the floor a good ten feet away. His sword had been transferred to his left hand.

"How the hell did that happen?" a low, hoarse voice remarked, speaking volumes about the situation.

Although D turned in the direction from which the attack had come, he couldn't discern the form of his foe. An enormous shadowy figure towered in the same spot as before.

"Think you can best me with your left hand?"

The chest of the mocking silhouette shook. The needles of rough wood that flew from D's hand pierced the shadowy figure, imbedding themselves in the wall behind him.

"That's two of them. We're still one short, aren't we?" the shadow said.

D charged. As the shadowy figure moved to the right, the sword in the Hunter's left hand mowed through his torso. Having gone halfway through the figure, the blade then jerked to a halt.

A thin needle protruded from the left side of D's chest.

"There's the third," said the shadow. "This is simply fate. Now do you see where your bones will lie, Hunter?"

Before the voice had finished speaking, D was down on one knee. The very same needle D had hurled ran through his back and out through his heart.

But how had that happened? At that moment, there had been no one at all directly behind D.

Slowly the shadowy figure circled around behind the Hunter. No matter what kind of attack he might make, it didn't seem that D could possibly respond. And yet, D braced his blade against the floor and tried to stand. The shadow couldn't help but admire that.

"Most impressive, being run through the heart like that. You are, indeed, the great one's—"

It was a heartbeat later that the voice became a cry of pain.

Between the pair, something black scattered like a mist.

Though pierced right through the heart, D had twisted around and slashed through the shadow's torso with his blade.

"You—you son of a bitch! I can't believe it!"

Though the reeling shadow retreated, D didn't give chase. Once again, he was kneeling on the floor. No Noble—or any other creature, for that matter—should be able to live with something driven through their heart. His last attack was not only impossible, it was miraculous.

"Out of respect for the great one, I had thought to dispatch you painlessly, but now that simply can't be allowed. I shall tear you to bits," the shadow howled, his voice shaking the whole room.

He rushed forward.

And just then, the world was rocked by a terrific impact. A warning siren resounded. Cracks raced across the ceiling, and then falling stonework and dust enveloped D.

Left with no other choice, the shadowy figure fell back to the door. The fissure that opened beneath his feet released a powerful stream of water.

"What was that?" he bellowed, and then he let out a groan.

Black blood trailed across the floor.

A Noble's body could immediately regenerate the damage from a simple blade wound. But there was nothing normal about the blow from the gorgeous Hunter.

"There's been an explosion in Dr. de Carriole's laboratory," the raven above him replied.

"Preposterous. Why should a mere explosion be felt so far as my own bedroom—"

"It was no ordinary explosion. It had dimensional repercussions."

"Dimensional?" the shadowy figure said, looking up.

Although Dr. de Carriole alone knew what he had wrought, surely he hadn't foreseen this result. The instant the mass of blue mist and the golem came into contact, the laboratory had been leveled. The doctor was saved by activating the molecular force field on his belt only a second earlier.

"Sai Fung! Are you there, Sai Fung?" he shouted.

"You betcha," came the somewhat flippant reply from a great hole that'd been opened in a wall bordering the courtyard.

It appeared the subordinate who now poked his head back in had made a hasty departure from the room a split second before it was filled by the explosion. Only instinct made something like that possible.

"What in the hairy hell—where's the golem?"

"Right here," de Carriole said as he knocked the dust off himself. "It seems to have been broken down to its constituent molecules. Gah, I'm choking on this dust. Has the Destroyer vanished as well? Once sucked into the dimensional rift, it won't be coming back again."

"You mean to tell me the golem disappeared because of the Destroyer, too?"

"Could anything else have done it?"

"No. But boss, if you were to set that thing free . . ."

"Precisely," de Carriole said, a smile beginning to break on his pale face. "Your crude brain finally comprehends, does it? What would ensue is nothing shy of the end of the world. You see, it was for that very purpose the Destroyer was created."

His smile was already that of the devil himself, but then it cut strangely deeper—becoming something that many would find far more intense than a mere grin. And then the great sorcerer blurted out a truly strange remark.

"Something capable of destroying the world could slay anyone. *Anyone at all*, you know."

Automated fire-suppression systems were spraying dry ice and extinguishing chemicals when the guard robots raced in, with the black figure of the lord coming just a short time later.

After explaining the situation, de Carriole gestured to Miska and said, "This young lady—I should like to bring her back to my house and examine her once again."

She alone had lain on the table without so much as a single hair displaced by the massive explosion.

"Do as you wish," the lord said, not because he was unaware of the fearsomeness of the Destroyer, but because he was confident that no matter how devious the experiments of the great sorcerer became, de Carriole could never betray him. Vlad went on to tell how the Vampire Hunter had paid a visit to his bedroom.

Intense flames suddenly dwelt in de Carriole's eyes. Ordering Sai Fung to keep Miska safe, he headed with his lord toward the latter's bedroom. Even the stairs and corridors appeared battered.

Presently the pair arrived at the bedroom, where they were greeted by nothing save the remains of destruction. Not only had the gorgeous Hunter in black disappeared as if he'd dissolved into the very darkness, but Taki had vanished from the coffin as well.

"Am I to believe he escaped on his own?" the lord asked.

As the pair stood there in a daze, cold water soaked the floor beneath their feet.

D was in the forest to the north of the manor.

He hadn't escaped under his own power. With a needle—to wit, a stake of wood—driven through his heart, there was no way on earth he'd be moving around with Taki over one shoulder. The stake had been pulled out of him and he'd been guided in his escape from the manor by the woman in the white dress whom he'd met underground. Where she'd come from he couldn't say.

Although it was the same woman he'd spoken with underwater, her image was somehow far fuzzier. And it was on account of this that soon after entering the forest, D asked, "Are you the woman in the water?"

Not answering him, the woman said in a crystal-clear tone, "Take care of yourself—"

She then turned her face slowly to the right.

D had already taken note of the cacophony of hoofbeats.

"Your colleagues are coming. I shall take my leave here."

Before D's very eyes, her form rapidly lost all definition, and in no time at all it was transformed into water that soaked the grass.

Seemingly giving no thought at all to that bizarre development, D stood up as if to protect Taki, who lay by his side.

The riders who halted a dozen feet ahead of D were the same men who'd paid a visit to the water-wheel shack.

"You look fit as can be," the leader of the black masks said from horseback. "You're only the second person ever to go into Lord Vlad's manor uninvited and come out again alive. I must say, we're impressed."

"What's your business?" D asked bluntly.

"Right after you headed off for the manor, we sent up recon birds to cover this whole area. That's why we were able to race right out here. We've got orders from our boss to do whatever you wish. There was probably no need, but we brought your horse along, too. Just say the word."

"Can you prepare a hut?" D asked.

Seeing the pale young lady who lay at the Hunter's feet, the mounted men knew what he was driving at.

"Indeed, we can."

"Put it up somewhere where your identities won't be discovered if the one who fed on her should come," said D.

Through the act of drinking blood, the victim and assailant were connected across time and space. The men probably wore masks more because of the trouble that would ensue if Vlad's people knew who they actually were than if D did.

"There's 'holy ground' on the west edge of the village. We'll take you there." Then the man with the black mask laughed and added, "We're ready any time. The hut's already been assembled."

"I'll take that horse," D said.

One of the black masks stepped forward, leading the Hunter's cyborg horse behind him.

Putting Taki over his shoulder and climbing easily into the saddle, D then took the reins and said, "Lead the way."

Although the others remained speechless, it wasn't because the Hunter's beauty and regal bearing didn't have the slightest impact on them. To the contrary, there was an air of unmistakable admiration coming from the masked men.

"Come with us—it's this way."

The leader's boots delivered a kick to his horse's flanks, and the group galloped west in a thunder of hoofbeats.

When they reached their destination, the men seemed to be dyed with the blue of twilight. Ruins that appeared to be the remnants of buildings were scattered here and there in the desolate expanse of land. Eroded foundations, stone walls, a portion of a tower—although it wouldn't have been unusual for the scene to look like a vision of haunted devastation in this bluish light, the air around this place was instead rather pure and refined.

On rare occasions there were places like this. In much the same way that there were accursed spots on which the Nobility had chosen to build many of their manors and fortresses, there were other places they would never dare approach—locations they could only ignore or gaze at in abhorrence. Tracing back through folklore, it became clear that these places housed the ruins of ancient religions. Apparently something had once existed in them that was diametrically opposed to the Nobility—something that had been held holy. We say "apparently" because almost all of them had been buried or destroyed by the Nobility, to the point where the number of places in the world with anything resembling such ruins could be counted on one hand. In their battle with the Nobility, it was these locations that the human race first thought to use, and the protective charms and icons they discovered there through their feverish excavations played such a vital role in getting a peace treaty with the Nobles that their true value could never be measured.

From the back of his mount, the leader pointed to a domed hut that appeared to be made of synthetic construction materials standing roughly in the center of the ruins. Its surface glistened a dull blue in the twilight.

"How will that do? It's a ready-made unit we just hauled out here, but it should serve reasonably well."

"You're well prepared," D said, letting a rare bit of admiration slip out as he advanced on his horse.

Leaving the masked men outside, D and Taki alone entered the hut. Inside, there was a smaller room for a caretaker furnished with a table, chair, and simple kitchen, while across from that was a cell ringed by steel bars. It could easily hold three people. There were no windows in the hut, for animate fog was among the pawns of the Nobility.

Laying Taki down on the caretaker's bed, D put his left hand to the nape of her neck.

Stretching out a bit, Taki quickly opened her eyes. Even after her vacant gaze finally focused on D, it still took a while before it filled with unclouded will.

"D . . . That's you, isn't it, D?" Looking around at her surroundings, she added, "Where am I? And what about *him*?"

"I got you out of the manor. This is a hut for isolating victims."

Taki's expression instantly darkened.

"Then . . . I was . . . by a Noble."

Reaching for the nape of her neck with one hand, she then stopped.

"You've received the kiss of the Nobility," D said coolly. "But I'm going to dispose of the one responsible."

"You—you're going to save me?"

D nodded in reply to Taki's desperately clinging tone. "Someone hired me for your sake. I have to honor that contract."

"Who in the world would do that?"

"May."

It was some time before Taki could open her mouth again.

"She did that . . . for me? But hiring you costs money, and—"

"Payment at a later date."

As Taki stared up intently at D, a glistening something began to well up in her eyes.

"Help me, D—I beg of you!"

"I thought I told you I'd honor that contract." Turning his gaze to the sky, D continued, "It'll be the land of darkness soon. That's when it all starts."

His soft voice was underpinned by the strength of a warrior who'd slain each and every prince in the land.

A Man Named Lagoon

CHAPTER 6

I

There was a man who had flames of hatred and longing burning in his eyes. Long hair covered half his face, yet he made no attempt to push it out of his field of view. The man was on a horse. Though his features could be described as handsome, all who passed him turned away with disgust on their faces due to his eerie paleness—the complexion of someone deathly ill. Glimpsed in the dark of night, the man was a veritable ghost. However, behind the man rode a boy who looked to be seven or eight-years-old and was the very picture of health, and the way he had his hands around the man's waist would be enough to set people's minds at ease.

Soon after entering the village of Krauhausen, the man went into the all-night bar in a hotel and asked the middle-aged bartender if he knew about a gorgeous young man visiting those parts recently. That was the quickest way to get information in a village you'd never visited before.

"I believe I do," the nodding bartender replied without ever asking the young man his name. "Word is he drove a carriage into Lord Vlad's manor, but met with violence. Rumor has it his corpse was thrown in the river; but, sad to say, Chlomo the Makeup Lover apparently pulled it out again."

"Chlomo? What happened then?"

"That'll cost you extra," the bartender said, turning away in a snit.

"Hmm," the pale man said, giving it some thought before adding, "If I were to, say, try and beat it out of you, I suppose your bodyguards would be all over me before I could leave the hotel, wouldn't they?"

His voice was as gloomy as damp, stifling rain.

"That they would," the bartender replied calmly, for they probably got a lot of this sort of customer in the hotel.

"And if that were to happen, I'd have to put up a fight. What do you think would happen then?"

"Good question."

A wide blade jabbed the end of the bartender's nose, making his features stiffen.

"Before you press your little alarm—watch this."

And saying that, the man put the blade to the base of his own neck and made a powerful slash.

"What the—?!" the bartender gasped as his bulging eyes confirmed that not a single drop of blood fell from the gaping wound.

"Okay, take a good look," the man said as he grabbed his own hair and pulled back, opening and closing the wound that cut half way through his neck like a mouth. "Now, how do you think your bodyguards would fare against a man who can do this?"

When he returned his head to the proper position, the wound swiftly closed, leaving a thin thread of a line that in turn vanished almost instantly.

"Don't tell me . . . You're that Vampire Hunter . . . Vince . . . aren't you?"

Having finally realized who he faced, the bartender found his face colored by the resignation and fear of one whose fate had already been decided.

"There are those who call me that. So, what became of that pretty boy?"

The sweat dripping from the bartender made it clear he'd suddenly become completely honest.

"If Chlomo put makeup on him, he should be back at his place. It's one of the abandoned warehouses on the west edge of town."

"Thank you," Vince said, clapping the bartender on the shoulder as his right hand flashed out. The tip he'd laid down earlier was back in his hand.

"Hey! That's a dirty thing to do."

"The best thing a man can do is to make an honest living. You're the kind that preys on the poor and gullible, aren't you?"

Grinning like a ghost, Vince exited the bar. As he walked toward where he'd left the boy sitting on his horse, he heard footsteps echoing behind him. Walking along undeterred, a pair of figures circled around in front of him. Two more were behind him.

"You guys bodyguards?" Vince asked as he halted.

"You had a lot of nerve pulling that in front of us," said one of the men to his rear—a guy with a beard. He kept opening and closing his right hand, which clenched something that resembled a big hairball. "But if we just sit back and let you leave, come tomorrow, we ain't gonna be drawing a salary anymore. So you've got your choice of either trotting back in there and apologizing, or throwing down with us."

Patrons and employees that'd followed them out of the bar had already formed a circle around them.

Vince chose a third option. He walked toward his horse.

Perhaps that figured into their plans, because the two ahead of him drew their longswords and started closing on him without a word. They didn't even have to think about what would come next. Slicing through the wind from either side, the blades should've cut diagonal paths through Vince's body. Their swords did, in fact, go right through him. The two of them stumbled in their respective locations. Having met so little resistance, the swings left them off balance.

On finally reaching his horse, Vince grabbed the old gunpowder rifle strapped to his saddle. The deafening reports left the spectators unsure of which way to run, while the two bodyguards hit the ground with half of each man's head missing.

Before Vince could bring the muzzle to bear on the other two, what seemed to be a fine net drifted down from the heavens and enveloped him completely. There was an explosion of light. Caught in the pale electromagnetic waves, his body looked like a rag doll as it blazed in the darkness.

"Half a million volts. That'd lay out even a fire dragon," the head bodyguard said, still gripping one edge of the net as he bared his yellowed teeth in a smile. Both the ultra-high-energy generator and discharge device were strapped to his right wrist.

Once Vince's body fell with bluish smoke rising from it, the man swung his right arm around. The daunting electric net quickly became a single ball again in his hand.

"Clean that mess up," he ordered the other bodyguard, and he was just starting back toward the bar when he noticed the expressions on the faces of the spectators. It was as he was turning around that something impossibly cold ran down his spine.

Vince was standing there. Though bluish smoke still rose from him, his skin had the pallor of a corpse, not blackened in the least.

"S—sonuvabitch . . ."

The rifle put a piece of hot lead right through the forehead of the paralyzed man.

Vince told the other immobilized bodyguard, "Clean *that* up," before mounting his horse and riding off to the west.

When the people finally began to gather around the corpses, one man still stood by the door to the bar, his gaze trained in the same direction in which the horse had ridden off.

"So, we've got another weirdo on our hands, do we? Looks like things are gonna get shaken up in town for the first time in ages."

These remarks were muttered by a figure in a dapper suit who was not only the owner of the bar, but the most prominent villager—Fisher Lagoon.

†

It took less than twenty minutes to reach the cluster of warehouses. Tethering the horse that carried the boy to a tree a short distance away, Vince began to walk between rows of half-fallen structures. He immediately recognized his goal. Several serviceable warehouses still remained, and a light burned in one of them.

After dashing over to the door without making a sound, he said, "Chlomo the Makeup Lover? That's an odd name."

The door wasn't locked. This wasn't a sign of carelessness, but rather it made manifest the owner's confidence that no one would come out there. The air that gusted out with that faint light had such a ghastliness to it, it actually sent chills through the invincible Vince.

Once through the door, there were seven-foot-high panels directly ahead lined up to form a partition and hide the depths of the warehouse from any visitors. In one spot alone a space wide enough for a single person to fit through had been left open, and the glow of an atomic lamp trickled out through it.

From where Vince was, he couldn't see anything. Keeping his footsteps muted as he approached the panels, Vince cautiously poked his head through the space and squinted.

In the room oddly filled by a glow close to natural light, more people than he could count lay on the floor or slumped against the walls, some alone, others stacked on top of one another, so that it looked like this was some sort of farmer's market where human beings were for sale. That alone would've been an unsettling sight, but what left Vince shaken was that every person's face had been covered with makeup. And each to a horrendous degree. Thick eyebrows sloping up, eyes ablaze—some burning with malice, others with lust—yet no one so much as moved a muscle.

From the midst of these motionless people, something like humming could be heard. Vince had already noticed the pair of figures seated on chairs in the center of the room. One of them—the rougher one—was running some sort of brush across the face of the other, who had a powerful and attractive build.

The Makeup Lover—Vince's eyes lit up. He began to walk forward, forgetting to keep himself hidden. Though he did continue to at least keep his footsteps muted, his behavior was to be expected from someone with supreme confidence that there was nothing his opponent might do to slay him.

The made-up people didn't move an inch.

When he finally stood in a spot where he could discern the face that'd been coated with the black of shadows, Vince gasped. Although he'd never seen the man applying the cosmetics, the one on the receiving end was—

"Baron Balazs . . ."

The same gorgeous prey he and the others had pursued for so long. However, while his clothes remained the same, his features had changed markedly. Bluish shadows had been painted on his skin, and the black circles that delineated his eyes gave them the dismal glow of a wraith, while his lips alone remained as red as some poisonous herb. At first glance, even those who'd been well-acquainted with the baron wouldn't have recognized him.

Though he stood there dumbstruck, Vince quickly sensed a mysterious phenomenon beginning to unfold in his heart. It was the cruel beauty of the baron's features—as Vince concentrated his gaze on them, he realized that the shocking impression the makeup had left was fading away. Just as those who stayed to watch an unsightly philosopher deliver his oratory for some time were left unable to deny the noble spirit within him, so the baron's heaven-sent beauty swiftly pierced the repulsive mask he'd been given, allowing him to shine once more.

The humming stopped.

Halting the hand that held the brush, the stern-looking man let his shoulders drop disappointedly.

"Ruined again. Lord Vlad, your son is someone to be feared."

Knowing nothing of the horrifying nature of this man's ability, Vince had a little grin on his lips as he said to him, "Are you Chlomo?"

Surely he'd been entirely focused on the baron's makeup, body and soul. The man turned and looked in amazement. Every bit as rough as his build, his face didn't look at all suited to someone in a field that demanded as much skill and refinement as cosmetics.

"Who are you?"

"Vince. I'm a Hunter. You're Chlomo the Makeup Lover, aren't you?"

"What do you want?" Chlomo inquired, his confidence now fully reclaimed.

"Him—we've been hunting that man. I'll take him from you."

After a quick glance at the baron, Chlomo said, "You went after someone I can't even put makeup on? Then it comes as no surprise you failed to run him down."

As the makeup lover smirked, his eyes reflected Vince's expression, which instantly became that of the devil himself.

II

"Oh, that's an interesting look you're giving me," Chlomo said as he stuck out his jaw. "My makeup would be simply perfect on someone with such a wicked expression. I can hardly wait."

Vince said nothing as he closed the distance between them. Though he didn't know what sort of ability his foe had, Vince had regenerating cells that could deal with any kind of wound, and this opponent shouldn't be able to deal a lethal blow to him. If this guy had such a keen interest in makeup, then the Hunter would rip his limbs off to get him all fixed up for a trip straight to hell.

Vince tightened his grip on the dagger he wore at his breast. It was a heartbeat later that movements became perceptible all around him. Keeping a fair portion of his attention focused on Chlomo as he spun around, Vince knit his brow. From the floor and wall, people in makeup were rising and slowly but determinedly heading toward him. There was no intellect in their vacant gazes. That in itself was extremely disturbing.

"Die!" Chlomo cried, and his voice was their signal.

The men closed on Vince with strangely stiff movements before piercing his neck and abdomen with longswords. Paying no attention to that the wounds, Vince slashed open the men's throats with the dagger in his right hand—and was shocked. The blood gushing from their carotid arteries didn't splatter across the floor, but rather it hung like a vermilion fog around him. It certainly was beautiful arterial spray. The color instantly drained from the men's complexions, but instead of falling, they leapt at Vince.

"Shit!"

Slipping through their hands and getting his back against the wall, Vince finally realized the gravity of the situation. He was invincible. But at the same time, so were they.

"You son of a bitch. You can do the 'deathless makeup.'"

Chlomo smirked.

The "deathless makeup" that Vince had mentioned was actually nothing special. In funeral rites performed widely across the Frontier, it was often applied to the face of the deceased to revitalize it. Though it could more accurately be called "renewing" rather than "deathless," it came as little surprise that those seeking to profit from the product had, like people in any day and age, changed the name to the more marketable "deathless makeup." Despite that, it shouldn't have made those who wore it immortal, but in Chlomo's hands, it could resurrect them as undying creatures of unearthly beauty.

Fanning out into a semicircle, the men prepared to once again assail Vince, who had longswords, daggers, and other weapons jutting out of countless parts of his body. A small black sphere rolled around at his feet.

A deafening explosion rocked both heaven and earth, blowing the artificial immortals to bits. The sphere had been a bomb.

"You—you bastard!"

As Chlomo stood there bolt-upright in shock and anger, the smoke-shrouded Vince pointed to his own chest and said, "Look."

"Oh shit!" Chlomo shouted, and he could hardly be blamed.

A foot-wide hole had been blown in Vince's chest, and you could see right through to the other side. But with one touch of Vince's hand the wound vanished without a trace, thanks to his amazing regenerative cells.

While his other hand toyed with a red sphere, Vince declared mockingly, "No one but me can fight like this. So, by all means, keep sending them at me."

Made up with the "deathless makeup" or not, there was no way the others could repair their damaged regions. The blasted bodies of men with arms torn off and chests shredded still wriggled, attempting to rise again.

Before Chlomo could give an order to the rest, three explosions occurred. An enormous hole opened in the wall, and the men went sailing through the air. Countless chunks of shrapnel bit into Vince's body, but they were quickly covered by new flesh. It took his body only about a minute to break them down.

Flames shot up here and there. Frozen in the lamplight, Chlomo looked like any other person paralyzed by a sudden twist of fate.

Vince kicked off the ground. When the Hunter landed right in front of Chlomo, he raised his right hand and prepared to bury his dagger in the Makeup Lover's chest. A golden light that'd come from behind Vince lanced through the Hunter's chest instead. Cells evaporated at the nearly one million degrees of heat, and were instantly replaced.

Turning to the warehouse entrance, Vince found a silver-haired old man standing there unassumingly. Although he had a cane to support his upper body, which was stooped over parallel to the ground, the light that filled his narrow eyes was so intense it would leech the color right from the face of even a professional warrior.

"I received your messenger pigeon. And after hastening here without a moment's delay, what should I find but this raucous affair. You really have gone too far this time."

"Dr. de Carriole!"

Not so much as glancing at Chlomo, the old man gazed at Vince, his eyes sparkling all the while with a curiosity so fervent it seemed to swell like a tidal wave.

"I've never seen a human being able to make such effective use of regenerative cells. Hmm. Could it be I've finally found that new receptacle?"

Vince paid no attention to the old man's words. In part it was because the Hunter couldn't understand what he was talking about, but it was also because a cold wind had stroked the nape of his neck.

The diminutive figure hobbled over, halting about a dozen feet shy of Vince.

The dagger limned an arc in Vince's hand. Taking hold of the blade, Vince prepared to hurl it at the old man. But his body stiffened in the blink of an eye. It was unclear if he saw the pure vermilion light emitted by de Carriole's eyes at that very instant.

When the old man turned to Chlomo, his eyes had already returned to normal.

"Useless oaf!"

At the naked contempt in his voice, Chlomo hung his head without saying a word.

"Put out the fires," de Carriole ordered as he approached the baron.

Throughout the deadly struggle, the young Nobleman had sat there without moving a muscle.

"Chlomo!" the old man bellowed to his subordinate, who had a fire extinguisher in one hand.

"Yes?" he said as he turned, and then the wooden cane seemed to sink halfway into his face.

As Chlomo's body tumbled backward, blows rained down on it, and he let out a scream as he rolled around on the floor. It seemed positively incomprehensible that a hunched old man could strike with such power and accuracy. Chlomo was numbed to the very brain.

"Do you know who this gentleman is, vermin?"

The old man was livid. His roar was like that of a lion.

"I fear I must inform you it is Master Byron Balazs—Lord Vlad's own legitimate offspring. To think that a wretched louse like you could make him, him of all people, your plaything—damn you, get those vile cosmetics off him this instant. What's taking you so long? I'll beat you day and night until Master Byron is back to his old self!"

Some idea of the force behind the cane he raised came when he brought it down, and Chlomo lost consciousness.

Catching his breath after the beating he'd just delivered to his subordinate—who was sprawled on the floor—de Carriole then prostrated himself at the baron's feet.

"Allow me to apologize from the bottom of my heart for my attempts to take your life—though you may not know that I did so—and for that lowly wretch laying his hands on your person. Please rest at my humble manse until such time as you feel better. This old fool de Carriole knows too well your lofty goal, milord. While it's out of the question at present, I give you my oath I will aid you in visiting your dear mother in the immediate future."

And then, the devilish eyes of the old scientist, possessed of such a bizarre character flooded with feverish tears that were completely genuine.

D had noticed that the wind had begun to carry hints of a certain air. *He* was coming. The Noble who'd drunk Taki's blood was rising from the sanguinary depths of the darkness to slake his thirst.

A whinny arose from the cyborg horse outside the hut. The men in the black masks hadn't noticed anything yet.

"D," Taki called through the iron bars.

D turned around.

"I'm sleepy. Really sleepy. Something's . . . strange."

Without even waiting for D's reply, the girl collapsed to the floor.

"This is a rare case," a hoarse voice brimming with curiosity said from the vicinity of D's left hand. "I've never, ever heard of a victim going to sleep like that. Especially when this girl's—"

"Think the enemy planted her with us?" D asked.

"Damn straight. No doubt that lousy magician set something up in her brain that even the girl herself didn't know about. I just hope her getting the kiss of the Nobility hasn't set it off. If that were to happen, it'd be bad news. We're talking a fire dragon at the front gate, and a water demon at the back. Should we set her right now?"

Approaching the bars that divided them, D stuck his left hand between them and touched Taki's face. After confirming that the breathing of the sleeping Taki had grown even deeper, D then stood up.

"I wonder what kind of dreams you have when you get knocked out on top of being asleep."

Leaving the thoughtful mutterings of his left hand behind, D stepped outside. An inky wind fluttered his black hair too forcefully. One could hardly say the moon was bright or the wind tranquil. D alone knew about the eerie aura knifing at them from the distant east—the direction of the manor.

One of the five shadowy figures that stood before him asked, "Any time now, would you say?"

"Stay out of this," D said.

"Afraid we can't do that. We've signed on to protect you at all costs. But we'll try to keep out of your way."

All of the shadowy figures standing in the moonlight looked daunting.

D said, "Let's hear your names."

"I'm Bross."

"Zecca."

"Schuma."

"I'm Byrne."

"Clarice here."

The last voice was that of a woman.

"We're dying to see Vampire Hunter D in battle," Bross told D before turning to his compatriots and saying, "Assume free-form deployment pattern."

Five shadowy figures, himself included, melted into the darkness.

"Kind of early, eh?" said a hoarse voice. The voice flowed out smoothly in the moonlight. "*For the dead travel fast . . .*"

And then, after about a minute had passed, the unmistakable sound of iron-shod hooves reached D's ears.

"All alone, right? Knowing what you're capable of—he seems pretty damned cocky. Either that, or he's just crazy about the girl's blood."

Not replying to the voice from his left hand, D concentrated his gaze on the depths of the darkness.

Even after entering the ruins, there was no change to the sound of the hoofbeats.

"Six hundred feet," the left hand said. "Four hundred fifty."

A crisp sound raced through the night. The ring of steel on steel was joined by the sound of flesh being hewn, and then there was the thud of something heavy hitting the ground. The hoofbeats never faltered as they drew nearer.

"Three hundred feet."

D's field of view had already closed on the huge mount and rider bulling their way through the darkness. The horse looked as if its head and body were connected by a savage, inky brush. The rider on the horse's back was a mass of dark clouds. Through the endlessly expanding and contracting swirl of darkness, a great black root of an arm could occasionally be glimpsed, and something like eyes and a nose could definitely be made out in the area that would correspond with a face. Pale blue lightning flew from the cloud, making the inky material that clung to its surface stand out starkly. Blood.

The mount and rider that surged forward like a jagged wave came to an impressive stop about fifteen feet from D. The bridle wrapped around the horse's head was fashioned from thick chain. The ends of it disappeared into the cloud, and the hands that worked the reins couldn't be seen. Even the feet planted in the stirrups were shrouded in dark clouds. That must've been the knight's armor.

"Are you D?" asked a voice that called to mind the distant rumble of thunder.

D didn't answer. He had already noticed that the foe before him wasn't Lord Vlad.

"I am Duke Greed," the cloud announced, introducing himself with a flash of lightning.

III

"Where is Vlad?" D asked.

Despite the arrival of this new foe—and given the fact he'd been dispatched to deal with this situation, as he was most assuredly a man of substantial ability—the Hunter's tone didn't carry any deeper emotion at all.

"That's 'Lord Vlad' to you," the black cloud knight—Duke Greed—bellowed.

"Where is Vlad?" D repeated.

Blue lightning bridged the space between them. Tiny flames rose from D's left shoulder.

"Lord Vlad told me you were far from common; but I wonder, are you so great that something like that last attack didn't even faze you? Or are you so terrified you're left unable to speak? I warrant it's the latter."

The flames on D's shoulder cast a blue light on his profile. Shifting shadows only made his heavenly beauty seem all the more exquisite. Perhaps even Greed was dazzled by it—that may have been what left such a gap between his attacks.

"Damnation!" the black cloud exclaimed in a tone of amazement when D closed on him, coming right up to his mount's muzzle.

The black horse reared up. Half beast and half machine though it was, it seemed even a cyborg horse could be enthralled by D's beauty.

In the split second it took for the entire length of D's sword to slash through the black cloud as the Hunter pounced, there was nothing Duke Greed could do.

However—the instant D felt a complete lack of resistance from his blade, rebounding shock waves transformed his body into a black mass flying through the air. Just as he was about to slam into the ground, black wings opened—the spreading of his coat.

As the young man smoothly sailed down poised for his next attack, the approaching black horse and rider were almost right on top of him, looming like a mountain. D or not, he wouldn't have time to deliver a fatal blow through that bizarre dark cloud of armor.

Lightning formed a spear that zipped toward D's chest. Just as it seemed to pierce him, it was sucked into his left hand, and naked steel split the moonlight in a straight, horizontal slash.

"My word!" the black cloud exclaimed on realizing that he was being pitched forward by the sudden impact. D's horizontal slash hadn't struck the cloud armor, but had instead hewn off the black horse's forelegs. Based on the speed and timing of his fall, it looked as if the rider was fated to slam against the earth.

Diving to one side to avoid the horse that sent out a bloody mist as it dropped, D saw something. The black cloud that'd sailed forward had hit the ground and was rolling like a ball toward the hut.

D ran, the wind swirling in his wake. And as he ran, his left hand rose. A small mouth opened in the palm of it, and then the air was drawn into it with a savage roar.

Just as the edge of the black cloud began to stream back toward the mouth, the rest of it impacted on the door of the hut. The way the hut collapsed, it looked as if it'd been caught in a massive tempest.

And then, a glowing ball of light fell from the sky as if drawn to the black cloud. The instant it made contact, it exploded into sparks, and a fog-like material was scattered across the surface of the cloud.

"Oof . . ."

The grunt of pain had definitely come from the cloud—and Duke Greed.

But who on earth was responsible?

Before either of them could ponder that question, D caught up to the cloud mass and drove his blade through it with all his might. He felt it make contact.

A scream rose into the sky, accompanied by a geyser of black blood.

Like a bird in flight, D sailed beneath the black light that shot out, ready to deliver a second blow. But a new sphere of light had been drawn to his blade. It exploded, and while he dodged the blast with both eyes shut, the dark cloud sailed far off into the darkness. Lightning flew two or three times, and then that too vanished.

Wiping both eyes with his left hand, D then looked off to his left. It was from that direction that he'd caught the sound of an engine drawing nearer.

What appeared was a stocky vehicle reminiscent of a beetle. The moonlight sent cold, hard ripples across its metallic surface. The wind.

Was this a friend or foe? Whichever it was, D should've been terribly curious about it. However, he only gave it a glance before going over to the hut.

Although it had collapsed, it hadn't merely been knocked over. Wreckage was scattered in all directions. Locating Taki was actually rather easy. She lay in essentially the same place as before, and in the same pose. The problem was the iron grate that lay on top of her. Though it weighed nearly five hundred pounds, D grabbed it with his left hand and effortlessly heaved it away. The bars jabbed into the ground right in front of the beetle, forcing a sudden stop. The squeal of hydraulic brakes split the night.

D didn't turn to look, but rather checked on Taki's condition. The effects on a human body would be very different depending on whether the iron mass had simply fallen on it or been hurled at it by an explosion.

Bright blood dripped from Taki's mouth. Her internal organs had undoubtedly ruptured. It was strange that no hint of pain could be gleaned from her expression.

Sliding his left hand from the top of Taki's head to the back of it, then from her neck to her spine, he touched her waist and thighs before ending at her toes.

"Two thoracic vertebrae are busted," a voice was heard to say from the palm of his left hand. "On top of that, her stomach and part of her small intestine have been damaged. She's hurt bad. Good thing she's not aware of it."

"See to it she holds on long enough to get her to a doctor," D said.

"I'm already on it. I've dropped her metabolic functions as far as they'll go. Call it a kind of hibernation, if you will."

In the meantime, a section of the beetle had lifted like the wing of a bird, and out stepped a figure so massive he called to mind a wall. From head to toe, he was neatly sheathed in silvery garb. Although its luster suggested it was metallic, it didn't have so much as a single joint to it, yet as the man walked closer, the action was perfectly smooth.

The massive form halted about fifteen feet away.

Rising, D turned to face the silvery giant.

"I'm the one who hired those five," the man said in a voice without inflection, having passed it through some kind of device.

"And are you the one who interfered, too?"

While D was referring to how Duke Greed's attack had been blocked, at the same time he was referring to how the man had also hindered his own parting shot.

"I suppose you could say that."

The giant grinned wryly. His metallic mask was featureless, like the perfectly smooth face of some monstrosity, but when he smiled, his nose and lips had clearly risen to the fore. Undoubtedly it was liquid metal.

"Man alive! Don't hit me with that killing lust. You'll make my heart burst." The giant backed away, saying, "I may have interfered with you, but you've gotta at least be able to tell I'm not your foe. Hear me out. But before any of that, we'd better get this girl to a doctor. Got anyone in mind? If not, we can take her to someone I know. How does that sound?"

After a few seconds, D said, "It's in your hands, then."

It wasn't clear whether or not he believed what the glittering giant had said. Taki's welfare was his primary concern. And he didn't ask who or what the giant was because it really didn't matter anyway.

"Follow me," the giant said as he walked back to the beetle with a quick gait.

By the time the door had been shut and the engine had begun to snarl, D was on his horse. He had Taki across his knees.

The beetle started a leisurely run. After following it for a step or two, D wheeled his mount around without warning. Galloping almost five hundred feet in another direction, he then stopped.

Five cool bodies lay on the black earth like stones. Bross. Zecca. Schuma. Byrne. And a short distance off, Clarice. Although the armor that covered her from the neck down had been charred black, the face that was turned upward didn't have a mark on it. Her loose red hair swayed dolefully against her cheek.

D changed direction without saying a word. The stars were shining. But this young man had no words to send the departed on their way.

The beetle slowly pulled out of the ruins. And after it came the horse and its exquisite rider.

There were three hours until daybreak.

The dawn-loathing darkness was now about to raise the curtain on an abominable play at the manse of one Jean de Carriole. The scene was the vast laboratory that occupied the topmost floor of the tower. On stage were de Carriole, Chlomo, Sai Fung, and a trio

of golem assistants. In a massive tank of water set in the center of the room floated a Noblewoman—Miska. And there was one other person present.

De Carriole was completely absorbed in giving commands to his golems, adjusting the cycles on the generator, and personally checking the tank's ionization field. Sai Fung looked askance at him and muttered, "Please, give it a rest already, boss."

Chlomo stood beside him, and on hearing that, he added with a calculated empathy, "I hear Lord Vlad's manor was a complete shambles."

"Oh yeah. Boss, you'd have to be out of your mind to want that to happen again. I swear, this time it'll be the death of us."

"Come now. You should be looking forward to seeing this."

"I would, if I could watch it from outside the tower," Sai Fung replied.

"Excellent! The preparations are complete," the old man proclaimed, his tone unusually triumphant as his words spread throughout the laboratory. "Quickly now—bring out our final subject."

A pair of golems jerkily yet hastily went over to a well-like structure on one side of the room. The rope that hung from a rail set against the ceiling disappeared into the darkness. One of the golems took the end of the rope that was secured to a cleat on the floor and gave it a pull. The pulley turned, and soon a figure thoroughly bound in rope came out of the well and into the light.

"Who the hell have you got there?" Sai Fung inquired.

"A Hunter named Vince. He was caught after coming out to my place to try and get the baron."

"Did you say Vince?"

Having forgotten his anger at being slapped awake in the middle of the night, Sai Fung now wore a look of understanding.

"I've heard rumors about him. They say he can instantly regenerate from any kind of wound at all. It seems Vince is a nickname he takes from 'invincible.' So, boss, you've got one hell of a scheme cooked up."

"You comprehend what it is that I attempt, do you?"

"More or less. Hey, we'd better hurry up and get the hell out of here. If it goes wrong this time, we'll be dead men!"

As he spoke, Sai Fung began backing toward the door, but Chlomo grabbed him by the arm. "You might be out to save your own skin, you bastard, but that's not the way it's gonna go. Like the saying goes, we're all in the same boat here."

"What are you two blathering about over there?" de Carriole bellowed abruptly, and his two henchmen snapped to attention. "I'll have you know, you are privileged to have been chosen to witness an unprecedented feat of science. Composure, lads. Try to show a bit more composure."

"Yes, I'm terribly sorry, sir."

"Ditto."

Though Chlomo didn't yet grasp the situation, Sai Fung's voice was coated with despair.

What did de Carriole intend to do? Hunched over at the waist as always, he waddled over to the water tank that restrained Miska and pulled a large lever set to one side of it. And once he did, every last window in the room opened in unison, and a wind laden with an unspeakably eldritch aura gusted in, racing around the chamber in a most unsettling manner.

As they tried to turn their faces from the wind that practically slapped at them, Chlomo and Sai Fung's thoughts quickly raced back to something that had struck them as incongruous since first entering the room—the beautiful woman adrift in the tank of water. Water was anathema to the Nobility. Nobles were robbed of their consciousness when they were trapped in it, and thus subjected to an endless sleep.

"Lady Miska has been sealed away," de Carriole muttered as he studied the lovely woman in the shifting waters of the tank. "As has the other entity. So long as it resides within a Noble, it should have difficulty dealing with water. And by 'it' I mean the Destroyer."

He rapped on the floor with his cane. From the tank of water, tubes beyond number looped out onto the floor, and they rose like serpents preparing to strike, raising their needle-tipped ends before moving toward where Vince dangled above the well.

On seeing the needle tips sink deep into every inch of the Hunter's body, Sai Fung clutched his throat and remarked somewhat uncharacteristically, "I think I'm gonna puke."

Another elbow jabbed against his.

"What the hell was that for?!" Sai Fung snarled, his teeth bared.

"Look," Chlomo said, pointing to the tank.

A blue light had begun to spill out into the water from Miska's mouth.

"The Destroyer," Sai Fung said, unable to keep the tremors out of his voice.

IV

The insane doomsday weapon the Nobility had brought into being—a monster so terrifying it would bring madness not only to our world but to this entire dimension—was once again trying to get free. However, on leaving the body of Miska—who was, in a manner of speaking, its "host"—the blue light twisted in obvious agony. As it dwelt now in the flesh of a water-loathing Noble, the Destroyer itself had become hydrophobic. Writhing and eddying, the blue light was drawn toward the tubes that had just gone into one end of the tank. The tubes themselves weren't sucking it up. In its pain, the Destroyer sought a means of escape. Miska's mouth continued to disgorge light, and now all the tubes were tinged with the pale blue as they carried the flow into Vince's body. And Vince's invincibility had only been bolstered by an immersion in the well, which had been filled with a liquid that enhanced cellular regeneration.

A minute. Two. And still the infusion continued.

When the last of the blue light had been disgorged by Miska's mouth, Vince's eyes snapped open. They were blue glows in the shape of eyes.

"No—it's too soon!" de Carriole shouted as all the tubes sprang away from Vince's body in unison. Each and every one of them returned to the tank, and the waters were instantly tinged with blue.

The rope snapped, and Vince's body fell to the floor. No. Look— the floor sank in a conical shape as cracks shot out from it in all directions. He was now an invincible Destroyer.

"It's not accustomed to that body yet," the aged scholar remarked. "It should stop presently."

The trio of golems closed on Vince, and the second they touched him, they were reduced to dust that fell in piles on the floor. When Vince reached for the ropes that still bound his body, they came loose easily, coiling like whips in his hand.

A hot wind that could've been a miasma, or an unearthly aura, or sheer insanity assailed the room, blowing the door down.

Sai Fung and Chlomo hit the floor without any further squabbling.

However, something horrible happened a second later. The tank shattered without a sound, and Miska went down toward the floor along with all the spilled water. But she didn't fall. Standing on her own two feet as water dripped from every inch of her, she stared at Vince.

There was nothing left in the water that covered the ground.

Miska opened her eyes. And they were choked with blue light.

"The Destroyer that remained in the tank has returned to Miska," de Carriole cried, his words carrying heartfelt fear and despair. "Yet neither has been fully assimilated by its body. Here! Here they shall fight. It's the end of the world!"

De Carriole spread both hands and dashed between the two blue-eyed beings. But his actions weren't prompted by thoughts of saving the world—as his next outrageous statements made clear.

"Destroyer! Hear me out. I have transferred you into an invincible form so that you might rid us of Lord Vlad."

Down on the floor, Sai Fung and Chlomo stared at the old man in amazement, and perhaps that was why neither of them noticed the ghostly figure who came in through the door just then.

Something awesome hung in the space between Miska and Vince. When it reached the saturation point, the world would most likely be obliterated.

Perhaps de Carriole couldn't do a thing there in the entity's sights, for the second he finished an arcane gesture in front of his own chest, the blue beams of light that surged from Vince's eyes sent him flying, smashing him against the wall.

Rousing his force-shielded body from the floor, the aged scientist cried, "Oh, my!"

And the gasps from Chlomo and Sai Fung mirrored his.

"You were sleeping down on the floor below—have these blustering auras brought you to the battlefield, milord? Yes, of course—you are a Noble, through and through."

The Nobleman to whom de Carriole's remarks were addressed—Baron Byron Balazs—had an utterly blank expression as he listened to the old man's words, which surpassed mere admiration and bordered on overwhelmed.

The beetle guided D and Taki to a room in a building that towered in the middle of the pleasure quarter. The door read "Lubeck Clinic."

"After she's been treated, we'll move her to another location," the giant told D.

Once he'd knocked on the door, a woman in a long white lab coat appeared and invited the little group inside.

"I'm Mireille Lubeck," the woman said, a hollow ring to her voice as she introduced herself naturally due to her having seen D.

D told her about Taki's condition and requested treatment.

After thirty minutes had passed, including the initial exam, Mireille told them she was finished.

"She needs complete bed rest for a month. Or that's what I'd normally tell you, but she's already half-recovered. That's par for the course for a girl who's received the kiss of the Nobility. I suppose another two days will be sufficient for a full recovery."

Then, shifting her gaze to the silvery giant, she said, "Is this the 'pretty boy' you had them out looking for?"

"That's right."

"Why would you do that?" she asked.

"None of your business."

At that, the doctor shrugged her shoulders.

"But when you get right down to it," the giant continued, "I don't suppose there's any point in me keeping up the act anymore. I'll have to come clean with you sooner or later. Should I tell you who I really am?"

A small spot formed at the top of the giant's head, and then the silver armor coursed down him like water, revealing the man beneath. With only one good eye, the face was one D had seen before.

"Well, I'm Fisher Lagoon."

D's complete lack of reaction apparently betrayed Lagoon's expectations.

"What? Did you know that?" he asked somewhat suspiciously.

"We met once," D said. "No two human beings have exactly the same build."

Shifting his eyes to his own torso, Lagoon gazed down intently for a few seconds, then said, "There are some scary folks out there in the wide world."

"I owe you for bringing us here. Let's hear what you have to say."

"Oh, don't make it sound as cold as all that," Lagoon said with a thin smile.

Though his expression was cruel, he also looked terribly human. In the presence of someone of such unearthly beauty, surely anyone would act the same way.

"Ordinarily, somebody would ask why it was I helped them out."

"If you've got nothing to say, then I guess I don't owe you anything."

"Hold up," Lagoon said in a composed tone. "I've met *the big guy*."

For the first time, emotion surfaced on D's face.

"When and where?"

"What was it, some thirty years back now? I was just a fresh-faced little punk, and it was right here in the village." Drawing a breath, he continued, "You know of anyplace else where there's a Noble's manor and the people can still raise such a ruckus at night? You see, not even Lord Vlad can raise a hand against me. Because *the big guy* has laid down the law."

"Laid down the law?"

"Firstly, the villagers aren't to be drained of their blood. Secondly, so long as Fisher Lagoon is in charge of the nighttime amusements, he's to be given free rein. There are others, too."

"Why is that?" D asked.

The expression that surfaced on Lagoon's face beggared description. Perhaps this man had had unrivaled good fortune, but no human could've been unhappier.

"Before I tell you that, D, could you show me just how good you really are?"

The gleam of liquid that crept up from the tips of his toes transformed him into a silver giant.

"Mireille, blast me with that bad boy," the giant said, his finger pointing to the gunpowder rifle that stood in the far corner of the room.

Perhaps the lady doctor was accustomed to his odd behavior, because she didn't hesitate at all, walking over to get the double-barreled weapon, then checking that it was loaded before shouldering it.

"All set," she said.

"Fire."

There were sparks as the deafening reports shook the room.

An armored man who'd asked to be shot in a doctor's examining room, a lady doctor who was only too happy to oblige, and a dashing young man who watched it all without raising so much as an eyebrow. This was just the sort of outré world conjured up by dream demons.

Two holes opened in Lagoon's chest. Strangely enough, ripples spread across the surface as if a pebble had been dropped in the water, and the bullet holes disappeared as if they, too, were water. Lagoon gave his right hand a shake. Ripples crossed the palm of his hand, and the pair of slugs were ejected to fall to the floor.

"No weapon can get through this. Except, that is, for a sword in the hands of the person I have in mind. Now it's your turn, D."

As he spoke, there was a silvery flash of light.

"Hot damn!" Lagoon exclaimed as he reeled backward, surprised that the attack had been so abrupt.

From the top of his head to his crotch a clean cut had opened up, but it quickly vanished.

D had already sheathed his blade.

Dr. Lubeck let out a sigh.

"I guess maybe I was wrong," Lagoon said, his tone cold.

And then he exclaimed, "Sonuvabitch!"

As his astonishment gave way to that cry, the line that appeared once more sent the liquid armor spilling to the giant's feet in a heartbeat.

Neither Lagoon nor the doctor could speak.

"So . . . it's just as I suspected," Lagoon said after a little while, his face lit up with a childlike delight. "Now, after thirty long years, a man has finally come along that I can tell my secret to. I'm glad. So glad I could cry."

The man's emotion was obviously rooted deep in his personal experience. Yet he had to choose his audience carefully.

"Let's hear your story," said a steely voice.

Apparently understanding, Lagoon gave a nod, then set right to his explanation.

"When I met him, the big guy seemed to be all wrapped up in certain experiments. After one look at me, this is what he told me: *I want your seed. To fertilize Noblewomen and create a new form of life!*"

Pale Fallen Angel

PART FOUR

Master of the House
of Ill Repute

I

T he chaos of the situation kept growing. And at the end, drawing cold breaths, naught but death waited. No, not death, but annihilation. Even Miska and Vince—both of whom housed the Destroyer—could only stare at him in amazement. A ghastly aura slapped them and de Carriole across the face.

"Kindly step back, milord Balazs."

The hand that came to rest on his shoulder to push him back was tossed off by a single shake from the Baron, following which de Carriole pedaled backward eight or ten feet in a kind of bizarre dance before finally coming to a halt.

"De Carriole," someone called out.

"Yes?" he replied, but he hesitated a few seconds because de Carriole himself knew that the person to whom that voice belonged couldn't be there. The voice was like that of a ghost rising from the depths of earth.

"De Carriole . . . who are these two?" the baron continued.

"You mustn't go near them, milord Balazs. Each carries within them the Destroyer."

"The Destroyer . . ."

The baron's gaze seemed to bore right through Miska and Vince.

"I was defeated . . . by Lord Vlad. I could never beat him . . . as things now stand . . . And there is no shame in that . . . but my ambitions shall remain unfulfilled . . . in the end." But in that wraithlike voice he added, "And this Destroyer . . . might it prevail? Over Vlad?"

"Good question," de Carriole answered reflexively, and then he numbed with shock.

The baron's intent had dawned on him.

"How about it?"

"Well . . ."

"De Carriole!"

Realizing he was beaten, the aged scientist replied, "I can't say for certain that it would win. The odds are fifty-fifty, I'd say."

The baron walked forward intently.

"These two—either one will do. Take the Destroyer out of one of their bodies and give it to me."

The old man's complexion grew as stark as his beard.

"I couldn't possibly!"

But as de Carriole protested, the baron only continued to advance. Gaunt as a specter, his expression was tinged with blue— the electric glow given off by the forms of Miska and Vince.

"You mean to tell me you can't, de Carriole? In that case, I shall take it upon myself to—"

But what exactly could he do? The effects of Chlomo's makeup and the humiliation of being defeated by his father had left the baron in an extremely strange and precarious state, both physically and mentally. The thought of taking in the Destroyer had sparked an obsession.

The legs that carried the young Nobleman across the floor were unsteady, and his knees hit the ground.

Vince smirked. Even before he'd been imbued with the Destroyer, he was hardly what anyone would call normal. A creature of pure blistering energy that ordinarily could be contained solely by the immortal form of a Noble seared his brain, driving him insane in its attempts to escape this frail meat cage. His muscles and internal organs blistered as well, melting away, regenerating in a millisecond, and then dissolving once again. Which force would triumph in that infinite repetition?

However, Vince's crazed mind recognized a "command" that had been branded into his subconscious as a Vampire Hunter. His eyes were shut. The smile that rose on his lips was the same one that could be found on so many religious statues from the ancient cultures of the east.

His eyelids opened . . . and unleashed the power of the Destroyer!

Heaven and earth were both bleached by the pale light. All things lost their shadows, and were turned into shadows themselves. Even the wind died. Every sound was silenced.

The baron's form was enveloped by a sphere of blue light. Within it, the baron could be dimly made out running. And when that light faded away, there would be one less Noble in the world.

The blue sphere of light rapidly lost its hue. Contracting in a matter of seconds, it broke into a million minute pieces that faded unexpectedly. Beyond them, a second sphere remained.

De Carriole shifted his gaze to it, and then looked at Miska.

Before the blue light that'd shielded the baron faded, Miska and Vince extended their arms simultaneously. Once again, the world dissolved into a single pale light. It took on a stark whiteness, and a split second before it was going to swallow everything in nothingness, color and shape returned.

The baron stood out on the floor, behind him and off to one side de Carriole had both hands out, and Chlomo and Sai Fung both poked their heads out from behind a massive cylinder of specially tempered glass. All noise had died out and no one spoke, creating a horribly quiet, yet peaceful, tableau.

Chlomo and Sai Fung moved. Gazing at the spot the two freaks had occupied, they then looked to either side before one of them groaned, "They're gone!"

"Where the hell did they go?" asked the other. "Damn! Look at the big-ass holes in either wall. They must've either escaped through them or been blasted to pieces."

"They escaped—or rather, they were both blown out of here," de Carriole said in a hoarse tone.

"What'll we do, just let 'em go?"

"Don't talk rubbish. They have the Destroyer within them. If we leave them to their own devices, it'll mean the end of the world. Although there's not a thing you two could do against them—damn it, find them anyway. Split up—no, never mind about Lady Miska. I'm sure her Noble blood will soon check the urge for destruction. It was that that saved the good baron. Find Vince first. You're to notify me as soon as you locate him. Just to be perfectly clear, make no move against him. You're not to so much as breathe on him."

After his two subordinates had vanished into the darkness like sparrows in flight, de Carriole turned back to where Baron Balazs stood on the floor. The baron's eyes were closed. He didn't even seem to be breathing. Though he stood there at the ready like a sculpted temple guardian, he'd lost consciousness.

"How unfortunate," de Carriole said, the pain in his voice all too genuine as his gaze was riveted to the Nobleman's haggard profile. "For you and your mother both. However, that's only for the time being. Some day very soon, your humble servant shall slay Lord Vlad. Please wait until then. I absolutely cannot allow you to make a demon of yourself, milord."

And then he walked over and put his hands on the baron's shoulders.

The baron went into action. This time, de Carriole's hands were not knocked away; but rather, they were seized around the wrists with a vise-like grip. Even as he heard his bones creaking, the old man couldn't help but be impressed.

"So, you want to attack the lord that badly, do you? Even while unconscious?"

He broke off there, running his gaze across a water tank that'd been destroyed. Twisting around, he then looked at the two huge holes in the walls.

"One of the two . . ."

Regardless of what he meant by that whispered remark, the aged scholar had the sort of dangerous glint in his eyes that would make even a weeping child faint dead away.

D was at a warehouse on Thornton Street. And though it was simply a warehouse, its contents looked like they would've brought down lightning bolts of wrath in any place besides this village.

When Lagoon got down off his beetle and gestured to D to follow him through the door next to the shutters, the Hunter's gaze leapt across all the items packed into a space that looked nearly large enough to hold a five-story building. The power shovel had a bucket fixed at the end of a rough one hundred-fifty-foot arm that looked like it could reduce a city block to dust in a mere five minutes. The gleaming black drill that seemed to stand alone was actually a machine for deep subterranean boring. At fifteen feet in diameter, it wouldn't stand very high, but the drill portion alone was a hundred feet long, and since the whole machine stretched to nearly one hundred and forty feet, it needed a heavy gantry to hold it upright. With a reputation for being able to pierce the earth's mantle and return unscathed, the drill was made of an alloy based on the mysterious orichalcum metal said to have been created in a legendary continent in the eastern sea in ancient times—Atlantis.

"Know what that is?"

As the speed of the moving sidewalk running into the depths of the building slowed, Lagoon pointed to a machine with a collection of countless rails surrounding a black mountain of a base. Its appearance reminiscent of a diagram of an atom, the path of its rails didn't appear to follow any set pattern at first glance, but on closer inspection, they were all laid out in accordance with a single guiding principle.

"A Big Bang Accelerator?"

Lagoon gave a hearty nod at D's reply. He was no longer wearing his liquid metal suit. His massive form was wrapped in a dazzling robe, as befitted such a prominent member of the village.

"Leave it to you. You're not like most of those uneducated Hunters kicking around. Just between you and me, there are times when I'd love to fire a blast from that bad boy into Lord Vlad's manor."

From Lagoon's flushed expression, it seemed he believed the resulting devastation might take the life of their lord.

This accelerator could produce the same results as the Big Bang—the enormous explosion that created the universe. Launched down rails that curved in arcs and angles determined by physical laws even beyond human comprehension, the "material" would exceed the speed of light once in flight and, on striking its target, it would impede the very flow of time. Although that was the greatest ability of the Big Bang Accelerator, the massive machine that smoothly slid through their view had been stripped of its time-impeding apparatus, leaving it a catastrophic death-bringer to be used solely for destruction.

"These are all devices of the Nobility," said D. "Were they brought here from the Capital?"

"Don't be ridiculous. I built all of them here in the village."

As D's eyes fell upon that grim visage, Lagoon's expression instantly gave way to childlike pride and joy. The owner and operator of the Frontier's preeminent pleasure quarter was almost certainly a surprisingly simple man at heart.

"Of course, the theory behind the machines was taught to me by *you-know-who*. Later on, I drew up plans, made a refinery, and brought in the raw materials. I even built a power station. I wish you could've seen the scale of the factory, sprawling out on the edge of the village!"

"So 'knowledge' was part of your compensation?"

D's query served to rob the man of some of his fire.

"Right you are. And thanks to that, the village stays safe from bandit and monster attacks without relying on Vlad's power. I know my place might look like some stupid little bumpkin strip joint at first glance, but it actually houses a few pearls of wisdom."

Just as his bragging was winding down, the automated walkway entered a narrow tunnel, and they presently halted before a metal door. Beyond the door lay two opulent rooms that were storehouses in name only, and in the first of these—a reception room—they were met by May.

"D—what about Taki?" the girl inquired anxiously.

"I rescued her, and she's in another location."

"That's great!" May exclaimed, leaning back against the armrest and weeping.

"But she was given the kiss of the Nobility," D continued in a cruelly soft tone.

May's body sprang up a bit as if with some sort of spasm while she stared at D.

"Then you'll have to . . ."

"As you requested, I rescued Taki. My work is done."

As if enslaved by D's handsome features, May didn't take her eyes off him, and she swallowed hard. It took some time for her little head to drop.

"Yes—I suppose you're right. It's all over now. Will Taki be put into an asylum? Is that how all this will end?"

"Do you have any intention of extending the contract?"

For a second, May stopped moving and knit her brow as if she hadn't caught what he'd said. She looked at D in disbelief.

"But—I mean, I don't have any money . . ."

"I believe I said you could pay me later."

"Say, would you like me to pay him for you, missy?" Lagoon said, fishing one hand into his pocket.

"No. I'll manage something or other. D—you have kids' rates, don't you?"

A gonglike sound reverberated through the room. Lagoon had thrown his head back in a great belly laugh.

But what was truly astonishing was what flitted across D's lips. No matter how you looked at it, it was clearly a smile.

"Pardon my asking, but just how do you propose to earn that money?" Lagoon asked with profound curiosity.

May smacked one foot against the floor, and then her tiny form flew straight up ten feet, executed an elegant flip, and, after planting one hand on Lagoon's shoulder, the girl flew across the room at an angle.

"Wow!" the big mover and shaker exclaimed when the girl landed on the shade of a lamp and maintained her balance exquisitely as she took a bow. "I've seen all manner of acrobats, but I've never seen such a cute little wunderkind. What do you say to coming to work at my place?"

"Well," May said, squinting at Lagoon, "I don't come cheap."

His great mitt-like hands slapped together.

"Great! Then we got ourselves a deal. The wages will take your breath away," Lagoon said gravely, but he gave her a smile of delight.

To D he said, "I don't imagine you have a problem with me making a star out of this splendid acrobat. Now, your job is to save Taki. From Lord Vlad."

It was difficult to tell whether that last remark carried scorn or sarcasm, but no sooner had it drawn a gasp from May than a slight tremor reached them from all sides.

"I'll be damned," Lagoon muttered as he gazed at D.

D was already headed for the door.

"If you're going to relocate May, you'd better be quick about it," the Hunter said.

D realized what had caused the explosion that he alone had heard. It was the same boom he'd heard on the outskirts of a certain town on the way to Krauhausen, when Miska—possessed by the Destroyer—had wiped the puppet master, Mario, out of existence.

II

The first reports on what threatened the ordinarily peaceful nights of Krauhausen came about ten minutes after the sound of the bizarre explosion. A farming family that lived out by the mansion of the aged scientist, de Carriole, got in their wagon and raced to the sheriff's office, foaming at the mouth as they relayed how nearby farms and sections of forest were disappearing one after another. Sheriff in name alone, the lawman immediately contacted Lagoon to request the mobilization of his private peacekeeping forces; and, once the sheriff had seen they were on the case, his men followed along after them. Although it wasn't really their fault, they had failed to pass along one very important piece of information obtained from the bloodless and nearly crazed farming family. As the family was on their way there, they'd encountered a young man of unearthly beauty astride a cyborg horse, and he'd gotten them to tell him about the mysterious disappearances.

D halted his horse in the midst of the ionized air. The scene spread before his eyes.

A section of earth roughly one hundred and fifty feet in diameter had sunken into a bowl-like depression. No. Seeing as there wasn't a single thing resembling a rock or tree to be found within the depression, perhaps it was more accurate to say it'd been scooped out; but the way the surface had been fused into a glassy substance made it clear that that wasn't correct either. A good thirty feet deep, it glowed bewitchingly in the moonlight, like particles of light that had coalesced. From the look of the rail fences, stepping stones, and wooden gates that remained beyond the rim of the mortar, what had been obliterated was undoubtedly a central house, an outbuilding, and a pen for animals. Near the brink of the hole, a two-story building that looked to be a barn was perfectly fine.

Advancing further on his horse, he saw that out in the moonlight, the eerie tableau went on. The glittering of the ground that'd melted down into a beehive shape challenged the light of the moon.

Who would do such a thing?

There was a crash. D's ultra-keen senses told him it came from a great distance away. From the direction of the village.

D wheeled his horse around. The sound of the first explosion had definitely come from whoever had left this hole. Was he on the move?

The conclusion D reached was a simple one.

"Why, there's two of them," a voice remarked from the vicinity of his left hand, but D raced off without even glancing down at it.

Having received orders from Lagoon to stop the intruder before he entered the village, the peacekeeping force formed a dragnet around the main road from the farm to the village as well as all side roads, but they soon realized it was too late. A roar was drawing closer from the dark forest where even they feared to tread by night. What's more, it was moving at an unusual speed. A number of men who ran out into the trees with the intention of establishing surveillance were obliterated, trees and all, leaving only a glittering mortar-shaped hole in the ground. Though it was clear some sort of energy was being released, not the slightest wind blew, and they didn't feel any heat on their skin. The survivors beat a hasty retreat, and though they peered hard into the night, they saw no sign of anyone moving around the hole. A second later, they too were reduced to nothingness. This was only about half a mile from the village.

On orders from the peacekeepers who'd remained in the village, all residents who lived in the direction from which the unknown being approached had been evacuated with naught save the clothes on their backs. But once the devastation had spread to within a few hundred yards of town, the explosions stopped dead.

Peacekeepers and members of the vigilance committee had crept into position with their weapons, and as they focused their fear-choked eyes, a tall, thin figure appeared from the darkness at the far end of the main road. Even by the moonlight, they could tell at a glance that it was an ordinary human being. But the bartender from the all-night watering hole in the hotel recalled the face that had been etched into his memory and let out a low cry. When that man had called on his bar at dusk, getting some information and easily dispatching the enforcers that came at him before leaving, the only way to describe the way he'd dominated his opponents was to say he was invincible. *Vince*—the bartender repeated the name.

The defenders were perplexed. Even on the demon- and monster-dominated Frontier, it seemed utterly unimaginable that the devastation the farmer had described could've been wrought by this man, who looked so dazed the very soul might've been sucked out of him.

And while that was going on, Vince reached the entrance to the pleasure quarter—the kingdom under Fisher Lagoon's direct control. The neon glared and music echoed because Lagoon swore this place would never be swayed by some unnamed threat. Halting, Vince was tinged with white from head-to-toe as he stood in a daze staring up at the glow.

A light a hundred times brighter than the midday sun hit his body with an almost palpable weight. It came from a searchlight the public peacekeepers had set up.

"Freeze," an amplified voice shouted down from the sky. "Who are you? You the one who blew the holy hell out of that farmhouse?"

As unbelievable as that seemed, it was still a possibility. One of the rules of the Frontier was that before trying to take anyone down, you asked your questions from a safe distance.

Vince didn't reply.

"Don't you have ears? I'm gonna give you to the count of three. Then we start shooting. Okay—one . . ."

It may have seemed a rough way to do things, but now that they knew the person they were dealing with wasn't a resident of the village, they owed him no mercy—that was also part of the Frontier code. From under cover, from behind the searchlights, from roofs and porches, the weapons aimed at Vince backed every potential bullet and laser beam with deadly determination.

And in response, Vince's reaction was—complete disregard.

Though his invincible flesh was another matter, the man's mind had been ravaged beyond salvation, leaving him utterly insane. The Destroyer required of its host not only the resilient flesh of a Noble, but an equally resolute psyche as well. Only the kind that'd brought it into existence had the wisdom to govern the Destroyer. When such control became impossible, its host became ruin and slaughter incarnate. The only thing that saved the village from complete destruction was some fragment of humanity that lingered in Vince's subconscious and remained active for a while.

And then that, too, vanished.

Vince's eyes glowed with a blue light, and then he took a step forward as if to crush the earth beneath his foot.

Light streaked at him from all directions, with the report of the guns following after. Flesh bunched up as massive slugs ripped into him. Struck by more than a thousand rounds almost simultaneously, his body seemed to instantly swell to twice its normal size.

The shooters' expressions were haunting. They continued pulling the triggers like men possessed—they couldn't take any chances. This character could be blown to ribbons and he still might come back. *Shoot! Shoot! Shoot!* They had to blow every last bit of him away with their bullets.

As if in answer to their prayers, the writhing body of Vince on the ground was indeed growing smaller. It already lacked a head. Both arms had been blown off, neither leg had more than the thigh remaining, and more than half of his torso was missing.

"Hold your fire! Particle cannons!" the commander called out at that point, entrusting the foe's final elimination to blasts of blistering heat.

Crimson streaks of light stabbed into the searchlight beam, ripping into the fleshy lump on the ground from all directions. Unlike lasers, particle beam cannons would also completely melt a wide area around the point where they made contact. The ground became a boiling pit of mud. And the bubbling soil swallowed Vince's remains.

"Good enough," a gruff voice said.

Some sixty feet above the scene, there hovered an airship the same hue as the darkness. The voice came from a loudspeaker set in its bottom.

"That takes care of that. We can look into just who he was later. For the moment, I'm more interested in the man who was headed into the forest. I wonder if he just wasted his time . . ."

And saying this, Fisher Lagoon turned his gaze in the same direction D had gone just as the subordinate who stood beside him on the observation deck exclaimed, "Boss—down there!"

"What?"

Twisting around a face that looked like a patch of rough rock, Lagoon saw the same thing his subordinate did, and his eyebrows rose.

The particle cannons had already ceased firing, and the circle of illumination thrown by the searchlight revealed the still-boiling ground, but out in the center of it something slowly rose. It had a head. And hands. It even had feet—it was clearly a human being. And all the while, flames rained down onto the baked ground from that slender form.

The second he realized that the face jerking up into the searchlight was that of the completely unscathed Vince, the commander bellowed, "Fire!"

Blue light flitted to space.

The hand of God sent the airship flying. Knocked out of shape, the light hydrogen-filled airship rose a good three hundred feet. Two things allowed it to narrowly escape destruction—it was fashioned from metal alloys using the Nobility's "knowledge," and it had only been struck by a plain physical shock.

"What—what the hell just happened?!" Lagoon asked angrily, gripping the handrail and barely managing to support himself.

"The street—the whole thing's been blown away," his subordinate said, his reply overlapping with the original question.

When Lagoon raced over to the window without another word, his eyes were greeted by nothing save the neon of the shopping district. What had happened to the searchlight? Worse yet, why was more than half the neon out?

"Get the ship's searchlight on!" he ordered.

For the first time in decades, he was met with an objection.

"That's too dangerous. I mean, that guy on the ground . . ."

"Damn it all, I don't care! Light it up!"

A beam of light shot down from the heavens to the earth. What it starkly illuminated was the mortar-shaped depression that'd been scooped out of the earth and the naked figure of Vince standing at the bottom of it. Standing there in the light spearing down from heaven, he might've been a god who'd come down to earth. However, this was no god of good fortune. This was a god of destruction who wouldn't leave so much as a single blade of grass. As evidence, one had but to look at how the rows of buildings around him had been obliterated without a trace and how the ground had sunk into a mortar-like depression in a three-hundred-foot radius.

Planting a foot on the smoothly sloping side, Vince began to slowly climb back up to ground level. The hole was twice the size of the one D had found. If these were to grow any larger, it seemed possible that one would be enough to wipe an entire village off the face of the earth.

"Should we attack the—" his underling began with trepidation.

"No, hold off. It'll be here soon," Lagoon told him.

Vince got out of the hole and looked up into the sky.

The subordinate let out a scream.

But it didn't seem that Vince turned on account of this noise. Down the same road he'd come by, a tremendous black shape had just come around the corner—a glistening black base surrounded by countless looping rails.

"Look there, boss—it's the Big Bang Accelerator!" the subordinate exclaimed in wonder as the airship finally regained stability.

"Looks like we don't have any other choice," Lagoon said, making it clear he could read a situation quickly.

To counter the power of a Destroyer who wouldn't rest until everything had been annihilated, here was the same Big Bang that'd created all of the planets in the universe and all life on them.

"Incredible. It's a regular showdown between God and the Devil!"

As if vouching for what Lagoon had said, the accelerator that'd halted thirty feet away began to let out a momentous groan, and the rails positioned themselves in sacrosanct angles that couldn't err by even a picometer. Ahead of it stood a god of destruction by the name of Vince, waiting to unleash more violence.

III

The moon hid behind a cloud. It was a second later that a golden light winked on somewhere on the accelerator. The light traveled down one of the rails, and there was a metallic *ting!* Once accelerated by electromagnetic waves, it took only one ten-millionth of a second for the minute charged particles the Nobility's science alone could've discovered to shift into hyper-acceleration. When Lagoon realized the golden glow clinging to all those rails was the afterimage of the accelerated body, it was already moving faster than the speed of light, and it slammed right into Vince's face.

It almost seemed a mirage, the way the blue light opened like the petals of a flower. If God's eyes had been trained on it, they would've seen that a split second before the accelerated mass scored a direct hit on Vince, the light enveloped his entire body— or rather, his body actually became that blue glow. And the bullet that was supposed to give life to the universe was swallowed by it.

Vince staggered. Just before it was annihilated, the shock wave from the accelerated mass's explosion had knifed through the wall of light, barely managing to strike him in the face. Clutching his eyes, he extended his right hand. What flew from his fingertips was a particle of light of exactly the same size. Once it had adhered to the base of the accelerator, it immediately expanded. Base and rails alike were tinged with blue, and then the color faded as if it were destiny, leaving no trace of the accelerator behind. The air danced with heat shimmers.

Not turning, Vince stared off in the direction from which the accelerator had come.

It's difficult to explain what happened next. Rows of houses in a three-hundred-foot radius vanished, and a huge hole was created in the ground. That's the only way to describe it. When and how the houses had been erased and the hole had been made remained a mystery. Perhaps the homes and soil had never existed in the first place.

"Boss, at this rate, the whole village—" the subordinate screamed, his voice ringing out even louder than Lagoon's, "no, the whole world could be finished!"

Vince began to advance. Far ahead of him towered Lagoon's place. The inhabitants of the village would've gone there when they were evacuated.

Then Vince turned around. The thunder of shod hooves was approaching from his rear.

At that point, moonlight spilled through a gap in the clouds to shine down on the figure who halted his cyborg horse at the rim of the great hole. Perhaps it was his good looks that made Vince stop. Though his face possessed the kind of beauty humans didn't even encounter in dreams, a fiercely eerie aura radiated from him as he glared at Vince. It was D! But could any Vampire Hunter, no matter how great, have the skill to stand against a fiend who could negate the very energy that'd created the universe?

Wrath filled Vince's face. Though his psyche had been ravaged, some final remaining fragment of his subconscious had recalled the connection between D and himself. And his eyes blazed with the pale and deadly light.

D didn't move.

In the airship in the sky, Lagoon was left breathless, and when May raced out of the warehouse, she paled at what was on the rim of the great hole. The instant that separated life and death required an appropriate ceremony.

WAIT! boomed a voice that called to mind the god of some evil domain.

The eyes of both D and Vince whipped around and focused for a second on a point in the huge hole.

While it was unclear how long he'd been there or how he'd appeared in the first place, the figure who suddenly stood there with a golden scepter in hand was none other than Lord Vlad Balazs.

Staring intently at D, Vlad told him, "Leave this to me, Hunter."

He seemed neither surprised nor angry that D remained alive. And there was no sign that he was afraid of Vince making an unexpected move against him. It seemed that this figure steeped in an overwhelming self-confidence and forcefulness left even Vince at a loss.

"Lowly worms though they may be, I have a duty as a Noble to protect the residents of my dominion. There's no point in you getting involved in this. What's more, at some point I shall have to do battle with you, so I thought this would be a perfect opportunity to kill some time while demonstrating my power to you."

The wind snarled. The scepter he'd held pointed straight at Vince.

D didn't move.

"I don't know how great your power is or who's given it to you—no, I actually have a fairly good idea regarding the latter—but the Nobility were born of accursed earth where everything else died off. And now you will feel in your bones how different that is from some upstart Destroyer!"

"This is unbelievable!" Lagoon's subordinate exclaimed up in the airship as he balled his hands into fists.

"Interesting," muttered a voice from the vicinity of D's left hand.

"Watch well, D. Witness the true power that we Nobility possess!"

Lord Vlad pulled back hard with his right arm. He held his scepter as if poised to hurl a javelin. Only three feet long, the scepter suddenly stretched—the part that extended was a golden spearhead. The whole scepter was probably some unknown form of coalesced energy. The lord's surroundings grew distorted, as if glimpsed through a heat shimmer.

Vince's right hand unleashed a blob of unholy light.

The scepter flew, too.

Changing direction, the point of light painted an arc as it zipped to the tip of the scepter. Even as it took on the pale hue, Vlad's scepter sped forward. The pale blue light fizzled like popping soap bubbles, leaving the golden tip exposed. Right in front of Vince.

Not only did it strike Vince squarely in the middle of the face, but it even came out through the back of his head. After a few seconds, he took a couple of steps backward, and then his body sank. He was at the brink of the pit.

"Get back!" Lord Vlad shouted as he leapt to the rear.

The explosion this time was terribly small.

As he felt a slight tremor pass through the airship three hundred feet in the air, Lagoon gazed at the scene that filled the windows of the observation deck. At the bottom of the opening yawned another hole, perhaps a third its size. And that was Vince's grave, plain and simple.

"Cut the searchlight. We're going home," Lagoon ordered.

Though he questioned the wisdom of not checking out the bottom of the hole, the subordinate realized he had no choice but to follow his boss's command and grabbed hold of the wheel.

Looking up at the departing craft with its tail fins gleaming in the moonlight, Lord Vlad spat, "Ha! That incompetent Lagoon's run off with his tail between his legs."

He then turned to D.

"How's that, Hunter? You can come at me if you like. If your nerve hasn't shrunk down to nothing, that is. See? I don't even have my scepter any longer!"

His challenge gave way to laughter, but then that stopped. Vlad was paralyzed by a ghastly aura that radiated from D.

"This . . . it's even more intense . . . than the Destroyer. You really are . . . the great one's—"

The lord was looking at D. Looking at the black horse and rider that'd raced forward sixty feet without giving any indication beforehand.

The lord's robe fluttered and a flash of white light shot from one sleeve to mow through the barrel of the horse.

Success! A feeling of relief the likes of which he'd never experienced with any foe in the past tempted the lord to drop his guard.

D was above his head. Coming straight down from above, his sword had incredible force behind it.

The lord held up his left arm to block it.

The second the Nobleman's armored limb was taken off at the elbow and blood spilled from his forehead like black ink, D reversed his sword so he could carve out his foe's heart, but the blade snapped off at the hilt and was lost in the darkness. As Lord Vlad leapt to a new location, D's coat spread like a supernatural bird and he flew back.

Now D had no sword, while Vlad had lost an arm and had a merciless torrent of black blood gushing from his brow. Given the situation, was D to be admired for the horrible force of his blow, or was the lord to be praised for his strength in stopping said blow?

"Well done," Vlad said, tearing the hem of his robe with one hand and pressing it to his brow. "You're everything I expected, I should say. However, this is hardly the full extent of *my* abilities. We shall meet again."

Although Vlad didn't appear to move his feet, he receded a good sixty feet in one fell swoop. D alone could see that beside him a horse and black-lacquered carriage waited. D didn't pursue him because he could see that even with his great speed, he'd never catch the Nobleman on foot.

As the black form of the driver cracked his whip and wheeled the horse around, a sharp line glittered through the moonlight. Though the needle of rough wood pierced the outer wall of the carriage and dropped the driver, the rattle of the vehicle's wheels rang out without respite as the carriage raced off into the darkness.

Walking over to where the driver had been left in the road, D pulled him up by his purple topcoat. Decaying bones rained noisily to the ground. Looking down at the figure that'd been reduced to dust as he'd fallen, D then turned his gaze to the darkness where the carriage had departed.

A small figure came out of the distance. May.

Just as she was about to call out to D, the girl became a statue. He was out in the moonlight. Though the tremendous aura that gushed from the young man in black was directed at the darkness before him, the girl was completely immobilized. What stood before her wasn't the handsome, unsociable and secretly kind man she looked up to like an older brother. It was a darkness-prowling killer who would sink his teeth into his prey and not let go through all its death throes. May saw only a Vampire Hunter.

The Plain of Slaughter

CHAPTER 2

I

Bringing the airship down at the airport to the north of his establishment, Lagoon had the contents of his bald head working ceaselessly as he headed for his bedroom. Losses to the village and his peacekeeping forces, compensation, plans for reconstruction—there were a million matters to consider. And yet another problem—one of the highest possible level—awaited his attention.

Luxurious was the only word to describe his bedroom, which was equipped with a gigantic circular bed. If the countless farmers who still slept on straw ever saw the beauty of that bed, riots would ensue. When Lagoon's troubled countenance turned toward it, a figure rose gracefully from its center. Lagoon froze in place, astonished.

"Surprised? For all your size, you're still only human," said the shadowy voice that rolled toward him. It wasn't until the next day that it came to light that the iron bars over the windows, proof against even the monstrous strength of the Nobility, had been melted.

"You—what do you want with me?" Lagoon asked, frozen stupidly in the process of taking a step forward.

"I came to ask you for something," the body in white replied.

†

A figure in a purplish-blue robe crossed the vast water-filled space without the use of a boat. From the elbow down, his left arm had been replaced with an electronic artificial limb.

As soon as Vlad halted, a woman's voice resounded in his ears like the rustling of a garment, saying, "Your arm and the wound on your brow—they're the work of the one as gorgeous as the very darkness, are they not?"

In spite of himself, Vlad put his hand to the deep gash that remained. Although the injury was obvious enough, she shouldn't have known about the arm, and yet she'd been entirely correct. And the wound on his brow—with his regenerative abilities, one ten times this deep should've long since healed over.

"You know about him? Just how did you and he come to—oh, never mind. It's a trivial matter, after all. I merely came here to tell you something: Byron has been destroyed."

For as far as the eye could see, all movement vanished from the surface of the water. Although there hadn't really been much to begin with, what now settled over the depths was the calm of true death. On account of this, the next remark rang out with a horrible clarity.

"You did this—you murdered our son with your own two hands?"

"Who else could've done so? Who but I would be up to the task of slaying the son Vlad Balazs raised with such tender care? By now, he's food for the fish in the river."

The water absorbed Vlad's words.

"You threw our child *into the water?*"

"Indeed I did."

"Then this night and for every night that follows, you shall never be able to let your guard down. The water cannot destroy him."

"What?"

"You have sealed your own wife away in the water. Trapped her in a world colder and harder than any hell for a Noble. But the streams that course through your domain, the lakes that dot it, yes, even the droplets of rain that cling to the leaves of the trees, all heed my will."

Her tone wasn't at all wrathful, and that in and of itself was enough to make anyone's hair rise on end.

Vlad snorted, "Do you mean to tell me your hatred has saved him? I have no problem with that. No matter how often he might rise again and call on me, I shall dispose of him each and every time. But that is not what I came here to tell you. I'll be moving to the mountain stronghold."

"Why?" the voice inquired. The surface of the water was calm.

The lord pointed to the wound on his forehead.

"You may remain in your hell if you so wish, but I must live in the world. In the days to come, backbreaking labor awaits. The man who did this to me—he *will* come again. If I'm to be ready to greet him, I shall need a suitable location."

"So you say, but that is the home of the 'mountain folk.' That is not good. Not good at all. If you make a foe of them, you'll be bringing death and destruction down on innocents."

"And that is precisely why I have need of such a place now. Especially against this Hunter. He descends from the great one!"

The woman said nothing.

"Such looks, such power, such presence—truly a breathtaking man. I fought him off once, but that isn't to say that I triumphed. You see, he came to rescue a girl I'd taken, and accomplishing that, he left. Hear me when I say that even Greed tasted defeat at his hands."

Once again, the woman said nothing. However, her lack of a response wasn't because she reveled in this information, but rather because Vlad's words instilled in her the same shock and awe.

"And knowing this, you can see the reason why I must relocate. To be ready for one of the great one's line, I must go to that fortress. Even then, there is fear in the depths of my heart. Not of the Hunter, but of the blood that flows through him. What's more, there have been disquieting movements within the village of Krauhausen. Someone has lent their strength to the Hunter—probably Lagoon."

"Impossible!"

"We are talking about humans here, after all," he chortled. "It wouldn't be at all surprising for them to do something we would never consider. I have already ordered de Carriole to do something about this, and I have taken measures myself. Yes, de Carriole himself has been acting strangely of late, but we shall see about that shortly. My wife—you are to remain here."

Silence descended.

Presently, the woman's voice replied, "With pleasure."

But who were the "mountain folk" waiting by the mountain stronghold? The woman's voice had sounded almost relieved.

Early the next morning, D and May were led by Lagoon as they headed for the isolation chamber beneath his establishment.

"Though 'isolation chamber' has a nicer ring to it, it's actually a jail for holding enemy prisoners of war," Lagoon laughed. "But seeing as this is a thousand feet underground with ten-foot-thick concrete walls, the Nobility can call to her all they want and there's no danger of her going anywhere. Naturally, getting themselves down here won't be easy either. Especially not with you around."

Feeling the chill that radiated from the boundless material beyond the special concrete walls, the trio peered through an observation window in the iron door before them and saw Taki lying on a spacious bed.

"It was a rush job, but in moving Taki in here, we tried to make it as comfy as possible. But no matter how good of a job we do of keeping him away, if we can't put down the Noble who bit her, it won't mean anything. And that, D, is your job."

Though Lagoon stole a glance at the exquisite Hunter's profile, he couldn't detect an iota of emotion in the gorgeous features turned toward the slumbering Taki. In fact, all it did was make him feel lightheaded.

"I'm heading out soon."

On hearing D's words, he finally returned to his senses.

"You're going?"

His question was pointless.

Giving no reply, D quietly stepped away from the door. The sword on his back was one he'd purchased from Lagoon.

"Oh, look at Taki," May said, pointing to the surveillance room. The girl was riding on one of D's shoulders.

Taki had risen from her bed, and it took no time at all for her to notice the group. Pressing her face to the window, she said, "You all look fine. You too, May."

"Yeah, well, you'll be fine soon too, Taki. Mr. D's gonna fix that bastard."

"I'm sure he will. I appreciate it. Until then, I guess I'll be out of commission, won't I?"

"I guess you will," May laughed, and she was about to put her hand in through the window. But she never reached it. D had drawn back. For Taki was a "victim."

"You're right, May. Take care," Taki said with a sad smile.

"The next time this door opens, you'll be back to your old self. Definitely. I'll unlock it for you myself."

While it was unclear how May's words sounded to anyone else, both D and Lagoon spun around at the same time. Entrusting the young woman to the subordinates Lagoon left down there, the three of them got into the elevator.

"I sure hope Taki gets back to normal soon," May said, gnawing on her lip.

"I'll second that," Lagoon responded. "That all rests squarely on the pretty boy here. Let's hope for his best effort out there."

Though what he said could've been taken in jest, such a remark could also be a grave matter. D wasn't the sort of person to appreciate sarcasm.

"Then everything will be fine," May said, looking up at the young man with eyes full of trust. She'd come down off his shoulder when they got in the elevator.

"But there's something I don't understand," she continued, the gaze she directed at Lagoon filled with suspicion.

"Oh? And what would that be?"

"You were gonna let a dirty old man have his way with me. And D saved me from that. But the people who protected me while D was off at the castle rescuing Taki were hired by you, right? And on top of that, you're giving shelter to Taki and me. I don't think you have any more slave trading in mind, so why are you suddenly on our side?"

People often refer to hitting someone where it hurts, and that's exactly what May's words did. Lagoon's face made him look like a bald sea monster carved from stone, but something rolled across it like a wave before the veins rose at his temples. Surely he'd never thought an eleven-year-old girl would put such a question to him. His squinting eye was invested with an unusual power as he looked at May. His look would be enough to freeze anyone but a Noble, but May met it with an innocent stare.

Lagoon grinned and told her, "Well, it's kinda complicated."

"Then uncomplicate it for us," May insisted. "You were gonna let some weirdo get freaky with me, you know. I'll thank you to take some responsibility for that. I wanna hear a good explanation."

"I bet you do," a hoarse voice said.

Lagoon gave D's left hand a suspicious glance, then quickly shifted his gaze to May. "You're a spirited little girl, ain't you? You'll have to ask pretty boy there for the details. All I can do is keep you folks safe here in my place behind the lord's back. And even at that, I'm putting my life on the line."

"Well, why can't you tell me yourself?" May asked, trying once more to get an answer from him.

Just then, the elevator halted. The floor indicator lamp told them quite clearly that they weren't at ground level.

"Sorry, but you're gonna have to leave by the underground passageway" Lagoon told the Hunter. "If it were to get out that you'd been here, it would be bad news. Just keep going straight and you'll come to the exit. The equipment you asked for will be waiting outside."

Once they'd parted company with D, Lagoon took May back to her room at his establishment, and then went into his office. Upon seeing a sealed envelope on the table, his eyes shone like a beast's. The crest pressed into the melted wax that sealed it was that of the Balazs family. Breaking the seal and reading the message, Lagoon felt the color drain from his face.

Come to the mountain stronghold at midnight tomorrow.

—Vlad

"Damn it!"

Suddenly forgetting all about the letter crumpled in his fist, Lagoon looked up to the heavens.

"So that's where you've gone—to the mountain stronghold? D, there's still time for you to turn back."

II

D was in the air, thanks to a device Lagoon had made available to him. Beneath the blue empyrean vault and the white clouds, he was like an ominous bird, riding and manipulating the wind as he flew along. The collapsible glider had a twenty-foot wingspan and was almost fifteen feet long—the scales from flying beasts that were attached to the wings made it simple to correct for the force and speed of the wind, so that even a child could easily enjoy an extended flight through the sky.

For his second time invading the castle, D planned to come in from the air.

The castle had come into view. Skillfully manipulating the wings, D started his descent. Of course, this was a Noble's fortress. It was sure to have anti-aircraft defenses. The enemy's approach would be caught on three-dimensional radar; and from hundreds of locations, lasers, particle beam cannons, and heavy artillery would be waiting to open fire. However, D landed at the base of a surveillance tower without the artillery even belching a single flame. The blue pendant on D's chest gave off a deep glow. All the electronic devices were rendered inoperable, and as D walked along, each and every door opened to let him pass.

A strange silence greeted D.

"There's no one here at all," his left hand said.

D also realized as much.

"Gone into hiding?" D muttered. He didn't seem to be talking to his hand.

"He's not exactly stupid. He's thought ahead to what would happen if you hit him during the day. But I can't tell what comes next. Will he just keep on running, or—"

D turned around. He was in the large hall on the first floor. A band of white had flowed around his feet. Fog. The pale figure that stood in its depths was the same woman he'd glimpsed in a subterranean passageway the previous day. He couldn't make out the face. Every inch of her was soaking wet, as if she had just come out of the water this very moment.

"Go north three miles—to Mount Blade. The lord awaits you in a castle on its slopes."

Without replying, D turned back in the direction he'd come.

"Wait," the woman called out behind him. In the voice of the fog. "Take me with you. Out there."

Her voice had a ring to it that was almost mournful.

Without ever halting, D went back up to the top of the castle by the same route. He'd hidden the collapsible glider in a recessed area below the surveillance tower.

As the wings snapped open, the pale woman stood behind D.

"Take me with you. If you're going to the mountain stronghold, you'll have no choice but to cross the Plain of Slaughter. When you're ambushed, I could prove useful."

"What is it you want?" D asked as he lifted the flying machine into the wind.

"I wish to go outside. Long have I waited for someone who might take me away from here."

"We could probably use her," the hoarse voice remarked.

"Come here."

When the pale woman approached, D wrapped his left arm around her waist from behind. She felt solid enough.

"We'll have need of a horse," the woman said. Her indistinct visage was turned toward the heavens above. "The Plain of Slaughter can't be flown across. There's no choice but to go by land."

D's gaze was on the nape of her neck, which was blurred as if underwater, and then he shot a glance to the sun in the sky above.

"Will you be okay?"

"You needn't worry about it. If it's a horse you need, there should be a few left in the stables to the west."

"Well, looks like you'll have to fold that sucker up again," a low voice remarked with interest, but at that moment, D's body took to the air.

It was about ten seconds later that they landed in front of the stable. Folding the glider without a word, D then chose a horse from those that remained and straddled it. The horse was bareback.

Though the woman got on behind D, she didn't put her arms around his waist, so as soon as the horse began to move, she nearly fell off. After D pulled her back into place, she finally grabbed hold of him.

"I'm sorry," she apologized, adding in a tiny murmur, "you're simply too beautiful."

The horse started to gallop. Less than thirty minutes later, a desolate plain spread before them. In the distance, a rocky mountain unmarked by even a fleck of green rose like a piece of obsidian, and halfway up it a castle could be seen. A lengthy and narrow flight of stairs stretched down from its gates.

"It's three miles there as the crow flies. And the Plain of Slaughter is a fearful place."

"Wow."

The woman turned her face for a second in the direction from which that remark had come in an odd tone, then continued, "Once upon a time, a battle took place here between villagers who opposed Lord Vlad and the lord's soldiers. The villagers were backed by Nobility from the western Frontier. Right in the very center of the plain they clashed—"

"When was it?" D asked, his voice making the woman's body grow rigid.

"At night."

"The Nobility's time."

The villagers would've been fighting as humans. Yet the time of the battle favored the Nobility.

"And the villagers were defeated. All the survivors were captured and buried alive out on this plain. They numbered more than a thousand. Some say the ground is red due to the blood they shed."

How this woman who'd been far beneath the castle knew this was anyone's guess.

Driving his heels into the horse's flanks, D spurred it forward. Before the Hunter had gone five hundred yards, he felt a minute but distinct vibration where he sat on the horse's back.

"Run. Get over to that big boulder!" the woman exclaimed, her voice falling sharply.

The ground had collapsed like sand. The way the dirt was sucked into the countless cracks, it looked like a sugary confection collapsing in on itself.

The woman let out a low gasp.

As they fell, the horse continued galloping. Its hooves pounded the collapsing ground, striking the earth just as it was about to fall away, and in that manner they were making their way across a pit that had to be a hundred and fifty feet wide. Was it due to the strength of the horse or the skill of its rider?

But once they were halfway across the hollow, only a black abyss yawned before them. They fell. The woman, however, was quite calm.

The ground had already crumbled deep into the bowels of the earth, but the horse and its riders floated in the abyss like something out of a painting. Around them, the wind groaned and bellowed angrily. And then the two riders and their mount drifted upward.

Looking up, the woman gave a louder cry of surprise this time.

A massive pair of wings had sprouted from D's back. The wings of the glider.

She realized he'd slung them over the horse's neck. And she also knew the device would open with the single touch of a button. However, this glider had no body—there hadn't been enough time for that. And it would be impossible for this type of glider to safely keep something in flight without tail fins, because it was the tail fins' job to stabilize and control heading.

D—this beautiful young man—completely disregarded the immutable laws of physics. What's more, he had his legs wrapped around the barrel of the cyborg horse and supported the weight of the woman as well, as they made a clear and powerful ascent out of the abyss.

"The Noble warriors who were supporting the villagers were swallowed by that hole. And the villagers were left here without any allies."

It wasn't clear whether or not D was listening to what the woman said.

Once they'd barely risen to the brink of the great pit, they coasted another thirty feet, and then quickly attempted a landing. The wings had already been folded up and their buoyancy lost by the time the cyborg horse touched its hooves to the ground, but the horse went right into a gallop. Flawless was the only way to describe the way the animal was handled without even a second's delay.

D yanked back on the reins and the horse came to a sudden halt right next to the big boulder the woman had indicated. But it soon became clear that the Hunter wasn't about to stop.

"Don't move," D told her as he dismounted.

He took five steps forward. From the third he was out in red grass that came up to his knees.

"The villagers rushed in headlong," the woman on the mount said in the lowest of tones. "There was nothing else they could do. But half of them were cut down instantly. And—"

A number of flashes leapt up from the grass. They were aimed at D's knees.

Evading them with a graceful leap, D drew in midair to cut them down. A semicircle of light slashed through the grass, while at the same time, cries of pain from nothing human and blue blood exploded into the air.

As D touched back down, he sensed that he was surrounded by a number of individuals—who then halted. His demonstration had struck fear in them.

However, the voice that rose all too naturally from the palm of the Hunter's left hand remarked, "Oh, this is gonna be a pain."

Apparently it had noticed they would be at a distinct disadvantage in this battle.

From what it sensed, the assassins hiding in the grass were less than a foot and a half tall.

When fighting opponents who didn't even come up to his knee, a swordsman's own height would be his greatest enemy. The body of the average human being simply wasn't constructed to use a sword against anything so small. Even a renowned swordsman would want to fight someone tall enough to give him a target around stomach-level or higher in order to demonstrate his skills to their fullest. At the very worst, he might settle for something that came up to his waist. Anything shorter than that would naturally force him to stoop and lower his center of gravity; and using both arms as a fulcrum when wielding the sword, his movements would be extremely restricted. No matter how expert a swordsman was, he would find the inability to strike with his full strength from the very onset a wholly new experience. On the other hand, his opponents were used to using that height to their advantage.

Long ago, the villagers must've had the very legs cut out from under them. The swords they should've raised against their enemies swept ineffectually through the air, and by a cruel trick of fate, they surely added to the fatalities.

The enemy's circle tightened. D's blade had been lowered.

"But among the bloodied blades of grass," the woman continued, "there also lay some of the foe. What had slain them was—"

The flash of light that shot up again was deflected by D's gleaming blade, and then the Hunter bounded once more. How gorgeous he looked as he froze at the zenith. Perhaps D's foes halted because they were in awe of his speed, but then again, it might've been because of the way he looked. Suddenly, they were pierced from the back and through the heart by needles of rough wood whistling through the air. Just like the spears and arrows of the villagers, the only thing that'd had even a negligible impact on the enemy.

Although another flash came at D like a silver snake after he came back to earth, the very instant it was simply batted away a strangled cry rang out, and then total stillness returned.

As D flicked his blade and sent the gore flying from it, a thin fog enveloped him.

"What a man . . ." the woman said, the tone of her praise practically a moan.

Returning to his horse without making a sound, D said coolly, "What'll be coming next?"

III

"I don't know," the woman replied, her answer clear and succinct.

D didn't respond. He hadn't really been asking her opinion in the first place. All she had to do was prove useful at the very end—that must have been his feeling.

Getting back on his mount, D stared straight ahead.

"We've got company!"

The hoarse voice made the woman's body stiffen. It was referring to the black specks rising from the distant mountain stronghold.

Against the backdrop of the blue sky, eerie flying creatures took shape, with four limbs in addition to their wings. In less than ten seconds' time the flyers came into contact with the horse and its riders. Taking no special formation, they flew straight down at once. Their bodies had an unusual number of bumps and pits. Their arms extended, and talons sprang from them. Clearly these were weapons meant to reach down from the sky and shred those on the ground. The talons were over three feet in length.

But the sword that gleamed in D's hand ready to greet them was the same unholy blade that'd hewn every manner of enemy into mountains of corpses and spilled rivers of blood. No matter what the foe, no matter how they attacked, they couldn't help but fall to that flashing steel.

Talons ripped down like a waxing crescent moon, and the sword went up like the same moon's waning crescent. There was no clang as they came together, but with a weird and unsettling sound three of the flying creatures thudded limply to the ground. By the time the bodies that'd been decapitated in midair finally sent up geysers of blood, the cyborg horse was pounding its way across the ground far ahead.

The remaining dozen or so continued to give chase, but they showed no sign of attacking right away. Who would've thought three of their kind could be dispatched so effortlessly?

However, the lead creature suddenly went into a sharp climb, with the rest following en masse. On reaching an altitude of roughly a hundred and fifty feet they turned, each going into a steep dive.

As intrepid as their tactics were, D had just shown how ineffective they were against him.

"Be careful. I don't like the looks of all those bumps on their bodies. They're—"

The rest of those hoarsely spoken words were obliterated by an immense shock wave from the figure that'd turned just above D's head.

The earth rumbled.

While the horse was sent flying, D clung to the reins, twisting the beast around. His hair billowed and his coat fluttered out. It was almost as if part of the shock wave's duty was to show him in all his grace.

As the horse miraculously landed on its feet, a great sledgehammer of air pressure slammed straight down from above. If D hadn't narrowly managed to work the reins so they continued to advance without any hesitation . . .

Grass and dirt went flying as the ground sank—fifty tons or more of pressure had been distributed there. But just before the impact, D's eyes had caught the creatures going from a steep dive to a steep climb. When a body moving at high speed executed such a sharp turn, it created a powerful shock wave ahead of it. And that was precisely what his foes used as an attack. However, based on their size and speed, such destructive power was unthinkable.

"It's the bumps," the hoarse voice said. "The air gets funneled between those bumps, pumping up the force in the same way that the wind is when channeled between buildings in a city. And here it comes!"

The voice flowed upward.

The third ruthless blast scored a direct hit on the raised palm of D's left hand.

A sound like thunder rolled across the earth.

As his steed galloped on, D clutched the folded glider in his left hand.

The creatures in the sky above were most definitely shaken. Their deadly shock waves had suddenly disappeared—or rather, it appeared they'd been swallowed by a certain spot on the palm of the Hunter's hand. No doubt it was impossible for even their sharp eyes to discern the mere speck of a mouth that'd formed there.

But it was a second later that the creatures were to know true astonishment. Three more went into a dive. Between them, the gorgeous figure in black flew up from the earth. Silvery flashes and bloody spray danced out, and the trio continued on in a new dive—to their deaths. D immediately launched himself into the rest of the flock, and four more plummeted with blood trailing from them like exhaust. Smashing through his confused foes, the Hunter turned in the sky above them.

This was what was meant by snatching life from the jaws of death. Opponents from the sky would be fought in the sky. Leaving the woman and horse on the ground below, D had put his trust in the artificial wings.

The Hunter dove toward the closest of his foes. The beast's fear-twisted face suddenly veered off to the right. A terrific blast of wind had just assailed D from the right.

Falling headfirst and essentially in a tailspin, D attempted to right himself.

As they watched the figure in black plummet steadily, the creatures laughed a silent laugh. Nothing that lived had ever escaped the turbulence they created. Even a giant roc with a wingspan of over three hundred feet could be driven to the ground, its bones already shattered in more than a thousand places. How much worse it would be for a lone human being! As D fell, they followed close behind him, to deliver the final blow and watch his cruel demise. The lumps covering their bodies shifted subtly, taking in the air currents, amplifying them, and then expelling them violently.

D's left hand came away from the glider, and his right hand now gripped it instead. The blade of his sword was clenched in his teeth.

The lethal turbulence that roared at him changed direction.

They saw something. Saw the mouth that opened in the pale palm of his hand. It sucked in the air, then expelled it. The turbulence that should've knocked D down to his death instead caught him, then lifted him high into the air.

As the creatures tried to flee, a powerful force tossed them in confusion—air expelled by the palm of D's hand.

The figure in black was drawn into the deadly dance of his foes. Blood spiraled out. It was several seconds after the last of his foes' corpses slammed into the earth that D came straight down to his horse.

The hazy form was slumped across the horse's back. Quickly righting herself, the woman gazed in the castle's direction.

"Shall we go?" she asked. "That was probably the last attack—and it seems even the Plain of Slaughter wasn't able to kill you."

"How goes it, de Carriole?" the lord's voice inquired.

"He's made it across the plain," the aged scientist replied.

"As I thought he might."

Though de Carriole tried to find some tiny hint of regret in the calm ring of those words, he had little luck.

"Though he may have human blood in him, for all his human airs, he is made of sterner stuff. You were terribly mistaken to believe any of your little tricks could slay him."

"Yes, I am horribly embarrassed to say."

"We've lost a great many of the servants you created."

For a second, de Carriole wanted to turn and look, but he couldn't. He was in a laboratory that'd been set up for him in the mountain stronghold. Although the light was thin, it filled the room to overflowing. This was not the time of day when the lord could take action. And yet, the scientist sensed his presence to his rear.

"This mountain stronghold certainly doesn't want for surprises. I'm counting on you, de Carriole. At the very least, don't let the Hunter run me through."

"Have no fear,"

"Ah, but I have a number of fears," the lord laughed. "Did Greed not tell you what happened? Five foes interfered with that errand—and I hardly think they sprang fully-formed from the foam. Somebody hired them."

"I have already sent someone to deal with that."

"And there is another matter. What of Lady Miska? Or rather, why was it that man last night had the same power as the Destroyer that possesses Lady Miska?"

"I have already explained that. You may punish me for my ineptitude—and my foolhardy curiosity."

"*Curiosity*—I see."

This was a repeat of the exchange he'd had with his lord the previous night as he treated the wounds Vlad still bore on his return.

"Well, it matters not. Instead of punishing you, I have another task for you."

"Excuse me?"

"This is the way we did things long ago—turn this way."

De Carriole complied. He sensed the lord stepping back, while at the same time the door behind him opened and a pair of figures entered timidly. It was a woman of about forty and a young boy.

"What's all this about?" the aged scholar asked his unseen master after a long look at the pair.

"I had them brought here from the Capital. A traveling songstress you were in love with a decade ago and her child. Apparently the boy will be ten this year."

"Surely you jest. For someone my age, a decade ago lies in a distant fog now. I couldn't remember her if I tried."

"Is that a fact? How about you, woman?"

Until she'd been addressed, the woman who seemed much younger and softer than her years had stared intently at de Carriole, but now she suddenly lowered her eyes and said, "No, I'm not acquainted with him at all."

When the lord spoke again, he sounded quite satisfied. "The child wouldn't know you, of course. In which case, this should be quite easy to do. De Carriole, kill them both."

"What's that you say?" the aged scholar asked, and not surprisingly there was an unsettling gleam in his eye.

Still clutching her child's hand, the woman grew stiff.

"I've looked into this. The woman clearly had feelings for you. However, for some reason, each of you claims not to know the other. Which is why I say it should be easy to kill them."

"Why would you have me do such a thing?"

"I feel a sudden urge to try your loyalty."

"No matter what you may believe, milord, all I can tell you is that I have no connection to this woman and her son. I find it quite difficult to believe that taking their lives would demonstrate my loyalty."

"Oh, but it *would*. And you know why that is."

"I'm quite sure I don't."

"Don't play dumb with me, de Carriole. However, for all your evasiveness, I don't imagine it's any use trying to physically threaten you. You're not the kind to value life. Why don't I put it to you in another way? I will forbid you from seeing my wife."

De Carriole closed his eyes. The die was cast.

"Long have I been aware of your feelings for my wife. I no longer have any use for the woman, as you could probably imagine when I built the grave she asked for—to give Byron some peace of mind—then destroyed it so soon after granting her request. Love her, bed her, do whatever you wish. But only after you have disposed of those two."

The old man said nothing, but his ugly face twisted as he stared at the woman and boy in a way that made their blood run cold. What rose from the wrinkled depths of his countenance was a shadowy mix of suffering and viciousness.

"Ah, now you're acting more like yourself, de Carriole. That's what I was after—that look upon your face!" the voice of his lord laughed. "I have no idea what it must be like for a human being to have feelings. Human and human or human and Noble—which do you choose?"

There was a strident clang at de Carriole's feet as something shiny fell there. It was a naked dagger with a golden grip.

"Hurry up before *he* gets here. *He* won't show you any mercy either. You might never see your beloved again!"

The aged scholar de Carriole had his eyes trained on the blade that'd been thrown at his feet, as motionless as if gazing into his own future. He remained that way for a long time.

Battling the Mountain Folk

CHAPTER 3

I

We just got in five new girls. If you'd be so good as to look them over," the manager of the house said with head bowed when he came to Lagoon's room.

As a massive pleasure complex, "Fisher Lagoon's" had a constant need for fresh entertainment and women. For instance, the "shock bath" powered by electric jellyfish that gave off just the right voltage for the ultimate in sexual stimulation, or the "jelly dance room" made of a material as supple to the touch as female flesh— to provide special event rooms like these, there wasn't a day this establishment wasn't under construction, and new girls were added once a week. While scouts from his place visited neighboring villages and even went all the way to the Capital, many women also came knocking on their doors when they heard rumors he was recruiting. Of the five new arrivals today, two were from the former group, and three from the latter.

"Bring 'em in."

Head still low, the manager quickly ushered in the women who'd been waiting outside, then left. In age they ranged from the teens to mid-thirties, each and every one of them an incomparable beauty, but out of them all, the thirty-ish woman named Ming and the innocent-looking Paige who said she was nineteen caught

Lagoon's eye. Apparently the women could tell, because Ming ground her hips purposefully in response to the master's gaze, while Paige bashfully looked away.

"Having come to 'Fisher Lagoon's,' you're no longer like the women outside. Say good-bye to sweaty farmhands and unpolished sweethearts. I'll see to it you have a life every bit as good as women in the Capital. What you'll have to sacrifice in return is great, but if it gets to be too much for you, leave whenever you like. However, once you've tasted the waters of my house, don't kid yourself that you'll ever again be able to live an upstanding life in the outside world. Because you have become inhabitants of another world. From this day forward, this house is your home. Aside from where the manager tells you you're not supposed to go, you're free to go wherever you like and do whatever you want. Any rat bastard who'd harm you or make you cry will have to answer to yours truly. So relax and make some money."

By the time he'd concluded the usual spiel, the women's faces glowed with a mix of confidence, trust, and allure—as was always the case.

"Go."

Once the women left at his command, Lagoon called in the manager and ordered that Ming and Paige be brought to him. Leading everyone into a waiting room for the time being, the knowing manager then brought the two girls back to Lagoon's office after explaining the situation. Lagoon wasn't there. After ordering them to take a seat and wait, the manager left.

"I wonder what he wants with us?" Paige said anxiously.

"Actually, it's pretty obvious. The dove of good fortune has landed right in front of us. Not with white feathers, but with pink, and carrying a bed on its back."

And saying that, Ming smirked.

"But I . . . It's really . . . I mean, right off the bat like this . . ."

"You must be pretty stupid, kid. You came here to sign yourself on, didn't you? Then show a little more gumption. If all goes well, you could be rolling in loot a hundred times faster than the other girls. Both of us could."

Turning away as she said the last part, she then glared at Paige from the corner of her eye.

That was when Lagoon came back. Looking them both over from head to toe in a way that gave them chills, he said, "You girls aren't snot-nosed little kids. You know this is the kind of chance that only comes once in a lifetime. What you make of it is up to you. Come with me, one at a time."

"Both at the same time wouldn't be bad either," Ming said in a husky voice.

"No way," Paige said, her cheeks flushing as she turned her face away.

"I'll start with you," Lagoon said, tossing his jaw to where Ming stood with a broad smile. After spending some "quality time" with her, he then led the reluctant Paige into his bedroom without any break at all. And on seeing his expression when he came out again a short time later, the smile was wiped from Ming's face.

"Go get to work," Lagoon ordered Ming frostily, and after she'd left in indignation, he came up behind Paige where she still stood and hugged her from behind.

"I'm scared," she said.

"Of me? Well, you were still pretty intense."

"No. Of the woman just now—Ms. Ming. She gave me such a look!"

"Just a jealous woman. Not much you can do about that. But all that aside—"

Lagoon must've been quite taken with this slender, innocent-looking girl, because his eyes were filled with a lecherous gleam as his rough fingers closed around a waist so thin it looked like he could snap her in two.

"No, I'm just not in the mood. This is all too fast," Paige said, madly tearing free of the man's hands to escape him.

She stopped in front of the door, and when Lagoon embraced her from behind once more, his hands were more forceful and more feverish than before.

"You've got nothing at all to fear. You're so cute. So long as we're in my place, I am king. I won't let anyone lay a finger on you."

"Really?" she asked, her face stiffening as she turned to stare at him with tears welling up. With huge, limpid eyes that seemed right off the cover of a fashion magazine, long eyelashes, a cute little nose, and lips like flower petals, the woman had such an unbelievable air of allure about her that Lagoon knew he just had to make her his own, and he seemed half-drunk as he pressed his lips to hers.

"You're going to look out for me, then?" she asked.

"Of course so."

"In that case, tell me everything about yourself. As proof that you're my man."

"No problem."

You're getting a little too big for your britches, miss, Lagoon thought, but he was surprised to find he was quite serious about her.

"But that's gonna cost you—okay?"

Without waiting for her reply, he swept her delicate form into his arms and carried her through the doorway to the bedroom, where the starting pistol for a manly endeavor was about to go off.

Letting out a sad little cry as she was tossed down on the bed, Paige smirked so that Lagoon wouldn't see it. For a second, a man's expression rose in the cute face of the cute young lady.

The girl who'd sold herself into service in the pleasure quarter was actually one of Chlomo the Makeup Lover's disguises. Only he hadn't applied the cosmetics to himself, but rather to Sai Fung of the Thousand Limbs. He'd snuck into the place on orders from de Carriole. Based on what the lord had told him, the aged scientist decided Fisher Lagoon was plotting treachery, and he ordered his two henchmen to get him irrefutable proof of that charge. The reason Sai Fung alone had been disguised was because Chlomo had been given an additional command: "Find Lady Miska!" And with that, the two of them had gone off to their respective tasks. The matter of who would handle each had been decided by a game of rock-paper-scissors.

In the same warehouse hideout where Chlomo had made up the Baron, Sai Fung was made up at dawn before making his way on foot to Fisher Lagoon's. As he was leaving, he saw Chlomo out in front of the warehouse looking around as if searching for something. He asked in a perfectly ladylike manner, "Whatever's the problem?"

"Nothing. It's just that when we took the baron and that Hunter that got in our way out of here last night, the bastard's horse was tied up. It was too much trouble at the time, so I figured I'd deal with it later, but now it's gone. Can't help feeling like I probably lost out on that one."

"Someone must've taken it," Sai Fung—or rather, the country girl by the name of Paige—replied promptly. When Chlomo's makeup worked its magic, Sai Fung's basic will and personality remained the same even as his voice and physical characteristics were transformed into those of the woman he was modeled after.

"I suppose you're right," Chlomo agreed, gazing steadily at the compatriot whose very gender he'd altered. "I was sort of curious as to what his horse was carrying, but it's too late to do anything about that now. Okay, go give 'em hell."

All of this had transpired as the dawn began to be tinged with blue.

In the bedroom, Lagoon was totally under the thrall of Paige/ Sai Fung. The woman Chlomo based his makeup on was a rare temptress—cute and a born nymphomaniac. She captivated hundreds of men and robbed them of their fortunes before she was eventually stabbed to death by the wife of one of the men.

"Stay with me," he ordered her, and as Paige/Sai Fung smiled joyfully, she cursed her luck in her heart of hearts.

From what Chlomo had said, anyone who went to bed with this temptress—male or female—had their brain dissolve while going mad and becoming a slave who would blindly follow her bidding. Needless to say, she quickly realized that Lagoon's incredible toughness was to blame for their miscalculations, but she/he didn't have the strength left to pull him back into bed once again.

Pawing Paige/Sai Fung's hair somewhat roughly, Lagoon said in a voice like stone, "From what I've seen, you've got even greater gifts than appearances would've led me to believe. At any rate, being my favorite, why don't we take a stroll around the whole place. If you happen to notice anything out there, tell me about it later, and I'll try to come up with the appropriate recompense."

And then, with the most dangerous of women/men by his side, he set out on a tour of his establishment. She was introduced to the people who ran things, and she also met the girls. The eyes of the younger ones burned with flames of jealousy and repulsion, and while those of the old hands should've burned several times more ferociously, they were calm instead. They knew in an instant the position any girl in Lagoon's company occupied. Once the personal introductions had been dispensed with, Lagoon showed the girl all the rooms in his establishment and explained how they were used. From the bordello to the casino, from the arcade to the offices and power center, Paige simply followed along meekly with her mouth agape. However, the one exception to this came in a bend in one of the corridors in the southern wing, where Lagoon would've been expected to keep going straight but instead made an awkward turn to the left.

"Um . . . What's down there?" Paige started to inquire.

She was speared by an intense look, but his eyes soon returned to a milder hue.

"It's under construction. Robot dogs are guarding it. Get too close and they'll tear you to pieces," he told her.

"I see."

As Lagoon turned his broad back to her and she continued to walk after him, Paige's lips twisted. But Lagoon didn't notice.

II

As they were galloping toward the mountain stronghold, D prepared to open the glider wings once more. But he was stopped by a crisp, clear voice that issued from the mountain stronghold.

192 | H I D E Y U K I   K I K U C H I

"The gate is open. There is nothing to hinder you, Hunter! Once you've entered the castle, find my immobilized form. However, you shall have to do it while you have the daylight as your ally. The evening will be long and dark, and for you, this night shall be your last."

The voice had told the truth, and D held onto the wings as the great gates opened to either side and ushered him to a staircase connecting the castle to the ground below. Seen from below, the stairs seemed to dwindle to a fine thread as they ran up to the castle.

"There are three thousand steps," the woman informed him.

D opened the wings above his head.

"Farewell," the woman's voice said, and the Hunter sensed the presence behind him departing.

"Aren't you coming?"

"No. There are a million things I should like to see, but your corpse isn't one of them."

"Thanks for getting me this far."

His words were suddenly thrown to the four winds. D rode that gust up the entire staircase, and at the head of it, the castle gate was open. The wind had been sent by Lord Vlad—he knew exactly what the Hunter was up to. It would've been easy enough to resist, but D played right into the enemy's hands.

Cutting across a front garden so small it couldn't begin to compare to those of the castle down on level ground, he was drawn into a hall. Suddenly the wind died and he dropped straight down to the floor. At the moment he landed, he trained a trenchant gaze straight ahead.

An old man hunched at the waist was just coming through a rough wooden door. Once the door had closed, he bowed his head deeply—so deeply, in fact, that it actually looked as if it had come free of his torso.

"I am a physician in the service of Lord Vlad; Jean de Carriole by name. I have been waiting for you . . . for the Hunter who was friendly with *him*."

His face rose sharply. Red light glittered in it–it was the same mysterious cat's eyes that'd made Miska and Vince his slaves. As they reflected the Hunter, D's eyes were tinged with red as well, and both men stopped dead.

Two streaks of red light stretched through the space between the old man and the gorgeous youth, and in the center of that a terrific battle of wills gave rise to unseen flames.

"That's an odd little trick you have," a hoarse voice chuckled. "But it won't work on my friend here."

As D kicked off the ground, de Carriole clutched his eyes and reeled. D's blade flew down at the top of his head—or started to, and then the Hunter turned around.

In front of the entrance doors stood someone he recognized.

"If it isn't the baron!" the hoarse voice exclaimed suspiciously. "He's acting funny. Better be careful."

Before the voice had even finished speaking, de Carriole shouted, "Kill him!"

The baron didn't move, and D also halted where he was.

Had one of them been immobilized by the murderous intent of the other? The intense concentration of ghastly emanations transformed even de Carriole into an icy sculpture.

A gap opened smoothly down the middle of the figure in blue. The instant the dazzling light burst from his cape and sailed toward D, the figure in black kicked off the floor. The light changed direction after slicing through D's afterimage, and fifteen feet still lay between the baron and where D hung in the air with his sword raised high.

"Gah!" the figure in blue groaned. Lowering his prim and proper face, he looked down at the blade that'd sliced him from the left side of his neck down through all of his thoracic vertebrae and even now still pierced him.

Before the baron dropped, D approached him with powerful strides and reached for the hilt of his sword. As the baron fell, the weight of his body left the sword in D's hand.

Without making a sound, D took his sword and pointed it behind himself.

As the tip of the weapon jabbed against de Carriole's throat, a thin sigh escaped him.

"I knew it . . . I just knew it . . ."

The tip sank into his wrinkly neck, drawing red blood. This young man wasn't the kind to pull punches simply because someone was old.

"Where is he?" D asked, strangely enough.

He wasn't talking about the lord—he wouldn't have referred to him as "he." And the baron was now the inhabitant of a bright bloody world colored by the fluid spouting from his body.

"You saw through that as well? The baron is in a different location," de Carriole replied.

The old man who seemed like he'd wear the same cold smile no matter what happened to him was now scared to the pit of his soul.

"Where?"

"A house . . . My house."

"That's a weird little dummy you had there. Even though the principal ingredient looks to be ectoplasm, its fighting ability's only a hair behind the baron's."

De Carriole's eyes shifted a tad toward D's left hand, but froze when the blade jabbed in even further.

"Doesn't look like a plain old homunculus or skill-transplanted body," the hoarse voice continued. "What is it, an artificially-made doppelganger?"

"Where is Vlad?" D asked.

"I don't know. There are simply too many parts of the mountain stronghold unknown to me."

"Then I have no use for you."

"W—wait! There's something I must tell you. I have information regarding the great one!"

This was de Carriole's ace in the hole. And he played it quickly because if he'd waited another tenth of a second, his head would've most likely been irrevocably parted from his body.

"And who would this 'great one' be?"

"The Sacred Ancestor."

"What do you know?"

"Then you *are* interested, just as I suspected. It looks like my skin is saved. Come to my room. I shall share with you all that I know. Truth be told, I never had any intention of fighting you from the very start."

"You go first," D commanded in a tone that made it clear he didn't need to hear any excuses.

Passing through the door at the far end of the hall, the pair traveled down a long corridor, presently arriving at de Carriole's lab. Though it came as little surprise it was smaller than that in the castle down on the plain, it was every bit as well-equipped.

"Just as I thought," the Hunter's left hand muttered in a tone no one would hear, having apparently spotted something that tied into the baron's other self they'd just encountered.

"Talk."

De Carriole nodded at D's low and pointed instruction. Although they had returned to the lab that could be called his private sanctum, he didn't appear a speck more relieved or relaxed. D's unearthly aura wouldn't allow him to feel either.

"I doubt the man they call D would fail to notice something in his travels with Baron Byron Balazs. His father was not Lord Vlad. It was the Sacred Ancestor!"

And saying this, he leaned back against one of the ropes that hung from the ceiling, wrapped one arm around it, and looked up toward the ceiling. There was a tinge of sadness in his eyes.

D had heard the better part of the story that followed from the woman in the water—wife to Vlad and mother of the baron.

"However, in the end, the lord could not love this son who'd been given something by the Sacred Ancestor. Or perhaps it would be better to say he wouldn't tolerate him. The lord treated the baron cruelly, ultimately plotting to take his life. But the baron was saved by his mother—Lady Cordelia. Thanks to her, he was able to escape with his servants, and today he follows the road to vengeance. However, the punishment Cordelia was given is enough to make anyone want to hide their eyes. For the Nobility, the fear of water is second only to that of the sun. The lord had Lady Cordelia's body surgically altered so that, while her fear of the water still remained, she would be strong enough to live forever submerged in it."

D saw that the aged scholar's shoulders quaked. His shaking was neither from grief nor anger, but rather from both.

"Who do you curse?" D asked.

"Myself," the aged scholar said, gnawing his lip.

"Who performed the operation on the lord's wife?"

"Me. That was me as well."

De Carriole gave a pull on the arm wrapped around the rope. A strident clang echoed from somewhere in the ceiling—the sole expression of suffering this old man was allowed.

"*He* wouldn't permit me to use anesthetic during Lady Cordelia's operation. Nobility or not, they still feel pain. Some of them even go mad from it. I swear to you, as I transformed her into a Noble that could live underwater, she surely tasted pain far worse than anything hell could hold for her. Moreover—"

The aged scholar turned around. The expression that surfaced on his waxy face wasn't that of any human.

"Moreover—oh, D, have you ever met her? Lady Cordelia—ever calm, ever gentle. Even as my scalpel visited insanity on her, her face twisting in agony as she lost consciousness time and again, she never once blamed me, guilty as I was. Once the procedure concluded, I was weeping apologies to her when she took my hand. I can still recall the look in her eyes as she asked me to look after her husband. Alas . . . even now, the sweet Lady Cordelia remains in the water. Laden with pain and grief that shall know no end—and it is *I* that did it to her. I, Jean de Carriole. You shall pay for that, Vlad Balazs!"

At that last flabbergasting comment, a cry of "Oh-ho!" rose from the vicinity of D's hip, but de Carriole didn't notice as his narrow, teary eyes bored into D's face.

"Lord Byron has returned. In all likelihood, he possesses the strength and skill of the Sacred Ancestor. The Sacred Ancestor has succeeded. But it will still take some time for his power to develop fully. And I shall buy him that time. However, before I do—"

The old man's wrinkled mouth moved sluggishly, like a cut of meat trying to speak.

"D, kill Lord Vlad."

No sooner had those words entered the ears of the youth of unearthly beauty than de Carriole cried, "Lady Cordelia, for you I now slay this Hunter!"

He'd specifically selected the rope from the very beginning. D and de Carriole rapidly drew apart, and a deep crevasse formed between them. The gap quickly grew wider, filled with the color of the sky and a deep green. Half of the room D was in had been blown outside by a jet engine set in the wall.

Slamming into the ground some sixty feet below, the room burst into flames.

D was in the air. The glider wings he'd kept close at hand had once again saved his life.

Avoiding the flames that shot up from the ground, the Hunter was soaring back up to de Carriole's lab when something from below snapped tight around his leg—ropes the same color as the bushes below where half of the lab had fallen. Once the first one had wound around D's ankle, scores more were swiftly tossed up from the ground, with a dozen of those coiling around the Hunter's body.

The sword in D's right hand slashed out.

Impossible—the ropes trembled, but weren't cut! Not only that, but they were fighting the flight power of the flying beast's wings as they began to pull D down toward the ground.

Who was manning the ropes? What kind of strength did they possess?

Seeing that it was no use, D finally let go of the wings. From a height of fifteen feet, he fell head over heels to the ground. But he landed on his feet.

He was in part of the forest that surrounded the castle. Each and every one of the ropes that bound him stretched off into the trees. The woods certainly seethed with madness and multiple presences. But why had they dragged their prey down to earth yet failed to attack immediately?

D's head was lowered. There was nothing at all unsettling about his pose, and yet the Hunter's presence seemed to freeze not only the air but even the rocks and trees—and when one of *them* did leap down from the trees, it was most likely because he could stand it no longer. He couldn't bear D's unearthly aura.

His physique was like that of a human being that'd regressed to some prehistoric era, and it was protected by a breastplate, gauntlets, and greaves that all had the same hue as the ropes and gave off the same sheen. In his hand a brutal hatchet glittered. Any form of resistance was useless, while his own attack would split open his prey's cranium—his brain was imprinted with a vivid picture of this preset course of death.

A flash of white light whistled up from the ground. The blade that should've been deflected by the protective coating of mountain beast fat and sand effortlessly split his chest protector, then his muscles and organs, severing his spinal column before it protruded from his back. The body that slammed into the earth sent out a bloody spray as it broke into two chunks of flesh.

Caught in the blood wind, D's form was stained vermilion.

Dead calm descended. Again. It was still. Truly still.

"What's wrong? Come get me," D was heard to say.

Beneath his lowered face, something red moved lithely. His tongue. He'd just licked off the blood that clung to his lips.

Slowly his face rose. His eyes had a glow more seductively red than de Carriole's gaze or the blood of anything in the world.

III

What D had tasted wasn't the blood of that sacrifice. He'd been wounded in the left shoulder by the copy of the baron. Just before he was pulled down to the ground, the Vampire Hunter had drunk the lifeblood that

spilled from that wound, transforming into a creature all abhorred and he himself cursed. A vampire. And there was more to it—late the previous night at the hospital where Lagoon had led D and Taki, the man had a mixed look of terror and nostalgia in his eyes as he gazed at the beauty of that heavenly visage and answered D's question.

"You know why I saved you? Because I get the same vibe from you as I did from *the big guy*. I gave him some help and got a ton in return. I'm still in his debt, you know. So I can't really consider you a complete stranger."

D still wasn't free of the ropes. From a distance, he looked like a graceful black butterfly snared in a spider's web. He seemed like no more than a creature waiting for the vile arachnid to rush in on unsightly legs with gnashing fangs as it attacked.

One of the ropes was given a sudden jerk. Though it was taut, D had no difficulty pulling it back.

Clearly shaken and loosing screams, a trio of figures made a murderous rush from the bushes around him in unison. Each was dressed exactly like the first man and wielded a hatchet and a sickle. D's sword flashed out and, unable to withstand the assault, the first two men were reduced to gobs of blood. The third man planted both feet on the shoulders of the man before him, made a leap to the tree trunk ahead of him, and then hurled his trenchant sickle. With such speed and timing the average person wouldn't have even been able to see them, as they attacked from unpredictable angles.

The sickle meant to decapitate D changed direction with a shower of metallic sparks, slicing the neck of the man in the tree with such speed he never even had a chance to move out of the way.

Suddenly, the ropes went slack. Cutting himself free of all of them with a single swipe of his blade, D stood alone on a narrow patch of rocky earth.

"These are the 'mountain folk,' I take it," his left hand said.

They were a tribe that never went to the world below, but rather made their own world in high mountain peaks and desolate passes.

Shunning contact with outsiders and interbreeding for generation upon generation, at some point they'd undergone physical and mental regression; and though they now resembled ape-men, some might say that their form was the best-adapted to their life in the mountains. Hating not only inhabited areas but all manner of human dwellings, perhaps the only reason they chose to live in the area around Vlad's mountain stronghold was to take on the role of his dark enforcers in exchange for food and clothing. Vlad must've relocated to the mountain stronghold knowing that D would pursue him and be attacked by them. But if that was the case, his plan had failed.

There was a strange look in his eye as it tracked across the four horrible corpses—actually, so far above and beyond horrid they had an artistic beauty to them. D raised his blade into a high guard posture.

From the grove directly ahead of him echoed what sounded like a steam locomotive.

What appeared less than five seconds later was a machine that called to mind a huge green caterpillar the same hue as the mountainous terrain, but it was most peculiar how it didn't snap even a single tree as it slowly advanced. In tighter spaces its body grew thinner as it twisted its way through, and its weight seemed to pose no problem for it at all—even though at fifteen feet in diameter and over thirty feet long, it had to weigh in excess of three tons. Conveyance or weapon of the mountain folk, it thudded to the ground beside a tree up ahead of D.

Out of bushes and trees figures leapt like monkeys, landing on the massive machine. The sides of it slowly split open and great folding scythes appeared. Easily twenty to twenty-five feet long, they were undoubtedly used for mowing through trees and carving through rock.

As the blades howled at him, D leapt over them and sailed backward. At the same time his form was slipping into a stand of trees, five or six enormous boles—each thicker than a man could fit his arms around—fell over, exposing perfectly smooth cuts. The earth trembled with the howling thuds.

A circle of flames shot up around D. Friction from the slices in the trees had caused them to catch fire.

No sooner had the Hunter's left hand groaned, "This thing's gonna be trouble," than wide horizontal streaks of light assailed them from either side.

The way D's sword bit into them and deflected them, it was almost too fortuitous to believe.

The green caterpillar of the mountains was preparing for its next onslaught, but when its legs stopped dead, a commotion broke out among the figures straddling its back. Each of the great scythes had been cut in half, with the severed portions now lying on the ground.

D closed the distance in one fell swoop.

Even more gripped with fear than the caterpillar, the men hurled their sickles and hatchets.

A flash of white light whined out to deflect every last one of them, and the men fell from the caterpillar's back with blood spraying everywhere. Perhaps it was his vampire blood that made D mercilessly cut down all who opposed him.

Ignoring those who dove out of the way or jumped down off the insect, D got on the caterpillar's back and reversed his grip on his sword before lifting it high above his head. The caterpillar may have sensed something, because the second it squealed shrilly and wriggled, the blade came straight down on it, sinking into a spot on the creature's wrinkly back all the way to the hilt. Where it had struck would be the nerve center of a living creature or the power circuits of a machine, or perhaps both in this case. A lump of white-hot material formed within the insect, and it began to run amok as if it'd lost its mind. Perhaps it knew it would die there.

Not even D noticed that a crevasse yawned between the stands of trees. The way the creature fell in, it looked as if it'd dived into the gap.

Only a second earlier, D had sprung, a length of black rope flying from his right hand to wind around a branch on a tree before him. With the dwindling form of the still-writhing caterpillar below him,

D swung in an arc like a pendulum and was about to leap to the far side of the crevasse when he suddenly sank. It was unclear exactly who'd thrown the sickle, but it'd severed the black rope.

Though the pale form of the caterpillar was still visible in the distance, as the gorgeous Hunter fell after it, he instantly melded with the pitch blackness, as befitted someone with his wardrobe.

Closing the iron door, de Carriole descended the stone staircases before him. He was in an underground burial chamber. The holes that opened in the majestically towering walls of stone were filled with a systematic arrangement of gorgeously adorned coffins. They were home to the witnesses to the Balazs clan's history of death that stretched back into antiquity, though not even de Carriole knew the names or genders of the occupants. Passing through a number of gates distorted into shapes that were practically impossible in three-dimensional space, de Carriole presently came to a graveyard with an especially high ceiling. Atop a waist-high dais sat a luxurious coffin the likes of which wouldn't be found even in the palaces of the Capital. It was Vlad Balazs's grave.

"It would seem that D was swallowed by a crevasse in the earth," he informed his master, bowing respectfully.

"Excellent. Then the mountain folk have played their part."

"However, they also suffered numerous losses."

"Give them more than adequate compensation. Furthermore, you're to search the crevasse and locate D's remains. Only then will this be over."

"Understood, milord. But as soon as we have confirmation, I should like to hasten back to my abode, if I may."

"Very well. However, you will have to wait a while longer. In addition to yourself, there is someone else whose loyalty must be put to the test."

"Yes, milord," de Carriole replied, bowing before he turned his back.

When he was almost to the point where the coffin would be swallowed by the limpid darkness of antiquity, a voice issued from it, saying, "Byron—I slew him, but I don't get the feeling he was destroyed. Look for him as well."

De Carriole was frozen in place for a brief time—he was trying to assess the true motives behind the remark. Byron Balazs was in his mansion at present. And it was for that reason de Carriole was in such a hurry to return home.

Holding his tongue and bowing his head, he then said, "Yes, milord," and began to walk away.

The coffin's occupant neither said nor did anything further.

It was shortly after de Carriole ordered his homunculi to search for the corpses of D and the baron that Lagoon arrived.

"Milord Vlad is in a lovely mood, I take it," the giant said, bowing toward the coffin in that underground lair while the lord watched him silently.

"Do you know why it is that I've called you here, Lagoon? It's been twenty years."

"No, I'm at a complete loss," the giant replied, head tilted to one side. His face sober, he inquired, "Let me guess—you're going to compensate us for all the buildings in town that were destroyed last night?"

"Whatever could you be talking about?"

"So far as I know, no creature possessing that kind of power lives anywhere near the village. And if it'd come from outside, it would've left the same sort of devastation all the way to our village, but there's no trace of that to be found. That 'thing' was a normal person already in town who either suddenly developed this monstrous power or was given it. I can hardly be blamed for thinking it the latter."

"Hmm."

"Well, who would do such a thing? de Carriole's mansion lies in the direction it came from."

Vlad said nothing.

While it was unclear what Lagoon made of the contemplative silence inside the coffin, he prodded, "Anything else?"

He didn't seem at all frightened by the creature within the coffin. In fact, he even seemed to be making light of him. You could say his reaction was simply perfect.

"You know a Hunter by the name of D, do you not?" the voice said in a decisive tone.

"No."

"Last night, he took a girl meant to slake my thirst from my manor down below."

"Impossible—"

Lagoon's surprise wasn't completely an act. Though he knew about what D had done, on hearing about it from another person involved—particularly from Vlad's own lips—he couldn't help but be awed. As it happened, this was extremely fortunate for him.

"I sent Greed out to reclaim her, but he was rebuffed. This man they call D is indeed quite intense. However, he had someone aiding him."

"Sounds like a real idiot."

"That real idiot, I suspect, is *you*."

"You must be joking!"

"Taking a variety of matters into consideration, it could be no one in the village save you. What's more, I've never heard of D calling on compatriots before."

"So, what do you intend to do?" Lagoon said, trying to cut to the chase. He was certain Lord Vlad's suspicions weren't easily aroused.

"The only human in the entire village who doesn't have to swear fealty to me is you. And as per my promise to the great one, I can't lay a hand on you. However, if you were to foment rebellion against me, that would be a different matter. Lagoon, will you swear fealty to me?"

"When pigs fly!"

"It's just as I thought, then," the voice laughed. "It would seem I have my proof of your treason, and now you must be wiped from the face of the earth."

"Then do it, here and now."

"I can't. Even I don't have the nerve to renege on a promise to the great one. Which brings me to another matter, Lagoon. Have you no wish to receive Noble blood?"

"Huh?"

"Don't play dumb. I'm talking about life eternal. Although in return, you won't be able to walk in the light of the sun."

"Heaven forbid."

"Take a good look," said the voice from the coffin.

As if in response, the creak of hinges rang out behind Lagoon.

Turning, the giant shouted, "Telena!"

Out of the dozen or so girlfriends he had, she was his favorite.

"Last night, she became my maidservant."

Like some pale, emaciated wraith who was somehow far more maddeningly beautiful than any healthy human, the woman approached Lagoon with a lethargic stride.

"How do you like her? Is she not even younger and more beautiful than when you loved her in your world? And that will not change for all eternity. What's more—"

A crimson beam of light shot down from the ceiling, striking the back of the woman's head and exiting again right between her eyes. Though white smoke rose from her, the woman never stopped walking, and the flames and wound on her forehead vanished almost immediately.

"—her brain can be cooked with a million-degree heat ray, and still she won't die. Living by night can have its pleasures, too."

"The Nobility have no life," Lagoon said, arms folded as he stared intently at the lovely woman who stood right in front of him. "Pardon me, Lord Vlad, but in my opinion, everything that has form comes to an end at some point. Come here."

Extending his left hand, he beckoned to the woman.

With a gorgeous and bewitching grin rising on her lips, the woman spread her arms wide.

Taking a step into her arms, the gigantic form was still in mid-stride when blue-black steel poked out through the woman's back.

Though her trembling fingers sank into Lagoon's shoulders, he didn't seem to mind at all as he worked the blade, then threw the woman to one side. The body that fell to the floor was already lifeless, its alluring beauty beginning to be replaced by the foreshadowing of death and decay.

"See? Look at that peaceful expression on her face. Sure enough, for humans, nothing beats a miserable human death," Lagoon said pensively as he returned a broad-bladed knife to his chest pocket.

"You've killed my maidservant," the voice groaned. "Now I have all the reason I need to rid myself of you. How do you intend to get out of here?"

"Don't be ridiculous. I only disposed of a woman who'd come down with a horrible affliction. And I couldn't very well have her come running back to my establishment, now could I?"

"You call my kiss a horrible affliction?"

"Just a slip of the tongue, Lord Vlad," Lagoon said with a grin. "Isn't it below the dignity of the great Balazs family to get bent out of shape over every little remark a mere human makes? Besides, I'd like to give some thought to the proposal you just made."

"Oh. In that case, why do that to the woman?"

"If anyone's going to get the immortality of a Noble, it ought to be me alone."

And with those words, Lagoon's smile deepened.

The voice of the Lord wasn't heard again.

A strange air of sympathy had begun to drift through the dimly lit tomb.

Miska's Circumstances

CHAPTER 4

I

D was in the hole. When he turned to look, the crack stretched above his head like a bolt of lightning—it must've been a sheer vertical drop of at least fifteen hundred feet. Just as the Hunter was about to slam into the earth, he'd spread his coat like a pair of wings in a braking maneuver. Nevertheless, the impact had been substantial, and although broken bones and ruptured organs had been unavoidable, there was no longer any sign of such injuries. His left hand and his Noble blood had seen to that.

"Hell of a place, ain't it?" his left hand remarked somewhat wearily.

A pair of tiny eyes formed in the palm of his hand, and they burned with curiosity as they studied their surroundings—although there was really only one direction where they focused. For this was no ordinary hole in the earth. The ground D's boots trod was covered by bricklike stones that had been highly polished, and though they'd been overrun by subterranean moss and grasses, it was clear they were the remains of human activity.

D advanced to the right.

Ahead of him lay a tunnel—and beyond it loomed a wall of stone that'd been carved with unknown patterns. Still further in lay wall upon wall on the brink of collapse, and what were apparently fallen pillars could be seen heaped on the stone floor.

From the style of the pillars, these ruins represented the height of the civilization.

"These remains are ancient. Roughly thirty thousand years old—they must've been here since before the age of man."

D touched the wall gently. The spot in question fell away like sand, and then the rest of it collapsed like a fragile confection, the remains spreading at his feet.

"This is dangerous. Gotta watch out for the ceiling, too. I wouldn't go this way."

"Would you rather climb out of the hole?"

"Nope."

Regardless, D kept going forward.

The ceiling to the left had collapsed, blanketing the floor with rock and black earth. What had initially supported it hadn't been able to weather shifts in the earth's crust. However, the ceiling itself was fairly high, and the higher it went, the larger the hole seemed to grow.

Though they were in the darkness where the light spilling down from the crack in the ground would no longer serve them, neither D nor his left hand seemed to be bothered at all.

"Ropes, pulleys, cranes . . . By the look of it, this was a probably a factory."

At the left hand's remark, D halted.

"There's still life in it, too."

"What?!"

The left hand's cry of surprise was answered by a base growl. A pair of green lights burned atop a length of pipe up ahead that ran off at an angle. Eyes.

The instant the creature pounced, D's blade flashed out, and the two chunks of meat it'd been reduced to skidded across the ground.

"From the feel of it, it was some sort of homunculus. Probably the factory's watchdog."

"As far as others go—there aren't any. Let's go," said D.

This time, they didn't even have to advance another thirty feet. When D stopped, a huge object lay on its side directly in front of him.

"You know, this thing kinda looks like that last critter," the Hunter's left hand remarked in the darkness in a tone that sounded quite impressed.

The *thing* enshrined atop the vast dais looked as if every part of it that could move was enclosed in a skeletal framework.

"Unfinished goods? No, that's not right."

D nodded at what his left hand said, stating, "It's finished."

Just then, he sensed something approaching him from behind that shouldn't have been there. Not bothering to turn, D let his left hand shoot out, and a stark needle snagged it in midair. Falling to the ground with its torso pierced was a homunculus that looked like a little demon with a pair of wings.

"It's got a TV eye set in its chest. We've been spotted," the left hand said with some relish. "Down in the bottom of this hole, we can't do a thing. They could fry us or boil us if they wanted to. So, how do you figure they'll come at us?"

Leaping up onto the dais, D climbed into the device.

"How many seconds?" he asked.

"Roughly thirty . . . twenty-nine . . . twenty-eight . . ."

It counted off the seconds until the enemy would respond.

On top of a box that called to mind an engine sat a cockpit made of stone. Most likely it was slightly oversized to leave room for a seat and back cushions. Apparently it was controlled by the steel levers that protruded from the cockpit floor. Maybe it was a unique property of the steel itself, or perhaps it had undergone some special treatment, but the levers didn't have a speck of rust on them.

D pulled a lever forward one position.

The stone gears in its locomotive section bit together, scattering sparks.

"Twenty-one . . . twenty . . . nineteen . . . eighteen . . ."

There was a tiny explosion inside the box. Giving three shudders in succession, it then halted. D returned the lever to its original position, and then pulled it again. This time it started. The explosion became a protracted and unwavering growl. The body of the vehicle shook.

"Fourteen . . . thirteen . . . twelve . . . Oh, my!"

The left hand's eyes shot a quick glance upward.

"Is that the sound of a missile I hear? They're a little quicker than I thought. Nine . . . eight . . ."

D's hand was reaching for the next lever.

"Seven . . . six . . ."

At the entrance to the tunnel, a flash of light welled up. The shock wave that surged from the light swallowed everything, rending and crushing all in its path as it surged forward. Pillars and walls dissolved like shadows, and then vanished.

The crushing surge of light was repelled by the device's hazy outer skin. The light waves coursed around it with seeming regret, snarling and eddying. However, the outer skin was also giving off smoke.

"This thing wasn't finished after all. It won't be able to handle a second hit! We've gotta reinforce it."

Apparently the source of the voice already understood how to operate the vehicle. But would they be in-time?

Precisely two seconds later, a second missile exploded at the bottom of the hole.

Soon after Lagoon left for the mountain stronghold, Paige/Sai Fung went into action. Her/his goal was the same south wing of the building where Lagoon had broken off the tour. After leaving Lagoon's room, she/he encountered a number of men and women on her/his way there. On sensing their approach, her/his body would climb straight up the wall and cling to the ceiling like a gecko. Surprisingly enough, this didn't require the use of either hand or either foot. As if using unseen limbs covered with suction cups, she/he stayed on the ceiling while the men or women passed below, and then continued on. She/he even crawled down from the ceiling at the destination and hung upside-down while opening the door.

None of them had been locked, and all the empty rooms were merely being used for storage.

Finally frustrated by the search, she/he was standing there absent-mindedly when suddenly someone asked, "What are you doing?"

She/he turned in astonishment, but not because the question had come from a young girl. Rather, the surprise came from her/his not noticing the girl sooner. Chlomo's makeup had made Sai Fung into another person, and his own senses and reflexes had come in part to reflect those of the woman he imitated.

Her/his eyes were filled with a look that could kill, but on noticing something, they looked instead with kindness on the young girl.

The girl was May.

"What are you doing in here?" she asked, suspicion on her childish face.

"Oh, nothing. I just went and got myself lost is all. See, I'm new around here."

"You work in the cathouse, then?" May asked unworriedly. For those who lived out on the Frontier, working in a brothel or any other sex trade wasn't necessarily evil.

"That's right."

"In that case, you're in completely the wrong place. It's that way," she said, pointing her finger.

"You know, a couple of minutes ago, I saw someone around here. A really, really handsome guy. He was just so gorgeous, I simply had to go find him."

"Oh, that's—" May was about to say his name, and then she bit her tongue.

"So, you know him, then?" Paige/Sai Fung whispered. She spoke for all the world like some sweet, gentle country girl. And the murderous whore that inspired the makeup had no doubt acted this way in her daily life.

May was easily taken in.

"No, it couldn't be him," she said with a shake of her head, but the gesture said that it actually was.

Paige smiled like an angel. "Okay, then. In that case, I'll just go on looking for him. Go about your business."

"Was he really here?" May asked this time.

Having parted company with D at the water wheel hut around noon the previous day and traveled here in secret with the warriors Lagoon had hired, she'd only seen the Hunter and Taki once since then. At present, Taki slumbered in the subterranean isolation chamber, while D had invaded Lord Vlad's castle, and even if he made it in, he might not make it out again. And though she wondered what would become of the two of them, there was something else that bothered May even more, troubling even her sleep. Hugh.

Her younger brother had gone missing during the trip, but where was he now? Instinctively she knew that D was the only one she could send to look for him. But now even D was gone. Unable to bear the anxiety, she left her room. Since she'd been forbidden to go outside, she'd intended to hide if she ran into anyone, but she was simply hanging around when she spotted Paige. The only reason she'd called out to her was because the woman had seemed even more lonesome and helpless than herself. She had no way of knowing that beneath that disguise was one of the pair that'd gotten her sold to Lagoon in the first place. That's how remarkable Chlomo's makeup was.

"Yes, I'm sure of it."

Once she had spoken, May's desire to see D again rose past the point where she could restrain herself.

"Where did you see him?" the girl asked.

"Around here—at least I think it was here, but I can't find him at all."

"It could be—"

"Huh?"

"Oh, never mind. Well, I'd better be going."

"Wait. Who are you, anyway?"

"May."

"I'm Paige. I sure hope we meet again."

"Me, too."

As the girl with the apple-red cheeks waved at her, the young woman waved back. However, once the girl had disappeared around a corner in the corridor, Paige/Sai Fung once again went up the wall, clinging to the ceiling as she began to follow May without making a sound.

Where May halted was the end of a corridor that Paige/Sai Fung had already finished investigating. A wall loomed at the end of the dead end. Taking a step forward, the girl melded with the wall. For the wall was some kind of holograph.

"I see."

Grinning sheepishly at her/his own failure to try that earlier, Paige/Sai Fung slipped through the wall up at the ceiling.

"Wow!" she/he said in spite of herself/himself when it became evident how tight the space was on the other side. There was room enough to conceal perhaps three people if they were packed in like sardines. At the real end of the hall, there was a door set in the wall that seemed to belong to an elevator, and it was in front of this that May stood.

There was something down below. No, someone. Odds were it was the girl named Taki. Though the mere discovery of May made Lagoon's treachery clear, if she/he could find out if he was harboring the other girl, her/his duty to de Carriole would be more than fulfilled.

Time to roll.

Paige/Sai Fung's eyes had a sinister gleam as behind her/his back, unseen fingers cracked one set of knuckles after another.

The elevator door opened. Not noticing that death was poised above her in the form of a country girl, May took a step forward. Paige/Sai Fung was about to leap—but then halted unexpectedly.

Footsteps were approaching from the corridor to her/his rear. While she/he was momentarily distracted, May stepped into the elevator and the door closed. Clucking disappointedly, Paige/Sai

Fung returned to the corridor's ceiling. She/he would see who the intruder was, and depending on the circumstances, she/he might then lay into them with a blade.

Standing there was a strange man. With a gray hood completely covering his head, the rest of his body was garbed in a robe of the same hue. The cord tied about his waist served as the sole accent to his wardrobe. On the roll of what might've been either paper or parchment that protruded from the chest of his robe, Paige/Sai Fung spied patterns that appeared to be part of some sort of map.

Tension knifed through every inch of her/him.

That guy . . . I saw him in picture books when I was a kid.

Fear brought the memories back with startling clarity. A tragic scene spread across the open pages. A hooded figure with its right hand raised high and left hand pointing back over its shoulder, and at its feet there knelt a Noble, offering prayers of thanksgiving. In the window behind it, golden mountain peaks and a palace could be seen. What the Noble sought and the hooded figure provided was the white strip of road that stretched from there. Come to think of it, the hooded figure was— And the boy's and girl's severed heads were upraised and the bloodied, decapitated bodies lay on the floor because—

What the hell is he doing here?

As Paige/Sai Fung froze like an insect pinned to the ceiling, the hooded one turned to look up at her/him. A creak of a voice said, "Don't lay a hand on the girl. If you do, I shall be the one to decide what road it is you take."

And then the hooded figure walked away.

Barely clinging to the ceiling, Paige/Sai Fung didn't have even the faintest intention of following him, as her/his dripping beads of sweat and the next words she/he uttered made perfectly clear.

"Just who in the hell would've called him here? A Guide of all things . . ."

†

"The sun will be setting soon. And I haven't found what we're looking for. I'm so thoroughly *screwed*."

Beneath a sky tinged with a hint of blue, the sound of hoofbeats and grumbled complaints had rung out for a long time. But they stopped unexpectedly.

"What's this?!" the rider cried in delighted surprise on peering into the thicket that grew to one side of the steep slope.

Flat saucer-like stones were set in the black earth, and atop them lay the black form of a youth of unearthly beauty. Somewhat bruised, his complexion was still almost completely white, and the lips, nose, and closed eyes that comprised his visage were exquisite in every respect. Long, supple eyelashes fluttered in the breeze, and the line of his nose was so perfect it had to be the work of some heavenly maker. After even one look at those lips parted for just a faint peek of white teeth, there wouldn't be a woman— or a man—alive who wouldn't want to press her own mouth to his. However, this beauty was dangerous. Gorgeous, alluring, and refreshing, it was decadent at the same time.

Though Chlomo felt many things—including lust—he didn't make a move right away because something the motionless young man exuded poked blades of ice into his spine. However, the terror was swiftly replaced by the bizarre artistic desires coursing through this murderer's blood, and he reached for the cosmetic case he had strapped to his mount's back.

"Such beauty. So this is D. I may have failed with the baron, but this time I'll succeed. Just watch my makeup—the work of the great Chlomo!"

And then he got down off his horse, keeping his footsteps muffled as he approached the soundly sleeping D.

It was an hour later that Chlomo arrived at the gates to Vlad's mountain stronghold with D. Twilight was already declaring its hegemony over the world. Everything had settled into a certain blueness. In less than thirty minutes, the Nobility would awaken. As soon as the TV eye above the main gates saw D's face, they were instantly granted permission to enter—it was clear he'd been adorned with Chlomo's makeup.

As homunculi scampered across the earth or buzzed through the air brandishing swords and spears, the pair advanced into the depths of the castle until at last they reached the same kind of subterranean resting place as before.

Bowing before the coffin, Chlomo stated, "I have brought you D."

"Why?" asked a voice.

With a ring that suited this forbidden resting place, the sound made Chlomo grow stiff.

"Why, you ask me?"

"This Hunter would take my life—so I question why you have brought him here instead of destroying him on the spot."

"I was simply . . ."

"Idiot!"

A bolt of purple lightning flew from somewhere in the coffin, piercing Chlomo's chest. Though the second blast caught D in midair—the Hunter having already kicked off the floor in a great leap—his blade bisected it, and as he landed next to the coffin, his sword went on to split the box itself in two lengthwise, as incredible as it sounds.

However, there was something D alone perceived. A heartbeat before he had taken flight, the lord's impostor had bounded from the coffin and landed on his feet on the floor some fifteen feet away.

"Duke Greed?"

"So, we meet again," the armored figure laughed, his entire form vested with a purple glow. "The lord is not here. Suspecting that you'd come, he returned to his manor. And by now he would've moved his coffin. Once hidden, you shall never find him."

The history of the conflict between mankind and the Nobility bore out the accuracy of Greed's statement. Even at the height of their prosperity, at a time when humans were viewed as lower than worms, there were still people who violated the graves of the Nobility and drove stakes through their hearts. And though many Nobles had never met with any aggression and had seen but a smattering of minor unrest, once they entered into the age of the Nobility's racial decline and these occurrences suddenly grew more and more frequent, Nobles began to take great pains to conceal their graves from both the eyes and the depredations of the savages.

Though vast subterranean crypts were standard, countless other resting places had been constructed: in dense forests, on desolate mountains, at the bottoms of frozen lakes, and in every other place imaginable. Some Nobility would even climb into modified coffins to slumber far from the earth in stations hovering high in the stratosphere. Even those who prized the ancient traditions used not only three-dimensional phantasms, hallucinatory zones, and labyrinths to try to stop the persistent defilement of graves, but also electronic devices, chemical weapons, and biological weapons—in fact, for a period of time, the Nobility's scientific elite focused solely on this problem.

Perhaps as a reaction to the time they'd been ruled, the humans grew extremely tenacious in their searches and investigations, but they ended with several targets on their lists never being located. When Nobles had an ace up their sleeve like the ability to access extra-dimensional spaces, it came as little surprise humanity couldn't beat them. Perhaps Vlad, too, had mastered such dimension control.

The resting place was tinged with blue. The shadows burnt by the lightning shooting straight at D made the subterranean world look for a moment like a land of shadowgraphs. The hue was horribly transient.

D pressed forward at full speed. His sword reduced the lightning to sparks, but his black garb burst into flames when it took a direct hit.

Giving a guttural cry, Greed sprang. Bringing both hands together in midair, he concentrated the lightning that'd been coursing all across his body into the tips of his fingers. A hundred billion volts—it didn't seem any living creature would be able to withstand that much.

The purple-blue streak seemed to seethe as it enveloped D. Everything glowed starkly blue, and in the midst of this strangely calming light, a gorgeous figure in black bled through like something out of a dream. His shape darkened, and the glow rapidly grew fainter. No, it was actually being inhaled. By the palm of D's upraised left hand. By the tiny mouth that had formed there.

Perhaps due to how ineffectual the attack that harnessed all his power had been, Duke Greed showed no sign at all of trying to dodge D's blade as the Hunter sprang up over him. A split second later, a vermilion line was scribed from the top of Duke Greed's head down to his chin, and he fell limply to the ground—landing on top of Lord Vlad's coffin.

II

Landing just after Greed, D gazed at the fallen forms of his two defeated foes. However, his black garb had been charred and even now was still burning, and it seemed fairly unlikely his warped and half-melted blade would fit back in its sheath. Though he stood there as still as a sculpted temple guardian, no one would've found anything strange about his horrible form.

"Damn it all! You tricked me!" came the groan that drifted from Chlomo down at his feet. "Never would've thought . . . you'd snapped out of it . . . Did I ever screw up . . ."

What Chlomo had seen was D resting after his narrow escape from the fiery hell the ancient subterranean ruins had become, understandably exhausted from the exertions of the previous night. Guessing that the Hunter was unconscious in his muddy and bloodied condition, he'd walked over with cosmetic case in-hand without incident. But when he went to apply the lipstick first, the hand he extended was caught firmly by the wrist. The rest probably went without saying. He'd been forced to do a harmless makeup job and serve as D's guide into the mountain stronghold. Of course, it helped that Chlomo couldn't really be described as a great Vlad sympathizer in the first place.

"Damn it . . . Just one more time . . . I'd like to do my thing . . . as I see fit. Let them see the great Chlomo's skill with cosmetics . . ."

As his cries of pain rolled across the ground, they were joined by someone calling out D's name.

D turned to face Duke Greed.

"D . . . kindly remove my mask . . . I can't see a thing."

The figure who'd stood there motionless then walked over to the one lying down, extending a hand to remove the face plate.

"I'll be damned!" a hoarse voice declared.

The face, now free of its armor, was that of a young woman. Her neatly trimmed blonde locks glistened in the gloom. The shadow of death already hung heavily on her paraffin visage.

"You . . . sound so strange . . . Be silent . . . and listen," she said, both words and blood spilling from her parted lips. "I am Siun Greed . . . Duke was my husband's title . . . Two hundred years ago . . . I was abducted from one of the western Nobility's masques by Vlad . . . I have been his guard . . . ever since . . ."

"What about your husband?" D asked.

The woman smiled thinly.

"How kind of you to ask . . . He came to rescue me . . . and was destroyed by Vlad . . . And now . . . at last . . . I may go to join him."

Raised abruptly, the woman's hand caught hold of D's ankle.

For some reason, D didn't move.

"Tell me, do I . . . do I still look okay? My love . . . Will he laugh when he sees me?"

"You're fine."

"That's a lie . . . I'm covered in blood. Come to think of it, these last few centuries . . . I haven't worn any makeup . . . I had no one to look good for . . . At the very least . . . I should try to look presentable . . ."

Bending over and taking the woman's hand from his ankle, D then walked over to Chlomo.

"You said you wanted to do one last makeup job. Come over here."

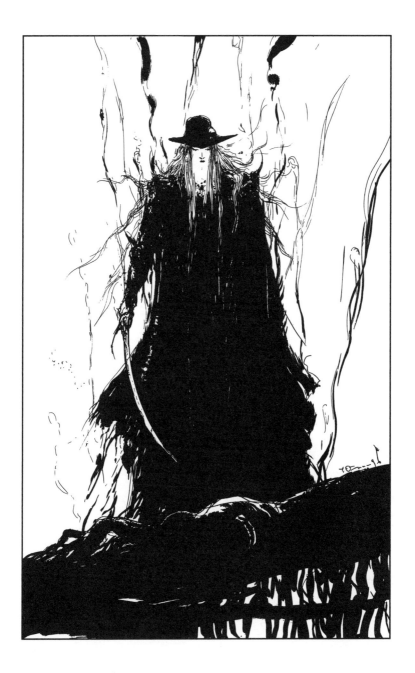

And saying this, he grabbed the man with one hand and dragged him back to Siun. While in-keeping with the young man's character, it was still an extremely rough way to handle things.

"Great. Leave it to me," Chlomo said with his eyes agleam after lifting his torso up off the floor for a brief look at his model. "Just leave everything to me . . . I'll give her the best death makeup . . . ever. Even one muscle spasm . . . can ruin the whole job . . . and I don't have time to fix it. My last gig . . . Hold still now."

Opening the cosmetic pouch he wore on his belt, he began to carefully work on Siun's face.

Both the artist and his client were half dead, and each was tormented by the agony of their death throes. However, in this world of darkness reeking of blood, the man who moved his hands as if he'd lost everything and the woman who lay there with a peaceful expression seemed to have far transcended their human situation to become something divine.

It was hard to say whether an incredibly long time passed or no time at all.

"Okay, I'm finished. It's my finest work," Chlomo could be heard to say.

Taking out a hand mirror, he held it out before Siun's face. Though the thin thread of breath she exhaled fogged it, it did nothing to extinguish the glow of what it reflected.

"This is . . . I'm so . . ."

Closing her eyes with clear satisfaction, Siun then looked at D once again.

"Thank you . . . I look a bit . . . like you now."

And then she was gone.

At the same time, Chlomo slumped forward and moved no more.

The burial ground greeted its two newest residents with stillness.

"Where's Lord Vlad? Looks like we've still got our work cut out for us, eh?"

Seemingly unbeknownst to the source of that hoarse voice, D touched the brim of his hat. Perhaps that was his way of bidding farewell. And then he quietly turned his back on the land of the dead.

More than the light that spilled in through the chapel windows, it was the blue fog enshrouding the coffin that spoke of a different caller. The coming of night—the time of the Nobility.

Heaving a sigh, de Carriole fell to his knees on the floor. Soon the baron would awaken. And overseeing that was his daily ritual. At least it had been, long ago.

When Byron Balazs was a boy, and later a young man, the old man had been his most capable servant, his teacher, his mentor. The sagacious youth had been gifted with a dignity and a magnanimous spirit to rival any Noble in the Capital. How he'd loved the young man who wanted to attend the funeral of villagers killed by a landslide. However, the reason the old man had been so devoted to the young Nobleman's education was because *she* had always been there. Now in the twilight of his life, de Carriole could plainly admit as much. As Byron sweated away at fencing practice, his mother had been close by, quietly watching her child. Her golden tresses swayed softly in the moonlight, with one or two locks resting sweetly on the pale nape of her neck. His heart grew feverish with the futile satisfaction that the proud look in her eyes as she watched over her child was also pointed in his own direction. And because *she* could live only by the light of the moon, he'd cursed the midday sun and refrained from going outdoors until evening. Even now his dreams were filled with the emotions he felt watching *her* furtively, loving *her* from afar as she strummed on the harp for Byron.

Now that time drew near once again, and though he stood and waited before Byron's coffin, how different the world had become. Why had he lived such a long, meaningless life and grown so decrepit, he wondered.

Before he could even utter a prayer he noticed that the chapel's door had opened. He knew of only one man who could make it all the way inside without tripping any of the profusion of security devices installed in his mansion. No, make that *two*.

"Is it you, D?" Jean de Carriole asked.

There was no answer.

The darkness seemed to swell in density.

"Concerned about Master Byron, are you? His circumstances are similar to your own."

"Where is Vlad's resting place?" said a steely voice that flowed through the twilight.

"That's impossible to say. At least, for me."

"There is someone who knows."

De Carriole turned, a bitter grin on his lips.

"Is that what you've come for? If you'll but wait a moment, the baron should be awakening soon. And though the good baron would hesitate to do so, there is something I must say to you. D, slay the great Vlad."

"Having a little change of heart?" a hoarse voice said, but the remark was directed neither at D nor at de Carriole.

"And help transfer the one who drifts in the waters of eternal torment to the accommodations that I've prepared. Please. Come."

Without waiting for a response, de Carriole rapped the cane in his right hand against the floor at his feet. The marble surface shook like a mirror. Reflected there was a great volume of crimson water.

"This solution has the same composition as blood. There is nothing I can do to ease *her* suffering even a whit, save to let her bathe in this. The red lake I've constructed beneath my mansion waits for her even now."

One of the aged scholar's hands balled into a fist while the other waved his cane. One tap of it against the ground made the vision of the lake vanish, while the second blow sent a spiderweb of cracks the color of darkness racing across the floor.

"I cannot stand to see Byron forced to slay his father. D, you must fight Vlad and destroy him. Toward that end, I shall offer any aid that I may."

"What I wish to know is the location of Lord Vlad's coffin—that's all I need."

A shade of bewilderment flickered through de Carriole's eyes.

"I do not know that."

"How about you, baron?" D called out.

The question had been directed at the coffin. The Nobleman was still injured, but the coffin replied.

"I believe I know. I probably know every last thing about the bastard."

"My good baron—so, your five senses have awakened before the sun has even set? As is to be expected from one for whom the great one had such hopes—"

"Hold your tongue, de Carriole."

"Aye, milord," the old man sputtered in reply, prostrating himself as if he'd been leveled by an electric shock.

"That may have been the start of all this trouble. D, I don't know what has transpired since my arrival here, but leave the matter of Lord Vlad to me."

"I've been hired to do it," D said.

"By whom? A victim of the lord?"

There was no reply. D didn't say that he'd been hired by May, that he had to save someone, or that that someone was Taki. As a Hunter performing his duty, none of that mattered.

"de Carriole?" the baron said, his tone rather insistent.

"I do not know who his employer is . . . but Vlad's mouth sullied a girl by the name of Taki."

A silence descended that could freeze blood. It was broken by the first sound of the Nobility's time—the creak of hinges that announced the coming of the world of night. The cover of the coffin was slowly opening.

Rising like a ghost, the figure who stood there was Byron Balazs by name.

"D—wait one night," the Noble in blue said in the voice of evening. "I swear by my name I shall slay my father—Vlad Balazs. And let that be proper atonement for what's happened to Taki."

"Where is his resting place?" D asked. He, too, had the voice of evening.

"I can't say. And if I were to tell you, you still wouldn't know it. Even the Balazs clan has but a hazy recollection of it. D, go back to Taki."

The Hunter said nothing.

"You mustn't underestimate the man known as Vlad Balazs. Do not think him the same as ordinary Nobility. He may already be on his way to visit his victim. I shall investigate the other possibility. But come what may, Vlad Balazs must die by my hand."

Gazing for a time at the figure in blue with whom he'd traveled, D then turned around.

"You have my thanks," said the baron.

"And you have just one night," came the stern reply from the depths of the darkness.

And that time was starting right now.

Distant Shangri-la

CHAPTER 5

I

I n her room, May got the feeling she could hear furtive footsteps. Those who lived on the Frontier occasionally felt this way. Coming down the corridor. From quite a distance. Oh, now it was on the other side of the door. Even the knock sounded furtive. It shouldn't be Lagoon. The only ones who could walk in such a way as to not stir the stillness of night were the people of the night.

She didn't call out to ask who it was. May stared at the door—just at its golden door knob. She couldn't even tell whether it turned or not.

The door opened.

Though the figure wore a white dress, May got only the most indistinct image of her, and she searched for the reason for this. She had no shadow. No doubt the light of the moon was insufficient.

"Have you been well?" Miska asked.

"Yeah," May replied, feeling relieved. "But what are you doing here? Didn't you go to that scholar guy's house or something?"

"No, this is where I meant to go. My grandfather entrusted an item to Mr. Lagoon long ago. I came to examine it," Miska said, gazing softly at the human girl.

"You don't say. Must've been really important. Was it safe?"

"Yes. It was here, surely enough. It's just a tiny censer, though."

"That's great, Miska. That's really great," the girl said, clapping her hands. "Stuff like that gets broken so easily. How nice. I'm sure your grandfather must be overjoyed, too."

The girl wore a docile smile.

Miska diverted her gaze. And like that, she said, "The censer contained a map. Where I was to go after losing my parents and everything else I had."

"Wow," May said, her eyes going wide. "Now that sure is something. So, where will you go?"

"I don't yet know. Someone shall bring me there. At present, he waits in another room. May, will you not go with me?"

"Me? No way!"

The Noblewoman turned a shocked expression to the girl who swung her head so vehemently from side to side.

"Why not?"

"Well, there are still a ton of things I wanna see in this world. And a million things I've gotta do, too."

"I've heard your mother and father are deceased."

"That's right. But a lot of other people are in the same boat. My mother, my father, and basically everyone older than me will probably die before I do. Well, when it happens a little too early like with my parents it makes me sad, but there's no helping that. I'll just have to live a good life and do all the things they didn't get to. If I were them, that's what I'd be thinking as I died."

After a short pause Miska inquired, "For someone your age, is life not painful?"

From her tone, she was expecting a certain answer.

"Of course it's painful," May replied in an exasperated manner. "Who wouldn't be hurt to be my age and have lost their parents? Only once in a blue moon does anything good happen to me."

"If such is the case, why go on?"

"Because once in a while something good *does* happen!"

Miska fell silent. The answer this girl of such a tender age had given was beyond her ability as a Noble to comprehend.

"Not everything in the world is good, but not everything is bad, either. It's the same for everyone. I have my hard times, and I'm sure even a Noble like you has some hard times, too. But somehow muddling through them is probably what life's all about. Thirty years from now, I'm sure I'll look back fondly on all the things that troubled me. That's the kind of person I wanna be. And I'm sure I'll remember you and the baron the same way and tell folks about you."

And then May looked Miska straight in the face and beamed. It was a most heartfelt smile.

"But it's nice that there's someplace so wonderful. You're hurting worse than I am. I can't go, but thank you for inviting me anyway. Let's go. I'll see you off."

"No, stay here," Miska said, resting a hand on the girl's shoulder. "I shall need more than one to send me off."

"Huh?"

As Miska receded, May gazed at her sadly.

The sound of a hard knock made the figure in white step off to one side.

"Sis—it's me, sis!" a quarrelsome voiced exclaimed.

May jumped up.

"Hugh—is that you, Hugh?!"

Scampering like a scared rabbit, she opened the door. And who should be taking cover behind Lagoon's enormous back? It was none other than Hugh.

The two of them embraced. As the siblings' cries rose like a thunderclap, Lagoon looked down at them for a while without saying a word.

"On the way back, my mount threw a shoe. I borrowed another horse from a nearby farmhouse, and that's when I got hold of him. Late the night before, the farmer was passing by the warehouses on Thornton Street when he saw a horse tied up there with a bag loaded on its back that was moving. He opened it up, and this is who he found. After listening to his tale, it turns out he was abducted by some villain. So he wasted no time in running off with the kid. And we won't pry too deeply into why he felt the need to make off with the horse at the same time. Apparently the farmer intended to bring him to the sheriff or me tomorrow."

After that clipped explanation, Lagoon gave an uncharacteristically warm smile.

"Tonight, you two get reacquainted. D should be back soon."

And saying that, he left.

It was then that another figure stood behind the pair, who held hands.

"Now that there are two of you, you could see me off," Miska declared, and it was to the pair's great fortune that they didn't turn and see the gleam that filled her eyes.

After leaving May's room, Lagoon headed toward Miska's hidden chamber. The events of the previous night replayed vividly in his brain.

Suddenly appearing before dawn, Miska had ordered Lagoon to produce the item her grandfather had entrusted to him a decade earlier. Long ago, when Miska's grandfather had desired a meeting with Lord Vlad, human assassins set their sights on him, and Lagoon had served as the Nobleman's guard at Vlad's behest. Seeing how reliable the man was, Miska's grandfather had entrusted him with an ancient metal censer, instructing him that if someone were to come for it with proof of their kinship, he was to hand it over with due haste and render what aid he could. And giving the man a vast sum in precious metal along with those directions, the Nobleman had then left.

Having received the censer, Miska then demanded a room where she might light it and that Lagoon accompany her there.

Halting, Lagoon caught his breath.

The black smoke that rose from the censer once it'd been lit didn't frighten him. It didn't spread, but rather stopped at human height, and even when he noticed that some kind of unknown chemical reaction must be taking place, he wasn't afraid. He wasn't even scared when it took the form of a person in an ash-gray hood and robe. But every hair on him stood on end the instant that person stated in a human tongue, "I am the Guide."

A Guide. Who would've thought they actually existed? Oh, if only D were here—or Lord Vlad.

He didn't want to think about what had come next. But he remembered anyway. His ears, his brain, his eyes all remembered.

"Take me away. Take me to the other side."

And to Miska's request the Guide had replied, "We shall require two children below the age of twelve."

That was the source of his horror. The great Fisher Lagoon stopped in his tracks, trying desperately to get a grip on the terror welling up within him.

The Guide required children, though that wasn't necessarily a rare occurrence. Until a century earlier, every village had done the same thing. However, the Guide was a different matter. What they *did* to children . . .

Oh, why did I have to read that book about them? Why did I have to be there with her? I've gotta stop her. No matter what happens, I can't let her seal the deal with the Guide.

It took several minutes for him to feel like himself again.

When Lagoon finally made it to Miska's room, he was shocked. She wasn't there.

"Damn it! Has it started already?"

The water seemed to spread forever. No one who saw it would've thought there could be any end to it. Visually and mentally, the surface of the water left just such an impression of vastness. And on it, a small boat came across from nowhere in particular. Standing almost at its center was the baron, and behind him was the robed form of Jean de Carriole. The two of them had slipped into the castle through a secret passageway that even de Carriole hadn't known about. This was where the baron wanted to go before doing battle with his father once again.

The boat stopped. de Carriole had cut the engine.

"Here?"

"Yes, milord," de Carriole said, his head bowed respectfully as he remained motionless so that the baron's eyes might be the first to look upon the woman who'd just then drifted to the water's surface.

"Byron."

The aged scholar plugged his ears, and the baron in blue turned a quiet look of heartfelt emotion to the pale and wavering figure in the water.

"I have returned now," he said. "Although you could say this is my second trip back here."

"I know," the woman in the water replied, looking like a mirage. "When you were defeated by your father and thrown into the waterway, did you think I wouldn't notice? Did you think I would do nothing?"

The baron was at a loss for words.

"I was constantly watching you. And I entrusted you to the flow of the water."

"Why?"

"I, who gave birth to you, knew better than anyone that it would take more than mere 'running water' to claim your life. So long as you were underwater, you would be safe from destruction by sunlight. And that being the case, I thought it would be best if you kept going and flowed right out of these lands. I tell you this in the full knowledge that, now that you've returned once more, nothing I say can dissuade you. Byron, my son—please, just leave the castle. Nothing can come of your battle."

"I am quite aware of that, mother."

From the very start, there was nothing to be won in this fight. A son would kill his father. Was it so the abused and banished son might be avenged, or so that his mother, who'd been relegated to a subterranean lake, would be vindicated? Whichever it was, it was so horrible it was deserving of the Nobility's most scornful expression—"oh so human."

"Byron," his mother said, her voice carrying a certain intent.

Your mother is going to share a great secret with you alone. Listen carefully—It was just such a tone.

"Your father despised you. Because you, who should've continued the family line, had been changed into something else. Your father did not refuse the great one's request. He was delighted to hand you over. And that was no mistake. However, I must tell you now that before your father, there was someone else who hated you and tried to destroy you."

The baron closed his eyes. He had always done so, accepting everything and bearing it quietly. For he was not a human being.

And that was why he inquired softly, "Was it de Carriole?"

"No."

"The great one, then?"

"No."

"Who then—?"

"Me."

II

There was nothing to disturb the silence. The water around the boat didn't move with even a hair of a ripple, and the baron was motionless as a rock. Apparently tragedy had frozen him.

"Impossible," the baron said, retaining his composure.

"Kindly ask de Carriole," the woman in the water said.

"Is this the truth, de Carriole?"

"Yes, milord," the aged scholar answered in a tortured tone.

For the first time, waves rocked the sides of the boat.

The baron let all the tension out of his body.

"At the behest of your mother—Lady Cordelia—it was I that drove a stake of ash into your chest. Had it been anyone but you, Master Byron, the stake would've left a substantial scar."

"He was unsuccessful. And I regretted doing it. For the instant your cries filled my ears, I awoke from a nightmare. To one school of thought, my being left trapped here in this condition through de Carriole's assistance was the wrath of heaven."

Byron Balazs, the baron in blue loathed by his father and nearly killed by his mother, stood there and didn't say a word.

"If you would slay your father, first you must kill your mother. That's all I wanted to say to you, Byron."

The baron and his mother and the aged scholar—each of the three seemed to have their thoughts take shape, flickering in and out of visibility in the faint light.

Suddenly the baron turned to the right. de Carriole raised his face. The woman swayed. All three of them had sensed a presence of staggeringly immense proportions. It became a booming voice that was drawing closer.

"Has your tragic episode reached its conclusion, my lovely wife and child?"

It was the voice of Vlad Balazs.

Though the baron focused every fiber of his being on the source of that voice, he was ultimately unable to pinpoint it.

"Well, I'm sure you've heard what your mother had to say for herself, my freakish son. Your father has come down here to do battle with you again. From the very start I was watching from up above as you came. And though I can't imagine what you're feeling now, since you are out to take my life, I can't let you leave here alive. Have no fear. Before the son can slay his father, the father shall destroy his son."

Suddenly the boat rocked like a fallen leaf. A tremendous shock wave struck the surface of the water, and seeking an outlet for its anger, the water surged violently.

"Ha ha! Can you see me, Bryon, my son? If not, you shall find slaying me to be most—"

The mocking remarks stopped abruptly.

"Where in blazes did you come from?"

The lord's shocked tone seemed to command the angry waves to be still.

The instant the bronze boat stopped on the water's graceful surface as if it'd remained that way all along, a black figure had shot up like a mystic bird from the water off the starboard side.

"D?!"

The lithe figure swept his left hand toward the unseen ceiling, executed a flip that sent his black raiment fluttering out around him, and then by some unguessed means landed feet-first on the surface of the water. Like some graceful black waterfowl, he didn't sink. The heels of his boots were only slightly dampened as he stood straight up on the water's surface.

Perhaps it was in response that the figure in deep purple came down from on high. He, too, stood straight on the surface of the water, causing only the faintest of ripples. And then, with a single wave of his right hand, he sent three fiery orange streaks coursing toward D.

Catching them, D's left hand was enveloped in flames, but those disappeared abruptly. Needles of rough wood the Hunter had thrown had been hurled back at nearly the speed of sound, and their friction with the air had made them burst into flames.

The beauty of that countenance by firelight made Lord Vlad woozy.

"D, what are you doing here?" the baron inquired.

"I tailed you," he replied, his answer reasonable and succinct.

Smiling wryly, the baron told him, "Stay out of this."

"I will if you can beat him."

"I'll beat him."

The baron no longer had any purpose save this battle.

Two transparent disks landed next to the boat—D had thrown them. The baron had no way of knowing they'd been cut from thick plastic panels the Hunter had found at de Carriole's mansion. D had prepared a second set for the baron because he understood the Nobleman's thoughts well enough to know he would call on his mother in the subterranean lake, and he reasoned there was a very good chance it was there that the battle would take place.

Though the circular disks lacked foot straps and didn't seem like they could support a rat, much less a human being, the baron stepped onto them completely naturally.

Now three men floated on the water, and the baron walked toward his father Vlad with a determined pace.

"Not feeling so well, are you, Father?" he asked. "No matter how great you may be, Father, the water is a detestable foe to the Nobility. However, to *me*—"

The Nobility feared running water, but the blood that coursed in Byron Balazs's veins had no terror of it.

The devilish face above the great purple robe twisted its lips.

"That in itself marks you as a freak. My son, may you be cursed for all eternity!"

Vlad swung the golden scepter in his hand down toward the baron's feet. An opening fifteen feet in diameter and of indeterminate depth was created, yawning there to swallow the baron.

But the baron was in the air. Ignoring the great chasm beneath him, he bounded toward Vlad's chest.

"What's this?!" Vlad exclaimed, finding this development so unexpected he forgot to brandish his deadly scepter.

Placing pressure on the lord's right arm that paralyzed it from the elbow down, the baron then twisted it around behind him sharply while wrapping his left arm around his father's neck. It felt like the root of a tree twisting around him. In the faint light, Vlad Balazs's face flushed bright red, then turned a more muddied purple.

"A choke hold, eh? That's a good approach," a hoarse voice commented from the vicinity of D's left hip.

Even if they were to suffocate, an immortal Noble would return to life in a matter of minutes, but that would be more than enough time to pound a stake through their heart.

One shadowy figure remained clinging to the other, the trembling stopped, and then another ten seconds passed. Just when the unexpected technique seemed about to deliver a somewhat disappointing denouement, Vlad's left arm—which was in the baron's grip—dropped unexpectedly. Not that it'd run out of power. Rather, it twisted around behind the lord's back, grabbed the scepter from his right hand, and sent it whistling into the water at his feet.

"What—?!" came the heartrending cry of pain from the pale figure who'd drifted under them at some point.

A red silk gauze of a cloud spread through the water.

"Lady Cordelia?!" de Carriole exclaimed.

And only a heartbeat later, the baron shouted, "Mother?!"

His voice and his physical form both sailed over Vlad's head as the lord bent over far, sending the young Nobleman arcing toward the water's surface.

A splash went up.

Vlad raised his right hand above the shadowy form of the baron, who'd sunk underwater. A crimson jewel glittered in the pommel of his slender dagger. Sinking or rising, the baron wouldn't be able to dodge it.

The flowing flash of silver and the explosive shower of sparks came at almost the same time. Going into a stroke right out of the sheath, D's blade came down on Vlad's left elbow—and was stopped by the arm the Hunter had supposedly taken from him once.

"My titanium alloy arm!" the lord gloated as he showed them the sheen of oxidized silver. "Better than my old one, and more powerful. Your sword will never get past this, D."

As if to test that, the Hunter brought down a second blow from the high posture.

As would be expected, the lord countered that with his left arm, then dipped the same hand into the water and squeezed it into a fist.

A single jet of water pierced D's chest as he still hung in the air. That was no ordinary water. Vlad's artificial arm actually had a mechanical force of fifty tons. Less than a millimeter in diameter, the stream of water reached a speed of Mach three. It burst from D's back, knocking him back some fifteen feet in the process.

Flames bursting from his chest, D sank into the water.

Without even bothering to verify D's death, Vlad turned his eyes to his son. His scepter protruded from the chest of the pale woman who drifted underwater.

Grabbing hold of it, the baron called out, "Mother—"

"It's no use. I took her straight through the heart—even if she's still breathing, she won't last long."

As Vlad stood there laughing like some guardian demon, the baron gazed fixedly at him. The water that shrouded his blue form was stained red.

"A-ha, you've finally got that look in your eye, Byron. However, you shouldn't feel that way. I've destroyed the woman who tried to harm you before I ever did. You should thank me."

"You're right, Vlad," the baron said, touching his hand to the woman's cheek. He didn't address his father by his title, but merely by his name. "The woman who would've murdered me in my infancy is dead. Now she lies here, truly my mother. I must thank you, Vlad. You are my real foe."

"And how will you slay that foe?" Vlad said, bending down to let the baron see his white teeth. "You're a traitor, descending from my blood but given another man's strength. Try using that strength to defeat me. What's wrong? Can't stand on the water?"

Once again a naked blade glittered in Vlad's right hand. But it halted in midair as he twisted around in amazement.

A figure in black was approaching in a mesmerizing fashion across the water's surface, a sword gripped in one hand.

"Interfering again, Hunter? No matter how many times you try, the same thing will—"

Discerning that D's blade was limning the exact same arc as before, Vlad donned a sardonic grin. Then his eyes bulged in their sockets. His titanium alloy arm had been severed at the elbow again.

Water dripped from every inch of D. But the stream of water that coursed by his lips had a dim vermilion tint.

"You filthy bastard . . ."

"I cut the same place," D said.

For the first time, Vlad looked with fear into the eyes that gave off that blood light. Was the gorgeous young man enjoying his terror?

"You bastard . . . So, your vampire blood has awakened, has it?"

Though the lord should've been frozen in place, reflex made him take a step back, and though he should've been able to narrowly avoid the blade coming down at the top of his head, a bloody mist suddenly shot out.

As the massive form staggered, the black cyclone dashed forward.

"Stop, D!"

Was the sword blow that could sever even steel thrown off by that cry, or was it the fault of the strange undulations that suddenly assailed the world? Up became down, and down became up.

And just as he felt as if gravity itself had been reversed, D saw something. He saw a different scene reflected in the depths of that vast expanse of water. A number of figures stood at the border between here and there—Miska, May, Hugh, and a hooded figure in a long gray robe.

III

Led by Miska, May and Hugh walked down a disused corridor beneath the pleasure complex. Mortar from the walls and ceiling had fallen to cover the floor, and the only light to speak of came from candles that burned in the candelabra Miska carried. She was like a restless ghost walking the rotting halls of some haunted castle. But both Hugh and May were cheery because they were together with Miska again. The conflict between the human race and the Nobility—although it was a filthy morass that would last forever, these two flexible psyches had easily escaped it armed with the experience of a few days spent together.

"Wow, Miska, I can't believe you're going someplace so cool!"

Not even bothering to glance at Hugh as he made this sudden exclamation, Miska walked on silently.

From what the boy's sister had told him, Miska was soon to depart for a distant Noble paradise. And they were to send her off.

"I sure hope you'll be happy there. I envy you. But it's kinda sad."

"Sad?" she said, her pale visage suddenly turning toward him. "How so?"

"Well, we have to part company with you, Miska." the boy said crossly. "Didn't we spend days together on the same dangerous journey? It's hard to just say, 'Well, see ya,' like we'd only shared a ride across town."

"But—I'm a *Noble*."

"Heck, I know that," the boy coughed. Something had welled up and blurred his eyes. "So you're a Noble. But you didn't drink our blood. As a matter of fact, I get the feeling you helped us out."

"I helped? Helped you?"

"Sure. I'm a guy, so I'm always ready for a bit of trouble or danger. Heck, my sister is too, because we've been out in the cold, hard world. Both of us have knife marks on our behinds. But you're a Noblewoman, Miska. You wear all that pretty white finery, and your hands are so soft. You've probably never had to lift anything heavier than a spoon or a fork. Yet a princess like you braved the same dangers as the rest of us. That made me think I had to hang in there, too."

"Finery? Princess? *I am a Noble*."

Miska grew confused. The reason she reiterated her point about being a Noble was to stress that she was something better and stronger than a human being. While daytime was another matter, with the coming of night the Nobility could see in complete darkness, had the strength to uproot even enormous trees, could float through the air like a bird, had the stamina to run sixty miles without resting, and worst of all, they had hypnotic abilities that could freeze their prey in place with just one stare. The human race couldn't even begin to compare with all that. Yet how did this human boy view her?

"Noble or what-have-you, you're still a woman. And with a woman giving it her all, I couldn't just sit around on my duff."

Hugh gave Miska a look that implored her not to make any more protests he couldn't understand. However, in the course of their journey, he himself had been beset by bizarre dragon creatures in the swamp, had been abducted by the magician, and after passing into Vince's hands he'd then spent several days unconscious and stuffed in a bag. When the farmer found him, he was nearly dead from hunger and thirst. But after just one day of sufficient food and rest Hugh was back to his old self, and that was something that could only be attributed to his youthful constitution and sunny disposition. As far as this boy was concerned, humans and Nobility were no different. And that's why he was sad. He would be parting company with Miska—a Noble.

"Say, Miska," May called out to her. "I'm gonna miss you, too."

Miska was speechless.

But that quickly came to an end. Before the trio, the hall entrance that'd been left open yawned like a great black maw. Inside, lamplight flickered. Candles burned in a tall candelabra in the center of the desolate hall, and beside it stood a figure in a long gray robe. His right hand was held behind his back.

"Is that the Guide? He's weird," Hugh said, expressing his opinion with a child's candor.

May merely tilted her head to one side.

"Come," Miska said, giving a push to the two children's backs and bringing them before the figure in the gray hood.

Not surprisingly, May found something disturbing about this and looked up at him cautiously, but Hugh merely greeted him with, "Hi there," then looked around the place somewhat restlessly.

"You're setting off on your trip from down here? Where in the world are you going, anyway? Ow!" the boy then exclaimed, clutching his right ear as he leapt up. "Hey! What do you think you're doing, you prick?"

Not even glancing over at the little outraged face, the Guide gazed down at the machete he'd concealed in his right hand, then licked the boy's blood that clung to it.

"Gross! What the hell is this freak up to?!"

"It is indeed the blood of a child under twelve," the Guide said with a nod. "Does the same hold true for that one?"

May looked up in surprise.

"Yes," Miska replied, her blossom of a face nodding assent.

"Very well. We have a contract, then. It's too late for second thoughts."

At the weird and otherworldly air that voice carried, the brother and sister finally began to suspect that something wasn't right.

"Miska—what's all this about a contract?"

In response to May's query, the Guide said, "I have been summoned by a Noble who has lost her place in this world."

From the beginning of their history, there had been Nobility who'd lost everything to which they might've returned. Relations with other Nobles were not always amicable. To the contrary, the days spent in grueling conflicts would probably be far longer. Long ago, in the time the ancients had referred to as the Middle Ages, nobility of another sort with the emblem of a beautiful rose on their swords and spears had watered those flowers with death and destruction, and the ageless Nobility seemed to live for unceasing and fruitless conflict precisely because they were immortal, as if they were stalking war-torn streets. In that each conflict produced both a winner and a loser, their world was no different from any other.

Just as victors in the Middle Ages had seemingly been lacking in mercy, so the contemporary Nobility were extremely thorough in rooting out and annihilating the vanquished. Fugitive Nobles at times defected to neighboring realms seeking aid, while at other times they fled to haunted passes high in the mountains and far from civilization, or caverns far underground, or cities in the depths of the sea. Ruins that could be found even now out on the Frontier in the mountains or beneath the earth were remnants of such places, and the murderous machines that roamed their vicinity were the last surviving examples of the devices of destruction sent out by the searchers. The giant whirlpools that swallowed mariners and the monstrous kraken up to sixty miles long were weapons of war born of the finest technology possessed by either the attackers or the defenders. Even now there were many who were chased across the face of the earth.

Realizing there was no place in the world to call their own, they decided to seek a safe haven in a place that was not of this world, as if resigned to their fate. Combining ancient tomes on demonology with the most advanced quantum mechanics and the fruits of mysterious engineering techniques, their efforts consumed thousands of years and tens of millions of lives before they finally succeeded in tearing through into another dimension—and it was said that those who fled there found a utopia. The promised land of Shangri-la—that image was always a sweet fantasy burning in the hearts of fugitive Nobility, though no concrete information was ever shared about it. A museum of antiquities was said to have a display of a few decaying letters from Nobility who had reached the other side, each addressed to friends or relatives who'd remained in our own callous world.

At present, the paradise of Shangri-la was said to be a mere legend—either that, or all who knew the method of reaching it had died out. In fact, the only thing connected to it that would fill the Nobles' hearts with real terror was talk of the Guides. Faces hidden by gray hoods and dressed in robes of the same hue, they were said to suddenly appear in answer to an ancient and secret rite, offering to show the way to Nobles seeking a path to the promised land, and at the same time entering into a fearsome contract. Essentially, they required that those who sought the promised land give up the lives of innocent children. Granted, that'd been a fairly common condition from ancient times. But that wasn't the horrifying part of entering a contract with the Guide. The single illustration that'd terrified both Sai Fung and Lagoon depicted a Guide raising the severed heads of children which, for some reason, even then continued to weep most vividly.

"Come with me," the Guide said, beckoning with his hand.

The brother and sister backed away reflexively. But their backs were blocked by Miska's hands.

"Miska?" one cried.

"What are you doing?" asked the other, but they were silenced by a voice that spread like the wings of death.

"The woman has entered into a contract. In exchange for my guidance, I am to receive your lives and your souls. And now that we have an agreement, there can be no escape. If the contract is broken, the contractee will also be subjected to a punishment the likes of which this world has never seen."

"He's lying, isn't he, miss?!"

"Help us, Miska."

Ordinarily, legs built up by acrobatics would've sent the pair flying through the air. But they remained on the ground as if they'd taken root partly because of Miska's strength as she held them by the scruffs of their necks, and partly due to the eerie aura surrounding the Guide.

The Guide's hands touched the heads of the pair. All strength then drained from the brother and sister, and they collapsed on the spot.

Starting with May, his blade drew a faint ring of blood around the base of her neck. Once he'd finished doing the same to Hugh, the Guide took a step back and said, "Watch closely."

He pointed to half of what appeared to be a large, vacant hall.

"Huh?"

As Miska gave a gasp of surprise, her eyes caught sight of an expanse of sea by night. The waves were a riot of white crests, but there was no telling what world this scene was from. Four moons shone in the heavens.

Suddenly the hall faded away. This was neither a dream nor an illusion. As they lay on the floor drained of all strength and sensibility, even May and Hugh knew that. The sound of the waves that reached their ears was real, as were the birds flapping across the disks of the moons. But what made it most real was the vast, unbridgeable distance of the entire tableau.

"Oof!" the pair groaned in unison.

How horrible it was. Fresh blood gushed out at once from the rings around their necks and began to soak every inch of them. Not only that, but it felt as if salt—no, acid—had been smeared in their wounds as acute pain shot through them.

"Now I shall cut off your heads," the Guide announced as he raised his machete. "But it will bring you no peace. Your heads will be tormented by the pain of death for all eternity. Even after this world is no more. But in exchange for that—there is *this!*"

Miska realized the last part was directed at her.

Beyond the sea fractured by the night waves, a hazy light had begun to come into focus. Land. In no time at all, it became a gleaming city.

And Miska was convinced.

Conspiracy of Dark Death

CHAPTER 6

I

The legendary city cast its reflection deep in the rapt eyes of the Noblewoman.

Did the groans of the young brother and sister rising plaintively from her feet not reach her ears? Could Miska not fathom the suffering of these children who'd taken her at her word about setting off on a journey of hope, going underground with her because the least they could do was send her off, and even going so far as to say how painful it would be to part company with her?

Her dignified face twisted in an ugly display of selfish joy, and she even licked her vermilion lips. The two children were already covered in blood.

Just then, the black surface of the water was pushed off to either side as a lone strip of white road appeared from the sea.

"That is the road to your Utopia. However, you can't cross it without my guidance. You would do well to consider yourself fortunate."

Even if those words reached Miska's ears, it was impossible to tell if her brain could make sense of them. Fixated on escaping reality, all the young Noblewoman did was stare at the distant land mass.

"Now, step onto the road," the Guide said, clutching Hugh's face and rolling him over onto his back. The tip of his blade brought a circle of blood.

"Stop it!" May cried out in a thin voice.

D wasn't there. Nor Balazs, nor Lagoon. That only left one person—

The machete that rose so smoothly halted in midair at that moment. It wasn't merely the physical stop required prior to striking with it. A slim, soft hand had seized the Guide's wrist.

"What is this—?" he asked Miska quite gently as he turned around.

Twisting his arm around, Miska sent the Guide flying, and then stepped in front of the children. Oh, who could've imagined the young woman in white shielding those two?

And then she shouted, "Flee!"

The emotions stirred by her voice and the sight of her gave the two bloody children strength. Rising unsteadily to her feet, the girl grabbed her brother's wrist and dashed toward the door.

As he watched all this, the Guide did nothing, but once the pair had vanished from his field of view, he turned to Miska and said, "You know what this means, do you not?"

Miska didn't reply, didn't even nod. Her blue eyes were filled with a powerful conviction that showed her the truth and a staunch determination to defend the others.

"Once a contract has been entered, if it is broken, both the sacrifices and the contractee shall be cursed for eternity. Your punishment will be dispensed immediately."

As he approached Miska, he raised the machete high. It was a terribly impudent combat pose when facing a Noblewoman, but for some reason, Miska didn't move. Although nothing could be seen within the hood save deep black darkness, now a pair of glows—incredibly profane gleams—transfixed her. The Guide's eyes. At that instant, Miska retained the ability to think, but lost control of her muscles and nerves. Even her heart stopped.

Whistling through the air toward what some might describe as the forlorn nape of the woman's neck, the machete sank deep into it. Blood gushed out. And though spasms rocked Miska's body, she didn't make a sound due to the pain. A blow from the Guide hurt thousands of times more than one from anyone else.

Jerking the gore-stained weapon back and forth to free it, the Guide then raised it unceremoniously for another blow to the top of Miska's head. The eyes in his hood gave off a particularly vile light. But the right one unexpectedly vanished.

As the Guide pressed one hand to it, a small rock fell at his feet. And at the same time, the grip of his evil gaze seemed to wane.

Letting out a horrible wail of pain, Miska fell to the floor.

A small red figure rushed over, pulling her up as he said, "Hold on, Miska!"

It was Hugh. The boy hadn't fled and left the woman to her fate.

However, before they'd even gone ten feet, the ash-gray figure stood before the pair, blocking the way.

"You may have been freed, but the pain the Guide has given you won't fade. My job, you see, also involves guiding pain."

The machete was swung.

Executing a back flip and narrowly dodging the blade, Hugh let the rock he held in his hand fly from midair. Although it was an exquisite display of acrobatics, the amount of speed Hugh's wounded and bleeding body put behind the missile wasn't enough to keep it from being effortlessly avoided.

The Guide approached.

"Stop," Miska called out feebly.

He brought the blade down—but luckily, the acrobatic Hugh was able to get out of its way.

"What's this?!" the Guide gasped in astonishment.

Hugh's position was at the boundary between the real world and the weird sea. Taking a step back, the boy's foot slipped toward the ocean, and Hugh fell headlong into the black water.

Both the spray and the sound of the waves were the real thing.

At that instant, a dimensional rift formed. The otherworldly sea summoned by the Guide sought something similar on this side, here in our world. The expanse of water filled with a sense of the bizarre.

Desperately thrusting his head from the sea, Hugh saw a reddish-black figure standing before him and exclaimed, "D?!"

Yes, D. What's more, D had just finished cutting off Lord Vlad's metallic arm.

The subterranean lake and the seawater had been mixed.

"Stop it!" the Guide shouted as he reached out for Hugh.

His strength and will both spent, the boy had latched onto the road across the sea—the path to Shangri-la—and pulled himself up.

Everything was stained blue and white. And in the midst of what could be described as calming colors, a human figure thrashed feebly.

The next thing Hugh knew, he was lying on the floor of a hall. Beside him lay the blood-soaked Miska, who May was looking after. And looking down at them was the gorgeous Vampire Hunter.

"D—I was . . ."

"I heard."

Getting the impression D had given him a little nod, the boy felt rewarded.

"Er . . ." he started to say, but he caught himself because both D and Miska were looking at the back of the hall—and the black sea.

But there was no sea there. The flames of the candelabra illuminated the baron in blue and woman in white on the cold stone floor. The woman lay there with what looked to be some kind of scepter jutting quite far from her chest. Yet the woman's dress remained white because all of her blood had apparently left her body and been diffused in the water. Clearly someone was bidding farewell to one who wasn't long for this world.

At that point, the woman in white opened her eyes a crack, despite the fact that her heart and lungs had already ceased functioning and not even a faint thread of breath whispered from her paling lips.

"In the end . . . it comes to this," the baron's mother said, her voice quiet and clear. "I can no longer do anything. Do as you like. While drifting underwater, I saw the stars. Your stars and your father's stars. They're completely incompatible. You and your father . . . No matter how you battle, eventually it will come to an end. But . . . what kind of end will it be? Byron, my son . . . I'm terribly afraid."

"Mother . . ." the baron murmured. One who knew what fate had in store could say no more than that.

"Please, don't follow along after me," she said, a hand damp with water rising to touch the baron's brow. "And please . . . forgive me. Forgive your mother . . ."

Her arm was about to slip away, but the baron caught hold of it and held it in place. His shoulders didn't quake, nor did he shed a single tear. Beneath his blue glove, his mother's arm lost its definition and turned into brown dust. Even then the baron didn't break his pose. For the longest time he remained as he was.

"D," he called out after even more time had passed. "Is de Carriole here?"

"No."

"Right now, it is he that I would like to see more than anyone," he said in a tone without cadence. "Lady Miska is here. With de Carriole's assistance, the Destroyer within her could be transferred to me."

"He stayed back at the underground lake. If Vlad's in his right mind, he'll probably have him executed as a traitor. Also—"

"What is it?"

"I think the gray hooded figure was a Guide. He's there with Vlad, too." Turning to the fallen Miska and the siblings, D said, "And she broke her contract with the Guide. No matter what, he won't give up until he's delivered the death penalty."

"You think he'll join forces with Vlad?"

"I don't know. My second blow split your father's head open. He's seriously injured, but he won't die."

The baron got to his feet. From his hands and his lap brown dust spilled, spreading across the floor. Not even looking down at it, the baron took what remained in his fist and put it in a pouch in his cape before stating, "I'm going to de Carriole's mansion."

"What'll you do there?" D asked.

"I intend to bring Lady Miska with me and transfer the Destroyer on my own."

"Even the Destroyer was powerless before the Guide."

"At the very least, I'll slay Vlad. Or battle him on equal terms. This is my fight. Once again, I ask that you stay out of this, D."

"And you intend on doing this even without de Carriole?"

"It may surprise you to learn I've always been quite good with machines. So long as there's a manual, I may be able to do something."

"Have his apprentice do it," D said, stepping to the right.

Smiling thinly, the baron said, "Now there's a thought."

As he spoke, a band of light shot from the interior of his cape. For a second, white illumination flashed across the surprised faces of May, Hugh, and Miska, and then the band of light turned right at the doorway.

A cry of pain rang out. It was followed by the sound of footsteps.

Having already broken into a run, D gave chase. He didn't need to run far.

Thirty feet ahead, the country girl with flowing blond hair had halted dead in her tracks. Standing before her, blocking her way like a wall, was the massive form of Fisher Lagoon.

"What are you doing down here, Paige?" he asked.

"Not a blessed thing. I was walking on the floor above and heard a strange sound, so I came down here, when all of a sudden . . ."

Seeing the wound that'd been opened on her right shoulder, Lagoon then turned his gaze to D and asked in a gruff tone, "You responsible for that?"

"No. But it's a hell of a disguise. Chlomo's makeup, is it?"

"What are you saying?!" the understandably shocked Lagoon exclaimed.

Before him, the girl shook her dainty, doleful face from side to side, saying, "No. It's not like that!"

"So—so that's how it is, eh?" Lagoon said in a hoarse voice that sounded utterly crushed. "Chlomo's makeup could make a woman out of a man. It'd even turn a nutsack into a woman's goodies. And if he used a real slut of a model . . . Hell, I fell for the wrong damned woman. People will be laughing about ol' Fisher Lagoon for the rest of my days, I bet."

Paige realized nothing she said would make any difference now—she *was* actually Sai Fung of the Thousand Limbs. As soon as the makeup was taken off, he'd be back to his old self. After seeing the Guide, he'd figured something was brewing and wouldn't let May out of his sight. As a result, he'd followed the trio she formed with Hugh and Miska and saw everything that happened thereafter from start to finish. He would've been better off not knowing that his presence had been detected.

"Out of my way," he said in a woman's voice, but with a man's mannerisms.

"So, we've seen through your disguise. I don't know who the hell you are, but I'll see to it you pay for making a fool of Fisher Lagoon."

"Shut your trap!" Paige said, kicking off the ground. With a woman's legs.

She would've been lucky to get two or three feet of vertical rise. But she just kept going. As she'd kicked off the floor, one hand had made a fist and wiped the makeup off. The leap had the power of a thousand limbs—the thousand arms and legs that Sai Fung possessed.

As he easily sailed over Lagoon's head, one of his unseen limbs landed a blow to the back of the giant's head that staggered him. Landing, Sai Fung turned. The kick that'd been intended to crush the man's skull had met something hard instead.

"Huh?!" the martial artist exclaimed.

Lagoon was no longer just an ordinary giant. The glittering silver that covered every inch of him was liquid metal armor. Moreover, it only took a thousandth of a second to don it.

For a heartbeat, a boundless animosity glowed in Sai Fung's evil glare, but he must've decided he was better off not testing his luck against this unknown material, because he stood up and tried to make a run for it. Before him, the massive silvery form landed after vaulting over *his* head. Behind him was D.

As he glided toward Lagoon, Sai Fung had a smile that brimmed with confidence pasted to his lips. His unseen hands had dispatched a stone colossus with just a single blow.

Both of Sai Fung's feet were absorbed by the silvery chest. A flying kick that could shift a fifty-ton boulder sent him sinking waist-deep into Lagoon's breastbone. Yet he didn't come out through the man's back.

"Is that liquid metal, you filthy traitor?" the man asked in a blaze of hatred, livid at having encountered such a resilient opponent— or rather, the material that covered him.

"Not quite what you're used to, eh?" the faceless silver figure mocked. "This time, I'll play your game. I won't dissolve anymore. Now, come get some!"

It was an open invitation.

Sai Fung didn't move. There were loud thuds as Lagoon's chest and stomach were dented. In the blink of an eye they'd taken hundreds of unseen kicks and punches. However, the bottom of the dents bubbled back up like water from a spring, quickly smoothing out again.

"That's not gonna work. It just won't cut it."

As if pushed by Lagoon's voice, Sai Fung backed away. His face was warped by pain—a number of his unseen hands and feet had been broken. It was like pounding on the ramparts of some titanic citadel. The liquid metal that encased Lagoon's body could alter its molecular arrangement at will, absorbing shocks at times like water, while at other times becoming ultra-hard armor to repulse blows.

"Is that the best Sai Fung of the Thousand Limbs can do? Then I guess it's my turn now."

The faceless giant extended his arms. His palms spread like a bolt of cloth and wrapped tightly around Sai Fung.

"Go on, just try to escape. That is, if the 'thousand limbs' in your nickname aren't all just hot air."

Pulling the man closer, the giant looked ready to crush him. It was the sort of half-playful action one might expect a drunk to pull on a hostess.

However, Lagoon cried out, "Oh!" despite himself.

Both his arms were slowly but steadily being pushed back. And he was putting enough strength into them to crush a boulder to bits.

"Now that's what I'd expect from the Thousand Limbs," he muttered, and at that instant both his arms were thrown open like a pair of wings, knocking his massive form off balance.

The way Sai Fung twisted his body, it looked like he was poised for a judo shoulder throw. Yet his hands didn't have a hold on anything, and there were still eight or twelve inches between him and Lagoon.

"Hi-yaaaah!" the martial artist cried, his earsplitting shriek a perfect companion to the enormous arc Lagoon's form traveled in.

The giant hit the stone floor back-first. A split second before he did, all the armor on his back spread across the floor, forming a cushion to absorb the impact. By the time he'd bounced back up to his feet like a human spring, Sai Fung had already dashed some thirty feet away.

A black figure closed on him from the rear. It was D. His eyes gave off blood light. The longsword he struck out with in a drawing cut came right down on the top of Sai Fung's head, blunt side first. When D called upon *that* power, those thousand hands and feet apparently counted for nothing and the blow landed easily, sending Sai Fung down to the floor still dressed in women's clothing.

II

Astride a borrowed horse, the baron turned to Lagoon, who was seeing him off, and told him, "You have my thanks."

They were in the courtyard of his establishment, where May and Hugh were receiving medical treatment from the physician. Sai

Fung was strapped to the horse's back. By the baron's side was a second mount that he also held the reins to, and Miska rode on that. Even by the dark of night, there were heavy shadows of pain on her. Nevertheless she had accepted the baron's proposal. She would cooperate with the effort to transfer the Destroyer within her to the baron.

"Come on. It's not that big of a deal. I've heard a lot of talk about you. Can't really consider you a stranger."

Noticing the focus of the baron's gaze at that point, the giant turned toward his establishment and added, "D's gone to stay with that girl named Taki. The night's still young. Your father might stir up more trouble yet. But that Hunter sure is a cold one, isn't he?"

After exiting the hall, the young man in black and the one in blue had parted company without exchanging a single word.

"The fight between you and your father has nothing to do with him. But if you slay your father, Taki will be saved. If it's the reverse, she'll be a target again. When you look at it that way, he really can't afford to be getting his nose out of joint. Always gotta do things his own way, I guess."

"It's fine," the baron said softly, wheeling his horse around to face the distant gates.

The moon shone up above like a silver platter. Off in the distance, birds sang.

"People gotta be cutting each other up all over the place on a nice night like this," Lagoon muttered. Those were the words with which he sent them off.

Just in front of the gates, an enormous camphor tree challenged the heavens. Beside it stood a figure in black raiment that seemed to dissolve into its shadow.

Even as he came to the shadowy figure, the baron didn't halt his horse. But as he passed, he turned and said, "I would've liked to have met you by day."

There was no answer. Instead, a black-gloved hand gently touched the brim of his traveler's hat.

The rider in blue went by with the two horses. Once he'd passed out of the Hunter's range of perception, D stepped away from the camphor tree and walked off to where Taki was. He had a job to do as a Hunter. What's more, the battle between the baron and his father had no bearing on him.

For some time now, the vast and lavishly appointed sitting room had been swimming in awful moans that sounded like they might've come from the spirits of hell.

"The drugs . . . won't work . . . Why not? Why won't the wound close? Does the bastard have some kind of special sword . . . de Carriole?"

After exhausting every possible means, the aged scholar stood beside an operating table stained vermilion smelling the stench of blood. He was about to reply but stopped himself, admiring the skill of the Hunter in black in his heart of hearts.

Vlad's face was swathed in bandages from the top of his head down to his chin, and he'd lost his left arm at the elbow. Though de Carriole had taken the arm off because it would only be in the way during his procedure, he hadn't been able to close the lord's head wound, and no matter what kind of anesthetic he gave the Noble, the pain wouldn't abate.

The ageless and immortal Nobility usually recovered from shallow cuts almost instantaneously, while graver injuries might take a few hours to heal fully. And aside from the instant in which they were wounded, they almost never felt any pain. Writhing in agony for the last two hours and having soaked the better part of the vast sitting room with his own blood, Vlad was an exception even among exceptions.

"De Carriole . . . you know what it is, don't you . . . Traitorous scientist . . . you have betrayed my trust. If by some chance something should happen to me . . . my underlings won't sit still for it . . . They're likely to tear you limb from limb . . . and throw you where the birds can pick your bones clean while you still live."

"I am aware of that. However, I have done my very best. The Hunter who goes by the name of D is indeed no ordinary person."

"D . . . D!" Vlad bellowed, his eyes snapping open to glare into space.

The look in them was so intense, it seemed as if the empty air might burst into flames.

"If only he weren't here . . . No, not him. de Carriole, this wound will heal, won't it? You can close it, right?"

"I shall do my best."

"Don't forget that your life hangs in the balance."

What a despicable way to behave, the aged scholar clucked to himself. Sooner or later, the wound should close and the pain subside. Until then, the best thing to do would be to simply leave the wound alone. Still, that Hunter called D—what on earth was he?

Bowing, he told the lord, "I must go and concoct a sedative."

As the old man walked to the door, a figure in gray rose to his feet at the head of the bed. He'd completely forgotten that the Guide Vlad had invited there from the subterranean lake had been sitting there. It certainly seemed as if the old man wished to drive every thought of him from his head. And although it might've been best if de Carriole had beaten a hasty retreat, he remained bound to the spot. As a profound scholar not only of science but of sorcerous inquiry, he wasn't about to miss any conversation between those two.

And apparently the Guide meant de Carriole no harm.

"Would you like me to heal that wound?" the hooded figured asked.

"Oh, that would be great—it was well worth bringing you along . . . Please . . . by all means. Let me . . . fight *him* . . . fight D one more time."

"You shall have to pay me in return."

For a second, not only de Carriole froze but Vlad did as well. What sort of payment the Guide would require—the mere thought of it was enough to stop their hearts.

"Wh-what do you intend to ask for as payment?" de Carriole inquired in spite of himself.

"That you become one with me."

Needless to say, the Guide was talking to Lord Vlad.

de Carriole turned in amazement. The way these coincidences overlapped—if you could call them coincidences—left him stupefied. To slay his father Vlad, the baron sought to become one with the Destroyer. On the other hand, here was Lord Vlad about to become one with the Guide. Father and son would finally become diametrically opposed forces.

Holding his breath and straining his ears, de Carriole was eager to hear what Vlad's reply would be.

"You would enter into me . . . and what would happen then?"

Although the lord's question bore a crushing weight of anxiety, that was only natural.

"Our power would be doubled . . . well, that's supposing that you and I were the same level."

"Ah, in that case—"

"However," the Guide interrupted him, "if your strength was far below my own, you would be killed in an instant. Or, as you Nobility say, 'destroyed.' And I would be left alone to slay the one who betrayed me."

Vlad fell silent.

I'm not surprised that's enough to make even you timid, de Carriole thought without any malice. And just then, he heard a rumble and felt a shock as if there were tremors deep in the earth. He soon realized it was an illusion. Nevertheless, none of his physical senses could be convinced that it wasn't real.

It was Vlad. Lord Vlad had made up his mind. The rumbling in the earth had been the harbinger of his decision.

As he glared at the figure in the long ashen robe with glittering eyes, his intensity and his ghastly air were not those of a man who'd been screaming moments earlier about how his head was split open.

"So, I would be destroyed? Hmm. Have you ever considered that my power might surpass your own? Very well, then. Enter me. If my flesh isn't destroyed, the psyche that controls it would of course be that of the stronger of us, would it not?"

"That is correct."

"Then enter me. I shall be most interested to see whether you claim my strength or I take control of yours."

He wasn't bluffing. Nor was he desperate or self-destructive. Though bloodless, Vlad's face was filled with such an overwhelming confidence it seemed liable to turn anyone he looked at to stone.

What was going to happen?

De Carriole was staring so intently at the two unearthly creatures, it looked like he might faint dead away from the strain. What if the Guide won and Lord Vlad's psyche was defeated? Or what if Lord Vlad triumphed, erasing all of the Guide but his strength? Whichever happened, a god of destruction with power beyond imagining would undoubtedly spread a whirlwind of slaughter across the face of the planet. Even supposing the baron were to be joined with the Destroyer, and D were to be on his side, it was uncertain whether or not they could stand toe-to-toe with the most vicious, evil fiend the world had ever seen.

As de Carriole watched the figure in gray leaning over Vlad's bed, he let himself slip into a tranquil despair.

III

"Think he'll come?" the hoarse voice asked.

The Hunter was in front of a set of bars. Behind them, Taki could be seen sleeping soundly.

"He'll come," D replied.

"I concur. But if he does come, he'll probably be three—no, five times as strong."

"How do you know that?"

"Just once, a long time ago, I saw it happen. A Guide taking possession of a Noble, I mean," the hoarse voice said wearily. "The

Noble lost and the Guide won. As a result, three villages were utterly destroyed. Fatalities topped two thousand."

"What happened to *it?*"

"It was taken care of."

"By *you?*"

"Could be," the hoarse voice replied evasively just as Taki began to stir behind the bars.

It was the middle of the night. In a room deep underground.

As she climbed out of bed and turned toward the Hunter, her body had a far more sensuous and alluring aura than ever before.

Why was it that women who'd been bitten by the Nobility lost all sexual inhibitions—the conclusion reached in answer to this seemingly eternal debate was that the actual sucking of blood set a woman's libido free, amplifying the sensual possibilities of her flesh. But why from something as simple as blood drinking? There was still only one answer to that: *It was unclear.* However, nothing could begin to compare to the sensuousness and debauchery of a woman who'd fallen into that state once, and it was said that among the decadent artists and religious cults in the Capital, there were those who secretly called in Nobility to drink the blood of their wives or female believers so they might admire the women who plunged into the beauteous hell of that corruption.

"D," Taki called out, pressing her face and ample bosom to the bars.

She extended a pale hand. The man she sought remained motionless, like a black mass of steel in human form.

"I'm so scared, D. Hold me!"

Though somewhat nasal, her sweet, lewd tone clung to D's body.

"That's funny," the hoarse voice could be heard to say from the palm of D's left hand.

"What is? "

"The way she's acting. For someone who's only been bitten once, she's in way too deep. Why is that?"

"Why won't you come over here?" Taki panted, eyes narrowing and mouth half open. Her red tongue wriggled in a mouth that looked upholstered in soft silk. "I'm begging you, hold me. I'm so scared and so cold. Please."

Sliding over her chest, Taki's left hand undid the buttons on her blouse one by one. The way she moved her hand and undid them was that of a she-beast skilled at arousing men. The alluring white swells peeked from the fabric as if they were about to burst right through it. Undoing the last button, Taki stared at D. Her expression, so filled with confidence and wanton lust, became a look of rage.

"Why won't you hold me? Don't you desire me? You pathetic, dickless Hunter!"

Seizing the bars with both hands, she rattled them with all her might.

"Kill . . . Kill the bastard already!"

At some point, the door behind D had opened from the outside. Two figures bounded in, firing rivet guns at D. What the lumps of iron they propelled at a thousand feet per second pierced was the hem of his coat.

Ducking, D delivered a blow to each in the shins with his still-sheathed sword, and the two of them toppled backward and stopped moving. The sheer pain had made them black out.

Taki gnashed her teeth behind the bars.

"She's quite a piece of work. What did she do, seduce the guards outside with her voice alone? D, this isn't normal at all."

D looked at Taki. His eyes were deep and dark.

Taki averted her gaze.

About to say something to her, D suddenly turned his head and looked up.

"He's here," his left hand said.

Saying nothing, D turned his back to Taki and walked away. Securing the two guards well with wire restraints that were on hand for making arrests, he then slipped through the doorway.

Just as he was about to close the door, someone called out, "D!"

Taki's cry was not that of a seductive harlot. And her eyes brimmed with tears.

"Save me, D!"

D turned around and closed the door.

The strength fled Taki's lower half, leaving her hanging from the bars by just her hands. Her fingers then sadly slipped off them. The young woman's ass hit the stone floor and she wept. Who could've known that it was partly out of relief? Just before he closed the door, D had responded to the girl's lucid cries with a slight but powerful nod.

The moon seemed to glow a whole notch more intensely than usual. Above the trees and rocks of the courtyard, moonlight swirled like silvery clouds. D stood at the edge of a glimmering circular pond nearly in the center of the garden. That alone was enough to make both the moonlight and all the artistic sculptures shipped from the Capital pale by comparison. The wind that stirred the water's surface ever so slightly swerved around him, embarrassed to look upon the young man's face—at least that was the impression it gave.

Lagoon's massive form was approaching from his establishment.

"Does it look like he'll be coming, D?" he asked as he looked toward the gates.

"Stay inside," the Hunter told him.

"Hey, don't be like that. I mean, this is *my* land."

"That's why I say it."

Blinking his eyes in surprise, Lagoon gazed intently at the emotionless Hunter and asked, "So, what do you think? Can you take him? If you like, I'll give you some of my younger guys to help out. Not a man among them loves his life too dearly."

"When you lose your life, it doesn't matter whether you loved it or not," said a strangely hoarse voice, and it caused Lagoon to involuntarily stare at the Hunter's left hand.

"Under no circumstances are you to get involved," D ordered him sternly.

"Okay, I follow you," Lagoon said, still looking back and forth between D's handsome features and his left hand as he made that reluctant nod. "The least I can do is stick around and watch you in action."

"I said stay inside—"

"Hey, now!"

As Lagoon leapt back a good ten feet, his body gleamed with silver in the moonlight. He'd donned his armor.

"We can't have you fanning your sword at anyone who tries doing you a favor. Hell, I might be your daddy. Huh?!"

Just then, he actually did feel the breeze of a blade narrowly missing his face. On realizing that it'd gone right through his armor, Lagoon was terrified. Cold sweat gushed from every inch of him. To think that anyone could swing a sword like that without evincing the slightest hint of murderous intent or premeditation.

"You're a freaking monster . . . *The big guy* might've collected my seed . . . but there's no way in hell you're my kid!"

Putting his sword back in its scabbard with a crisp click, D headed for the entrance.

"Back then . . . I asked *him* a question, you see," Lagoon continued. "I asked if he was collecting human seed to make human/Noble half-breeds. He didn't answer, but I kept dogging him about it. Asked him if it could really work. Asked if it'd ever gone well. And then he answered me."

D stood there like a black sculpture.

"'There has been but one success,'" Lagoon said in a probing tone. "Hey, D, look out at the pond. My reflection's clear as day, but yours is fuzzy. Is that a dhampir's lot? A cross between a human and Nobility—was that *you* he was talking about? "

Wary of the next attack, Lagoon was already poised to leap at any second. But it never came.

A bizarre sensation froze the moonlight.

"He's coming," a hoarse voice informed them. "But there's something strange here. Though I sense his presence, I can't say just where he is . . ."

D made a quick move to the left, just in front of the gates.

The black shape of a horse with a hunched-over rider came barreling into the courtyard. In a sumptuous robe that stretched all the way to the ground and clutching a scepter in his right hand, the rider had the form of none other than Vlad Balazs. But what was on the inside?

"Is the girl down below?" said a voice that seemed to blow from the icy caverns of the northern extremes.

The tone was that of Vlad. The strength of the Noble's will had gained control of the Guide.

"Don't interfere! Out of my way!" he said, then added with a lick of his lips, "On second thought, stay right there. I'll pay you back now for what you did to my arm and head. Lagoon, are you in league with this scoundrel?"

"D-don't be ridiculous."

The same man who hadn't given an inch while talking with Vlad the other day at his mountain fortress had dropped his armor to stand there exposed in a show of obedience, so he likely sensed something was not the same as before.

"Well, it matters not. I'll see to you later."

Exhaling sharply, the rider then lined his horse up directly across from D. The barrel and legs of the black steed were covered with titanium armor.

The scepter stretched toward D—and D's right hand reached for its shaft.

"Wait!" someone shouted, but it was unclear if it was Lagoon or the hoarse voice.

And it was at that very instant the earth rumbled.

"Did they come from below ground, too?"

Even as D realized what that cry meant, his body sank.

The black steed had gone into a charge. A flash of light ran straight under its iron-shod hooves.

Look! Vampire Hunter D's drawing cut was a technique that all who'd witnessed spoke of—and that same skill took the horse's forelegs off at the knee, sending them flying. As the horse thudded forward, a dazzling glint parried the moonlight as it danced out in into space.

A black cyclone flew from the ground.

Where the two men met, there was the cold ring of steel on steel, and then a splash went up from the nearby pond. The pair had dropped into the middle of it.

Lagoon ran over and prepared to throw himself into the water when he noticed something.

"Damn!" he exclaimed, dashing off in a determined fashion to the chamber where Taki slumbered.

The pond was sixty feet deep and set up so that bathing beauties could put on a show for patrons in a subterranean viewing room. But what kind of deadly battle was now being waged at the center of that normally pleasant stage? What Lagoon had seen on the moonlit surface of that pond was a deep red cloud of blood that called to mind a dark destiny.

Angel with a Blue Shadow

CHAPTER 7

I

O n regaining consciousness, Sai Fung immediately realized he was in de Carriole's mansion. Beside him stood the baron in blue and Miska, and they had an incredible question for him. They wanted to know whether or not there was a manual to explain how to transfer the Destroyer within Miska over to the baron. When he replied quite honestly that he didn't know, the baron thought for a moment before ordering him, "Help out."

With a ghastly, blood-chilling aura blustering at him from a face every bit as handsome as D's, Sai Fung was only too happy to agree.

Surprisingly enough, the baron was familiar with the use of each and every piece of machinery in de Carriole's laboratory. In no time at all, atomic candles burned in the reactor and a mysterious mix of chemicals and herbs began to boil in a large cauldron.

"Tachyon injector: energy charged to ninety percent—okay," a machine called out, announcing the result of its checks.

"Mental wave conversion mode at highest setting—okay."

"Psycho transference zone alpha: Unity ratio of 1/99,999,999—okay."

Although he'd been told to help out, Sai Fung's role only went as far as moving unnecessary tables and equipment out of the way. For him, the work was a piece of cake. Simply standing in one spot, he effortlessly moved the massive centrifuge and maser-based stabilizer.

It didn't even take ten minutes to complete the preparations. Once the baron had finished adjusting a servomechanism, he went over to where Miska lay on a couch.

"I'm sorry, but it's almost time."

With one arm missing and her neck half-severed, the beautiful woman with the paraffin-pale complexion still managed to nod. Although the bleeding had stopped and the wounds were closing, she remained in hellish agony. That was the fearsome might of the Guide.

"The thing within me still slumbers—will that be okay?"

"We'd better do it while it's still groggy," the baron said, and then he grinned. "I heard from the children's own mouths how you came to be injured. You were superb."

"No, merely foolish. And it was only on account of the Destroyer that's within me."

"Is that a fact?"

"Pardon me?" the woman said, crinkling her elegant brow.

"The Nobility may still have possibilities. Something other than a simple run down the road to decline. Possibilities for the whole species. You and I, or you at the very least, might've served as an unexpectedly positive example. And I suppose the way you risked your life to save a human boy and girl is another expression of that. Perhaps it's just a tiny something sleeping somewhere in our genes that no one would ever know about if it were left alone. But there was *one* who took note of it and planned to use it to change the fate of his declining species. My lack of desire for human blood may be one phenomenon connected to something *that being* awoke in me. Your protecting the children might be, too."

"But I . . ."

"It is conceivable that the Destroyer somehow triggered this. And given what that being represents, I can only say I find it highly ironic."

"I don't know . . . I simply can't fathom Nobles sympathizing with human beings . . ."

But after saying this, she held her tongue. Because she was talking about something she herself had done.

The baron guided Miska over to an operating table hooked to countless cables.

"Lie down. This should all be over soon."

"I wonder if you're right about that," Sai Fung called out from behind an enormous distillation rig. "Trying to transfer this Destroyer without even an instruction manual isn't the sort of thing a sane person would do. I don't care how good you are with machines; this deal's gotta require a certain amount of know-how. If you screw it up, what'll you do then? There's no telling what'll become of the world if the Destroyer runs amok in some half-assed form. You think you'd be up to stopping it?"

"Step back," the baron commanded sharply. "I'm finished with you. You may go."

"Yessir. No way in hell am I gonna hang around here and get mixed up in any of this. You'll have to excuse me for making an early exit, O wise baron."

As he headed for the door, he suddenly turned and said, "What you said just now—you really think that could happen?" He was wearing a very strange expression—a sober face.

"I certainly hope so. Now go."

Shrugging his shoulders, Sai Fung walked out muttering, "Humans and Nobility . . . that's just stupid . . . Sympathizing . . . Hey, you've gotta be pulling my leg . . ."

The baron stood before the control panel and threw the switch to start the nuclear power. The whir of a motor rose from nowhere in particular, and pale blue current connected one cylindrical electromagnet to another.

On the operating table, Miska closed her eyes—then, after a moment, opened them again to gaze at the baron.

"What's wrong?" she asked.

"Now, I might never be a match for Vlad Balazs. I can't. Suddenly, I simply can't bring myself to do it."

Choked with distress, the baron's expression was enough to make Miska forget her own pain.

The Noblewoman sat up, saying, "Why all of a sudden? Do you fear the Destroyer running amok?"

"More than that—I'm afraid for you."

"Me?" Miska asked in shock, but something quickly occurred to her. "You mean of me returning to normal?"

The baron nodded. A shade of suffering flickered in his handsome features.

"You are one of the great possibilities of linking the Nobility and the human race. And being possessed by the Destroyer plays a large part in that. I don't want to remove it."

"Then you will never accomplish your aim. Or avenge your mother."

"I will still strike at Vlad Balazs. However—"

As the baron gnawed at his lip, Miska focused a gaze on him that was beyond description, but suddenly she let out a low laugh.

"What is it?"

"I was—my dear baron, I have no desire to become an exquisite link joining the Nobility to the human race."

"But you—"

"I saved those two merely on impulse—or to be more accurate, from the same kind of sentiment as someone who won't abandon their pet dog to be killed by someone else. But they aren't even my pets. While I cannot say that I don't care for them more than the average human, still, they are naught but a burden to me. I will thank you to return me to my old self as swiftly as possible," she said in a gelid tone.

The baron stared at Miska, but then he shook his head and said, "You make a poor liar."

"Ridiculous."

"No. Your eyes are too soft. Now that you know what it's like to save a human life, you can't return to your cold ways. And it's best that you don't. Kindly wait at Lagoon's place. You may not get to go to the Promised Land, but you might become someone of great promise yourself. I will dispose of the Guide without fail."

"But . . ." Miska began, but she broke off there.

It was just as the baron said. The instinctive scorn and hatred of human beings no longer existed in her psyche. The boy and girl were doing everything they could, trying their best to survive— and she loved those two kids.

"Let me help you down," the baron said, stepping away from the control panel and walking over to Miska before offering her one hand.

It was just then that the operating table gave off a glow. An unseen force suddenly laid Miska flat on the table. A spasm rocked her body, and she arched her back like a bow.

Turning in amazement, the baron couldn't believe who he saw standing before the control panel, and he shouted, "de Carriole?!"

"It would seem this old fool has given you too much credit, my good baron. What a foolish, pathetic mind I fostered in you. What a Noble needs is a psyche of ice and steel to make the lowly humans kneel, and to feel no remorse about drinking their lifeblood down to the very last drop. If not, then why did your mother have such regrets? Baron—kindly leave this to me. I, Jean de Carriole, will take that power from Lady Miska and transfer it to you, milord."

"De Carriole, you mustn't!"

The baron advanced two steps. A band of light flew from the interior of his cape, splitting open de Carriole's left shoulder.

Though the aged scholar spilled bright blood everywhere, his madness didn't waver in the slightest.

"Master of the dark skies, immortal Sacred Ancestor! In your name, I now offer Baron Byron Balazs the most powerful Destroyer."

He prepared to slam his right hand down on a switch on the display. but it stopped in midair. The old man turned in shock. There was no one behind him stopping him.

"Give it up, boss."

Sai Fung stood in the doorway.

"You—you wretch! Are you trying to interfere, you miserable traitor?!"

Madly thrashing his arms and legs all the while, de Carriole was pulled away from the device.

"Why don't you act your age and wither away already? You've still got too much interest in romance."

"Why do you interfere?" the old man asked.

"Let me tell you a little story. My mother got bitten by a Noble, too. But even though she hadn't gone over to the Nobility herself yet, she wound up having a stake shoved through her heart by the same villagers who'd been her friends. Now, I don't know who was right and who was wrong, but if the Nobility and humans could get along, there'd probably be a whole lot fewer kids that'd have to go through something like I did. I was only nine at the time."

The building shook unexpectedly. Ripples passed through the floor and walls as if they'd been turned to liquid, and a second later, the area around the door rose in a point like the head of a squid and rocks and earth were thrown aside as a colossal caterpillar-like device wriggled into the room.

Sai Fung immediately shoved de Carriole away as a few thousand tons of rock rained down on him, but they all halted three feet above him. However, having all his attention focused on that load proved to be the undoing of the grinning Sai Fung.

The great scythes whooshed out of the caterpillar before any of those thousand limbs could react—no, actually it felt like a number of those unseen arms and legs were severed as Sai Fung's torso was bisected horizontally.

"That's a just reward for interfering with me—that's what you get for being a traitor," a voice called down from atop the green caterpillar.

Though he'd been cut in half, Sai Fung's superhuman tenacity allowed him to open his eyes and turn, at which point the man gasped out loud.

The misshapen figure standing on the mountain folk tank was de Carriole. The other one—the de Carriole Sai Fung had hampered—had been buried beneath rocks and dirt by the caterpillar. Undoubtedly his death had been instantaneous. In which case—who was this?

"My lord knows better than anyone the results of my research. Kindly come out here."

As de Carriole spoke, Vlad arose from somewhere in the caterpillar. There could be no mistaking that the young woman he cradled in his arms was Taki.

Then whom had D defeated?

Without even glancing at Sai Fung or the remains of the other de Carriole, Vlad glared at his son on the floor.

"Why do you think I've come? Fear not, it isn't to dispose of you. As punishment for betraying me, I have come to send you into even deeper despair. Look at the girl who was hidden in Lagoon's basement, yet I took possession of her oh so easily. Tomorrow night, I shall make her my bride. What's more—oh, is that the young Noblewoman who came seeking Shangri-la? The Guide has told me all about that."

The grin that skimmed across his lips was that of a good-natured old man—something rarely seen from him.

"Don't!" the baron exclaimed as a white flash shot from his cape.

Deflecting it in flight, the scepter pierced Miska's chest as she lay on the operating table, running through the table and into the floor below.

"Miska?"

As the baron was about to dash over, his body was knocked away by a blast of light from the side of the scepter. Flames engulfed his cape, but he quickly returned to his feet. His hair was singed, his flesh melted and dripping.

"Oh, as defiant as ever, I see. Very well, Byron. I won't run, and I won't hide. If you still intend to get me, come to the Field of Bones at midnight tomorrow evening—that nostalgic spot where I walked with you nestled in my arms. Come alone if you wish, or bring assistance if you will. However, keep in mind that if you are even a second late, I shall sink my fangs into this young lady's throat. Give up, Byron! Forget about me and everything else and leave the village. You have but to go to some distant backwoods Nobility and introduce yourself and you'll not want for human blood for the rest of your days. However, the name you should give them is *mine*."

Once again a streak of light flew from the baron's chest, but Lord Vlad had already disappeared into the caterpillar, and de Carriole had also vanished.

When the massive vehicle caused the ground to rumble and began to return to the depths of the earth, the baron raced over to Miska. Her frail form was pinned to the operating table like an insect. Just like the baron's mother.

"Baron . . ." Miska said, opening her eyes.

Byron must've wanted to plug his ears. Because he now had to listen to the final words of another woman he loved dying in exactly the same manner as the last.

"Please . . . go," Miska rasped in a thread-thin voice. "Leave the village . . . as your father said . . . You must not . . . be destroyed. If Nobles and humans . . . can reach some understanding . . . that will be your task in the future . . . I wish . . . I could've helped, too . . ."

Miska's body suddenly grew heavy.

"My dear baron . . . just before I was stabbed . . . I restrained the Destroyer. No more blood should be spilled . . . I beg of you . . . Just leave the village."

The baron made no effort to look at the beautiful woman as she rotted away. Seizing the scepter, he pulled it out with one jerk. And then he slowly headed toward the control panel, saying, "You have made a mistake, Father."

He had changed the way that he referred to Vlad. But could anyone in this world ever give the word "father" such a ghastly and mournful ring?

"Tomorrow I shall slay you. Father, you shall see with your own two eyes the power of Nobility and humans."

And then he calmly walked back to a device he had apparently renounced—the control panel for transferring the Destroyer.

II

The sun rose, the sun set.

Tonight the lights burned once more at Lagoon's sleepless pleasure quarter, and D awoke just as its halls were being festooned with the coquettish laughter of women and the murmur of bumpkins in their best clothes. At the end of their underwater battle, he'd dispatched Vlad. In return he'd been seriously injured as well, and his wounded form lay in a woodshed in one corner of the courtyard. Although Lagoon had been rather insistent about finding someplace more comfortable and having a doctor examine him, D had already fallen asleep.

The Hunter was aware that the massive subterranean tank-like creature had broken into the underground isolation chamber and that Taki had been abducted. No matter how badly wounded, this young man would bravely go off to rescue her. The reason he hadn't was because of something odd Vlad had said underwater in his death throes: *I may be destroyed, but tomorrow at midnight I shall wait at the Field of Bones. With the girl who's underground. If you're even a second late, I shall make her my bride.*

As he'd finished speaking, D's blade had taken off his head. However, astounding was the only way to describe the sight of D heading back to the surface after seeing to it that Vlad had disintegrated underwater. Vlad's scepter had cut halfway through the Hunter's neck.

Turning his back to the astonished Lagoon, D had gone into the woodshed and closed the door.

Lagoon had peeked in through a gap in the frame. And what he witnessed was a sight weirder than anything even he'd ever seen.

Lying on the floor, D held his shredded neck closed with his right hand and pressed his left hand to the wound. Blood still gushed from it. But none of it was spilled. Every last drop of it was being sucked up by the palm of his left hand—the giant realized that was the source of the slurping sounds the left hand was making.

Lagoon was fully aware that D was a dhampir. But could anything in the world be more loathsome than a creature that drunk its own blood?

And that wasn't the only thing that astonished him. When the left hand came away, the Hunter's neck was partially healed. And then the left hand—clearly of its own volition, not D's—dropped to the ground, clawing up dirt with all of its fingers and spitting the blood it'd just drank out on the loosened soil. At that point the palm was turned toward him, and the eyes, nose, and mouth that'd distinctly formed on its surface made Lagoon rigid as a corpse beyond the door. It was a miracle he didn't suffer a heart attack.

The left hand's bizarre ritual continued, with the hand being thrust into the muddy blood that the pile of dirt had become, and the soil instantly being wolfed down by its tiny mouth. When it'd stuffed the last mouthful into its cheeks, Lagoon saw a pale blue flame blazing in the depths of its mouth. It was clearly the burning of an overwhelmingly mystic and powerful force. The wound on the neck of soundly slumbering D vanished in less than a second.

And now, as D stepped out of the woodshed with the coming of evening, Lagoon alone was there to greet him.

"At any rate, what do you say we *have a drink?*" the giant said, and even he thought his voice sounded funny. After all, he'd seen what D—or his left hand—had consumed.

"Why didn't you run me through?" D asked.

"Huh?!"

"There was murderous intent in your eyes as you looked at me. Orders from Vlad? Were you to be compensated with the power of the Nobility?"

"You've got me!" Lagoon said, slapping his forehead. "That's what I'd planned on doing until I saw you fight, and then I gave it up. With a guy like you after me, I'd have to live in fear for the rest of my days. Plus, I never was very fond of Vlad."

While it was unclear whether D believed him or not, he changed the topic, asking, "Where's the Field of Bones?"

"Oh, that's the plain that lies to the west of Vlad's castle. Bang a left just in front of the castle and you'll be there in a snap. But who's gonna be waiting there? You slew Vlad, right?"

"One of them."

"Huh?!"

"There are two of him."

Lagoon only grew more and more confused.

"What was de Carriole researching?"

After thinking for a while, the giant smacked his fist into his hand.

"Now that you mention it, he did order a weird text from the Capital. Some book about doppelgangers, I believe. Hey, you don't mean to tell me there are two freaking Vlads, do you?"

D said nothing as he straddled the horse tethered there. Then, in a terribly blunt manner, he said, "Thanks for everything."

"I didn't do much. But—Godspeed to you. Even I couldn't live the way you do."

As the Hunter began to ride away, the giant called out from behind him, "I suppose there's no sense saying this, but if you ever get tired, stop by anytime. You're always welcome. I'll even set you up with a good woman."

D raised one hand. His left.

On seeing the grinning face that formed on palm of that hand, Lagoon almost fell over.

From the windows of a lab in the lord's manor de Carriole gazed out at the twilight tinting the western sky. His decrepit form—heavily-wrinkled face and stooped-over silhouette—was bathed in the red glow, looking like it might melt away entirely. In reality, he was already an empty shell. The second Cordelia was impaled before his very eyes, the fires of enthusiasm that'd burned in that elderly body of his had been snuffed. Now, he intended to die. The cane he held in his right hand had a knife built into its handle. One thrust of it into his aged, feebly beating heart, and he could bid farewell to his pointless life.

When he turned that blade toward himself without any great determination, a voice called out his name behind him.

De Carriole turned, and his eyes bulged in their sockets.

Standing about ten feet away was a woman in white with water dripping from every inch of her. Although he couldn't see her face for some reason, he knew at first glance who she was.

"Madam—is that you, Lady Cordelia?"

"Indeed, it is," the woman nodded in reply.

In the same voice with which he'd addressed D early in the afternoon the previous day, the old man said, "If that's the case, then it actually worked. Ah, and I never knew it for this last decade . . ."

"And with good reason. I didn't appear until a year after you believed you'd failed."

A doppelganger—de Carriole had been so obsessed with the idea of creating one because Vlad's wife was hopelessly condemned to a life drifting underwater. He wanted to make another Cordelia and give her a different life. The fervor born of his longing only grew more obsessive with each passing day, until the genius succeeded in animal tests and his brain turned to making a copy of the valiant Cordelia. And that ended in failure.

De Carriole wasn't discouraged, though. After all, he'd succeeded with Vlad and himself. Of course, in Vlad's case, it'd manifested as merely a voice at first, becoming a complete physical entity only after news had reached them that the baron would return home, and it was at about that time de Carriole conducted similar experiments on himself. Naturally, every time he'd made a new breakthrough he'd asked the woman in the water if he might attempt the experiment again, but he'd always met with the same calm refusal.

However, it seemed impossible that the failed experiment he'd conducted for the one he loved most had actually succeeded.

"Cordelia," the old man said, forgetting the ironclad rules of master and servant and addressing her solely by her first name. "Why didn't you tell me? If you had, I might've escaped much of this pain. The pain of making you live underwater."

Perhaps that was the very reason why Cordelia hadn't told him.

"You mustn't die, de Carriole," the woman from the water said. Neither cold nor kind, her voice was like the water itself. "There's one thing you must still do. A creator must take responsibility for his creations up to the bitter end. Destroy the doppelganger of *him*."

De Carriole shook. He had guessed what the woman would want. Still, hearing someone actually say it now, he couldn't help but shudder.

Dispose of Lord Vlad's doppelganger—

"For the longest time, I was unable to leave that underworld. But it became possible after my other self met that gorgeous young man. I went outside with him. If I so desire, I can make it so no one at all can detect my presence. De Carriole, your experiments have proven more successful than you ever imagined. I rode with him on a horse out in the sunlight. And on returning to the manor, I saw and heard everything that you and my husband undertook."

De Carriole was speechless.

"I have nothing to say regarding that. Except this—de Carriole, you must destroy the copies you created of my husband and myself."

The old man swallowed hard. His Adam's apple was a horrible sight, bobbing up and down.

"But that's . . . Milady . . . I cannot do that. Nay, I mustn't. To start, even I don't know if the Vlad that remains is the doppelganger or not. Milady, it might well be that you alone would disappear . . . and that would only serve to subject this old fool to the pain of having his soul torn asunder once more."

"Do it, de Carriole."

The old man turned his back on the dripping wet woman. It was soon afterward that a pale hand touched his shoulder gently. Perhaps the woman who'd drifted underwater had the devilish nature of the Nobility after all. As that hand slowly groped his neck and stroked his chest, the color returned to the old man's cheeks, and his breathing became as ragged as a beast's.

"You destroyed me once. With your hands and your scalpel. Do away with me again—that shall be your recompense. And when you do, you shall die as well. At least let us set out on the journey into death together."

De Carriole's eyes filled with a confused vigor. It had a horribly dark hue to it.

III

Regarding the Field of Bones, there were those who said it was so named because that was where the bodies of the villagers who'd fought the Nobility had been left to rot, while another theory had it that the remains of creatures used in the Nobility's bizarre experiments had been discarded there. Whatever the case, the soil in that region was as red as if it'd been soaked with blood, and perhaps the grass that grew there had sucked that up, as it was unusually high and deeply verdant.

The wind had picked up with the coming of night. Though many flying animals had abandoned the field, being unable to fight those winds, a number of lizard-like creatures deftly rooted at the red earth and began snatching up grubs and insects. Suddenly, they sensed something.

Abandoning their prey, the creatures scampered off en masse while behind them, an object that resembled a titanic green caterpillar appeared, halting almost in the dead-center of the field. Of all the cruelty—Taki was completely naked and spread-eagle, bound hand and foot to the front of the vehicle. Opening the hatch, Vlad stuck his head out. Standing on the mountain folk vehicle with scepter in hand, garbed in an opulent robe, and with his hair billowing in the wind, he was the very picture of a demon king about to sacrifice a young beauty in some accursed ritual.

After gazing off in all directions, he said, "Only one more minute—I never thought both of them would fail to show up."

From the way he phrased it, it seemed he'd expected both D and the baron to come and had intended to fight both at the same time from the very start. His self-confidence was chilling.

Going to the front of the caterpillar, Vlad then leered down at Taki and said, "As promised, I refrained from slaking my thirst last night. And as I also swore, if they are even a second late—"

The way his grin left his lengthy incisors exposed, it made him look like a demon. After making an easy leap down to the ground, something must've happened, because his lips warped once more into a smile and he approached Taki.

Guessing who it was, Taki opened her eyes.

"Stop it . . . Stay away from me!"

The gaze Lord Vlad played across her full breasts and the face she tried so desperately to avert could only be described as that of a lustful fiend.

"There's no problem so long as I don't feed on you," he chortled.

He pressed a pair of thick purple lips to her right breast.

Taki was anguished by the pain of flesh being punctured, and two streaks of blood coursed out between the lips and the supple skin.

"I haven't drunk from you. Haven't drunk a drop."

When his mouth came away from her, two dark, swollen fang marks remained. And then he pressed his disgusting lips to the impressive swell of her left breast.

"Aaaah!" Taki cried as she tried to pull away.

Common opinion was that the thing about the kiss of the Nobility that sent the victim into rapture was the magical power of the actual act of drinking blood. Bites delivered without that feeding were nothing but the agonizing act of a wild beast tearing into flesh.

The writhing girl's entire body was covered with blood, with teeth marks ruthlessly carved into her smooth belly, her armpits, and her thighs.

Intoxicated, perhaps, by the scent of blood, Vlad had a look of sheer ecstasy on his face. Although this act was meant to check his desire, the way he subjected a completely immobilized girl to the torture of being pierced by his fangs without bothering to hypnotize her only seemed to illustrate the cruelty of the Nobility.

Taki fainted from the fear and pain.

Feeling the time, Vlad muttered into the wind, "Only three more seconds . . . Two . . . One . . . And now—"

His chest made a strange sound. A wooden spear flying at lightning speed had penetrated it. The spear was over six feet long.

Driven back two or three steps by the impact, he said, "So, someone came?!"

His bloodshot eyes turned toward the waves of grass before him. Every time they undulated in the wind, it scattered the moonlight, so it looked as beautiful as the dance of the fireflies.

Seeming to push his way through the grass was a figure in black who gripped a sword in his right hand.

"D."

Taking hold of the spear, Vlad pulled it back out.

"So good of you to come. And what of Byron?"

"I'm here," a voice called out from behind him.

Not bothering to turn around, Vlad said, "What are you waiting for? Have at me!"

D's wooden spear had clearly pierced him through the heart, yet he didn't show a hint of pain.

"D, stand back," the baron called out to the Hunter.

Gazing at the young Nobleman's distant face, D gave a nod.

Perhaps taking it as some kind of signal, Vlad pivoted. He saw the face of his son. And he groaned.

Although there'd been no change to his gorgeous features, which could be described as the glory of youth personified, Byron's cheeks seemed to have lost some of their meat and his skin some of its color, so he looked like a wraith from the underworld. But more startling than anything was the intensity of his eyes, which glittered with pain and the hue of blood as he stared at Vlad.

Had the baron decided that the only way to slay the devil was to become a demon himself?

"What happened, Byron? Did you take on the Destroyer?" Vlad asked. It was only natural.

"No, it's just me."

And saying that, he let a streak of light fly from the chest of his cape—and in response, the scepter flew from Vlad's right hand.

Were life and death separated by an eternity or a split second?

Vlad's body opened to a vertical flash of light.

At the same time the baron was pierced by the scepter and blown backward. For an instant the young Nobleman's body appeared to swell up—but a second later a boom resounded within him like a great drum being struck. Still, the baron managed to maintain his pose, narrowly avoiding collapse.

"You bastard—you took in the Destroyer after all," Vlad groaned as the band of light kept flying right through him. It had pushed straight through the middle of his massive frame.

"What's this?!" he cried, pressing his hands to either side of his head.

The lord was using every ounce of his strength to try and hold the two halves of his body from splitting apart.

"Do you see this, Byron? This is your father."

As he laughed aloud a band of light split his chest. Vlad's body was literally split in a cross.

"Arrrgh!" he cried.

His scream of agony was like a howl from the heavens and the earth. The night wind buffeted his face.

"It won't close! The wound won't close! What are you doing, Guide?!"

Staggering, he collapsed in the grass. The baron lay about fifteen feet to his rear. The light the young Nobleman had just hit him with had taken the last strength he could muster.

Crawling over to him, Vlad grabbed hold of the scepter protruding from the baron's chest and used it to pull himself up onto his feet.

"You or I—which of us will follow after Cordelia?" the lord said, giving a powerful twist to the scepter he still grasped.

There was nothing the baron could do but bend backward in pain and writhe.

Pulling out the scepter, Vlad raised it high over his head for the coup de grace. One more thrust—to the heart. Even possessed by the Destroyer, the young Nobleman couldn't survive a second blow.

His body shook. Another scepter had pierced his heart from behind. The same scepter that'd destroyed Lady Miska.

"You—you bastard . . ."

He tried to turn, but there was no need. In the raging wind, the imposing figure in the black coat circled around in front of him.

"Looks like there was no need for me," D said in a low voice, taking Vlad's head off with a single stroke of his blade.

Even after the head landed on the red soil far away, the body didn't fall. Still impaled on the scepter, it slowly began to walk. Toward the head it had lost.

"I won't be destroyed . . . I won't be . . . ," came a distant voice. The head lying on the red soil had spoken. "Guide . . . take me away . . . to the promised land . . ."

"Oh," the wind groaned. In the vicinity of D's left hand.

Look at how the space ahead of the decapitated torso shimmered like a mirage, forming an image—was that a land mass coming into view far beyond the black-and-white tips of the waves? The crystal palaces off in the distance had an eternal glow. And the waves parted as the path rose from them.

D said nothing as he walked over to the baron and propped him up. Picking up what Vlad had dropped, he put it in the Nobleman's bloodless right hand.

"You can use this, can't you?" he asked.

The baron opened his eyes a crack, nodded, and said, "This isn't the Destroyer's power."

He hadn't borrowed the strength of that shuddersome entity—there had been fears it might unleash limitless destruction. His powerful desire to slay his father had been checked by clear thinking. However, his hatred remained. At this rate, he couldn't beat his father. When despair and hatred overlapped and his seething emotions reached their peak, another power had awakened in him. And that was—

"In that case, you're the same as me," D said.

When the baron planted both feet firmly on the ground and raised the scepter high with his right hand, D let go of him.

As he watched the howling scepter smash Vlad's severed head into a million pieces, the baron tumbled to the ground face-first.

The massive form of Vlad fell as well. His hand trembling feebly all the while, he reached out for the glittering Shangri-la. However, before he could touch that dreamlike space his fingertips dropped with a sudden lack of power. The Noble's hands slapped the red ground ineffectually before he moved no more.

The confrontation between father and son had come to a conclusion.

On seeing that it was indeed finished, D was about to walk back to the baron when he suddenly turned his attention to a sound on the breeze.

"It was a woman's voice," his left hand said. "Sounded kinda like the baron's mother."

Later it was discovered that the aged scholar de Carriole had died after severing his carotid artery in his laboratory in Vlad's manor. By his side was a smashed machine the purpose of which no one knew, and in addition to that, it was said there were signs that water had been splashed across the floor. Seeing that the puddle in question was in the shape of a person, the farmers who'd discovered it shuddered in fear. They never did learn that in keeping with a request from the woman he'd secretly loved, the aged scholar had destroyed his own device for creating doppelgangers. In the end, he'd probably died without ever knowing that the Lord Vlad that remained was the real one. What de Carriole's thoughts were as he watched the woman who'd once been relegated to an unnatural fate under his scalpel turned to water once again by his destructive act remained a mystery. They had set out on their voyage to the hereafter together. However, no one knew whether or not they'd held hands as they did so.

It was at dawn two days later that D bid farewell to the baron. In the courtyard of Lagoon's establishment, Hugh, May, and the owner had come out to see him off.

The baron had already recovered his strength. His recuperation came with the same remarkable speed as D's own.

"Just like you," the left hand said with deep admiration. "So, was there *another success?*"

"Will you stay here?" D asked the baron.

"No, I'll be setting off on a trip soon. There's no place for the Nobility now," the baron said with a smile.

"You're not a Noble anymore. You should stay," Lagoon said as he gazed at the young Nobleman with a look that said he regretted this parting from the bottom of his heart.

The garden was filled by the light of winter. A day brimming with life was just beginning.

And in the past two days, the baron had discovered that whatever "a certain great personage" had given him, it'd done more than just give him the power to slay Lord Vlad; it also allowed him to walk in the light of the sun. He hadn't borrowed the power of the Destroyer. The strength of his will had kept him from inviting limitless destruction. And that's what Lagoon had meant.

"We'll be staying here instead," Hugh stated proudly as May gently rubbed his head. The two of them were going to be doing acrobatics shows at Lagoon's establishment.

"Just a word of warning . . ."

At that from D, Lagoon stuck both hands out in front of himself.

"I know. In no way, shape, or form am I gonna let anything weird happen to those two. I'm sure if I did, you'd blow in here like a gale and chop my head right off."

"Miss Taki's not here. But she said she'd be out in a minute," May said as she turned back toward the door to the establishment.

"I'll go have a look," Hugh said, and he started walking that way, but the baron put a hand on his shoulder to stop him, then turned.

The wintry light threw blue shadows on the ground.

The Nobleman disappeared through the doorway and several minutes passed.

Taki's room was the third from the door.

"I'll go," Lagoon said, but just as he was about to do so, a figure in an ink-black coat passed him.

Slipping through the doorway, D halted in front of Taki's room. He'd caught a certain odor.

Quietly he pushed open the door. The light spearing in through the window focused on the white bed. Taki's upper body had fallen back against it. Apparently she'd changed into a gray sweater to see D off, and the garment was speckled with red dots.

Walking over, he looked down at her. Taki had already expired.

"The girl—she was a victim before she ever joined us," a shadowy voice echoed behind him.

Apparently the baron was standing behind the door.

"The one who called himself Lord Yohan used his hypnotism to repress her memories of being a victim, but it would seem the shock the other day brought them back. When I got near her, she suddenly threw herself at me."

To lull D and the baron into a false sense of security, the "victim" had most likely had a keyword implanted in her mind that would awaken her true nature, but in all this time it hadn't been used.

D turned around.

The baron had one hand pressed to the nape of his neck, and the chest of his shirt was speckled with drops of blood.

"Were you bitten?"

"Yes."

His face was pale, his lips colorless, and from them poked a pair of bloody red fangs—Taki's throat had been torn open.

"And that awoke it in you, too?"

D's ears caught a distant voice. *You were my only success.*

Taki's voice came back to him. *Save me, D.*

D heard the blue voice.

"D—destroy me."

"No one has hired me."

"I'll be the client."

"I see."

For an instant, two streaks of light adorned the transparent morn. The light from the baron skimmed by D as the Hunter bent back far, imbedding itself in the floor, while D's blade pinned the Nobleman's chest to the wall.

The baron's cape tinged D's eyes with blue.

When he got up again, D laid Taki's body out on the bed, and then left the room. He didn't watch as the baron's end came. For D knew that he'd intentionally missed with his light attack.

"What did you come here to do, baron?"

There was no one there to hear that muttered query.

A figure of immeasurable darkness and beauty walked down the corridor.

Through the doorway, the sound of May and Hugh's laughter was growing closer as the children rushed to find their friends.

END

Postscript

Here we have the second half of *Pale Fallen Angel*. When I think about how the story was published in four volumes in Japan, I'm somewhat stunned, but quite some time has passed since the printing of the first half, so time-wise it probably took about as long as the Japanese edition. And that's about all I have to say about that.

D's stage is the Frontier. If someone were to ask me exactly where that is, I'd be at a loss, but you can think of it as the entire Eurasian continent if you like. That's why the descriptions of some places call to mind the forest regions of Europe, and then suddenly you have a location where the snow is piled thirty feet deep like you'd only find in Siberia.

But the image I have in my head of the Frontier comes from a scene in director F.W. Murnau's 1922 classic *Nosferatu the Vampire*—the part where the realtor protagonist traverses the desolate plains of Transylvania. In the half century since 1958's *Horror of Dracula*, I've seen Transylvania in scads of movies, but not one of them presented a tableau as stark, wild, and cold as that single scene. One reason for that might be because it was a black-and-white movie. The key difference between this variety of film that so admirably makes symbols of "darkness" and "light" and the color film that replicates the hues of our daily existence is that the former creates a strange land that is sharp and isolated.

When I traveled to Transylvania twice in the past, it didn't give me the same sense of an otherworldly reality as Murnau's film of eighty years earlier. For me, D travels constantly through a world of black-and-white film. Whether his exquisite features are glowing a pale blue in the moonlight, the skin of a beautiful woman is taking a rosy flush in the light of day, D's blade is sending out bright blood, or a Noble's manor is crafted of gold, D is still a resident of a world of darkness and light. A world where everything last creature that draws breath in the white world melts in a heartbeat into a world of darkness. Those who dwell there are shadows. D's tale is told in beautiful silhouettes.

Pale Fallen Angel was penned as a tale of just such a world as well. I can only hope that you agree with me on that point, dear readers.

Hideyuki Kikuchi
November 13, 2008
while watching *Nosferatu the Vampire*

And now, a preview of the next book in the
Vampire Hunter D series

VAMPIRE HUNTER D

VOLUME 13
TWIN-SHADOWED KNIGHT PART ONE

Written by
Hideyuki Kikuchi

Illustrations by
Yoshitaka Amano

English translation by
Kevin Leahy

Coming in October 2009
from Dark Horse Books and Digital Manga Publishing

Numa

I

T he wind raced by, and it was heavy. It had weight because it bore molecules of what was termed a killing lust.

Two shadowy figures squared off on a desolate patch of earth. Whenever it passed them, the wind grew furious.

The sky was as dark as the afterworld.

Suddenly, one of the shadowy figures pounced. As he rose ten feet straight up, he swung both arms down.

Two spiteful flames erupted from the black earth, shooting straight for the figure still on the ground. Like lines drawn by a talented artist, the fiery streaks came together on the figure.

Silver flashes crossed. Two of them.

If fire is a physical phenomenon, it has mass and substance. Thus, it's possible for a greater mass and harder substance to deflect it.

The light from the flames bouncing off the stark cutting edge became a sword rising into the air. A simple leap made the second figure a sparrow in flight.

Faster than the figure in midair could rise to greater heights, the sword came straight down on him, splitting him from the crown of his head to the base of his neck.

The wind was stained red. When it slapped bright blood against the black earth, the two figures had landed on their feet a dozen yards apart. One of them collapsed, while the other stalked across the ground.

Not even bothering to wipe his blade, the victor returned it to the sheath on his back. There wasn't a speck of gore on it. There was nothing special about the blade, but its speed had prevailed over the cohesive powers of blood.

The wind had a flattering glow to it as it blew across the shadowy figure's face: deep, dark eyes gleaming beneath the wide-brimmed traveler's hat, the line of a nose that was sure to send tens of millions of artists into despair, lips that quietly brimmed with a will heavier than anyone would ever know—

The wind had a request. *Tell me your name*, it said.

"D . . ." a voice called out.

The figure with his head split in two had called to him. Already a death mask, his face wore a smile.

"D . . . Listen to me," he said, even his voice that of the departed.

The heavens and earth roared, and the hem of the black coat hid D's face, as if to shield him from the words of the dead. As if to keep him from hearing.

There was a sharp slap. A hand in a black glove had knocked his coat out of the way.

"Oh . . . so you intend to hear me out . . . One word will say it all . . . Of course . . . for you . . . that one word . . . might send you to hell."

The figure on the ground was an old man with white hair and a white beard. The long robe he wore was woven from metallic threads in a wide range of hues, and its distinctive color scheme declared that even among the Nobility, he was a necromancer of some stature.

The beautiful figure stood there without saying a word. As if he'd heard these words ten thousand times before.

The bisected and bloodied face split to either side, and the old man raised his hands to hold it together again.

"Go to . . . 'Muma' . . ." he said, his voice sounding like it came straight up from hell.

And as he finished speaking, he took his hands away, and something that might've been blood or brains oozed from the reopened split.

A life that'd lasted who knew how long had ended.

Only the wind growled across the wilderness until a new voice was heard, saying, "Did he say 'Muma'?"

It sounded like it came from D's left hand, which hung at ease by his side.

"What's that mean?" D asked.

Signs of surprise seemed to rise from his hand for a second.

"Damned if I know," the dried, cracked voice then responded. "Just the babbling of some guy about to die. A little memento to mess with you."

The voice then mixed with groans of pain. D had squeezed his left hand into a tight fist.

"D-don't . . . do . . . anything . . . stupid . . ."

The fist trembled. Finger and finger pressed together, and nails broke through skin and muscle. A thin red stream had begun to drip to the ground.

"Answer me," D said.

"About what? Ow! I don't know . . . anything at all . . ."

"What is 'Muma'? A person? The name of a place? Or is it . . ."

"I . . . don't . . . know . . ." the hoarse voice said, its manner changed so that it now sounded like it might throw up.

He gave his fist one more squeeze. Silence resulted. After maintaining that fearsome tension for several seconds, D opened his fingers. The blood that covered the palm of his hand was scattered by the wind.

D squinted. He had no memories of this word *Muma*. And yet, his body told him of subtle changes. His blood was coursing faster—by a thousandth of a second. D's body knew when something that small had changed.

Was it his heart or his genes? He'd felt a mysterious excitement from the second he'd heard the word *Muma*.

D turned his gaze to the far reaches of the gloom-shrouded plain.

Something roiled like smoke all along the horizon. A mob of countless figures shaken by the wind. Their vile forms were evident to D's eyes

296 | HIDEYUKI KIKUCHI

alone. Arms like withered branches, fingers tapering into claws, skin that seemed born of corruption, cloudy eyes reminiscent of a dead fish, bodies covered with pustules—all of these creatures had been summoned from their graves deep in the earth by the necromancer who'd just been slain. Even D didn't know what they actually were. Nor did he know what they were supposed to accomplish. Their overlord had just been reduced to a blood-soaked cadaver.

D gave a brief whistle. Somewhere, the sound of iron-shod hooves approaching rang out. Before the white cyborg horse could come to a stop, D was in the saddle. As he took up the reins, the horse went right into a gallop—in the opposite direction from the mob of misbegotten dead. And most likely toward the hell the necromancer had mentioned.

It was after midnight when the white horse and black rider blew into the village of Gilhagen like a monochrome cyclone. Street lamps glowed through the weighty darkness of the wee hours.

Atop a hill that was rather high even for a village in the rolling terrain at the foot of a mountain, the house with roof and walls painted black squatted like the darkness. It didn't have windows, either. It was impossible to tell if it had a door or not, but D stood in front of the house and brought his fist down just once.

A thin crack of light spread through the dark. The door that'd opened in response to that single knock couldn't even be seen.

Standing there with a soot-stained lamp in hand was a gray-haired crone. She had a face that looked like leather pasted on a skull. The black leaf that covered her left eye must've served as an eye patch.

Opening a crack of a mouth, she said, "To be calling on the home of Origa, the greatest sorceress in the southern Frontier, at this hour, you must be prepared to sacrifice your life . . .if not your very soul."

Her voice was like a chill wind gusting from a dark grotto.

"I will, if that's your wish," D said.

Just then the sorceress's eyes snapped wide open.

"That voice—" the crone said, blinking vigorously behind the light. "Yes, and that beautiful face—It can't be . . . You're—"

"I've come because there's something I'd like to ask Origa the Sorceress."

Before D had even finished speaking, the door opened wide.

A few minutes later, D sat at a heavy table and the sorceress brought him a hot cup of tea. As she turned a mysterious look at a countenance so gorgeous it seemed to drink up darkness and light and even sound, she asked, "What can I do for you?"

"I've heard Origa the Sorceress specializes in memory regression."

"That's right. Humans, horses, birds, flame beasts, shadow-eaters— hell, I can slip into the memories of any supernatural creature and make 'em recall the past. But—"

After stopping there, Origa had the expression wiped right off her face, as if she'd just committed some unpardonable sin. A face of unearthly beauty was right before her. The woman's next words would be a betrayal—a betrayal of a beauty that couldn't possibly be human.

"But . . ." the old woman sputtered, trying desperately to retain her pride, "but . . . I won't for you. Be on your way. I didn't meet anyone tonight. Didn't see anyone, no matter how gorgeous. I'll believe that to my dying day."

"Why are you afraid?" D asked from the other side of the little round table.

"I'm not afraid of anything, I'll have you know."

"I don't believe we've met before. Or have we—"

"Hell, I've never laid eyes on you before. At any rate, kindly be on your way now. Or if you won't leave, I will!"

"Please, restore my memory."

The crone quaked at D's words as if struck with palsy.

"I already told you . . . No more of this foolishness!"

"I'll pay you ten times your normal rate. And I'll do you a favor as well."

"A favor?"

"I'll give you a look into your own past."

"You're talking nonsense!" the crone said with a low laugh.

The laws of nature had decreed that sorcerers who could restore the memories of others couldn't go back through their own.

D wasn't smiling.

The crone stopped smiling, too. Licking her puckered mouth, she said in a parched, cracked voice, "You mean to tell me . . . you could do that? No, you could . . . I believe you could . . . you of all people. Nearly thirty bandits were cut down before my very eyes . . . back when I was five—and that's the only thing I remember from my past."

"How about it?"

As that question was put to her, the crone suddenly turned her gaze to the vicinity of D's left hip. She'd gotten the feeling the hoarse query she'd just heard had come from there.

After a bit of consideration, the crone nodded and said, "Okay, my beautiful demon. My normal fee will suffice . . . that and the return of my past. Not that I doubt you or anything, but would you be so kind as to show me a little proof you can really do it?"

D's left hand rose before the crone's eyes, which were rocked by puzzlement. There was no glove on it.

At the moment he reached across the table and touched that hand to her right temple, the crone's body arched in her chair. Her expression changed. The changes came at intervals of a fraction of a second. Anger, hatred, fear, joy, and finally sadness skimmed ruthlessly across her deeply wrinkled face, hammering her, teasing her, and then leaving.

Somewhere, the lid of a pot rattled quietly. Apparently she was boiling medicinal herbs. Before it rattled a second time, the crone sat back in her chair normally. Her whole body was suffused by a mysterious kind of peace unconnected to the relaxation of her muscles, and tears rolled from her eyes.

What had she seen?

Blinking repeatedly to stem the flow of tears, the crone then focused her gaze on D.

"You pass muster, D," she said in a perfectly clear tone. "I remembered all manner of things. But instead of thanking you, I'll see to it I give you what you want for certain. Come this way."

Rising with the lamp in one hand, the crone began to walk toward the doorway, and then stumbled. Falling to the right before she could even regain her balance, she was caught by the figure in black. D.

"You're a surprisingly good person at heart, D. Right this way."

Stepping through the doorway and walking down the dark corridor a bit, the crone opened a door at the end.

The room was a dreary affair, with nothing but a metal bed and a chair.

"Lie down," the crone told D, gesturing to the bed.

She then took a bamboo flute out of a niche in the wall.

"This is called the returning flute. It has a unique construction that allows it to extract memories from the brain. To date, I've used it on nearly twenty thousand people and supernatural critters, and not once has it failed."

And yet, she hadn't wanted to use it on D. The incredible swordsman the crone had seen when she was five must've been him after all. But what was it she feared she might glimpse in his past?

"Lie back," Origa said, pointing to the bed and readying the flute.

In no time at all, the thin strains of a melody echoed from the instrument, moving to the ceiling and walls as it flowed through the room.

"First layer of the subconscious—passed," Origa muttered in a low tone, although how she managed that with the flute still to her lips was a mystery.

The melody changed.

The secret of the famed flute that could restore lost memories was inner mechanisms that made memories replay and this tune known only to the sorceress's clan.

D didn't move. Was he sleeping? Was he even breathing, for that matter?

As if entranced by his handsome visage, the crone said, "Second layer—no, let's just dive straight down to the mystic layer."

There was a ghastly ring to the voice of Origa the Sorceress, like she was sick with the smell of blood.

The mystic layer—that was a mysterious zone of the human mind only those of her line could reach.

Adjusting her grip on the instrument, Origa began to pipe a short, strange rhythm wholly unlike what she'd played up to this point. Accompanied by light, the arrows of sound slipped into the ears of the gorgeous Hunter—no, they battered his brain directly.

Origa's features grew indistinct. They'd been blurred by the sweat that covered every inch of her in a split second.

Look what kind of misery had to be endured to call back lost memories! The body of the sorceress contorted and grew dehydrated, and she might shed as much as a tenth of her weight. And in exchange for that fearsome price, the notes produced by the magic flute seemed enough to make even a rock shudder, echoing an eerie melody like the marching tune of a demonic army, orderly and awe-inspiring.

The first thing that could be called emotion suddenly raced across the face of the sleeping D. His right hand reached for the sword by his side.

"Don't!"

Whose shout was that?

The woman's screams exploding from the little black house were swallowed by a far deeper darkness. The sounds dragged long, long tails after them—then vanished unexpectedly.

Aside from that, the night had been particularly quiet.

Past noon on the following day—when the Hunter in black was more than one hundred and twenty miles from the village—a villager who called on the home of Origa the Sorceress was left standing frozen and speechless on discovering the crone's body in pieces in the blood-spattered living room.

II

Surprisingly, there were many types of travelers that one could expect to see on the highway: medicine peddlers dressed in white with drug cases of the same hue slung from their shoulders and tri-colored pennants of red, white, and blue flying high off the poles on their backs; contract fighters in old-fashioned armored cars with heavy machine guns and the barrels of rivet guns protruding from their sides and the words "warriors available" written in large letters on their coats; traveling performers who did flips on top of their carriage, disgorging flowers from their mouths, then striking them down with knives or gouts of flame; and so on, and so forth. And the eyes of all of them bulged in their sockets.

What some saw from the front and others from the rear was a cyborg horse galloping at terrific speed. But even those who recognized it as a horse still didn't believe it. Cyborg horses couldn't keep that kind of pace, and what's more, as it was passing them, a number of people saw a figure of unearthly beauty, and to some it looked as if said figure was actually running right alongside the horse. Whatever the case, by the time they could focus their eyes, both the cyborg horse and the human figure were dwindling in the distance.

Not even the bands of warriors astride their vaunted steeds or the riders of the Pony Express—who were said to have the fastest horses on the road—felt like challenging that pair. They literally galloped along as if possessed by the dark lord of the winds.

It was D. However, the gorgeous young man had never raced like this in the past. When he commanded his mount to run at full speed, the cyborg horse entered a mad gallop, as if in the grip of some unearthly aura. His horse moved as swiftly as a swallow in flight. But it couldn't continue like that forever. When he saw that his horse had grown exhausted, D got down off his mount and ran alongside it to lighten its load. Needless to say, those times were few and his horse slowed down a bit, but keeping pace with a wildly galloping horse was something no human—or even Noble, for that matter—could do.

Nevertheless, the horse had been ruined.

Beside the towns and villages, there were rest stops along the highway where travelers might obtain cyborg horses or energy bikes. The proprietor glanced at the cyborg horse that'd collapsed after it galloped in, but by the time he realized it'd died of excessive exhaustion, D had already selected a new mount and left a pile of coins that would also cover the burial costs of the horse, and disappeared into the distance in a cloud of dust.

In the past three days, he'd ridden twelve hundred miles without a moment's rest, and he was on his third cyborg horse—he truly was riding at an insane pace. D's unearthly aura took hold of the steed. But what was the purpose of that aura, and what was it directed at? Where are you going, D? And what is waiting there?

The far end of the desolate night plains had begun to take on a watery hue.

Wherever this young man went, people always met their fate. But whose will it be this time? Will it be yours, D?

In the village of Sedoc—or to be precise, on the outskirts of the village—an incredible change took place on the twenty-sixth day of the third month of season A. A group of elderly women on a pilgrimage from the east were staying at Sedoc House, the village inn, when all twenty of them suddenly suffered heart attacks that night and died. After the sheriff's department wrote up a perfunctory report, they were carted off to the morgue.

In the middle of the night, the janitor from the morgue rode to the sheriff's office with bizarre news. One after another, the corpses in the morgue had gotten up, smashed through a stone wall, and begun to march off in single file toward "the red wasteland" on the village outskirts, by his account.

The sheriff railed about how they'd been bitten by a Noble and grilled the janitor on what the hell he'd been doing, but the poor janitor insisted there was absolutely no way a Noble could've gotten near them.

At any rate, talk turned to forming a search team and rounding up the corpses, but just then, the caretaker from a cemetery near the sheriff's office bolted in with a face as pale as a dead man. He told them that every corpse in the entire cemetery had risen from its grave. Clawing up through ten feet of heavy dirt, they reached the surface and started walking.

The sheriff asked him where they were headed. But he already knew the answer.

"The red wasteland," the cemetery caretaker replied.

An urgent appeal went out, and more than thirty men responded immediately, taking up their inevitable task as residents of the Frontier. They came with sharpened stakes, spears, and bows in hand, quickly proceeding toward the outskirts of the village.

They were a third of the way to their destination when the massive earthquake struck. Heaven and earth rumbled. The ground undulated like waves across fabric, rapidly pitching from side to side. It was a miracle that no one in the search party was harmed. Not even the horses had been able to flee; they'd fallen to the ground and rolled around on their sides for what'd seemed like an eternity, though it was later learned that the trembling of the earth hadn't lasted five seconds.

Still, the sheriff and a number of other brave souls were to be lauded for the way they decided to press on less than five minutes after the great quake had passed. Driving their cyborg horses as fast as they could, they arrived at the edge of a red plain, where the composition of the soil made it look like blood, and were struck by a terror that effaced all other thoughts of strangeness in their minds as they froze on their mounts—or rather, *along with* their mounts.

The red ground was missing.

What they saw was an outer ring that seemed to go on forever, dropping at a sharp angle into a great mortar-shaped depression. But from the standpoint of natural phenomena, such an occurrence wasn't inconceivable. What terrified the group was that along that vast brink—later the hole would be found to be a mile and a quarter in diameter—there was a mob of shadowy figures. Some clad in rags, others fairly well dressed, and still others nearly completely naked, they stood peering down at the bottom of that subsidence without moving a muscle. Irrespective of age or sex, there was nothing about them that had the slightest semblance of human life—eyes as cloudy as those of dead fish, sunken cheeks with bones laid bare, and pale shapes wriggling in holes through their chests and bellies that could only be maggots.

All their dead.

No, the caretaker said in a flat tone. *That's not right. They aren't just from our village cemetery. There are too many of them.*

It was at that point that the sheriff sensed the presence of countless people behind him and heard their footsteps.

Corpses, someone shouted. The moonlight drank up his voice.

Behind them, dead beyond numbering were coming down the highway. And although the sheriff and his men didn't notice it, they must've traveled quite some distance, since each was stark-white with dust from the ankles down.

"What are they up to? What the hell are these things?"

Ignoring the sheriff's muttered remarks, the walking dead marched on, trudging right past the living. And then, as if they'd been given a push from behind, all the dead who stood at the brink of the mortar-like depression leapt in at once. The row behind them followed suit. As did the one after that, and another, and another.

Their brains assailed by egregious horror and the foul stench, most of the search party passed out. They were brought back to the village by the remaining members of their group.

And for two full days after that, the sheriff watched the procession of the dead to their mass grave.

Were there really that many bodies buried around the area? How much longer would this go on?

These concerns ate at every brain, leaving the townsfolk on the edge of madness that dusk. The next thing they knew, the procession of the dead had ended, but the villagers were left in a state of shock, roaming the streets like the new dead.

A young man in black with heavenly beauty and an exhausted horse had come into town with the wind whirling in his wake. Halting his horse in front of Sedoc House, the rider grabbed one of the unsteady villagers and asked, "What happened?"

The young man's tone and his handsome features returned the stupefied villager to his senses. He told the young man everything he knew, from start to finish.

"Am I too late?" D muttered in a tone devoid of emotion—a voice of iron—and he prepared to get back on his horse.

"Wait!" a voice called out to him. Though it was low, the voice had a faint tinge of something to it.

Not even looking, D put his heels to his horse's flanks.

As the gorgeous rider and his mount tore up the ground, the voice called out once more.

"Wait, *D!*"

III

The girl introduced herself as Mia. She also said she was the daughter of a fortune-teller who lived about sixty miles to the north. Her smock and the skirt she wore below it were both embroidered with a mysterious crest representing where she came from, and her numerous necklaces and bracelets were set with stones that possessed a deep luster that seemed to hold a dark history. She knew D's name because when her mother predicted a strange occurrence in this region, she'd told the girl that that would be the name of the man who'd race there from afar.

"From what Mother says, the key to solving this mysterious occurrence is held by a man who comes from far away," Mia said in a hard tone. "This case is something no one can handle. No one except the man named D. D—if that's the name that you go by—what in the world are you?"

"Can you see the future?" D asked.

"A little," Mia replied, her tone carrying very restrained pride and self-confidence.

"In that case, do you know how this all ends?"

"No, not even Mother knows that. But it's not because she's not powerful enough to see it. Something interfered." After a short pause, the girl continued, "As far as what happened, I asked the villagers before you got here. Mother had pointed to a spot on the map and said that an incredibly evil power was at work. It was the same area where there was that massive subsidence. That's probably the center of it."

"What kind of power?"

"An evil one is all she said."

"It probably would've been better if your mother came."

"I think so too," Mia conceded, not seeming the least bit angry. "But unfortunately, she can't do that. Right after predicting this incident, Mother coughed up blood and collapsed. She's probably passed away by now."

"And you came here instead of tending to her?"

"Mother's orders were explicit," Mia replied with her eyes still focused straight ahead.

Her age had to be sixteen or seventeen. Some childish innocence still remained, but a strength of will that hardly suited her had also spread across her face.

"She doesn't view this incident as merely another great catastrophe. Mother said it's a major event that could have repercussions on a global scale. Ordinarily, she'd have gone herself. Even though going might not accomplish anything, as someone with the power to catch a glimpse of people's future—society's future—she has to try and do whatever she can. But since she couldn't possibly move, she told me to go."

A mother had sent her own daughter into an incident that might shake the very world.

A girl had raced here even though she knew her mother was fated to die.

D tugged back on the reins.

A split second before her face was about to hit his back, Mia swiftly turned it away, so that only her right cheek took the impact. She could feel the swell of his muscles through the fabric. For just a second, she grew dizzy.

"We're there," D said.

"Okay."

Taking away the hands she'd had wrapped around his waist, Mia put them on the saddle's cantle and braced her body. Before D could dismount, the girl flew into action.

Not bothering to call out to the girl who'd hit the ground before him, D began to walk.

Their entire conversation up to this point had taken place on the back of his horse.

His left arm rose naturally and from the vicinity of its wrist a hoarse voice humans wouldn't hear squeaked, "She's a hell of a girl. For one thing, you've got a little slip of a lass like her racing into a place like this. For another, she didn't even bother to wait for you to offer her a hand getting down from the horse. She's been schooled in how to live on her own. If you ever take a wife, one like that'll—"

The voice broke off there. D had made his hand into a tight fist.

As he walked quietly but gravely, ahead of him yawned the great subsidence that'd swallowed so many dead.

"This place is incredible, isn't it?" Mia remarked pensively as she peered down from D's right side.

Compared to the diameter of the depression, its depth wasn't great at all. Only about a thousand feet. Blending with the sloping sides, the bottom was a chaotic mix of boulders and sand, with the red soil filling in the spaces between them.

"It's like a sea of blood," Mia remarked as she rubbed her cheek with her right hand.

"You saying the dead can bleed, too?"

Mia looked at D's hip out of the corner of her eye, and then stared at his face. Perhaps aware of the rosy glow suffusing her cheeks, she swiftly averted her gaze, saying, "You do a weird little voice, don't you? Are you teasing me?"

Making no reply, D planted one foot at the edge of the incline.

"No, I'm serious," Mia continued. "And I'll thank you to answer me."

Saying nothing, D stared downward.

Piqued at being ignored, Mia undertook a reckless course of action. With unexpected speed she came up behind D and told him, "You're rude!"

She'd aimed a kick at his ass. But it met nothing. Nothing but the empty space over the pit.

"Wha—?!"

As she reflexively put her strength into the leg that still supported her, the supposedly firm ground gave way.

The second she heard her own cry above her and felt the sensation of falling, her body suddenly stopped dead. On realizing that D's left hand had caught her by the collar, she madly reached around with her hands to latch onto him. Just as it dawned on her that she was floating through the air, and her feet came down on solid ground. No sooner had a feeling of relief flooded through her than the hand came away from her collar and Mia staggered.

As her eyes stared fixedly at D, they began to hold hints of a bottomless terror and rage—and a gleam of admiration.

"What do you think this depression's for?"

The voice that posed that question was tinged with trust—and even a bit of affection.

Once again there was no reply. But even though he didn't answer, no anger bubbled up in the girl.

"You said you were the daughter of a fortune-teller, didn't you?"

"Yeah," she said, feeling silly for getting so excited that he'd turned the conversation to her.

"The dead left every graveyard in the region to throw themselves from here. There would've been thousands of them. Why do you think that was?"

There was a short pause.

The next thing Mia knew, she had one hand to her chest. Her heart was racing. She had to do something to slow it down.

Pressing a finger gently to one part of the heart—the left ventricle—she made her breathing as shallow as possible. Her heartbeat returned to normal immediately. But then, she was a strong-willed and courageous individual to begin with.

"Is it okay if it's pure conjecture?"

D nodded.

"I think they were a sacrifice."

"That's it, all right."

The hoarse response definitely sounded like it'd come from the vicinity of D's left hand.

Though she looked, naturally she didn't see anything.

"That's right."

This time the reply came in a rusty, masculine tone—D's voice. So, was that other one just her ears playing tricks on her?

"Last time, corpses sufficed, but next time it'll probably be living people jumping in."

"Thousands of them . . ." Mia muttered, her remark a question at the same time.

There was no reply, of course. You could say *that* was her answer.

"But . . . why in the world?"

"It's the will of the one down below this."

"Down below?"

Mia couldn't help forgetting her present terror and peering down past the brink of the hole. But as she quickly recalled it again, she backed away, then stared at D.

"You know what it is?" she asked.

Not answering her, D stood there like an exquisite statue, but then he told her, "Go home."

And then, without further ado, he dove headfirst from the rim of the hole into its interior.

"D?!" Mia called out in spite of herself, and she was paused at the very brink of the hole ready to go after him when something white got in her eyes.

Gas.

Covering her mouth, the fortune-teller's daughter made a great leap back.

It looked like the white pillars of smoke rising from the brink of the depression numbered in the hundreds. All those geysers of gas couldn't have suddenly erupted from the ground in unison. They'd been triggered mechanically. And the one who'd set them off was—

"D . . ."

Still unsure just what was in the gas, Mia took a deep breath and raced back to the rim of the hole. She turned her gaze downward.

He'd probably been crushed. Why was she so determined to find this young man? Because his actions were so extreme. Like what he'd done just now. She couldn't help thinking that whatever he really was, it was tremendously unsettling and of great importance—just as he'd appeared in the fortune-telling. And the last thing that occurred to Mia was something the girl tried vehemently to ignore so it wouldn't rise to the fore of her consciousness. *Because he's gorgeous. More than anyone has a right to be.*

Mia couldn't see D anywhere, and she had to back away again. The gas had grown thicker and jetted out even harder. Luckily for her, it was only intended as a smoke screen.

She couldn't go after him. Should she wait, or should she go back to the village?

That decision wasn't Mia's to make. From behind her came the thunder of approaching hooves. There were also the echoes of what sounded like a motor.

Mia turned around.

The figures she could see down at the far end of the highway halted before Mia less than ten seconds later. It was the same group of village peacekeepers who'd discovered the depression. And they'd brought a rare item with them.

The source of the motor sounds was an armored car. With iron plates riveted to a car chassis, the strangely rough-looking vehicle was apparently an antiquated model, with the edges of some plates starting to pull free, and both the sturdy turret and the forty-millimeter cannon that jutted a foot and a half from it were flecked with rust. The scorches and countless bullet marks that covered its armor plates were undoubtedly shining proof it had been fighting off aggressors in the form of bandits and supernatural creatures for decades. And it looked as if it was still more than capable of serving as the little village's guardian angel.

Mia's eyes were drawn to the wagon that rode alongside it. She could read the words *High Explosives* branded onto the sides of the wooden boxes piled high on it. Some kinds of munitions were often obtained from military installations and battlefields where the Nobility had fought their own kind, and it wasn't particularly unusual for towns and villages to have them on hand. Weapons that were especially easy to use, such as rifles and various kinds of grenades, could make an impressive show of force when the situation called for it. To the north of the village were wild plains and the ruins of what had once apparently been a testing ground for the Nobility, and normally no one dared set foot there.

The sheriff got down off his horse. As he moved toward Mia, he called over to the group forming around the wagon, "Get yourselves some explosives and line up along the drop-off. We'll be pitching them in soon."

"Wait just a minute," Mia called out as she dashed over to the sheriff instead of waiting for him to come to her. "What do you think you're doing? If you throw a bunch of bombs into this weird hole, there's no way of knowing what kind of reaction you'll get. Plus, someone just fell in there."

"Someone? And just who might that be?"

"A man named D. He's a Hunter."

Actually, Mia didn't know for a fact that D was a Vampire Hunter. But his good looks, the way he carried himself, and the way he called to mind ice and steel made her say it on impulse.

"Why'd he fall in the hole? No, before we get to that—who are you anyway?" the sheriff asked, knitting his thick eyebrows suspiciously.

"Mia, isn't it? You're the daughter of a fortune-teller who lives up north. I had her tell my fortune before," called out a young man who'd been staring at the girl all along from the driver's seat of the wagon. He wore a heavy wool shirt and had a red scarf wound about his neck. And as befitted someone so dapper, his countenance was a good deal more attractive than the rest of the men.

"This fortune-teller up north—would that be Noa Simon? I've heard the name before. Seems quite a few people are in her debt," the sheriff remarked; and, seeing a smile break on the lawman's face, Mia was somewhat relieved. "This Hunter you mentioned, is he some friend of yours? What in blazes brings him here?"

And having said this, the sheriff then held his tongue.

In fact, everyone froze right where they were. Though white smoke poured over the brink of the great subsidence, covering everything up to three feet from the ground, they could make out a human shape on the other side of it. The hem of a coat swayed around the knees of the powerfully built form. Mia alone could tell whose silhouette it was by the longsword on its back.

"D?"

How many of them heard her say that?

As Mia reflexively started to step forward, someone behind her grabbed her right arm.

"Don't go," said the young man who'd been in the driver's seat.

"But—"

"When did he fall? "

"Not five minutes ago."

"You think after falling in there it'd be that easy to get back up again?"

"Maybe if he got hung up on something halfway down."

"Think that's what happened?"

"No."

"Stand back."

Pushing Mia out of the way, the young man put his hand to his waist. He had a gunpowder pistol in a special holster. After drawing it, he called out to the shadowy figure in the fog, "Hey, I'm from the village!"

At the same time, the color of the silhouette darkened—and a heartbeat later, it slipped out of the fog to stand face to face with the young man.

A rumble went through the crowd. Murmured exclamations of rapture. For the villagers had seen the face of the shadowy figure.

"D . . ."

That name was known to Mia alone.

To be continued in

Vampire Hunter D
Volume 13
Twin-Shadowed Knight Part One

About the Author

Hideyuki Kikuchi was born in Chiba, Japan, in 1949. He attended the prestigious Aoyama University and wrote his first novel, *Demon City Shinjuku*, in 1982. Over the past two decades, Kikuchi has written numerous horror novels, and is one of Japan's leading horror masters, working in the tradition of occidental horror writers like Fritz Leiber, Robert Bloch, H. P. Lovecraft, and Stephen King. As of 2004, there are seventeen novels in his hugely popular ongoing Vampire Hunter D series. Many live-action and anime movies of the 1980s and 1990s have been based on Kikuchi's novels.

About the Illustrator

Yoshitaka Amano was born in Shizuoka, Japan. He is well known as a manga and anime artist, and is the famed designer for the Final Fantasy game series. Amano took part in designing characters for many of Tatsunoko Productions' greatest cartoons, including *Gatchaman* (released in the U.S. as *G-Force* and *Battle of the Planets*). Amano became a freelancer at the age of thirty and has collaborated with numerous writers, creating nearly twenty illustrated books that have sold millions of copies. Since the late 1990s, Amano has worked with several American comics publishers, including DC Comics on the illustrated Sandman novel *Sandman: The Dream Hunters* with Neil Gaiman, and Marvel Comics on *Elektra and Wolverine: The Redeemer* with best-selling author Greg Rucka.